The Angle Quickest for Flight

Steven Kotler

FOUR WALLS EIGHT WINDOWS

NEW YORK/LONDON

Published in the United States by
Four Walls Eight Windows
39 West 14th Street, room 503
New York, NY 10011
http://www.fourwallseightwindows.com

U.K. offices:
Four Walls Eight Windows/Turnaround
Unit 3 Olympia Trading Estate
Coburg Road, Wood Green
London N22 6TZ

First printing March 1999.

Library of Congress Cataloguing-in-Publication Data:
Kotler, Steven, 1967-
The angle quickest for flight / by Steven Kotler.
p.   cm.
ISBN 1-56858-129-7
I. Title.
PS3561.08459A85   1999
813'.54—dc21   98-55984
                            CIP

10 9 8 7 6 5 4 3 2 1
Printed in the United States

Interior design by Ink, Inc.

"I'll have none on my boat who doth not fear the whale."

—Herman Melville

HE CAME WEST, TRAVELING IN A LONG
pocket of dawn that never strays far from a sallow gray.
Behind him a set of mountains reaches high into a wide sky
and on certain peaks are footprints and patches of grass
pressed flat against the earth where he had made his camp.
Behind these places are other camps and other footsteps and
a long walk without a good reason and somewhere back
there are his parents, alone now, in a house too big for them,
wondering where their son has gone.

It is no longer winter. Soon his picture will begin appear-
ing in leaflets and grocery stores among so many other lost
or left or no longer wanting to be found. But it's not much
use, he dyed his hair in the bathroom of a Texaco and lost his
virginity to a long-legged bull rider named Linda in the
hayloft of a Texas panhandle barn and is about as gone as
gone can get.

Now, it's morning in Santa Fe and he sits in plain sight
on a shaky park bench under a sad willow. There's a wind in
the trees and a dull roar to the north where a storm's been
building. This is the main plaza, a plunk of grass surrounded by a square of streets. It's early and except for a
stalled pickup in the northwest corner, the roads are empty
of cars. In the distance, salsa plays. There's a rhythm there,
but it's too soon and no one moves to it.

Across from him, under a long verandah, Indians are
setting out wares. Fresh bread, pottery, jewelry, brushed
wool blankets in neat rows on a hard ground. They're slow

and old and sick of it all. They know that the weather won't hold and the few tourists left in town are still asleep in their hotel rooms, but it's been a long time since they have had any choice in the matter. He watches them slump, that's the word for it, knowing that the silence and the gray and the approaching storm hold something for them that will never be his.

He cups a cigarette deep in his fingers, the smoke hanging in the heavy breeze, hanging close to his mouth a moment longer than it should. It isn't much of a trick, rather something that happened to him. Just the way the world works now.

An old woman watches him from the opposite corner of the plaza. Not one of the Indians, though at a glance there's almost no telling. Lean and taut. Eyes the color of ash. She wears old jeans and cowboy boots scuffed at odd angles as if they had been drawn and quartered and restitched out of sentiment. He understands this, the need for things attached.

He's been here a week and seen her for most of it: a far shadow that is always there. The way she moves like an old history teacher makes him think there is no way she should be able to keep up.

She watches him with nonchalance, as if this is another thing in a long list of things she does, as if he were to stand and turn and walk out of her life forever it would be no different than if she never bothered to read today's paper.

He isn't going to do anything about her, or not yet. There's a part of him that will always like such games.

The rain starts as sound. At first he thinks it's coming from a radio, a canteen band playing a chutney of Latin rhythm. It comes slowly and there's even a pause between drops, but he hears the hiss of grass: cold rain and black skies, the way it happens in the desert. Maybe it will start slowly and he'll have time to make it back to his camp or wait it out in the library; he doesn't really know what to do with this day. He doesn't have time. The rain falls hard and fast. And he understands this too, the need to seek level ground.

Only the Indians don't move. This is just another storm they'll have to wait out.

He walks across the street and up the stairs of a bar. He doesn't have a gait as much as a motion, not slick or slow or shambling or shuttling or anything quite. He walks with his square shoulders square and his chin up and eyes the color of lawn grass always looking into some medium distance, just beyond the edge of sight. The street is already wet, his boots track water into the bar. It's a little early for a drink and he doesn't have ID and, even if he did, he's still only seventeen. But in this rain it doesn't matter, before anyone notices he's sitting on a stool, beside three or four others, sipping a cup of hot coffee.

The bar is old, held together by nostalgia, sawdust, brass spittoons. There are tall barrels stacked in corners and a few rodeo trophies on the wall. Coffee comes in mismatched mugs and some mugs have names written in black ink across their bottoms. The names correspond to another set of names written on masking tape and stuck to the wall behind the bar. Above the tape small wooden dowels stick out. Some have mugs hanging on them, others are just names staring into empty space. It looks like a seating chart for the Alamo.

He's watching the bar's door when Father Yohji Amo SJ

arrives. There is a clunking on the stairs or a rush of wind or something else that gathers the boy's attention. Today Amo doesn't look like a father, there's no clerical collar and nothing to distinguish him. Instead, he looks like a man cut down from a mast on some sailing ship that had blown through too many hurricanes. His hair is stark black and his eyes oriental. There's an angle to his body and he walks with a forward thrust as if something large and invisible is blocking his every move and he has to push past it continuously.

Amo walks into the room and crosses towards the bar and once there holds a hand up, two fingers extending toward victory, long, clean, lunulas the color of opal.

"Two snorts of whiskey," glancing around the room while the bartender pours, "and a coffee, please."

He pays and lifts the drinks and moves to the stool beside the boy. His hair is wet and water is slowly leaking onto his face.

"You got a napkin or something?"

The bartender hands him a dry rag. Amo tousles his hair, his brow, his hand moving in concentric circles like a man polishing silver. He wears wool trousers and a wool fisherman's sweater, both black and beaded with water. He picks water from worn elbows and clumps his boots together with an odd smile.

"Thanks," he says, tossing the towel onto the bar.

He looks down at the whiskey glasses as if surprised to see them.

"Here," sliding one of the shots towards the boy, "takes the chill away."

The boy looks around, uncertain, finding no one beside him turns back to the stranger.

"You're buying me a drink?"

"Hate drinking alone."

"Thank you." A nod of the head, more dash than dot. An edge of hair falls forward, normally lighter in color, but now damp with rain. He lifts a hand to brush it from his forehead or has he always been lifting a hand, something about him making it impossible to tell, and all the while his eyes never stray from the man.

"Yohji Amo."

"Nice to meet you."

"Veteran of special forces campaign in occupied Germany, of the war in Chubut, of Jakarta, the New York Public, Congress, and the Kirghiz Steppe."

The same odd smile. His teeth are thin, or appear thin, as if ground and shaped from so much odd smiling.

"That's quite a list."

"Yes, it is."

"New York Public?"

"Library. That and Congress, both of them a bitch. Tougher than war, not as many mosquitoes though."

"You should print calling cards."

"Did. Ran out."

A blur as Amo lifts his arm towards his mouth. He drinks by throwing the whiskey into his throat.

"Got yourself a name?" asks Amo.

"Say again?"

"A name."

The boy says nothing for a while, he wanders his eyes across the coffee cups, weighs the options, then shakes his head slowly and keeps shaking it slowly until he finally hears himself say, "nah."

This isn't a great decision, but it is the first time since he's left that he has had to think it through. There is a tingling in his shoulders, a weightlessness. This, he supposes, is the sensation of being cut free, just for a second, from one of the things meant to keep.

Amo taps the bar, long fingers again, a soft sound. "Well, good for you. No sense being the same old person, not in times like these."

The boy measures his sip of whiskey, feeling the liquid slot into his mouth, his throat, the thing that whiskey always does to him, the moment of being alone in a hot desert. He's never drunk alcohol this early in the day before.

The bartender refills the coffee and looks at the empty glasses. Amo winks and a small scar appears on his left eyelid. It looks like three lines from a Paul Klee drawing. The bartender sets two more shots in front of them. The boy ignores his, reaching for the mug. The coffee tastes black to him and he considers this for a moment, how easily colors become tastes.

"Angel," and Amo pronounces it with a Spanish twist so the *e* is more a whisper than a vowel.

"Pardon?"

"Mind if I call you Angel? I used to know an Angel, he's not around anymore." Amo watches the rain for a moment. "Probably could use another one right now."

"Angel?"

"Angel," Amo says again.

This is how people are with him, how they have always been. Somehow he will always fill their holes. It is something he had grown used to long before he ever could make the decision.

Steven Kotler

"Nothing personal, but I think you got the wrong guy."

Amo nods at that. "Opinions vary."

Outside the rain slows. Light, flowing in through a row of large windows, dampens and brightens. A shadow sweeps the room, stopping on an old world map tacked beyond the bar. The corners are bent inward to the place where the tacks pierce oceans and the shadow lays a sigh across Antarctica. The far-flung edge of the earth.

"My father died there," says Amo, pointing to the shadow's edge. He stares at the map, his eyes squint and crunch, and Angel watches the lines fan out across the sides of his face.

"Where?"

"South Georgia Island," pointing to a speck at map's bottom, "but he wasn't all there."

Angel understands, without having to be told, that there and there are not just two different places, but on different maps altogether.

"He was a Pi mystic," as if it were as natural as being a baker.

"Uh-huh," says Angel, a little light in his eyes. "I think I'm going to need a cigarette."

Amo tosses a pack onto the bar, lights a match. The cigarettes are foreign, smell faintly of turpentine, hard on the lungs.

"He was born in Japan, lived hand-to-mouth, traveled the countryside, found the occasional pupil. He taught bellyfuls of obfuscating mathematics. Awful stuff. His private cult of Pi."

Amo smokes like he drinks, like a man who has spent his life starving. The first cigarette disappears and a second comes up to replace it. He shakes away the smoke and his hair drops into his face. He shakes away the hair and keeps talking.

"Not much left of the old cult now. Had something to do with the radius of the Buddha's fingers and a numerical vision kept taut and locked by deep, deep concentration."

"What happened?"

"The war came, he volunteered for the Kamikaze ranks. Had to be the oldest fuck they ever put in an airplane. Got a headband and a destiny. But it didn't work out like they planned."

Amo smiles and Angel waits.

"He broke course early and somehow," Amo raises his hands, the ancient symbol for god-knows-what, "crash landed on South Georgia Island." His finger juts out, pointing at a dot in the lower edge of the South Atlantic Ocean. "Never been anything to see there. Seals. Ice. A few transplanted Welshmen who think Tierra del Fuego too populous. It's less than seventy miles off the crush of Antarctica. When winter comes the ice shelf jostles the island. In the glare of summer's thaw there are floods."

Amo taps his cigarette and some of the ash spills over onto the bar.

"He's a mess. Nearly broken in half. Found by a sealer who tosses him in his sled and drags him back to his tin igloo for his wife to nurse. Wife's name is Elena. Feisty, solid woman. Won't let the old man die. He's a handsome bastard and she falls in love. One day husband comes home to find them in bed together. By now she's two-months pregnant, tells her husband this like it's going to make a difference. Takes the guy thirty seconds to put a harpoon through my father's skull. Elena escapes only by chance.

She runs to Cumberland Bay and hops a whaler to the Falklands and another to Argentina. I'm born on a coastal trawler given to touring the Straits of Magellan in search of sunken treasure galleys."

There's more to the story, but it will be months before Angel hears the ending. How Elena wades ashore in Tierra del Fuego wearing white sailor's pants rolled above slender knees. It is little more than twenty-five feet to shore but when she reaches the sand her toes are blue with cold and she hugs the child close for warmth. She walks up the beach and up a flight of steps cut into the cliff. A Jesuit mission perches atop the bluff. A small metal gate rims the front of the property and two gargoyles look down at her from fence posts. One has a crack running up its wing, despite the good currents and the open sky this is a place it will never fly away from. There's rust on the gate hinge and a sweet squeaking sound when it opens. Condors nest nearby. They don't move at the noise. They have no natural born predators and are not hunted. This is just another sound they have learned not to fear. She leaves Amo on the church stoop. He wears swaddling rags and a blue cap. Deep Patagonia. He has birds and priests and cold for company.

Though he doesn't think this way, for Amo, Santa Fe was a long time coming. But which way does he think? Amo wonders this sometimes, sitting with strangers in strange bars and drinking too much or too soon or both, and all the while the rain falling down on his life. That is what he thinks of when he recalls the Jesuits, the incessant sound of water falling through sky. In Patagonia, he was always certain about the ranking of the elements. He wonders after this too, the things that are now certain. There has always been the fear that sooner or later his life would evade him, that one day he would find himself on a fool's errand, doing something, possibly idiotic, possibly not much different from this errand, and after that nothing would ever quite fit.

"You all right over there?" asks Angel. Sometime in the telling Amo had turned his head away, offering only a scruff of neck, an ear, a wedge of brow that has become increasingly furrowed.

Amo looks hard at Angel and asks a gruff question from the middle of nowhere. "You like books, kid?"

"You asking me if I can read?"

"It'd be a start."

"Yeah, I can read."

"What about old books?" Amo starts to qualify this, then stops.

Angel smiles at him. "Just what does any of this have anything to do with me?"

"Maybe it doesn't." Amo coughs and rolls the empty tumbler between his palms. "More whiskey?"

"Little early for me."

"Never too early for more whiskey."

Another pair of shots appear. Amo slams his down with a flourish, Angel lets his lie on the counter. Neither say anything. Amo pulls a long, twisted cigar from his breast pocket. It could be a churro or a dried snake. He reaches to his waist and undoes his belt buckle. There's a long blade tucked inside. The belt's leather is lined with steel to form a sheath and when Amo slides the blade out, it rides across the metal like a sneeze. The buckle collapses from a hollow square of silver bars into a thin handle that looks like a fancy *H* steamrolled into an *I*. He snips the cigar's end with a fast, clean motion. When he's finished the knife goes back to being a buckle and his pants go back to being tight along the waist and the cigar pours smoke into the room.

A group of tourists have been watching from the corner, the knife makes them huddle and whisper. It's been a long vacation and despite the new boots and the miles and the shitty beds in podunk motels this is as close to the American West as they've come.

"Truth is, kid, I could give a shit. This wasn't even my idea." Then he stands and walks towards the bathroom. Angel sips his coffee. Time passes. The tourists watch Amo walk back to the bar, he puts a roll in his stride for their benefit and later they'll believe him to be a bronco buster, a good one, who has taken some nasty falls and walks funny as proof.

"Angel."

"Yes sir."

"You're being watched."

Angel whirls the stirrer in his coffee and lets go, it makes large circles around the cup's edge before dragging to a stop.

"Probably not worth the effort," looking up from his cup, "I'll send up a flare if I do something interesting."

"You've seen the old woman?" asks Amo.

"I have at that."

"She's a friend of mine."

Angel says nothing, just offers the slight, bemused curve of his mouth.

"She doesn't mean any harm."

Angel takes another cigarette from the pack on the bar. Amo lights a match and Angel leans towards it. Smoke like frost seeping between his fingers.

"Where I come from meaning and harm have very little relation, they both just seem to happen."

Amo picks up his cigar and chews and suddenly knows what it is she sees in Angel. The smoke pulls at the corners of his eyes. All night he's been awake trying to solve an equation, one belonging to the great Russian mathematician Georg Cantor who, in the end, went a little crazy and Amo's wondering if he will too.

"She asked me to come in here and find you."

"You're trying to get me drunk so she can have her way with me?"

"Not like that at all. " He splays his fingers and lifts his hand slightly from its perch on the bar. A small glimmer of gesture that Angel finds strangely beautiful.

"She just wants to speak with you."

"Why didn't she come herself?"

"She's a strange woman."

"She's your friend."

"Yeah, but I'm a strange man."

"What does she want to talk about?"

"Look," says Amo, standing and striding towards the door, "there ain't a thing in the world that makes sense if you look at it the wrong way." And then, already starting down the stairs, he stops and turns his head back towards the room. "See ya round kid."

At the bottom of the steps he thinks I'm a lousy priest, and this cracks him up.

of town. The rain has moved on. Amo has taken a fine room at a nice hotel. Quiet and respectable. A winding row of adobe cottages. The cottages are designed for isolation—an artist's retreat for the idle rich. Certainly, you could paint here but at prices few artists would pay.

The thin desert darkness stretches all around. There is the feeling that you could poke right through it, tear just a corner away and back would rush the hot, hard day. But for now Amo sits looking at a sliver of moon. His head rests on the seatback and his feet are propped up on another chair. Behind him there is a six-foot stone fence that separates cottage from world and world from cottage. He drinks his wine slowly now that this morning's show is over, humming "When the Saints Go Marching In," and doesn't turn around when Angel slips over the wall and pads up in bare feet.

"Howdy sailor. You follow me home?" still not turning around to look at him.

Angel grabs a chair and squats on it, feet splayed at a hard angle, the rest of him riding just above his heels. They pass a few moments watching the shiver of moon's glow.

After a while Amo says, "You should put shoes on, there are scorpions."

"Tell me about her," says Angel.

"Her name is Pena."

"Pena?"

"I don't know what it means," shaking his head, "but you can be sure it means something." Amo uncorks the bottle and pours himself another glass. "Would you like some wine?"

"No, thank you."

Something creaks along the wall behind them, but neither turn. Amo brushes at a crease in his pants. "Her story's been lost and found for years."

Angel can see that he means it like a question, but he doesn't answer or have an answer and they sit in silence.

"There have been rumors," Amo says finally.

"Like what?"

"Extravagant, grand schemes."

Angel wonders what it would be like to have people make up great lies about him, what kind of life would he have to live to get to that point.

"Some say she's here only to bear witness. There was a story that she was Catherine the Great's first female lover, an impossibility, of course, but the rumor of that romance ran fever up and down the Baltic corridor. I've heard she's the last descendant of Ghengis Khan. You know Khan's treasure has never been found, still hidden somewhere in Mongolia."

He stops to light up a cigarette, to plume smoke into the dark. "Maybe in the Altai Mountains," smiling now, like that was an adventure he'd really like to be a part of. "And that the location of this secret treasure is inked on the inside of her womb."

"Imagine that," says Angel and he does.

The orange glow of Amo's cigarette rises in inhalation. Recently Angel had learned of organisms that live in the boiling pools of hot springs, in a world made from steam and heat.

"Do you know about the Di?" asks Amo.

"Di or Pi? Here we go again."

"The Di people," the words smacking with enunication, "were natives of the Min Shan in China. Pena has a lot of their blood in her. A pretty insular tribe, fairly peaceful, fabled for their calligraphy. Spring of 420 AD—someone—something—happened. There's no way to tell, but when it was done the Di had simply quit. In less than a week they stripped their homes and packed up their lives and left. They began raiding other villages. Kidnapping. Making strangers teach them strange things. Want to know what they were stealing?"

"You want to tell me?"

"Languages. They stopped speaking their own. They took the best of what was around and went on. They erased their own history, they forgot—intentionally." He takes his feet off the chair and places them on the hard stone. "This is a people who walked out on history, who said, 'No, this is no longer mine.'"

Amo stands up and walks thirty-five steps across the garden and reaches a far wall and turns and walks thirty-five steps back. He stops right in front of Angel and looks him right in the eye and says, "Kabbalah."

Angel looks right back. "Kabbalah—Jewish mysticism. Yeah, I know what that is."

"Holy books aren't just about what they can teach, they're about lines of power. May I tell you a story?"

What else, Angel thinks, have you been doing?

"The largest accumulation of Jewish mystics to put pen to paper was in Spain just before Ferdinand and Isabella. Middle of the twelfth century. Until then the Kabbalah was mostly an oral tradition, but the thirteenth and fourteenth centuries was the first time stuff got written down. Imagine that, a religion nearly 4000 years old and they don't write down their most sacred traditions for 3600 of those years."

"So why then?"

"The Moors were running the show, Jews felt safe with them. It didn't matter. Maybe there was a sign from God, maybe just a literary fever, who knows. When the Inquisition came Isabella paid her tithe to the Church with Jewish art and Jewish books. The Inquisitioners stole everything. They did it right out in the open for anybody to see. Most of those books are still under lock and key inside the Vatican's secret archives. They don't belong to the Vatican and most of them aren't much use to it, but it's a question of sovereignty."

"The Vatican's?"

"Not every last priest is involved, if that's what you're asking, but a group within a group within a group. What I want to tell you is sometimes it doesn't matter what's true and what's not. Those are just end points. The black and white. Pena is all gray."

Angel thinks about it a while. "What do you believe?"

"Me," says Amo, "I believe everything."

A SPRING RAIN BROODS IN FROM THE north bringing a cold light to an old cafe. Shadows lie about at odd angles and the air is thick for this time of year. A waitress brings coffee. Her shoes tap a clatter on the cold, stone floors. Angel watches her walk away, pretty legs, but they won't last, not here. Ten tables spread out over the place and there's a counter like a streamrolled rickshaw propped across one corner. On a high shelf sits an old tin radio. There's a ball game on, the Patrons or the Silvers or some other farm league team, and the only reason anyone pays attention is because the hundred-and-fifty cash a week and the chance to swing a bat works almost as well as a green card. The managers have some sham deal worked out with the INS, enough to keep the players sober most of the time. People round here listen because everyone's got a cousin or a sister's kid or a friend or two coming up in the league and this is a part of the country where fortune, good or bad, runs in streaks wide enough that it helps to know when to duck.

Pena wears a fantastic scarf over her silver hair. It looks like an inkblot test or a Gauguin print that spent days lost at sea. Her eyes always seem fixed on the horizon. Points standing out from a face hard and wrinkled, the skin stretches tight over bones that seem elevated by stilts. She must have been beautiful when she was twenty, thirty, forty—but that was a long time ago and there's no telling how old she is now. She sits across from him with her sleeves rolled and her elbows resting on the table. People who don't know might try to find a numbered tattoo across her wrist, but there is none. That is one tragedy she managed to avoid.

A wind carries in through an open window. The waitress leans down to push it shut and as she does a fleck of paint on the frame cracks into a canyon the size of a child's eyebrow. Angel watches her as she walks by.

"I'm Pena," the old woman says by way of introduction.

"Angel."

"Is that your real name?"

"Hard to tell."

She sits very still, he's never met anyone so still.

"Amo give it to you?"

Angel nods.

"He does that," her eyes narrow and fall towards him, as if he were suddenly very far away, some distant sight. "It's a good name, though, fitting. May I ask you something?"

He is watching her, patient in this, happy with the small mystery. Eventually he nods again.

"Are you a drifter? Because it's a drifter's town. Indians, Mexicans, miners, artists. A good outlaw history."

"I've had a few moments." He doesn't bother to clarify.

"A long crossing—those mountains in the winter."

"You couldn't possibly know that."

"Eventually drifting whittles down curiosity," she says in the pause. "I think it's better to have a purpose. I know purposes, everyone has one. It is my belief that each person comes into this world with the ability to do one thing, one small thing, but each of us can do that thing better than anyone else. This is what I see when I look at people."

"That sounds like a lot of work, maybe you should stop

looking." To his great surprise she laughs and it comes to him that this is something she has done quite a bit of, this laughter, and isn't it amazing how everything you think about a person dissolves in a moment.

"You're right, of course," she says. Which is when he realizes she possesses a very dangerous quality—she's really likable.

Around them the light changes, it's a product of the desert and there's an old Navajo word for it that Pena knows and Angel doesn't and it will be a few months before he's settled enough to do more than notice and when he does get around to asking she'll smile and nod and tell him that "Yes, there is a word for it." But for now it is just a subtle change, a dampening perhaps, that turns her features strangely marble. She has the ability to look like a Catholic statue.

Outside, the sidewalk is starting to fill with rain. Pena's hand drops to her side and she fiddles with a bundle of coins that she keeps tied up in a leather satchel. They're the same coins Angel saw her tossing about the plaza and the same coins Pena's mother gave to her back in the twenties with a little instruction book on the ruminations of the I Ching and a lecture on the righteous properties of the Gypsy blood coursing through their veins. Those coins bought her passage into Earle Warren's smuggler's court in Istanbul in the late thirties and later brought her across oceans to South American shores and up the Argentine spine and into the central portions of the New World where she became more of a fable than a myth. They feel tough to the touch, a hardened metal seeped in the smells of a million disguises. She takes her hand away and folds it into the other and they sit together on the table as if she were thinking about praying but didn't or doesn't and instead leaves her hands there as a reminder of the bigger things to come.

"Where do you sleep?" But she already knows the answer to this question. As much as Angel's been seeing her around she's been seeing him. Just last night she watched him creep up a fire escape and spread out his sleeping bag on the roof of an old firehouse.

"I'll be all right," he says, with an ironic little smile that lets her know that he might and she might and maybe not and sometimes that is the way of the world.

"I got a place outside of town, there's a shed in the back, it's about half fixed up. You could finish it, if you feel the need to pay your way." She pauses, thinking something through. "That is if you'd like a roof over your head."

Angel says no and thanks her and pays for his coffee and leaves. He doesn't see her again for a few days but when he does what else can he do; he says yes and walks home with her on a jackrabbit path that cuts through the sage and the dust to the edge of town just as the last light is leaving the sky and in the distance the mountains are turning to the color of blood.

LIFE HERE IS A GREAT, SEAMLESS
migration. A streaming of doorway faces and anomie hung
together inside a throbbing ticktock passage of time long
since passed by. It is sundown in the back alleys of Old
Jerusalem and Friday, the beginning of another Sabbath.

Johnii Rush passes through hooka smoke and stone pro-
files. Dust leaps around his shoes. Everywhere are eyes
strung out on extended last chances—miracle junkies
unable to get by on faith alone, eyes that track, that skulk
and know as he knows that there are things that will always
await him. He stops for cigarettes at a corner store. The
prices have already risen from what they were this morning
and he finds himself needing extra change, which, alongside a folded Colorado tourism brochure, sits in the back
pocket of his trousers. He pays, rubbing at the nicotine stains
on his forefinger, lighting another cigarette, waiting for the
full of night. It comes quickly in these winter months,
there's already snow in the mountains to the north. He tilts
his head back and looks for a familiar pocket of the sky. But
the angles are all wrong and he sees only a new night and
tastes the crisp air in the far corners of his mouth.

His stride is long and fast. Noiseless, in its way, as if he
is the last of a long line of silent men. He has it in him to
follow footsteps into brick walls, that old magician's feat, to
turn slackjawed and so seemingly unprepared to find the
vanished truly gone. It's ingrained into his copy of the I
Ching—now tattered and hanging inside a velveteen

The Angle Quickest for Flight   *21*

satchel tied to his belt by wizened leather—this trait of distance and meant to be read like card sharks read cards. In truth, it's what all the old Taoists knew—this lesson of ramshackle lives and too much time spent in high, thin air.

Around him the air has grown thick and heavy, a storm is moving in from the west. The streets are a cobbled redbrick and wider now as he comes out of the Old City. He finds the lane he's been looking for and a doorway and passes through a short line and into a bar.

The place is owned by an American named Max. They've done business for years, drunk together for longer. Max is a short man with an old sailor's face, a wide mouth curling up at the corners, eyes lost at sea. It's a small place, this jazz joint, with a bandstand in a far corner holding a couple of horns, a drummer, a bassist. A good crowd though, always, rumpled and shaking on a dance floor the size of a dime.

Johnii stands in the doorway for a moment, letting his eyes adjust to the dark. The doorman points him towards an enormous oak table, thick with bodies, piled near the room's center.

A man stands, an arm the size of a small country rises to wave hello.

"Welcome to the Good Ship Lollipop," a deep baritone. "Name's Coyote Blú, how do you do?" Johnii sees an easy smile and an old silk tie, dark blue, and an elegant suit to match.

"Please, have some champagne. It's pretty good."

The words emerge as English but with a long twirl. Drawl. He must be six-five or six-six, well over two hundred pounds, a good man in a fight, a war. The name is one Johnii's heard before, somewhere, but he doesn't ask and just says hello. The glass is cold to the touch, the champagne colder.

"It's very good," says Johnii.

"Actually," says Max, arriving with another bottle, "it's a 1976 Tattinger Comtes De Champagne Blanc de Blancs. So rare that the fact that he's here drinking it could be construed as a miracle."

"I didn't know," says Johnii, turning towards Coyote. "Thank you very much."

Coyote tips his glass and moves to welcome another guest.

Coyote Blú. It's just a name, but Johnii has a thing for just names. Later, he'll ask a couple more questions and come no closer. Even if you press Coyote, all he can tell you is he likes American cars, had a worthless shit for a father, and has seen *Butch Cassidy and the Sundance Kid* forty-nine times this year alone, and the only problem he's ever had in the world is deciding which one he'd rather be. When it finally dawns on Johnii that it really doesn't matter which one Coyote is, that they both get their asses shot off in the end, it will be too late.

Max passes Johnii a set of keys to a small house at the base of Aspen Mountain along with a bundle of airline tickets. Johnii passes him the Colorado tourism brochure and folded inside is a list of names and a passport for a mutual friend, which—though neither of them know it—was actually procured by Coyote after passing hands and countries and all the while Coyote just sips his drink and keeps another secret.

Johnii feels Max's hand on his shoulder. "Have you met Christiana?"

"Christiana?"

In a chair beside him is a woman with fingers like silk and a hand extended towards Johnii, which he meets and shakes and she smiles and laces her fingers between his before setting them back on the table together.

"Christiana," she says.

The song ends. Applause. Someone walks to his microphone and invites Coyote to join in. Cheers as he stands. Christiana whistles, teeth of bone white, the sound high and sharp.

Coyote pulls a blues harp out of a silver case in his lap, walks to the stage playing the begining notes, a slow version of "Bye-Bye Blackbird." One of Johnii's favorites. He falls for the first few bars before remembering Christiana and their hands, still woven and sitting on the table, and he looks down at them before looking at her. She has pale hair, silver in the dim, worn long and straight. A curve to her eyebrows, to her hips, the lips of a great actress.

"Good evening," says Johnii.

"Good evening."

When she speaks her words come out and linger and Johnii can almost watch them form. She speaks English with a light inflection that he first thinks is South African then recognizes as a Londoner's tongue, but far back in years, maybe a mother or an aunt, and now weathered.

"Where are you going?" Christiana unlaces her fingers to point at the plane tickets.

"I was thinking about skiing."

"When?"

"Soon, maybe sooner, there's been snow in Colorado for almost a month. It's part of a project."

"And how long are you staying?" teasing him slightly.

"Don't really know. The ticket's are open-ended and I have a place for the whole of the winter."

"Are you a skier?"

He smiles. "As compared to what?"

She takes a cigarette from a deck lying on the table and drops it between her lips. Statues of small camels stand braying in the center of each table, a bundle of blue tips rising from a black basket tethered to the hump. He lights a match. She leans in to take the light.

She says thank you—does she say thank you? Does she mouth the words? Is there sound? He will never be sure.

She moves like a soft calypso, so soft if you're not looking dead on, if you're not completely open to it, if you happen to have the bad fortune to blink, or sneeze, or sip your coffee, you'll miss it. Can't take his eyes from her, can't believe anybody ever could. Later, when he stops to think about it, he'll be a little amazed at how easy it was, but then he'll stop kidding himself and remember that she took his hand and then, maybe, he'll start to wonder what kind of game this was.

The band pauses. The front door opens and closes. The room smells of winter. A silver note arrives, and another. Coyote plays "Trouble in Mind."

They sit quietly, watching, sounds arrive, hoist, teeter. He misses the touch of her hand. Disorienting, he thinks, glancing quickly down towards his satchel, what would the book tell him now?

"What were you thinking?" she asks.

"When?"

"Just then. Don't tell me this is your favorite song because you liked the last one better."

He nods.

She smokes patiently.

"I was thinking about what it would be like to kiss you."

"And?"

And the trumpet plays blue and low and almost from a different song or era and sounds close to something Johnii almost remembers. They don't kiss. The music ends. Coyote reappears with a fresh drink and a line of sweat. He loosens his tie and offers his hand to Christiana. On the dance floor she moves and moves and moves.

Max walks up, standing beside Johnii with his eyes following the room, the pulse, pausing on Coyote and Christiana.

"Good people?" asks Johnii.

"My friend, you'll only find the very best at Max's."

The band plays on, a strange song for a strange land. Johnii, thinking about making the patterns fit, watches them dance, thinking how he'd like to see her again. Afterwards they stroll to the table arm in arm, Christiana somehow not lost in the crook of Coyote's elbow. He holds a chair for her. They sit beside Johnii, smiling slightly, at ease with their place in this world.

Johnii looks at them. "May I ask an odd question?"

"Always."

"I'm having a party—an event—next week." He hears himself speaking the words, not really thinking them through, and maybe, later, there will be time to wonder, but for now it's just Friday night.

"I thought you were going to Colorado?" She dribbles her fingers along the rim of her glass, her nails unpainted.

"I am going to Colorado, that's where it is."

"Parties are good." Coyote leans forward with his words. "Tell me what you want."

"Skiers."

"I'm not sure I follow."

"Granted, my idea of a party is pretty weird, but I'm a weird guy. I'm working out a pet theory here. For years I've tried to enact each of the hexagrams of the I Ching. Six lines to a hexagram, six possibilities, so I need six skiers. Already have four."

"You want to tell us why?"

"Everybody needs a hobby."

"Some hobby," says Coyote.

"You folks ski?"

"Does a rabbit hop?" says Coyote.

Christiana laughs, clear and free.

"I'd like you to be my guests."

"Just like that?" though, of course, Coyote knows with certain things and certain people it's always just like that.

"The plane tickets are already taken care of," removing them from his pocket, "Max gave you the nod, that's all I need."

Christiana says nothing and Coyote pushes back from the table, crossing arms across his chest. He mutters something about wanting to see an old woman again. Maybe or not quite. Johnii can't tell and doesn't ask.

"I could loose my expat status," says Coyote.

"Stay at my place, it's neutral, there's too much room already."

Coyote takes the tickets, they shake hands. A pause in the music matches a crack of lightening.

"The darkness is only Kether," says Johnii.

It's an strange statement and not one Johnii would normally make. Something about this evening, this company, and perhaps Johnii's understanding of this, the first of the Sefirot is rudimentary, but his relationship to darkness is exquisite.

"Keep telling yourself that," Coyote says quietly and then stands and strolls towards the bar.

Guests arrive, depart. Coyote returns with another bottle. They drink and smoke and act as friends. At a lull in the music he grins and turns to face Johnii again.

"So you know something of Kabbalah?"

"This is Jerusalem, the world's been coming here to make deals with God for about as long as anyone's been making deals with God."

"So you pick things up along the way."

"Doesn't everyone?"

Max moves through the crowd, nods towards the table. Coyote touches a finger to his forehead, tipping his hat. A smack of thunder flickers the lights. Johnii feels the darkness creep. "The descent of the yod?"

"No," Coyote shakes his head. "Not yet at least."

Certainly they're talking in code here and an old one at that. The story is one of the most complicated in Jewish lore. The idea being that the essence of God leaves no room for Creation, that any derivation from this fact constitutes a limitation of God's powers. An ancient idea and maybe not even a Hebrew one. Most of what we know comes from Nahmanides, from Genoa in the middle of the twelfth century, from a time when people liked to hold ideas up to the light, to see where things fit. In order to create the universe God must have pulled himself into himself leaving behind a primordial gap and it's within the darkness of this gap that God breathed life. All life. Everything. The entire universe in all of its subtlety.

"Think about it," says Coyote. "If God is everything and everything is God and God wants to create something new—where does this something new go? It's the paradox of omnipresence. Now I don't know what any of that means. But it sounds really serious."

That's not how he really sees it. He knows the almost heretical truth that this first act of Creation was not one of revelation and emanation, that, despite all the thrill and magic, this was a moment of concealment and retreat, that, in truth, what was left behind was an eternity of shivering darkness and the lost nuances of Kether.

Outside, in the cold Israeli night, soldiers brace as another rumble comes. Christiana slides her arms into the sleeves of an old suede jacket.

"What happens now?" she asks.

"We wait."

"It's just thunder," says Coyote. "This God of the Hebrews has always been a bellowing fellow."

"The ten Sefirot," says Johnii, again thinking out loud. He's a little outside his discipline, a little outside anyone's discipline.

Christiana watches the words crease Johnii's brow, the excitement in his eyes. It's no wonder he's of interest to the Russian.

"Kether, crown; Hokhmah, wisdom; Binah, understanding; Hesed, grace; Gevurah, strength; Tifereth, beauty; Netsah, victory; Hod, glory; Yesod, foundation; Malkuth, kingdom," counting Sefirot on his fingers as he speaks. "They are the hidden aspects of God. The chain of descent that leads to the world of man. Kether is the first rung of the ladder."

"Descent?" asks Christiana.

Coyote smiles. "Descent and ascent. They may be the funnel through which God breathed the world, but they're also a ladder that can lead back. According to the Bible God spoke Creation into being. 'In the beginning was the word and the word was God.' This is the first of the mysteries of Kabbalah—if you want to climb the ladder, if you want to return to God on the mystical path, then you must learn to speak God's language. Like the Sefirot, it's a backwards puzzle; God gave the Torah to the angels, they gave it to us. The faithful believe that all of God's power is contained within the Torah, thus to be able to correctly read and pronounce the Torah in the same order as God did would give one the same power as God."

"Have you seen the Orthodox?" asks Johnii. "All day long mumbling through prayer. Their slow bowing. It's for rhythm. An internal metronome. An attempt to capture the rhythm of the universe."

Coyote places a finger to his lips, thinks for a minute.

"This is what the Orthodox are doing, even if they don't know it themselves. In the beginning God pronounced his name, an amalgamation of four Hebrew letters: yod, he, vav, he. The tetragrammaton, Yahweh; the name of God; the beginning. The chief concern of Kabbalah is the combination of letters, pronunciations, purifications—the only map is the Torah, the puzzle itself. It's the old joke—like having a map of the earth drawn to scale. But even great mysteries have points of origins, places where the multiplicity of threads are still one fiber. The descent of the yod refers to the moment in the Creation when God pushed air through moist lips, forming the first of the tetragrammaton, the yod, forming and descending the ladder of Sefirot, simultaneously the gate and the Creation."

There's a hard crack, and the lights flicker and fail. The bar goes dark. The music stops. Max, already on the phone, a nearly instinctive reaction by now, and has learned that this, for once, is nothing more than a power failure brought on by fallen wires. Still, the crowd packs around, edgy.

Coyote watches the whole scene.

"Bad place for a fight," says Johnii.

"Stay here," and then Coyote's gone.

Under cover of the darkness, Christiana leans over and kisses Johnii. It is a soft kiss that lingers, leaving his lips warm. He leans back slowly, watching Coyote as he crosses the room and crosses the stage and lifts his big arms towards his mouth. He cannot see the harmonica, but he hears the sound.

"Taps," says Johnii.

"What's that?" asks Christiana.

"That chap over there," pointing to Coyote, "he's playing taps."

The room goes quiet. They kiss again. He doesn't know what this is about and if you were to ask her the same question she too might have difficulties. There are things and there are things and really does it matter so much that you want to kiss a stranger?

Max walks to the stage and stands up to explain the situation. He has a box of candles in his left hand and when he's finished talking he passes them into the crowd. The box moves around the room. A fumble for matches. As the candles light the thunder dies and the voices too, but there's another sound present, not readily identifiable, a melody of all that's forgotten in the world, come down from on high to grace tonight's darkness. Perhaps, later, if you need something to cling to, this is the tune that can help you through the night. It's a lonely sound. A lost song sung without background music or dance and don't bother looking because there's no one around who can promise you a happy ending.

ANGEL SITS BY A WINDOW IN A SMALL adobe, not much more than one room: a cot, a small bookshelf, and his pack in the corner. There is nothing to cook with, he takes most of his meals with Pena in the house, a hundred yards closer to the road. The bathroom is an outhouse, nailed wood with a creaky door and holes for windows and the whole thing lilts to one side and looks like an ancient phone booth. Over a month has passed. She never asks for rent. He helps with the garden, puts a new door on the outhouse, lays tile on the floor. She brings him books to read, he reads them. Odd assortments. Ancient topologies; Inquisition histories; astronomy; teleology; the Old Testament; Roman glories—aqueducts and architecture and ways to dismember a man; desert survival; books on Jews and their exodus; scattered books on the papacy; spelunking guides. The first time he ran low on money she figured it out and tried to offer him some, instead he asked if she could help him dig up some work. She spent twenty minutes on the phone and a week later he was earning a hundred dollars a day on a documentary film about desert life. Two weeks worth of lugging equipment across the whole of the plateau and rats chewing through yucca leaves.

Today, he sits in a straight backed wooden chair, facing the first of evening clouds and the far mountains. The door is open, crows line a fence to his left, and the ground beneath is hard, red dirt. A book rests in his lap.

Pena leaves the house and walks quietly through her

garden and when she stands in the doorway there's twilight at her back. Her question comes to him from a shadow.

"Is it done then?"

This was her way, to ask just what she meant and let him work forwards to meet her.

"Done?"

"You've been thinking about things far away?"

He nods, taking off the hat he'd been wearing, setting it down. Its wide straw strands lie across the table's oak.

Her hand is wrinkled and long and Angel knows, even though he hasn't turned to look, that it rides on the thin satchel she keeps tied to her waist. Inside, always, are coins for the I Ching, close to her like a scent. Last night he watched her sitting at the kitchen table, a sprawl of wood long enough for ten children with crayons, and the coins spread out from a throw like street corner dice. Pena uses heavy metal coins, obsolete, big as a fist around. One time, after he asked, she told him the oracle dates to 1000 BC. Originally bones were tossed, then forty-nine yarrow sticks, now three coins. The system contains sixty-four hexagrams—six lines stacked on top of each other. The lines are either considered broken and represented by two side-by-side dashes (- -) or solid and thus appear as one long line (—). The result of a toss is the divination of one hexagram. Each hexagram reflects a universal category, specifically a conflux of energies caught in time which represent archetypal circumstances. "The I Ching is the oldest preserved human abstract sequence," she had said. When Angel wrinkled a brow at her answer she added, "Not my words, read them in a book," and walked from the room.

She moves lightly, in the doorframe, the coins touch as a chime.

"Thinking of things long behind you?" she asks. It had taken him most of the month to get used to her speech.

"Do you ever talk like normal people?"

"Hah."

"Does anyone you know?"

"I know a lot of people."

"Subject, verb, object—thank you very much."

"You're welcome."

He takes a cigarette from a pack on the table, taps it against his wrist.

"Yeah," he says finally, "woolgathering."

"You miss them. Nostalgic for a life not your own. Hard thoughts—those." She has never once come out and asked a straight forward question about his family, about why he left.

"Hard not to miss them, to miss something. They were all right, not mean, I didn't leave because they were mean."

Pena walks up behind him, she doesn't touch him, just stands there, sharing the air.

"I was looking for something to keep," says Angel.

Pena nods, but she's behind him so he sees nothing but a darker sky and a horizon. The crows sit murder still.

"Rilke says, in the ninth *Duino Elegy*, 'Perhaps we are here in order to say: house, bridge, fountain, gate, pitcher, fruit-tree, window'—perhaps that is how it is for you now, perhaps you need a larger vocabulary."

Pena lays a wooden box on the table. The paint is scraped and the hinges stay dull and flat even in lamplight. Outside the sky goes to a deep blue and the mountains black and the clouds hang limp. He knows she likes this time of day and leaves the doors open to let as much of it in as possible.

"Maybe you will look through that when you have some time, there are some things inside," and she moves out the door and whistles for her dogs and they come bounding across the yard and together they set out into the desert for their evening walk.

The light is starting to go, he stands and walks to a tall iron lamp, reedy and plain with a sloped shade that could be made of moth's wings. The light is the flowing, pale kind that looks like it's been washed in a river. Angel sits down again and pulls the box towards himself. It is over a foot long and half of one wide and three inches deep and very elegant. It looks nothing like a coffin. He picks it up and lets it spin on its corners until the wood digs into his palms and he has to put it back down. The latch is silver and appears wet. It opens with a thin, cricket's chirp.

Inside is a brick of papers and on top of that yellowed scrolls rolled into tubes tied with thin, soft leather twine that doesn't bite through, but holds fast. The tubes are maps and Angel unrolls them one at a time and fastens them to the table with a book for each corner. He has pulled out a notebook to catalogue everything.

He wonders if it is a puzzle. Pena likes puzzles. "Riddle me this," she'll say, smiling. Once, gardening, she asked, "What do the following things have in common: President James Buchanan; the two-toed sloth; the chow chow; the hyoid bone; mercury; -40 degrees; Kahoolawe; the pyramids; *Midnight Cowboy*; the flags of Nepal, Libya, and Ohio." Then she repeated it slowly. Angel had no pen, so he scratched shorthand into the dirt and ran to recopy it after she had finished. She left him weeding and took the dogs for a walk. Angel took to the game and went to the library to sift through possibilities. It took him almost two weeks to put it together.

"President James Buchanan was the only bachelor president; the two-toed sloth is the only land mammal besides man that mates face to face; the chow chow is the only dog with a black tongue; the hyoid bone, which supports the tongue, is the only bone in the human body that doesn't touch another bone; mercury is the only metal that's a liquid at room temperature; -40 degrees is the only temperature where Fahrenheit and Celsius thermometers read the same; Kahoolawe is the only uninhabited Hawaiian island; the pyramids are the only one of the seven wonders of the ancient world still standing; *Midnight Cowboy* is the only X-rated film to win the Academy Award for Best Picture; Nepal is the only country with a nonrectangular flag; Libya is the only country with a single-color flag; and Ohio is the only state with a nonrectangular flag." He read the answers from a yellow legal pad and tapped his left foot as he did so. "Chow chow and mercury were the hardest, had to find a dog specialist in Albuquerque, mercury took a chemistry student I met at the library. One of a kinds, all of them."

She'd been standing in the garden then and had to sit down in the dirt. He watched her bury her hands in the dark soil, he watched the earth cover this small part of her flesh, and he heard her laughter. When she finally did catch her breath all she could say was "dog specialist in Albuquerque," and then the hot trill running through her again. "You could have just asked," she told him, her laughter finally stilled, but she smiled when she said it, smiled so he knew that she knew that sometimes it's nice to have someone who would fall down in the dirt, who would revel in a two-hundred mile crossing to discover the color of a dog's tongue.

He looks back at the box. There are seven maps in all. One of ancient Rome, waterways and aqueducts; one of Rome present day, printed on clear plastic to be overlaid atop other maps; four of the Vatican, too detailed for tourists, too detailed for most purposes; and one, the last, hand drawn and labeled Hidden Passages Below the Tower of Winds.

He chooses this one first, holding it in his hands, feeling a dizzy rush like the needles of sleep, a giddiness in his fingertips. He follows the lines with his eyes, playing them over a tight section in the middle. Penciled across the map's bottom in faint, looping script are the words Jewish Voodoo. On the side, to the right of the gate leading to St. Peter's square, lies a small stamp, a bird of some kind holding a small child in its mouth. On the child's forehead is a small letter in a language Angel's unsure of—Hebrew, Sanskrit—no way to be certain. It catches him, tugs at the wrong places. He unrolls each of the other maps and looks over them; there is nothing in comparison.

For close to two hours he's at it. When he's done, his eyes hurt from the strain and there's a hard rumbling in his belly. He walks to the house, cactus and white sage in dark shadow, like an small army on its belly. Pena is in bed, but Angel finds hot coffee and a thick corn chowder, good cold, which he carries in a wooden bowl back through the garden to his table. He comes back and gets a hurricane lamp, which is fueled and ready and smells of kerosene even before he lights it. He finishes the stew and smokes a cigarette and watches all the stars. Venus bright in the distance though he doesn't know it.

He rolls the maps again and puts them in an empty jar, away from the windows and out of reach of tomorrow's sun. They should go back in the case, but he likes the way they look. Their shadows coat the walls.

Next is a thick envelope labeled "Padré Isosceles" in dark ink. Angel finds a picture of a man, very tall with a dark beard, close-cropped hair and lips set tight as if sewn shut or capable of great anger. Like a stick figure drawn by a crow, something out of Poe or Lovecraft. There is a description of a compound in Baja. It's an old mission built in the eighteenth century and left alone after its initial occupants died from hepatitis. There were no locals around and superstitious Catholics, believing it cursed, stayed far away. Isosceles moved in almost twenty years ago, cleaned the rooms one at a time, over fifty of them, finding bones and lizards and old books, weeds growing through cracked walls, places that hadn't seen light in a century. He is a passionate man, the kind of man about which word manages to spread. Others came to join him. Strange, sad devotees. Hope was their final curse. Refugees, Isosceles called them. He taught them to follow the traditional Catholic rites, days and nights filled with incense and Latin. There was little money, not much for food, hard soil to till, some fish from the sea, cactus.

Pena found him then, found the little out-of-the-way monastery, a place where books had been hidden so many years ago. Answers she needed. She found Isosceles saner then, a willing listener, a man in need, a man who saw Jesus in a thin cold light but somehow liked what he saw. A man who had things he might be willing to sell.

That time Pena was looking for a copy of a cargo manifest, a lone ship sailing from Barcelona through the

Ligurian Sea to Vatican City in August of 1493. Seventeen months after the fall of the Muslim Kingdom of Grenada, fourteen months after the 100,000 Spanish Jews were given a choice between exodus and Christianity, Christianity or death. Fourteen months after the start of the Spanish Inquisition. Fourteen months after Isabella had decided to pay her tithe to the Church with Jewish books and Jewish art. Caught up in that transaction was a book Pena was tracking, a book smuggled out of Alexandria, before the burning of the library, a long, complicated story. The book was somehow preserved, perhaps recopied. The only thing for certain is it disappeared in Spain during the Inquisition.

"That's over three hundred years ago," said Isosceles.

Pena agreed.

They were drinking cherry brandy.

Inside Isosceles' envelope is a copy of the manifest. The books have titles in all languages, many are in Hebrew and one of the Hebrew titles has a little question mark beside it and beside the question mark, in a different ink, a small star. There is a bundle of letters, these are in English as is ten years of correspondence between Pena and the Vatican. They denied all existence of the book. She stopped short of calling them names.

Angel hefts the file, looking for a hidden weight, as if he could hold the pages upside down and shake out an extra secret or two. He could not believe the detail, could not believe what she is asking of him.

But, in truth, he doesn't know what she really wants and she keeps it just that way. He will go along anyway. Anywhere. He's just a boy and this is just a grand adventure and isn't it pretty to think so.

In the file is a short essay on Gematria written by an anonymous author and published in an underground newspaper. The original essay is in Latin, of all things, and beside it is a second printing, this one in Italian. The title has been translated in fine pencil. Dull gray letters pulled flatter by time.

Angel stands and walks over to his bookcase. Pena had given him a dictionary of religious terms, it was one of her first gifts and one he cherishes. A dictionary of religion bound in dark leather. Something that would offer just enough information, would tantalize and abandon, would not prattle onwards about the how and the why, but would rather leave open a myriad of the possible.

On his second day in Santa Fe, he walked into a second-hand bookstore and saw the book for the first time. He wanted to steal it, not having the cover price, and had even thought up a plan, but all the elements were too crude—if he were going to steal he wanted stealth, dexterity, charm for the job. Simple thuggery wouldn't do. On that day, he did no more than a cursory examination of the book, a few glances and he knew. Then he just stood there, holding the cover shut, thinking himself lucky. He had one-hundred-and-eighty-six-dollars worth of a purpose—enough money to buy an oversized, overweight dictionary and then, maybe, be on his way. Four days later he went back to the shop and the book was gone. Pena had seen the whole thing. It was the first time she noticed him. She bought the dictionary on the spot.

Gematria is one of the aggadic hermeneutic rules for interpreting the Torah. Kabbalah. It's a system of exchange. Letters signify numbers. Hebrew words take on a numerical value. Connections can be made. Sometimes Gematria is no more than simple substitution: number for letter. Sometimes the numbers fall into sets and equations and became involved in long and powerful calculations. The Babylonians did it first. Later the Greeks. It caught on in rabbinical literature in the second century. As time passed, systems of Gematria became more and more complicated, the square of the numerical values lead from word to word. In that way, the four letters of the tetragrammaton become numbers that when squared and added become 186. 186 is the word *place* so *place* becomes another of the names for God.

"After all, He is everywhere," says Angel out loud to the empty room.

Gematria rose and fell in popularity and wasn't codified into anything rigorous until the imagination of Rabbi Eleazar of Worms arrived at the beginning of the thirteenth century. Eleazar developed a system of meditation based on numeric representations of the names of the angels and the names of God. Numbers were visualized during prayer. The system was so powerful that Eleazar advised, as was the Kabbalists' rule for many years, that neither the divine names nor their vocalizations be written down. Critics railed against his innovations, claiming that such obvious power would lead to abuse. This is one of the secrets of Kabbalah, that it in itself is secret.

There's something about the whole newsletter that bothers Angel, but he's too tired to think about it now. His eyes have blurred and the box lies empty. He stands and stretches, then bends over to blow out the hurricane lantern. The lamp goes hush and everything seems quieter in the new dark-ness. He crawls onto the bed, his shoes already off, and buck-les the covers over him like a seatbelt at a carnival ride.

"THAT NEWSLETTER CAME FROM THE Vatican, didn't it?" asks Angel.

"Which newsletter?" but Pena's teasing him and he can see it in her eyes. "Certainly did," bending down to pick up a stick. She folds her knees and keeps her eyes level, fixing the stick with some inner radar so her hand goes right to it but her eyes stay steady in the world. It is the type of thing that would take practice to do as casually as she does. She passes Angel the stick and he throws it as far as he can.

They are out walking the dogs. It is cold enough that the breath from their nostrils plumes white in the thin air. If the dogs see it, they're not paying attention. Angel has seen dogs chase their own breath before, but then again he once saw a man drink seven shots of whiskey for breakfast. They trot the stick back, Angel having to dart quickly to get a hold of it, then straining his wrist back and forth while wrestling it free. This brings a cascade of yapping and then a silence and a stealth as these two bob up and down, moving backwards as Angel goes forward, focusing, intent, watching only his fingers, the stick, waiting to run. Angel throws towards the east, the air at the desert's edge just starting to turn bright in the sun's rise. An occasional ray makes it over and out onto the long flats of this cactus prairie to brighten the dull patches of night still caught in sage brambles and yucca spines. The stick sails in a dumb arc, end over end in the early sky.

The noise has flushed a jackrabbit and the dogs nose off

towards it, leaving the stick alone in midair. The jackrabbit has a huge, loping stride that the dogs can't match so they spread out to cut it off, but the rabbit switches and crosses and finds a burrow in the ground and is gone. The Labrador, the one Pena calls JP for John Paul, trots over to Angel and gives him a half-hearted cant of the head and Angel laughs and stops to rub between his ears.

The other one she calls Tatra, which is actually the kind of dog she is, rather than a name. Tatra is a Baltic sheepdog. A big, hearty animal with thick fur that likes it when you bury your hands deep in that shag and twist and turn. It's a kind of wrestling that the dog can appreciate. So Pena calls her Tatra—Tatra. It's a reminder and Angel knows enough never to ask her of what.

In the distance they hear church bells and Angel realizes it's Sunday, funny to him because the last time he thought about it, it was Sunday also and somehow seven days had been shoved between these thoughts and he hardly knew it.

"Where did it come from?" asks Angel, still thinking about the newsletter.

"A good question indeed," Pena says, her eyes lighting up in the memory. "Hard to answer, though, I mean hard to dig around something like this without arousing too much suspicion."

"Are there more?"

"Hard to come by, not many are printed and what is distributed goes directly to scholars. Though I'm not certain it's genuine."

"Why?"

"Think about it."

The sky in the distance has started to color. The light rises high enough to catch the dogs' vision, so they stumble mid-trot, loosing the stick and the game to a fast flash, and then stand dead steady as if they could pause the moment and the soaring arc until their senses return.

"Why go to all that trouble, why not just steal the books?"

"My thoughts exactly."

"Because your access isn't that good?

He watches as she puts a whole world together, making small connections, amazing how familiar it sounds, how a certain boyish impulse wants things to be that way, wants a hidden door behind a special panel and the buried treasure.

"Someone's secretary, a clerk or a guard?"

"Most likely a Jesuit, they have the best access to the library, and the longest tradition of such things."

"Why do I care?" she asks, blatantly quizzing him now. "Tatra, No!" her voice is not shrill, just a low grunt that seems to match the dog's own growl. Fighting JP for a stick, the dog's tone had changed, just for a second, but Pena heard it and knows what comes next. Tatras are raised to fight wolves, one little Labrador isn't going to offer any problems.

"Come." Tatra looks at Pena for half a second, but isn't about to disobey, not over a stick, not after whatever it is that they've been through together.

Pena crouches down as the dog trots over, it's that same fluid motion and even the dog knows enough to not obscure her view of the horizon. She swaggers close to Pena, but out of the way of her line of sight. Pena whispers something to the dog, the whole while holding her still, hands on the outside of her legs bracing inward, then she rubs the top of Tatra's head and stands up again.

"You have no answer?" she asks Angel.

"Where's Amo been?"

"That's not an answer."

"I was trying a different technique."

"He's trying to find a friend."

"How about the phone book?"

"He's not that kind of friend."

"Unlisted?"

"Off the map—no pun intended. Give Amo a few weeks, he'll show up."

"Every time he shows up I get a hangover."

"You don't have to join him."

"Because," finally returning to her question, "if you can find the network then maybe you can get inside or maybe you can get information about the book that you want."

"And where would you look?"

Angel thinks about it a while, watching the horizon come to life in the new morning. The distance has a flat shimmer to it, a magician's trick, he watches plants turn to horses to card tables to plants again.

"You would want to work backwards, so as not to draw heat to the source." He takes the day's first cigarette from a pack in his breast pocket. The dogs back away from the lighter's flame and won't play catch with him when he smokes. They run circles off to the side of Pena, mad at the interruption of the game. "So you would look for scholars with really good information, people doing speculative religious history."

"The kid's getting good," says Pena.

Pena's a woman of sparce praise, Angel starts to redden, and she just glances at him, smiles through old teeth.

"Publish or perish," she says. "A scholar's whole world is information. And this isn't just any information: sacred books, lost magic, things that could do so much harm to the Catholic Church. The stuff they've hidden for centuries. Scholars, especially the kind who are getting this kind of material, would feel very blessed and probably a little nervous. Religion on its own breeds secrecy, this thing is a whole other ball game. They won't be so fast to give away their sources."

"No, but they have to get the thing from somewhere, even if it just appears in their mailboxes at night, someone has to put it there."

"A courier, probably double-blind, unable to burn anyone."

"So you source the courier, watch the pickup spots, see who else uses them. If you have enough time you could build the network backwards."

"We have to be really careful with this, I've been thinking it through for nearly a year and I can't figure a better way, but it's a mess, one way or the other, it's a mess."

In the distance a small plane. So far away they barely can hear its tiny, nasal whine. It banks hard and turns toward Taos. The dogs see it, run with their heads bent towards the sky.

"There was a small fishing village in Poland called Drensk. No more than four hundred people, begging a living from the river Bug. Most of the village was Jewish, though you would have to spend a long time among these people to figure that out. From the looks of things they were a people who went into hiding before the birth of Christ. They hid their synagogue inside their church. A wooden Jesus on the altar, well crafted, but not so ornate that anyone would want to take it with them. The spike through his foot works as a lever, releases a catch, spins the whole altar around."

The sun pulls over the horizon. So big out here in the open flat, nothing for comparison, so able to fill the whole of the sky.

"The village cobbler had escaped from Turkey with a book said to detail a journey Jesus made through Tibet. It's an old story and probably there's some truth to it. Christ spent a huge chunk of his life wandering around and somewhere along the way he learned a great deal of mysticism. People have written whole books on the subject, but there was never any proof. The book was supposed to be real proof, but who knows, who could tell you a thing like that. This guy comes from Turkey, he knows something of the village's reputation for secrecy and thinks he'll be safe there. Four hundred people all good at keeping secrets, there would be so many things hidden in that village you would never know where to look. They could have built the Taj Mahal in the center of town and all you'd see is an ugly brown shack and fish hanging from brown thread. But the Vatican wants the book, it's wanted it for so long that it scared some poor man into hiding in Turkey. Could you think of a worse thing for a Jew?

"He makes it to Poland and sets up shop. The Vatican waits until he's comfortable, until he no longer stays awake half the night, until he stops sleeping with a shotgun in the bed beside him. Middle of the night men come to him and ask for the book. He won't give in. A lifetime worth of hiding can make a man stubborn. They tell him if he doesn't give them the book they'll destroy the village. 'Why would you do a thing like that,' he says, 'nobody is that mad.'

"In the center of town was a small fountain, a young girl holding three fish, water squirts from their mouths. They tie him to the fountain and burn the whole village to the ground. Three hundred people die. Everything is lost. When the survivors cut him loose he's crazy with grief, lasts three days before drowning himself in the fountain. It doesn't matter. For the few that survived the fire, winter kills them off. By spring there's no one left who can remember the village."

Angel knows stories like this, knows the ending even before she finishes the telling. It's always been this way.

What would you do if you were pope? Would you tour around the world in an endless Thanksgiving parade? Would your flock become so large that only the devil could count its numbers? Would you wander out into the cold Italian streets at night, puzzling through a problem created twenty centuries before your birth? Would you burn down a village to prove a point?

The executive suites in the Kingdom of God—they belong to book thieves and liars.

ANGEL STANDS BAREFOOT ON THE kitchen's rough floor pouring a cup of coffee when the phone rings.

"Want to talk to you, Angel." Amo's voice clear and loud like he was beside him, having coffee of his own.

"Little too early for whiskey," says Angel, laughing as he does. Something about Amo's voice, after the time that has passed, the fact that he's back maybe, makes Angel giddy.

"Breakfast, I'll buy, huevos and those loco pancakes they make at OJ Sarah's. You know the place?"

"Do you guys ever speak in complete sentences?"

"Rarely."

"It'll take me half an hour to walk there," says Angel.

"I'll pick you up."

"I'd rather walk, I need to clear my head, if you don't mind."

"Wear good shoes. Pena buy you those boots like I told her?" But Amo clicks off before Angel can answer. He glances down at his cold toes, he thinks they're flatter from his crossing, all those miles pressing down on them.

The wind blows dry and empty. There's sunlight over the desert and farther away a gray roil swamping over the mountains. He finds Amo at a far table well into a monster stack of pancakes. He's wearing a wool poncho and looking like a pirate, but older and slightly out of business. Amo raises a head and a hand, stands to clap Angel on the back and whirl him into a chair. Food piles between them.

"Beat around the bush or get right to it?" asks Amo.

"You don't say," says Angel.

"That's what I thought. I want you to go to Baja with Pena," says Amo, holding still for a moment.

"You want me to find Padré Isosceles?"

"Not much finding to do. He doesn't get out much. Look, I'd go, but Isosceles doesn't like me much."

"Imagine that."

"He knows I wouldn't show up without a good reason and unfortunately we have one."

"Which is?"

"We need to know what he's doing."

"Sounds like a good reason to me," says Angel.

"You're not the only one."

Through the window, Angel watches a bird lazy in the high sky. A silver line heading into a storm, silent, then gone.

"We need to know if he's going to move on the Vatican and if he is going to move on the Vatican we need to be there first."

"We?" says Angel.

Amo waves his question off. "Look, I don't think Isosceles is going to be too happy about seeing anyone. If you and Pena show up it might buy a little time, throw him off a bit. What I want to know is what he knows. The list of people in the world who have similiar interests is rather small."

" 'Similiar interests?' "

"Rare books," says Amo, tapping his fork against the table for emphasis. "He owes Pena, he probably won't make a play for her. He doesn't know you, which is about the only edge I can think of, but don't kid yourself, he's going to figure it out pretty quick." Amo smiles at the thought. "Did you read the file?"

Angel nods.

"Isosceles never dropped the ball, he's too much of a scientist. Pena got him curious and he just got more curious and then his curiosity got curious. Lately he's been collecting maps, rare ones at that, and recently turned up on some interesting mail-order lists."

Angel raises an eyebrow at this.

"He put the word out that he was looking for an explosives expert, safecracker style, carefully directed blasts, especially rock, must be a Catholic, faithful but at odds," as if reading a list.

"Maybe he's going to rob a bank," says Angel.

"Maybe he is."

"Look," says Angel, "I might be the new kid in town, but isn't there a better way? I mean can't we just infiltrate the compound, little nighttime stealth mission, maybe send in a plant?"

"You seem to think we're some kind of big organization with unlimited resources and government contacts."

"Well?" says Angel, raising his arms, palms towards the ceiling.

"OK. Good point. So what. We still don't have the resources and Pena doesn't think we can just steal what we want, she needs to see Isosceles, see his reaction to her. The book we want has been a big secret for a long time. We get one shot at it. The Vatican figures out that we want it and it's going to disappear and disappear for good."

"And if Isosceles gets his hands on it?"

"Yeah, well, that obviously can't happen." Amo pushes

back from the table, lights a cigarette. "Look, I don't know if you've noticed, but Pena's not so young anymore."

"She's not that old."

"Angel, she was in her early twenties at the start of WWII."

"She's not that old."

"Fine," says Amo, "she's not that old, but she's not that young either. A plant takes time and training and effort. Even if we forget the cost, we would need to create false histories and this isn't like setting up a banker in some shit-hole midwestern town. This isn't the witness protection program we're talking about. The people around Isosceles are bad guys with bad histories. To set up someone in that world takes years. We don't have years. We may not even have months."

Amo leans back to sigh, but doesn't. The air is starting to cool, like the day never made it all the way in. They level eyes across the table. The waitress picks up empty plates and pours fresh coffee. Her hair hangs long down her back and sways as she walks away.

"So you want me to go down there with Pena."

"I want you to go down there with Pena and once you're there just don't make too many sudden movements."

THE PHONE'S RINGING AS JOHNII WALKS
into his flat. He doesn't hear it at first, it just registers as
another siren. Since the blackout, the city's been a mess.
Under cover of the darkness some hero decided to slip into
the Arab quarter. Naked women drawn on the doors of a
mosque in goat's blood and of course you can't insult Allah
like that. A day later someone painted naked women on the
doors of a synagogue—this time with human blood. Panic,
neighborhood sweeps, searches, roadblocks: everyone
wants the guilty caught, wants to be able to sleep at night,
wants it all just to go away. It's been nearly a week and
tonight the curfew finally got lifted. Still, it isn't as bad as
when someone decided to let a couple of lunatics into the
country and they got drunk and spray painted *Arbeit Mach
Frei* across the doors of a synagogue. That was so bad that
the Arab community started beating up every tourist in
sight. Swedish, Polish, English, French, American, German—playing all the angles, it didn't matter, they just
wanted everyone to know it wasn't them. They knew all
about that line, knew better than to cross it.

"Shalom," finally finding the phone under a pile of
papers on his desk.

"Shalom," the voice is Baltic, deep and choking, and
not one he recognizes. "My name is Parvitz, I am a friend
of Kendra's, she asked that I call you."

Johnii knows no one named Kendra, but after a second
he recognizes the code. "Hello Parvitz, why did Kendra ask
you to call?"

"She had to leave the country on business, something about patent rights and distribution, she's in New York for the month. She said that you had lent her *Pale Fire* by Nabokov."

"I did."

"She asked me to return it for her."

"Please, I'm not worried, it can stay in her apartment for a few more weeks."

"Would you mind if I read it? I have heard it's very good."

"Enjoy, it's great, and just give it back to Kendra when you're done in case she didn't get a chance to finish it."

"Thank you very much."

"You're welcome."

"Goodbye."

"Goodbye," and then a soft click and a dial tone.

In the distance another siren. Johnii almost answers the phone. Some things you never get used to. He looks down at his notepad. It takes him a second to count up letters. Kendra starts with *K* which is the eleventh letter in the English alphabet and Parvitz starts with *P* meaning plus. Eleven becomes one plus one equaling two. The second week of the month.

Pale Fire starts with *P* which is sixteen and Fire with *F* which is six, added together is twenty-two and again for four. Fourth day of the second week which would be Thursday which would be tonight.

Johnii switches off the phone's ringer and shakes his head and looks around the apartment for earplugs, something to keep the sound of the sirens away. It's going to be a long evening. He really should take a nap.

HE IS ASLEEP OR AT THE EDGE OF IT, with a T-shirt draped across his eyes to keep out the light and a set of earplugs to keep out the sound. A pillow lies between his knees, there's something about how bone rides on bone that he doesn't much like, the buildup of heat, whatever, he doesn't really know. He's a damn particular sleeper and so what, it only seems to bother his girlfriends, and he hasn't had too many of those around recently. The phone is ringing again. He rolls toward the nightstand, T-shirt wrapping around his head, he flings it away, finds the receiver, tries to sit up.

"Shalom."

A dull muffle, a hint of sound angling away, the feeling of being in a deep pit.

"Shit," he says, "hold on a second."

He takes out the earplugs, shaking his head for a second, trying to return from wherever it was he had been.

"Hello," repeats Johnii.

"You all right there, partner?"

"Yeah, sorry about that, just a little Greco-Roman wrestling practice."

"Got some company?"

"No," says Johnii, "nothing like that. I'm alone. Wait a minute, who is this?"

"It's Coyote."

"Huh?"

"Coyote. The other night, Max's, plane tickets to Colorado, you met my friend Christiana."

"No. I know who you are, I was wondering how you got my number."

"Ways and means."

Johnii says nothing, his head barely clear, not sure what to do. Outside the window the day is finding a way to end.

Coyote continues. "I'm around the corner, was wondering if we could talk for a minute."

"Well, if you want me coherent you might want to pick up some coffee."

"Already did. How do you take it?"

"Often."

"Yeah, me too."

"I'm on the top floor."

"I'll see you in a sec."

Johnii rolls out of bed and yanks on clothes and looks around the room and says, "Yeah, well, I'm up," to no one in particular.

He can hear Coyote on the stairs and stands to meet him, checking the room to make sure that everything that needs be out of sight is out of sight and then he remembers his conversation with Max and what difference does it make. He had, eventually, asked after the champagne, and Max had let him know that Coyote's history was as a smuggler and a broker. Getting anything anywhere was his specialty.

Then Johnii told Max he had gotten a little drunk and a little headstrong and maybe a little too taken with Christiana and invited them to Colorado.

"Good choice" was what Max had said.

Johnii still not used to second-guessing himself.

"Well, you've made a friend for life, and Coyote's not the kind of friend that is easily made and one thing is for certain, whatever happens, your life will be better for it."

Coyote knocks twice at the door and waits. Johnii opens the door. They shake hands and Johnii takes the coffee from Coyote and walks to the kitchen where he pours it from the styrofoam cups into big mugs and passes one back.

"I think it tastes better this way," says Johnii.

"Probably does."

Coyote looks around the room. The open kitchen, glasses and plates and heavy bowls stacked on shelves. He lifts a hand to touch a row of pots hung from hooks, the bottoms long burnt black, Johnii being someone who liked to cook with the flame high.

"I never got used to the Turkish tradition, the small glasses, small portions. I need a mug I can get my hands around."

On the wall a framed photo of a man standing atop a rock outcropping. The land rolls away, far below, in shadowy stretches. The figure is nearly in silhouette, his back to the camera, thin, white dreadlocks rolling down his back. Coyote walks over and looks closer. On the bottom edge a date and the words Devil's Tower and beside that the six small lines of a hexagram. Written in pencil.

Johnii and Coyote cross to chairs and sit in a slant of afternoon light. Simple chairs made from heavy wood, a table to match. Coyote wears a straw boater that he lifts from his head. He crosses his legs and rests the hat on the bend of his knee and uses two hands to cradle his coffee.

"What can I do for you?"

"I was wondering about Colorado," says Coyote evenly.

"What were you wondering?"

"Well, I'm wondering how to ask this diplomatically."

"Best way is to come out and say it."

"I've seen a lot of things," says Coyote. "But I'm not used to strangers passing me plane tickets."

In daylight Coyote still as big as a house. He looks stacked more than made.

"So you still want us there?"

"Unless you want to give me a reason to change my mind."

"Can't think of one."

"Neither can I."

"What the hell, I've got a little shack up in Montana. Lately I've had a feeling I need get up there again." He sips his coffee and looks around the room thinking arrangements will have to be made, mail gathered, everything outside the normal channels.

Coyote eyes Johnii. "So you asked Max about me?"

"We go back aways."

"Can I ask what he said?"

"Yeah," says Johnii, "you can ask."

Johnii stands and walks out of the room and comes back with a cigarette and offers the pack to Coyote.

"He said you were a man not afraid to discharge his pistol in the line of duty."

Coyote laughs at that. "Is that supposed to be a good reference?"

"Worked for me."

"What did he say about Christiana?"

"He said she was your friend and that you trusted her explicitly."

"Then you know everything."

THEY LEAVE SANTA FE IN AN OLD JEEP, heading border south across a hundred miles of New Mexico before the sun prickles over a far ridge. Night bends at hard angles, the stars above are just beginning to fade. A flat light sweeps across the desert, Angel sees a silver-back fox, fat from the easy winter, creeping through mesquite after lizards or mice. Abandoned shacks in the distance, no more than planks of bleached wood, still standing for some unknown reason.

In the late afternoon a cackle of heat lightning falls in the distance, but there is no thunder and no rain to follow. It falls hard and flat. Angel drives wearing a straw hat, the brim starting to shred, strands pulling loose in the wind. There is no radio, nothing to fidget with until he remembers he smokes. It can be that way on long journeys, you forget things about yourself, come back to them later, maybe never.

Down near Las Cruces they see the Rio Grande for the first time. River the color of dust with flashes of steel in the day's fading light. In the distance are canyons. The road curves alongside the water. They pass a rusted car, the doors torn off and the front seats removed. It looks like a couch in a Soho loft.

"'64 Dodge, not much under the hood, but good for the long ride," Pena tells him. "Less than ten percent of the cars stolen down here are recovered."

Angel turns toward her, his neck stiff from bumps and daydream twistings.

"They're driven to Mexico, across the border."

"Smugglers," says Angel, happy with the word, the sounds, says it again to the sky, his head tipped back and watching for the first of the night's stars.

Later in the afternoon they stop at a small post office in a smaller town. Angel buys a soda from an old machine and drops off a letter for Pena. The envelope is white and reads "My Old Friend" and beneath that an address somewhere in Israel.

All she says is "just something I had to do, while I still have the time."

They drive until dark, pull off the road and hide the jeep behind shadows and cottonwoods. The darkness is mossy. Beneath them, the ground still arid and hot. Angel stops unrolling ground sheets and sleeping bags to press his palm flat. Dry heat, he feels the sweat get sucked from his hands, feels water turn to dust. Pena makes coffee on a small stove. Then pulls tortillas and beans from a cooler in the jeep, a block of cheese which she tosses to him for grating. They eat as the night starts to cool. Angel lost to the sky. Pena hangs a small lantern from a low branch, sits with her back to a tree, her reading glasses pushed tight towards her eyes and the book held close.

The air feels thick with fog or dust, turning brittle as they sleep. Angel wakes to Pena coughing, a heavy lumbering from deep in her chest. She raises her head to spits phlegm.

"You okay?" he asks, but she's still asleep and doesn't know.

In the morning she's worse. They cross into Arizona on backroads, Angel drives and Pena rides beside, her hand a tight fist, her chest and throat heave. Dirt, rolled into balls by the last rain, crunches under the wheels. For fifty miles they pass nothing but flat land. Angel sees a can of Wolf Brand chili sitting roadside like a watchdog. A tiny splotch of red left on its label, dusty and hollow inside, amazing to him that it's still there. At a small market Pena speaks Spanish with a woman who disappears into a small house behind the store, comes back ten minutes later with a few packets of herbs and a steaming cup of tea. Pena drinks in silence, her cough subsiding. Angel can see her shudder with relief, doesn't want to look, instead finds a paper from El Paso, ten months old and starting to yellow. Reads foreclosures, want ads, walks far away from her to smoke.

Pena buys a case of lemons and Angel carries them to the car, the scent the first clean thing of the day. All morning they pass through gutted towns, stopping in diners for hot water. Dark men at counters, no one speaks when they walk in. In the jeep Pena mixes thick remedies, things that stink, float in her cup. Lemon slices as garnish until the dashboard smells of citrus.

Angel watches the horizon's edge as he drives, likes seeing things cross over from nothingness. Red desert walls, a hundred feet tall, lifted from a speck no bigger than a thumbprint. Wind blows hot in their ears. Sun everywhere you could think to look. He lights a cigarette. Smoke passes. Pena sits with an old Indian blanket over her legs, shivering. Angel wants to stop, find a doctor. Pena won't allow it, wants to make California by sundown, wants a hundred things, none of them Angel can imagine. Toward afternoon they find an old picnic table under an old pine, the needles half dried and blown, like torn stuffing for an old scarecrow. Someone has carved a pentagram into the table top, below that a message of love. They unpack lunch, Pena coughs from the movement. Angel stops and stares at her, there are lines drawing tight from his mouth that were not there before.

"You gonna be okay?"

"This has happened before," coughing and waving her hand for him to wait, "this cough. Once in Istanbul in the forties."

She sits down stiffly, working with some inner balance that's not to be upset. "The war created a cult of information, informal trading floors, huge profits. I worked for Earle Warren, anything you wanted to know, he was the business. He had the finest taste," her head shaking back and forth, smiling with the memory.

"With the Nazis raiding every town they went through we were getting blackmarket everything. Most people didn't care who got the stuff, as long as it wasn't the Germans. There was a period where we got enough nails and thorns and splinters and whatnot from the original cross to crucify half the Russian army."

She coughs, spits.

"One day he asked me to take an envelope across town to a Jesuit that we had never had any dealings with before. I sassed him about what was inside— more splinters from the cross—asked him if he finally found a buyer."

She stops to sip tea, stares at the horizon. "Earle didn't even look up, he just slid me the envelope, said 'Kabbalah. Jewish voodoo.' Sometimes you see these things coming, sometimes they get you. We were sitting in a bar, I was drinking a Wabash Sidecar Twist. It was a light orange color, served in a martini glass. The barkeep was an exiled trainman from the Midwest, made up his own drinks." Her hands rising up in the air so Angel can see. "These great, fantastic things that no one else in all Europe could copy. He used to do it so he could name them after trains—or women—no one was ever certain. Right after Earle said that I started coughing. Spilled my drink. My whole chest wracked with pain."

"He poisoned you?"

"No, I don't think so. Earle said he tested the drink and it was clean. I coughed for twenty minutes straight, phlegmatic, awful. I started to shake and couldn't stop. Finally Earle picked me up, tossed me over his shoulder, and carried me cross town to a troop of Gypsies. It lasted three days, I would have died if it weren't for the Gypsies. They made special teas, said prayers. I spent one night sleeping in skunk fat, don't ask why."

In three months she has never told Angel more. He rolls sliced meat into a tortilla, adds cheese, a little mustard. Pena offers him two slices of bread, he shakes his head no and starts eating. The food hangs out of his open mouth when he stops to ask a question.

"Did you open the envelope?"

"Jewish voodoo," she says with a smile. "Someone shot the Jesuit while I was sick, hung his cloak from a church spire, and left him face down in a mud puddle. Earle got the cloak down, two hundred feet in the air and he did the whole thing with a cigar in his mouth. Use a leather belt to wrap round the spire, old logger's trick, just walked up the side. The stuff of legend," she says, winking at Angel. "He never asked for the envelope back."

As she speaks she leans forward with the Indian blanket

now wrapped about her shoulders and her fingers running quiet over the wool's hairs, tying invisible knots. There is a gap between her front teeth, no more than a razor's width, and her final words seem to come from there, as if she won't put her whole mouth around them.

They find Route 10 and drive smooth highway into California. That evening they camp in Yuma, near the border. Angel wants to stay in a hotel, Pena's cough comes back around sunset and he thinks she should be inside, but she won't hear of it. Instead he spends an hour finding a grove of trees thick enough to stop the wind, but it has the whole of a continent to build up speed and nothing short of a mountains will keep it away.

The next day they cross into Mexico. Pena tells him that the monastery is six hundred miles down, stuck right in the middle, hidden by a chorus of low rises and the fact that there is nothing, not even room for life, in the middle of the Baja. She is still too tired to drive, so she just sleeps in the passenger seat, saying Isosceles will care for her—a small smile—not to worry.

They stop on the Bahía del Rosario, a few miles down from a fisherman's camp. Angel buys yellowtail and makes a thin soup for Pena, eats little more than a tortilla and a few spoonfuls himself. At sunset a family walks down the beach, the father plays a soft violin, the wood pale and thin in the last light. Mother and daughter watch the final sky. The music is a wan bolero, a far journey. Angel walks up to them, offers them soup, they decline, saying they have a long walk ahead and a long walk behind and the fisherman fed them fresh shrimp with chiles. The man stops playing long enough to smoke a cigarette. Angel walks a little ways down the beach with them. They all know the night.

Pena sits with a sleeping bag across her shoulders looking old. There are bags under her eyes and a sallowness that wasn't there this morning. When she speaks her voice is a soft mush, words from a faraway radio. She tells Angel about Catavina and the boulder field at the north end of the central desert. She says there are boulders the size of buildings and thousands of them and people to say that the dead sit atop these rocks and sing to each other.

"Maybe they need the company," she says when he asks why.

The sun has dropped away, Angel digs a small sand pit to build a fire. A rock crab clips by, drawn by the light, then scuttles back to sea. Angel spreads Pena's sleeping bag out, watches her lie down. Her breathing makes a crushing sound that reminds Angel of an ant colony on fire, only thicker. She doesn't really sleep or wake. Angel gets up every hour to boil water, make tea. The wind picks up, carries light spray from the ocean. He doesn't remember setting up the tent, its long poles shiny and pale in the moonlight. Pena's weight no more than a scrap as he carries her inside.

By first light she has a fever. Angel wants a doctor, but Pena says the mission is only a day trip away and it is easier to go there and they'll have medicine and she is too firm about it for him to argue. At noon they arrive in Mulege and head west across broken canyons, driving between high walls where a carpet of scrub mesquite and cactus and the thirst of the land becomes a force unto itself. The road has all but vanished and at a jagged sandstone arch they turn south and off it for good. They drive between narrow rock walls and Pena points to petroglyphs—bicolored humans with top-knotted hair, their left side black, the right red.

"Cochimí Indians lived here, most of the central region was theirs. But that's not their work." Her hand shakes as it rises to point at the petroglyphs. "Their legends says it was done by a race of giants who lived here long before them. Archeologists call the tribe responsible 'The painters.'"

"'The painters,'" playing it over in his throat, trying to feel what it would be like spending all of history with that as a nickname. Not as bad as some, he decides.

Now, Pena speaks slowly, a creak to her voice that Angel's never heard before. "Most petroglyphs, especially the early ones, have a purpose, offer a warning, but not these."

"What do you mean? They painted them as art?"

Pena says, "art for art's sake," and looks back toward the desert.

"How do you know a thing like that?"

"You don't."

Angel smiles and reaches for a cigarette. The road loops back and forth, a gentle rocking that follows the flow of a river long dry and even the wash it has carved has opened in places and if by dread punishment water were to once again flood this land it would form little lakes and pools rather than roar down the canyon's gullet.

In the afternoon they crest a low rise and in the distance there is a simmering, gray shadow not made by the desert. Pena sleeps, sweating and slumped, the fever having taken most of her strength. Angel wants to wake her, but doesn't. Less than ten miles away a church is visible. Pale dust spurts from their tires. The road becomes a switchback torture, a flight of fancy with packed dirt paths shooting down tremendous cliffs, wind following like tag. Beside them sand streaks in smooth sheets at places where boulders have dropped and plan to stay, crushed under their own weight into pale cicatrix. They do no more than five miles per hour. The rock walls rise all around them and Angel feels as if he were driving down into the earth, feels short of breath, a man slowly submerging in water. Pena stays asleep. The light comes from far above, as if torn from the sky and carried here, a thin slit between two massive gates. Shadows lay about. He drives between shapes broken and twisted, poured over harsh descents, a topography of a slow, violent time. The whole way cigarette smoke plumes from his hand and mouth. Somehow the light forms a calendar out of the risen walls, he sees shadowy dates marked off. Thinks about his birthday, less than a month away, eighteen years old, he didn't expect to see Mexico so soon.

Less than a mile away Pena wakes. She takes a thin flask from inside her jacket and unscrews the top in big, hearty turns. The flask is of polished silver and across its bottom runs an engraving. She swigs and takes out a bandanna which she dips into water, then wipes the mouth of the container off and then passes it to Angel. The flask is oddly cool in his hand, he balances the cap on his knee, as he drinks he sees the engraving in the rearview mirror.

"It tastes like smoke," he says.

"Sipping whiskey."

"Still tastes like smoke."

"It's supposed to," she says. "Keep it."

Angel raises an eyebrow but doesn't say anything. He has an old denim jacket lying across the backseat and he reaches round a hand and slips the flask into the inside pocket.

"You ever do much fishing?" she asks him.

"What?"

"I was just curious."

"Yeah, I did some fishing as a kid, my father liked to go after largemouth bass. He used to go out with a group of guys, stay drunk for three days, usually caught something. I went along a couple times."

"I have a friend who is a great fisherman. Coyote Blú, he's a big, steely-eyed Texan, wears the craziest hats."

"'Coyote Blú?'" he turns to look at her, but her head is turned away from him. She's watching a building emerge from the flat land. It shivers in the heat, then drops behind a rise.

There is no gate around the monastery, the road levels out for a while, bends and becomes a driveway. No one stands outside to greet them. Angel doesn't know what to expect and Pena just stares. She coughs as he stops the jeep, spits thick phlegm into the dirt. Angel hops down, an ache spreads out from his feet as they touch hard ground, the pain bone deep. Rubs the cramp as he shuffles. There is no bell, only a thick iron knocker. Metal smooth and black and hanging in the center of a twelve-foot door. Hard wood. The knocker is a seated gargoyle, wings half folded, head bent down, watching for something on the ground. There is a long echo as sound hollows and folds in on itself, not what he expected, he thought flat and thick, ineffective, worried about standing in the desert for hours waiting on the invisible.

"We're low on water." His back to the door, he's looking over his shoulder at the six two-gallon drums they carried.

"Isosceles will have some."

The hinges are well-oiled and don't creak. When Angel

looks again there is a brown cloak hovering in midair. Beneath the cloak is a man, but Angel doesn't see him at first, sees only dark cloth and dark stone behind. The air feels surprising cool.

"Yes?"

Angel's eyes start to adjust, he can make out a short beard and hazel eyes with scars running off the left one like hatch marks, almost hidden unless the light hits just right.

"She's very ill," jerking a thumb back towards the jeep. "She knows Padré Isosceles and says he can help."

The door stays open but the monk seems to vanish as if he were walking along and suddenly dropped into a deep hole. Inside a bell rings. Six men come rushing out the door, there's no order to it, but Angel sees a trace of a formation. No more than timed footsteps. They have a stretcher and Pena gets lifted and lain, then they are back inside and Angel stands wanting.

He watches the door, looking for something else. The hallway inside is bulk stone: heavy, gray brick, and not indigenous. Carted here, the long haul. Walls higher than the doors, over fifteen feet. He hears a quiet babble. Sees a long white taper lit in the background, a specter passes through its light, face cut off at angles, no eyes visible, skin white, terrible.

"Creepy," Angel says aloud.

"What's creepy?"

Angel startles, spins to see a man standing before him. Shorter than he is, five-ten maybe. Face like a drunk chipmunk. Angel can't answer the question, just shakes his head, and steps towards the truck to begin unloading. Stops, walks back.

"I've been driving too long." Extending his hand, "Angel."

"Brother."

They shake. Angel thinks he could like a man named Brother.

"Are you hungry?" asks Brother.

"Yeah. No. We're low on water," shaken by how thin Pena looked on the stretcher. "I'm sorry, I meant that if we have to leave quickly to get Pena to a hospital we're going to need more water. I'm a little dazed."

"You can refill your water jugs in the shed," says Brother, pointing to a pile of gray boards about a hundred yards off. Four walls and a sloped roof, not much threat from rain around here, another mystery. "But we have the best doctor for three hundred miles."

Angel starts carrying jugs anyway, Brother follows with the others. Inside are gardening tools, hoes, spades, shovels, things Angel doesn't know the names of—sees a whole rack of needle-nose pliers and asks.

"Pulling the spines out of cactus, we all help, they make a good salad."

The pump sits in the center, shiny red like wet paint. Brother primes it and Angel sees the shadow of a tattoo under his sleeve. Thick wrists and maps for veins. The water comes out clear, very cold and clean, up from someplace far underground and Angel knows this one must of been a bitch to drill. They finish refilling and Angel reloads the jeep. He needs to know he can leave at any time and Brother doesn't seem to ask any questions. Just here to help or watch.

"They've taken her to the tower, she's a woman, we're celibate here." There is no judgment in his voice.

Angel sees the tower, a lookout post rising above the left side of the church. Near the top is a trim of red, could be paint or tile, he can't tell. Above it the open archways and the thick iron of the bell.

Angel asks if she's okay and clenches his teeth—as if there's been a change in the last five minutes.

"Doctor's with her now," says Brother. "I'll take you to her, but she'll be asleep, he'll give her codeine for the cough and she'll go right out."

Angel pulls a bandanna from his pocket, wipes sweat off his forehead, puts the bandanna back in his pocket.

"Is there somewhere I could wash up?"

They walk towards the mission in silence. Dirt rises from their heels in thin clouds. The canyon breaks the plain to the north into shadow, the other directions are low rises, small hills with low tumble shrubs. Angel smokes as he walks, the cigarette lodged between his fingers. A black mutt trots out to meet them, eyes Angel from ten paces, and rushes over to lick and bounce. Angel stops to play and then rises and they all walk together. The sun beginning to settle into the horizon, light in bands like stacked pancakes and a flush of drifting crimson births a migration of crows.

IN JERUSALEM, THAT MONTH, IT RAINS.
But once the thunder has gone, no one notices.

"For four thousand years people try to kill the Jews. They've been plagued and stoned and driven across deserts, there was that big flood and who can remember how many wars. Who's gonna notice a little rain, Johnii?"

Johnii raises his hands and smiles, as if that's his purpose, that's what he's been waiting for all this time. He, alone, is here to notice the rain.

Amazing that the man can recall his name, they met only once and that must have been three months ago, but that's how things are in a country tearing away at itself, people remember small kindnesses, handshakes, drinks: after a while it becomes a currency all its own.

A small cafe near the west gate of the Old City, a place of old stone cut at odd angles, what would be a bad part of town if that phrase mattered here. It's late and the lights have been off for hours. They sit in the dark, drinking bitter Turkish coffee from paper cups. This place is an impossibility, a throwback to a time of constant threat, and one that's been kept alive simply out of tradition. It's part of the job, but Johnii likes to come. What could be better than a roomful of brave old men gathered to watch old movies?

Tonight's bill is *To Have and Have Not* and Johnii's companion wants to know if he's a Bogart fan.

"I came out to see Lauren Bacall."

"She's more than enough of a reason."

"Men have crossed oceans for less."

"I did," says the old man, a tilt of the head, a crease at the edge of his mouth. "They're starting, let's go inside."

They get up and shuffle through a beaded curtain into a smoky room full of old couches. There are ten, maybe fifteen people in there and Johnii looks around for his contact and spots no one wearing a green beret. He checks his watch, but knows his timing is exact. There are a few seats open by the door, Johnii chooses an overstuffed armchair with a split seam and a pale blanket thrown across its backside. They use a blank wall as a screen and every week someone slaps a fresh coat of white paint up to make the showing as good as can be.

His companion picks a battered love seat directly in front of him and drags an old coffee can beside him to use as an ashtray. He puts his feet up on an ottoman and sits deep in the chair so as not to block Johnii's view. The lights dim, someone lights a match and pulls on a cigar. Johnii watches the coal grow bright. On the love seat, the old man reaches into his jacket pocket and comes out with a green fisherman's cap, glances back at Johnii, shrugs and puts it on. Halfway through the second reel he slides a manila folder behind him, it goes into Johnii's coat before anyone can notice.

Such a great movie, it's a shame to leave early. The night is cool and the rain falls slowly in fat drops. Johnii drives south towards Hebron, then east towards a sleepy hamlet perched beside the Dead Sea. This is a terrible place for machinery, even the air smells of salt. Metal turns to rust in a season, cars don't last an hour. The way in is a graveyard of fallen axles, rotting interiors, cars whose wheels have fallen off midstride and have been pushed just off the road, waiting to be sold for scrap. One of the least likely places to look for expensive printing apparatus, only a fool would try to run that kind of operation here.

Johnii leaves the car at the end of a long road, pops open his umbrella, and makes sure the envelope stays deep inside his coat. The sign outside reads boat repair and there's a full workshop inside and a couple of dusty hulls. You could bring an engine here and get it back in better condition. They were good with saltwater damage, dings and nicks. The pier out back has a few freshly painted boats tied to it. He can see them bobbing in the pale wash of the new moon as he makes his way up two hundred yards of fresh mud. No one would bother paving a driveway out here, no one who didn't want a little extra attention.

A thin key hangs round his neck, riding the same chain as an old pair of dog tags, he unsnaps the clasp and lets it slide into his hand. The locks tend to change—especially on that old side door—rather frequently. Not that it's too much trouble, lock repair comes easily to these boatmen and they do most of the work themselves. He gets his key in the mail and leaves a light burning all night to confirm arrival.

Inside is a small printer's shop, a small workstation, a few presses, and two store rooms: one holds barrels of gray ink labeled as machinist's oil and the other a thorough selection of paper. Someone has left a small table lamp on low, the bulb not more than forty watts, not bright enough to shine through anything, let alone the steel reinforced door and the solid concrete walls. Johnii dumps himself into a small couch positioned beside the lamp and pulls the envelope from his coat. The usual trade around here is in paper products, a little documentation for citizens wishing to travel through the world unmolested. A Jew, even an Israeli Jew, still has to be free to do a little business. The original shop was set up for Holocaust survivors—people who wanted to insure that if anything like that ever happened again they had ways of presenting themselves as others: as Russians or Italians or Samoans for all it mattered, anybody but who they were.

Johnii finishes his cigarette and unlocks the storeroom door. He walks past the barrels of ink to a small worktable at the far side of the room. The left leg of the table is hollow and inside is a spare pair of reading glasses. The world changes a little when he puts them on. He can no longer see, but he can smell. Saltwater and musk and something that's not quite lilac.

The ink is stacked in barrels three high and five deep, enough to last two years. It's hard to procure, when they can get a good price they buy all they can. A risky deal, but they don't have a choice in the matter. This ink dries a light gray and their contact inside the Vatican demands it be used, maybe it's made by a brother or a cousin and he's getting some kind of a kickback, but that doesn't feel right to Johnii.

Another small mystery, the world's full of them.

Twenty-seven sheets of paper slide out of the envelope, not much longer than a college term paper. It's funny how thin some lives can become. The writing is in columns, Latin on one side and Italian on the other. Johnii reads over the Italian, it's some of the only practice he gets.

There's an article about a treatise by Isaac Luria. A passage of commentary on the demon Lilith. It's a little article and not of much importance to anyone but a handful of scholars. Lilith appears only once in the Torah, deep within

Isaac, she is among the beasts that lay waste to the land on the day of vengeance. The counterpart to the white goddess, the demon female come to strangle children in the night.

Johnii holds the paper in his hand, feeling the old parchment. A new text written on old paper. By the end of the second page he's got most of it. Luria's work details Lilith's relation to the world of the kelipoth.

Kelipoth is a favorite topic, one that often shows up in these papers. There are those that believed the world was poured into existence. That vessels were filled and life given. It is another way of looking at the moment of Creation. In Kabbalah, it is said, these vessels couldn't hold on to the divine light. They shattered on impact. Afterwards nothing remained in its proper place. Exiled, erring, in need of return. It is the moment that Creation became unfinished, flawed, broken. Some of the divine light managed to return to its source, but some was lost—hurled into existence with the shards of the vessels themselves. The combination of the two—broken aspects of the divine—became known as the kelipoth, the realm of evil, the vessels of the dead.

Luria assigns Lilith a position within the shattering. It is a casual study, an attempt at understanding conception. The paper doesn't offer much more information, just this brief summary of the contents and the original book's location within the Vatican. A locked room, deep beneath something called the Tower of Winds. It just so happens that the Tower of Winds is the main structure in the Vatican's secret archives, a fact that anyone with a guidebook to Rome could learn. The only difficulty being that the locked room doesn't appear in any guide book or in any book whatsoever, not even if you looked through the entire history of Christendom.

Beside the Luria article there is a short history of a painting done by a particular Flemish master and taken from a private collection by the Nazis on another trip through Belgium. It was the end of 1944. They were Nazis and they were losing. The painting, along with countless others, was sold by Hitler to the Vatican to finance his flailing war efforts. The money got dumped into Swiss banks, changed hands, reemerged. Some of it went south, to Argentina, some sat around, waiting out the war. It was all standard practice.

No signature follows these articles, but Johnii supposes the author a Jesuit by dint of his ferocity and thorough scholarship. The work is smuggled out of the Vatican once a month, makes its way via Malta to Jerusalem where Johnii is responsible for getting it from the courier—different every time—to the printer. He has held this position for almost five years. In that time, he's had no close calls. It's a living and some days a good one at that. He's made some contacts, traded his access to printed goods for information, a few well-timed investments, enough so, should he ever need to vanish, he could live out the rest of his days in comfort.

Somewhere, he knows, he has a boss. Someone who is in charge, someone who tells someone who tells someone and then a phone rings, a man coughs, motion begins. Who runs the show? He only asked once, for his effort he heard laughter, he heard only that the man was Eastern European, a Russian perhaps, he heard that he's to know no more, to not ask, to not think along those lines. And that's interesting too, a discipline of sorts, something from which to learn.

He originally took the job to have access to early commentaries on the I Ching, hoarded like so much other information, deep within the Vatican.

It started a long time ago, at a time when Johnii wanted a second-century treatise written by a Tibetan monk and given to the Chinese emperor as a present. A detailed commentary on the first ten hexagrams of the oracle and their relation to the calendar year. The truth was that the whole of the scroll was little more than a bribe in support of a new calendar issued by His Majesty. It proved great diplomacy to support another's intellectual folly, especially, in fact, if that support took the form of some of the finest astrological scholarship to date. Johnii found out that the item he was looking for was secreted in the Vatican's collection. He didn't understand. He asked questions. No one wanted to answer and because he knew right when to stop asking, knew how to keep his mouth shut afterwards, someone noticed. Someone called someone who called someone and he got a job that paid in US dollars. A real blessing in a country that has as much luck with currency as it does with neighbors.

The whole thing amazed Johnii. The Catholic Church and how many people know its secrets? Johnii knows of rooms within the Vatican locked for all of time. Knows that the Swiss Guard are set to task. Men would spend lives outside of closed doors, would forbid all. Clerics and demons and angels found themselves at the sharp end of a halberd, found a stranger's menace, found a part of their world denied. It's not a joke. Johnii heard stories of the pope finding himself barred from certain rooms. Certainly he may be the spiritual emissary of the Lord, but the Lord has an agenda all his own.

Johnii looks back through the pages one at a time, just another set of eyes in a long operation. He's partially reading for information relevant to his interests but mainly he's looking for stylistic variations, changes from all the previous months, anything that would signal the organization had been caught. A wrong word, a badly adjusted sentence, a rhythm that doesn't match—he knows his Jesuit. There's no fun in being had. It is after three AM when he finishes reading, he signs off on the bottom with a legible *C* for courier and a neat square drawn round it—an Americanism from the fifties: square, dull, same as it ever was. If he were to draw a circle, well then someone would understand that they had sprung a leak.

The safe lies in the floor beneath the couch and the couch, being bolted down, requires the release of a jigsaw clasp on its hind leg. He dials in the combination and puts the newsletter inside, removing another small envelope, this one containing five thousand dollars in cash and a smattering of other documents to be distributed around the city over the next few days. Not usually his responsibility, but he wants a little extra spending money for the trip to Colorado and it's been a long time since he's had a vacation.

Christiana comes into his head all on her own, but he doesn't want her there, he has business in Colorado, he has a long week ahead of him, he has the taste of her buried deep inside. The twenty-second hexagram of the I Ching is known as *Pi*—grace. Fire below, mountain above. A sweet heat rising, a sky illuminated, a woman he just met. She is not a part of that, his world made from broken lines, and he wonders if he can keep it that way.

He took off his boots when he came in and now he bends to put them back on. A dirty rag hangs on a small hook beside the door for wiping off mud on nights like this, but Johnii has to trudge back to his car and his boots will only get dirty again. As he reaches for the door, his other hand trails inside his shirt to a small leather pouch hanging round his neck. Inside, his original copy of the I Ching, written in Chinese, a language, strangely, that he has always known. It's become a talisman to him and he just feels for its presence and lets go, stepping out into the wet night. All that excitement and it turned out to be a routine evening after all. He'll be back in Jerusalem before people start waking up for their workdays and just in case he messes his hair and unbuttons the top few buttons on his shirt. Another lover sneaking back home late at night, always a good sign in a country at war.

ALL NIGHT, ANGEL SITS IN THIS MONK'S cell watching Pena's gray sleep in her iron bed. She clutches the coins of the I Ching to her breast, earlier Angel tried prying them loose, but her grip was too tight. A small dresser sits in the corner with their bags shoved beneath. They carry very little, Pena almost nothing at all. On top a small, white taper that doesn't drip, gives off a slow glow. Angel sits in a straight backed wooden chair, the kind they had in school, with an ashtray at his feet. Besides these things the room is bare. Outside, it starts to rain.

He yawns, stands, walks to her side. The slow urge to touch her brow from above.

"I'm gonna go find some coffee, would you like anything?"

But there's no answer and he wasn't expecting one.

The hallway is dark, made of high stone, offering no lit torches or arrow slits to guide his way. He almost goes back for the candle but thinks better of it. Instead, he lights a Lucky Strike, one of his last, and starts towards the end of the corridor. It is an immense hall and his footsteps create a rough flow that peels round him. At the hall's end Mary rests in a deep alcove, a lunula bent across the straight lines of the wall's corner. Her face hidden by the shadows, but there is a window round the bend and a slate of pale dusk angles across the floor leading to her. A fading spotlight from a performance old and forgotten, but still, there's something to it and enough of something that Angel steps around the light, does not disturb her curtain calls.

He finds the stairway, a wide spiral carved into the rock without banister or guardrail, and descends with one hand dragging along the cool stone wall. The rain is louder now, but through it he hears the deep toll of the vespers' bell and below a shuffle of feet marches into the chapel. He stays on the stairs, out of sight. The ritual doesn't frighten him, but the seriousness of these men does—as if, for them, this church is all that remains of their lives.

The kitchen is off to the left, past the chapel and "one, two, three," doors down, counting in his head. Then down another dim walkway, a right and a final left and he finds the kitchen door, rough wood, a cool, brass knob.

He must have gotten lost, a wrong turn, a missed step. He knows right away what he's found. No matter what else, he was coming this way sooner or later, so now it's sooner. He almost shrugs as he steps through the doorway.

Isosceles' private chamber is a medium-size room from an eighteenth-century manor: a hard bed and a huge desk, bookshelves from floor to ceiling with the books often two deep in places and loose papers in mounds. On the desk, a small lamp already lit. Angel sits beside it, in another straight backed chair, not unlike the one he passed last night in. Spread across the thick wood is a small Torah, unfurled, with pen lines running frantic over its words. He has never seen a desecrated Torah, not one printed on vellum. Isosceles, he thinks, is a man who likes to roll the dice. Beside it a calculator, scratch paper full of equations, Hebrew letters and a steel ashtray holding a half-smoked cigarette that Angel, unthinking, promptly relights. There's a small shelf above the desk, more books, several on the great Russian mathematician Georg Cantor, a collection of Einstein's early writings, a few books on Kabbalah, and a series of stuffed manila folders. Angel runs a thumb across the folders looking at the docket names. Mostly they're places: Cairo, Alexandria, Spain, France; towards the end he sees one entitled "The Templar" and just past that, "Pena and Angel."

"Fuck me," staring at his name on a folder in a monastery at the ass end of Mexico.

Outside a dog barks, the rain, a reedy shuffle. Or was it... but there's no time and he doesn't really think about it anyway. He grabs the Pena and Angel folder, thicker than he thought, and shoves it between pants and back, pulling out his shirttail to hide the protrusion. He hears footsteps. Cigarette extinguished and back out the way he came.

But what was the way he came? The light's changed, the day has become brighter and he's starting to sweat. Past the tapestry, the old wooden crucifix, then around the corner, take the right fork, the bright copper kettle, then a left and a right, down this hall, through the archway and shit this isn't the way back at all. But there really is no way back and there hasn't been for quite some time. Angel does, eventually, not only find his way out, he actually finds the kitchen and a hot cup of coffee—his original purpose—which he manages to carry to the bottom of the stairs before someone finds him.

"Amigo."

Angel turns to find another cloaked monk.

"Did you come down to pray with us?"

Angel raises the coffee cup. "In a manner of speaking."

"Ahh."

"It was a long night, I'm sorry I helped myself, didn't want to disturb your morning prayers."

The monk pauses, thinking about something, starts to turn away, then looks back at Angel. "All the nights are long around here." He leaves Angel before he can ask.

Angel spends the rest of the day with Pena. She's not doing any better. Her breathing is a shallow dream, a muttering, but the voice is soft and the language is not one he knows. Around sunset a plate of food and a fresh taper appeared outside the door, but that was hours ago. It is well past dark now. The monastery has settled in for the night. Angel's tucked the folder into his bag and is doing his best to forget about it for now. Around nine o'clock Pena's sleep becomes restless. Angel has taken to sitting beside her, mopping her brow with an old shirt. One less thing to carry out with him. Behind him the room is a wash of damp space and behind that there is a knock at the door. Angel turns as it opens.

"Come in."

But it's Padre Isosceles and in is something he already is. He stands staring and thinking, then moves like an elongated bird. His breath smells of rum. His eyes are red as if from crying, but not crying, from study and toil and long strain over difficult books that have brought him nowhere or closer to something that is still so far away the gain of distance is not measurable in any metric Angel can understand.

"How is she?" asks Isosceles, his voice a primitive instrument: two steel wires stretched between a casing made of human bone, played with a hacksaw.

"Well, she's either dying or living or both and managing to take her own sweet time about it."

"Yes."

"What?" asks Angel.

"Yes."

Angel shrugs and starts to turn away. He wants a cigarette but they're across the room and well . . .

"I meant Pena's always been a difficult woman."

"I wouldn't know."

"I would," and with that Isosceles turns and heads towards the door and turns again with his shoulders leaning against the frame and sighs and looks at Angel.

"I came up to tell you we've decided to say a midnight mass for her, you'll hear the bells, you can come join us if you'd like."

Angel pauses, considering this.

"Will it help?" not angry, just sad.

"I could lie to you and tell you that it's up to God to decide, but I've been in the business quite a while now and no, I don't think it will help."

Angel looks at him for a long time, then starts to ask the next question, but Isosceles says, "Respect, out of respect," but he says it so softly that Angel has to think about the words before he can actually hear them and by then the door is shut and Isosceles' footsteps are going down the hall.

"I am really not sure about that man," says Angel, but Pena's not listening.

He walks over to his backpack, to the folder sticking out of it. Whoever Padre Isosceles is, he's certainly done his homework. But that's not what catches Angel, what pulls him up short. It's a note paper-clipped to the top of the pile, just a few handwritten words. And what would *nobody goes home* mean? It's almost funny to Angel, the thought of going home, now where would that be? But then if they aren't going to be allowed to go, what then?

By midnight the rain has stopped. Angel opens the window to darkness and wet air. He senses the bells approaching more than he hears them. There is a change in the feel of things, but then he notices, pulling his head in from the window, a new shadow in the room, one that wasn't there and shouldn't be there and on the wall beside Pena's bed. He turns and sees her sitting straight up, still clutching the coins to her chest. She is wide-eyed and sickly, her face ashen and drawn. She is smiling, but it's not a smile Angel's ever seen before. Angel tries to whisper something, *Mba-kayere*, but the phrase came to him in a dream and does not come back to him now. Still, he knows what it means—I am passed over—and knows enough to utter it at times like these.

Pena doesn't die as much as she evaporates. A light comes in the window and perhaps there are bells, but he doesn't hear them. Later, he'll remember his cigarette falling and the thin shower of sparks arcing from the cold stone floor into a stretched orange shower, but for now he sees nothing but Pena. Steam rises from her body. She throws her hand toward the window, releasing the I Ching, four thousand and ninety-six interrelationships falling and turning into night and some crack in the wind or leave before Angel can see them, but the others turn to birds and for a moment the sky is full of them, then there is nothing and Pena puts herself to bed. It is a soft motion, a lying down followed by her hand closing her eyes. Then all her gestures turn to smoke.

He doesn't know how long he waits, not thinking or smoking or doing much of anything with his head on her cold breast and the only sound left in this hollow room is his own lonely breath.

There is another knock at the door. He sees the stolen folder sticking out of his backpack. Should have hidden it better. He tries to now, but somehow he finds himself zipping what's left of his belongings into the backpack and then it's over his shoulder and on his back and he buckles the waist strap as he steps through the window and onto a cold stone ledge with a hundred feet of dark yawn remaining between him and the ground below.

Nobody goes home. Well, fuck them, is all he can think. There is wet stone beneath his hand and a long fall below. Everything works by instinct. It's only much later that it comes to him that Pena did, after all, manage to go home.

He can hear them inside, hear them prodding at the cold body, their boots on the floor, presently he makes out a dull scuttling noise followed by a distinct curse which is the overflowing ashtray being kicked across the floor. He has managed to work his way across the ledge to the building's edge and an iron drainpipe. The rain is heavier now, muffling the rusted whine of his added weight on the pipe. The spray comes off everything, miniature explosions that sound like hiccups, coming off his forehead and shoulders, his hands already cut by the flaked metal, arms extended straight with feet flat on the building, one on each side of the pipe taking, slogging, against fast gravity. Whatever moon there was is now gone behind a sheath of clouds. A bright light appears in the window above and, as he touches ground, he can just make out the boom of Isosceles' voice.

His plan is simple and clear, the kind you make up when you have no other choices, just run like hell and find someplace to hide out. The jeep is where he parked it and the keys are still in his pocket. As he starts the engine he catches a glance of the gargoyle door knocker hanging free in midair as the door yanks open. Through the rain, he hears the hard pop of a gun, a pistol of some kind, but doesn't notice the bullet hole in the passenger seat until the next day. He's not certain they'll come after him, not until a week later, when he's curled up for the night in the arms of a pale-eyed surfer girl who thinks Angel's not a bad way to end the day.

It's then, after a long tangled night and too much of a peculiar rum punch that everyone down here seems especially keen on, that he sneaks off into a closet and sits reading the folder under the hard light of a bare bulb. He reads slowly and carefully and boy is he in deep shit.

IT IS NEARLY TIME FOR SUPPER. THE windows are open and the air already cool. Isosceles stands alone in the bell tower, staring at the bed where Pena once lay. Downstairs, his men are waiting for him to arrive and say grace and he lets them wait. He is playing the angles. There is already talk that he killed Pena himself. It's not true, but he has left them to wonder.

It is in this room that he originally uncovered the manuscripts. Here that he first learned of the Kabbalah. Well, what of it?

The bed frame has already been disassembled and is stacked outside the door. Tomorrow he will have someone carry it to the cellar. He has dragged the mattress to the center of the stone floor. At his feet lies a small gas can that he bends to pick up, unscrewing the cap as he does. He pours the gas slowly, covering the mattress, letting the stain spread onto the floor. This is something else for his men to wonder about, why he has chosen to burn the mattress here, why not throw it out the window and burn it with the rest of the garbage? Whatever killed Pena is not contagious, not in any viral sense. In the corner of the room is an old life preserver, faded orange, with a rip running down one of its pillows. He crosses the floor and picks it up, throwing it onto the center of the bed. He empties the gas can on it, then walks back to the doorway and strikes a match, tosses it inside. The mattress catches all at once, flames rising in a wall, licking high, the room instantly full of smoke.

He shields his face with a hand, the heat too much to bear, backing him into the hallway. The smoke will stain the ceiling and the walls and no matter how often he has the room washed it will never go away. Soot will coat the windowsill. The floor will turn black with ash, but the fire will not spread. It's an old monastary, all stone, there is nothing here left to burn besides an old bed, a roomful of memory. There was a birth and a death and everything in between. Just a gesture, he thinks, starting to walk away.

games, so it comes as no surprise, but to find oneself so squarely in the middle of it? Angel rests with one hand at his side, his bare feet have found a piano's brass pedals, the slick cold to match his spine. The tingling that is now always there.

He sits in the back room of a surfer's honky-tonk, somewhere near Magdalena Bay. The front door hangs half open, roughshod, angling off its hinges, pouring into other rooms. A front counter and the few chairs, fewer customers. Grandma watches him from her table in the back. The piano sits in the middle of a sagging wooden floor, rocking on a perch bent by its own weight. Someday the piano will pull itself through the floor and people will point to the hole where the music once stood. For now Angel plunks at broken keys. It's not nearly as out of tune as he supposed and there's still some tension to the pedals. He always liked the slow echo, the fade out. The bench is a cherry brown, a slash of lighter wood showing through where a splinter has torn out. There is no cushion to sit on.

How did he get in so deep, knowing so little. The society was set up by the Borghese, was so secret that it was never given a name and so, for the few who ever knew, they grew up calling it just that. The Society. Angel imagines that with the passage of years it must have earned the capital letter. His father had played poker on Tuesday nights. They were the Society of Inebriation, Tradition and—but Angel can't remember all of it and it didn't matter because he too took to saying he was off to a society meeting or off to society and now Angel is haunted by the word.

It's hard to tell if Isosceles has anything to do with the Society or not, if he does it's a tangential connection. The file sets them too clearly apart, the us and the them. Perhaps there is competition. Certainly the Society was founded by a pope, but Isosceles was chosen by a god. However, that's a part of the story Angel doesn't know yet and if he did? Hard to tell what he would have done differently. Right now he only knows that he misses Pena and if she wanted him for a protégé, well, that might be fun too.

He shakes it all out of his head, starts to play the opening to "Mr. Bojangles" and laughs at the thought. Grandma stands in the doorway for a moment and he understands that someone wants to hear that song so he plays on and when he's done he plays a few other songs and then he sits in the cool of the room and thinks about things.

During the Renaissance there was a flowering of knowledge and there were men who wanted some of it hidden. An entirely new art form for them, another unnamed thing, the art of concealment, of hiding in plain sight. They built a library within a library.

Who knows what the original purpose was—to know thine enemy as thyself, to generally misbehave, to own and possess and deny. In the middle of the richest time in history they wanted their own abandon. They wanted an endless wasteland and the vacancy. They wanted to know what was so special that an entire people would walk out of Egypt to spend a lifetime wandering a desert. They wanted the treasures of another people living high on a plateau above the Himalayas. They wanted the mysteries of spice.

They wanted and wanted and wanted and in the end they found they had not the soul for it. They had come to possess empty treasure and that too became a calling, when there is nothing else there is still possession.

under a gaunt sky. A heavy light that's thick enough to blow on, that weighs everything differently, that comes in from the ocean, from the islands, from some all night ju-ju cauldron and the fishermen on the beach can feel it and know enough to head home. Here at the border there is no place to head, no shelter, just the inevitable back and forth and the feeling of being always caught in the middle. They've turned the lights on early, big spotlights that bleach the skin. They rise above the checkpoint, hot white, light that splinters at off angles. The pavement glows. It's dazzling all right, there are Mexicans lined up for miles just to watch.

The jeep broke down in Ensenada and it took him two days to walk up the coast. He's caught a ride out of Tijuana from a cacti broker with a business card that reads exotic plants, but both he and Angel know that there's nothing legal about this—coming out of Mexico and all. The guy says he's just a broker, a money changer and there's nothing to worry about. He doesn't wink, which is the only reason Angel stays in the car. Behind them idles a rusty station wagon full of kids, their small fingers dotting the windows, then a Ford Bronco with fat tires and then the line trails off and Angel can't really see. But somewhere back there, somewhere in a mad desert, somewhere—asking questions of stubborn surfers, following his own tired trail is Isosceles.

He thought to travel back to New Mexico, but instead decides to stick near the Pacific. Oregon maybe. Small clapboard towns with cafes that open early for the loggers. Something in the desert's flat spaces no longer feels right, something he would add to Isosceles' bill when the time came. He's grown a beard, or tried, thin across his cheeks and upper lip: spaced weeds of hair. Everything is a disguise now.

So he gets to San Luis Obispo in the back of a Pinto and is dropped in the center of town, right in front of a church. It's Sunday afternoon. Small children on bicycles, girls with pastel haltertops and breasts the size of dollhouse teacups, people who hold hands under a silken sky that will never rain on their parade. Angel buys supplies and catches a short lift to the base of the Seven Sisters, a small chain of extinct volcanoes just outside of town. The evening will bring a fog over their tops, but for now they are big teeth half-yanked out of flat earth. He puts his pack on and humps it until he's high enough to watch the sunset from a rocky perch on Bishop's Peak and want a drink. It's then that he remembers Pena's flask sitting in the pocket of his jacket. Whiskey on a cold night. The flask is almost full, enough to be soggy drunk and in terrible pain tomorrow if need be, but he doesn't think it has to go that far. The metal lies cool in his hand, cooler than the whiskey in his throat. He screws the cap back on tight, turns it upsidedown, the liquor inside makes a slosh. There is an engraving on the bottom, he remembers seeing it in Mexico. "Ask the Fisherman—Red Lodge, Montana." Store where she bought it, maybe. Later, about to fall asleep, he remembers his last conversation with Pena, how she said her friend Coyote was a great fisherman, how strange it was that she gave him the flask, how two and two make four. A soft breeze winds up the mountain, whistling through short grass, carries a dog's bark in from town. Angel's never been to Montana.

He can't sleep much and dreams of Isosceles all night. Sees himself as a cowboy and sees Isosceles on a gray steed with his hat worn low across the eyes. Not too hard to figure that one out. He's awake by four. Walks into town to clear his head, has pancakes and eggs and sausage and bacon and a double side of potatoes and six cups of coffee and then an order of rye toast with butter and a slice of pie. Hunger pouring out of everywhere. Finishing the pie and thinking of ordering a second slice and can't believe he's eating like this when he sees an old red car creep past the cafe. The driver has dark glasses and a nose like a beak. Angel knows the face. The man from the kitchen, after he had stolen the folder, the man who called him amigo. Can't believe they could actually follow him here, two weeks since he left the monastery, he could be anywhere. But here he is, paying his check and ducking across the street to a grove of fir trees in a park where he dumps out his pack. Two hours combing everything for some type of tracking device. Nothing to be found, unless it's too small to be found—doesn't like where these thoughts go.

On his way out of town he walks by the Mission San Luis Obispo de Tolosa, the red-tiled roof bright in the noon sun. The tiles were developed to replace the thatch that fell to flame so easily under Native American arson attacks. How many churches did it take until they learned, how many houses of God were lost? He didn't used to feel this way.

Both buses and trains are options, time-savers at least, but he's running low on cash and doesn't think he can stomach three days bottled up. Instead he wears sunglasses and treks alongside a marginal road figuring he can get a ride to Las Vegas and another to Montana when a '64 Valiant painted steel blue stops beside him. Inside the wood on the dash is authentic and baby smooth and he asks if he can smoke.

"Ain't nothing in the world you can't do," says the driver, turning towards Angel, twinkling eyes, gray hair cut short and thick and curled into little springs. "Jack Crawford."

"Angel."

"Get in. I'd be honored if you smoked in my car."

Angel climbs in offering his hand and they shake and then he pulls cigarettes from his pocket and offers one of those as well. Jack takes the smoke and slides it between his lips, his eyebrows thick and peering, his hand reaching into the backseat, swatting, coming out with a wide-brimmed hat, a gangster appendage, what his father used to call a Cagney.

"I think I'm gonna need my smoking hat."

Angel grins, the seat soft beneath him.

They drive all day and later the land turns ocher in the last light. Music on the tape deck and Angel asking questions. Jack speaks in lazy turns, his words form and hang in a friendly, raspy gate.

"Got a thing for cards of all sorts. I can read the future in truck stop postcards—tell you if it's cancer or marriage by spreading out Welcome to Doohickee, Idaho, population 3 or the ones with girls in pink bikinis, the whole of Florida stamped across their butts. Can't even get near most tarot decks, vibrations are too strong, damn things fly outta my hands. Poker's about the stupidest way to pass the time I know of, but in a few hours at a decent table I can make my rent."

A short hammering of the accelerator gives rise to a furious engine growl. Jack bangs knuckles against the wheel, sheer celebration in pointing the thing straight down a road. "Sometimes I gotta make my rent."

"So we're going to Vegas?"

"Vegas, Salt Lake, Vernal, Dinosaur National, in that order," ticking off his list.

"Why?"

"Why? Cash, family, necessity, pleasure, of course."

Jack glances over, eyes squinting in amusement.

"Vegas is obvious. I have a little money in my pocket and plan on having more when I leave. My sister's in Salt Lake and needs cash. Vernal's where I meet my river guides and Dinosaur National Monument runs the Utah-Colorado border. Green River slices down the middle. It's not much in the way of big rapids, but Ladore Canyon is supposed to be one of the better ones."

"Ladore Canyon," says Angel.

Jack nods.

"Pressure and time." Angel's hands wrap a blue bandanna into tight spirals, watching as it spins itself free.

Jack taps fingers as he drives. Whole notes, quarter notes, short staccato blasts with the back of his hand. Keeping time with the music rolling through the speakers. Fat guitars in layers, thick like waves. Angel watches California through the window, thinks he should come back some time. They pass an abandoned mining shack, Jack watches it fade in the rear-view mirror. He uses the road like an encyclopedia. It's something Angel notices, a fact that arrives, how Jack sees sparrows on telephone poles, blowing trash, the flat of the horizon, how they open up memory, how the road retells his life, changing the order, always insistent.

"Want to know how this little card thing of mine developed?" A curious smile spreading across Jack's face, angling into all corners. He looks like a man governed by the moon. "'Tis an odd tale."

"Says the man who's already told me tarot cards sail from him unaided."

Jack takes his hand off the wheel to turn down the music.

"I was driving from El Paso over to Carlsbad in an old beater which died somewhere in the Dakotas about three years later. I had to walk for two days before anyone would give me a ride." He swats his hand to shoo away the tangents. "Different story.

"Anyway, I wanted to see Carlsbad Caverns. Those big, bad caves. I came through Texas from the west to drive over Crow Flats, nothing special to there, just liked the name. Crow Flats. Had some extra time, so instead of going straight there I stopped off at the El Paso Gap, right on the Texas-New Mexico border. A place called Dog Canyon, in the Guadalupe Mountains. From the highway all you can see is a wall of red rock rising straight up from the desert floor. I buy my topos from the ranger station. My pack's already loaded, three-day's worth of provisions. High country canyon, well-forested. Saw Apache mescal-roasting pits. Waisthigh grass."

Jack pauses for a second, chewing something over.

"It's not a big park, but somehow I get all spun around. My compass seems to be spinning at random. Don't understand it. Remember, this was twenty years ago and a lot of the hiking trails that are now trampled weren't even there. Later found out I had walked over a pass out of Dog Canyon and into South McKittrick Canyon. Didn't matter to me, I was lost. Hot sun, running out of water, thirsty as hell, starting to get scared."

The tape ends and Jack pops it out, puts in a tape of old tangos, full-bodied and mournful. "Music to swoon to."

Angel shakes his head. "I don't think I know how to swoon."

"Not matter. Not important." Jack sucks in a gulp of air, blowing it out slowly, trying to stay on track. "By the third day I'm starting to figure it's all over. I know the park isn't big, tried walking in one direction, following the sun, heading west, all of it, keep getting lost. I think everything's crazy—I mean I've been canyoneering for almost a decade, I never got lost, used to be a point of pride. I pull out my compass, I'd been looking at the thing for two days straight, was sure it was broken. This time the needle's spinning in circles, not slow either. I just sit and stare. Five minutes pass and it's still spinning. Then it stops. Points north-east. I don't know what to do, but somehow I know this thing is giving me directions. Don't ask me how, I couldn't tell you, but I know. I walk, watching the compass the whole time. Couple hours later it starts spinning again, stops, pointing west. I go off in that direction. That's how the day goes. Middle of the afternoon I find a stream with water like glass. Thank God. As I'm drinking I notice a playing card in the middle of the stream, wedged between two rocks. Strange-looking card, looks old, two of hearts, but the hearts are big and fat. When I yank it out the card's completely dry. Been in that stream for who knows how long and it's dry. Weird huh? After that my compass went back to normal, I was out of the canyon before sunset. That's when my relationship with the cards developed."

"When you got back to the parking lot you kissed your truck."

"Yeah," says Jack, his jaw slackening. "Yeah I did."

Angel reaches for a cigarette, unaware.

"How did you know that?"

Angel stops, the lighter lit, the flame a few inches from his face. Shadows waver across his nose.

"I don't know," says Angel, "maybe it's what I would have done."

Night comes quietly. Angel's been sleeping, wakes up to blackness and a rushing vertigo. Like falling from distant skies back into his life. Jack pulls into a truck stop for coffee and Angel takes the next shift and by morning Vegas is a shiver on the horizon. Light that grows, unstoppable. Angel understands why they tested the atomic bomb in the desert, how terrible more light can be here, how they wanted that terror, needed the proof.

They break for breakfast and Jack drinks coffee black, more cups than Angel can believe. They check into a hotel on the outskirts of town, Angel falls into a lumpy bed, sheets the color of trout. Jack prepares to head into the glitter. Says he needs to visit four casinos, should take all day. If Angel wants a ride to Salt Lake he can wait, if not it was nice to meet him. Angel tells him he'll wait. He hands Jack a hundred, asks him to bet if he wants, keep a percentage of the take, give him the rest.

"Feeling lucky?" asks Jack.

"Feeling something, that's for certain."

Jack walks out the door in a white silk shirt and expensive

trousers, his shoes click in the hallway, the last sound Angel hears before sleep.

He wakes to three thousand dollars in hundreds landing on his head and Jack's voice saying, "Feeling something is for damn certain. Blackjack, fifty-dollar ante, I figured I play your money for an hour and walk. Every bet I placed with your cash came back in spades. No pun intended. I took twenty-five percent off the top, sounded fair, you want to disagree shoot me after I've had something to eat."

They wash up and head into town for steak which Angel buys. By nine they're back on the highway with Angel driving and Jack asleep in the back, both happy to be leaving, happy for the road and the darkness and the feeling of Las Vegas behind them, fading to a lantern then a nightlight then a firefly.

Morning brings them to the entrance to Kolob Canyon. Jack wakes with his hat slanted over his left eye blurring the sandstone walls of the Hurricane Cliffs which rim the west entrance. Angel knows that deep in the heart of this canyon are the narrows. Two-thousand-foot-high walls of stone, at places less than eighteen feet wide. He can feel all that rock in his chest. At the bottom rolls a pale stream, quick to rise and roar and sweep away anything in its path. Hikers have drowned. There are trees lodged hundreds of feet in the air, wedged between walls, branches resting on air.

Angel had stopped in the night to buy fresh fruit and coffee and pancake mix. They hike in for a few miles to a rock wall that juts forward with a crooked slant. From the ground it looks like a broken nose. Box elder and cottonwood grow in the distance. His stove makes a loud hiss that rattles around the canyon until breakfast is ready.

"Good pancakes," says Jack.

"Thanks."

"Fresh strawberries are a nice touch."

It is early evening when they roll into Salt Lake City. The house is roomy and old with cotton drapes and open windows. Jack's sister is close to sixty and blind and stuck to a rocking chair on a wide white porch. There is a dull light above her head and a circle of bugs like a halo. Her fingers are bent and taunt around the rocker's armrests as if the chair could suddenly dart forward on a high-speed frolic. She wears a small wedding ring backwards, the diamond cutting into the chair's hard wood, leaving a thumbnail dent that will grow. If she had ten million years she could carve a canyon. Her name is Matilda and she smiles at Jack, but doesn't say much. Her fingers stay tight on the chair. Jack goes inside to make tea and Angel watches the night come across the world.

He sits beside Matilda, in another rocking chair, listening to the early evening sounds. "You have a lovely home," he says finally.

Jack returns with tea but Angel can't stay awake and excuses himself and falls into a fast slumber between clean sheets smelling of baby powder and lilac. He wakes around five when the night is darkest and walks downstairs through its clutch. Sitting at a low oak table, he watches the sun climb over the mountains and at first light stands and stumbles about the kitchen looking for coffee. When he does find the pot, it's already on and full. The cups are on small brass hooks hanging in a neat row. They are gray and hearty and the coffee fits nicely inside. He sees Jack awake on the porch, sitting in the rocking chair, a rough wool blanket spread across his legs.

"Morning."

"Morning."

Jack's fedora is ten feet from him, upside down on the white slats of the porch. Its bowl is half full of playing cards and Angel notices the other half of the deck in Jack's hand. Jack cocks his wrist and spins the five of clubs end over end over end and into the hat.

"Matilda sleeps most of the day, we'll both be gone by then so I told her goodbye for you last night."

"Thanks," sorry he didn't say so himself.

They drive into town for breakfast and then Jack takes him to the Greyhound station and buys a one-way ticket to Red Lodge. They share a bench and a couple of cigarettes and a tired patch of yellowed light that has fallen through high windows and down onto their laps.

Eventually, Jack winks at him and says, "Go on, get outta here, you're late for the rest of your life."

The bus departs with a jolt. Jack stands with the sun behind him, a lean silhouette, his arm waving in a great arc. The windows on the bus are well-oiled, slick to touch and Angel struggles to wave before the bus pulls too far away. Cold air swamps his fingers. He lets them rest outside as the bus rides away. They pass through quick streets then onto the highway. He does the crossword puzzle. Padnag is a six-letter word for a good old horse. Utah passes behind tinted windows, the freeway empty, above the clouds the color of steel. The night comes, then another day. In his sleep, Pena comes to him, looking younger and spry, skipping down a path in the woods, tearing pages from an old book as she goes. The bus climbs to ten thousand feet and drops through the great barrenness of Hellroaring Pass. It looks like the end of the world. Drab rocks and sky, a whole bus full of people and no one knows what to say. Land drops away on the other side of the guardrail. At seven thousand feet rain falls. At five thousand feet they leave the highway to pull into Red Lodge. Home to the fisherman. The air is cool and sweet. Droplets land on Angel's neck as he bends to stretch. Small puddles form on clean ground. Pena once said she could see the future in a patch of rainwater, Angel hasn't tried.

THE SUN PULLS AT A DEAD-TIRED DRAG.
Pockmarks of night are starting to appear, but mist from the afternoon's rain, still chewy and languid, holds the light at odd angles. Angel reels through town in worn-out flannel, creased with frustration, dead ends, sleeves rolled high from the work. His eyes are drawn and bleary, there is mud on his knees from tripping over the only wino in Red Lodge.

It has been two days and there is no place he hasn't been. He paced the streets reading names off mailboxes. There was nothing at the post office or the county registrar. No sign of the fisherman. For the first time in a year he feels a clock in his life.

He goes to the hotel and packs up everything dirty and heads out to wash his clothes. He buys a heavy terry cloth bathrobe at the WalMart and wraps himself tightly inside while his clothes dry. There aren't many people in the laundromat, but the few who do come in give him hard looks and shake their heads. He doesn't care. When he was growing up his mother used to wrap him inside her robe while she washed their clothes. Sometimes the past creeps up on him, sometimes he gives in.

It didn't do all that much good. The robe went into the hotel closet and the clean clothes went on, the sun went down and now he's sitting on a wobbly stool, drinking George Dickel #8 as a brace against the things to come.

Not much of a bar, ragged music plays on the jukebox and men are spread out like hunter's trophies. A woman holds the pool table, playing eight ball against any and all challengers. The balls drop into pockets with a lush thud. She wears a Cleveland Indians cap and peace signs hang from her ears. The most remarkable thing she's ever done is a three-rail combo to bank the six ball into the eight and then off the eight and into the two for a soft slice towards the corner pocket.

The men here tonight have been losing to her for years now and take it as part of the scenery.

The bar is wooden and dull, scratched by age and long winter drunks. Above it hangs a pulaski—half-hatchet, half-hoe, used by the smoke jumpers to fight forest fire. This one belonged to Bob Salee, one of three survivors of the 1949 Mann Gulch fire. Its ends are black with carbon, years of cigarette smoke, neglect. Another wall holds a Zebra head, shot on safari in Africa, brought to Montana at the hunter's expense. Sam stands behind the bar, he owns this place, a pile of T-shirts, some long underwear, two red and black checkered logging shirts, three pairs of jeans, boots, coat, a burnished rifle, a picture of his wife who ran away to Toledo—Spain or Ohio, he can't recall, and a black lab with bad hips. He's seventy-one years old and serves twelve kinds of bourbon and two kinds of beer. On Saturday night he lets people bring in colas to cut their whiskey, but doesn't encourage the practice. Angel's been here for three hours and Sam has spent all of it buried in an algebra textbook. The numbers make him feel better. The one time he got drunk in this bar he told three different people he was an abacus counter from old Egypt, a past life he said. They carried him to his bed and set him to sleep with his boots on and he never mentioned it again. When Angel orders his fourth whiskey, Sam looks at him for a moment. "If you pass out I'll leave you where you lie."

He's a mean, old man, but he's right. Angel's drunk. He's discovered a wonderful new viscosity, a thick fluid replacing his blood. The stool has become unsteady purchase. His mad priest is everywhere, in every fissure and tint, in every amber sip. There is a burning in his throat, a bile of some kind, just to remind him.

The jukebox plays Blind Willie Johnson.

"Have you had enough of their kindness?" a woman's voice and not much louder than a whisper.

Angel looks up and realizes he's been looking down, watching for tide pools in his drink, small currents. An August landscape hangs at eye level. Hair cut like fresh straw. Sunny more than golden. He looks down to see hips curved. She puts a hand under his chin, lifts his head to her level. He's looking at a woman he's never seen before. He feels her breath on his cheek and sees green eyes.

"Did Isosceles send you?" asks Angel.

"Let's take a walk," she says, taking his hand.

Despite a round moon and plump stars, there is little to see with. He stops her and totters a few steps forward, turns to get a good look. Wants a good look. Lithe and subtle and something that makes his heart beat. Lips that could stop time. He has that charming look in his eye, that slight smile, that angle to his head—the things that always works so well. Then he falls on his ass in the dirt.

She smiles at him, with some women you cannot measure their patience, there are no instruments known.

"Some night we're having." he says.

The smell of woodsmoke comes across the basin.

PADRE ISOSCELES LEARNED TO DRINK
rum in a rundown bumba shack in the Caribbean, where he retreated after meeting Jesus. There was no door and only half a roof. The room was a skinny rectangle, forty-feet long and ten wide with three ratty booths and a smattering of bar stools propped against a makeshift counter. The smell of skunk cabbage and wet hemp crept from the walls and the floor. Isosceles sat tall in a back corner speaking to no one. Above him the light fell through a rift in the rafters, but the angle was off and he sat in a mute darkness.

He was drawn to the darkness, the absence, it was his own gravitational pull. As a child he would sit in a closet with his head ducked beneath old coats and a blanket covering the crack between door and floor. He would sit and have conversations with himself, speaking different languages for different parts. He had a gift that way. Learned Latin and English and Portuguese by the time he was six. His mother, once a promising anthropologist, had abandoned academia for a drunken poet who left her poor and pregnant giving birth on cold straw in an old attic with the ticks and the door mice and the whine of horses for company. Though she never told him, it came to her mind to name her new child Whelp.

One spring, while sitting in a park, he met his father. A tall man in a long coat. He gave him a plastic abacus, told him he had been away at sea and had brought the present from the Far East. Isosceles was five. The abacus said

"Made in Korea" across its bottom. He remembers shaking his father's hand, the rough fingers and the slicked-back hair and the slight limp as he walked away and never came back. Even Isosceles saw the irony. He didn't see him again until he was seven. Then his father showed up at their house one night, stayed for two weeks, got drunk and began beating first his mother, then him. Neither cried. It lasted most of the night. Isosceles survived by counting then adding then subtracting—the last memory he has of his father was 12 times 12 is 144. He had eleven broken bones. 11 times 11 is 121. He was in the hospital for three months, then taken to a rigorous boarding school with hard Catholic nuns. He found out his God and his father came from the same country.

Science and math and language became his world. By his fifteenth birthday he knew all the great names by heart, the old grays as they were called: Chandrasekhar, Bohr, Oppenheimer, Penrose, Sciama, Schwarzschild, Zel'dovich, Wheeler and Einstein—like a litany. Mouthing the words and waiting for the day when his name would cascade off another's tongue. He fought for a scholarship to college and spent four years as a promising Brazilian physics student with a lanky gait. His only affectation a thick mustache and those dark eyes. He graduated at the top of his class, pulled strings, begged, got a partial scholarship to Princeton for graduate study and a chance to do general relativity research with John Wheeler. Isosceles was drawn to Wheeler's catalogue, completed a decade earlier, of cold, dead stars. He liked the idea of caught time. It was hot August when he arrived and he didn't go outside again until the leaves had colored. Often, he slept on the lab's stone floor, his bones creaking and his mind forming sharp edges. He was at work on a notion of bent time, of gravity, of endless numbers and the thought that there might be something to be learned from Georg Cantor's infinite set theory, perhaps a way to merge the idea with Einstein's field equations. The two together could explain how time behaved inside a black hole.

Winter came, Wheeler bought Isosceles a coat when he noticed him shivering and hunched over a stack of papers in the library. By Christmas, he was stuck, hard-problemed as they called it, and was beginning to take it personally. Every now and again he would catch himself talking aloud, often in Latin, not noticing at first. He began drinking tea, waking at all hours for a fresh cup, watching the patterns of leaves on cup's bottom too carefully. One day, in late February, he noticed the snow on the ground, thought it a wonder, thought a walk would do him good. He wrapped himself warmly and went out to spend the afternoon with the world. Behind his building the red brick gave way to a gentle slope and a wood. Bare branches stretched in long, crinkled arcs above his head. The air smelled of pine. He walked slowly. A light snow was falling. A simple mistake led him to believe he couldn't get lost in his own backyard, but the fresh flakes smoothed his tracks and after an hour the trees all looked the same.

He came upon a pale stream, the water clear and slow beneath a patina of ice. The trees bent far over, leaning in, listening. A puzzle of branches blocked the light. Below, Isosceles stood on cracking ice, lightless, listening to his weight fracture the world. It was then that he knew he was right about the field equation, right about the Cantor sets, but that he would not come closer to the solution, that he would forever remain outside of the bigger mysteries. He shed his shoes and socks and began walking in the creek. The ice cracked beneath his feet, reaching up with a sharp tongue, drawing blood. The skin on his toes went white then pink then blue. He ignored the pain and kept walking. Wind crept up his back. The stream wrapped a curved path, a downsloped question mark that suddenly ended, curving underground, and Isosceles looked up to find himself directly behind the physics building.

Inside, he found a bucket in a janitor's closet and filled it with hot water from the bathroom sink. Stopped at his workstation on the third floor to pick up a book. No one was around. He carried the book and the bucket to a stool in the back labs. They were empty rooms mainly with big oaken counters and the occasional abandoned piece of equipment. Microscopes from the eighteenth century, oscilloscopes with broken screens, a lens from an abandoned telescope, now cracked and awaiting the trash, textbooks that are out of date and out of print piled into Precambrian shapes in corners of thick dust. Isosceles plucked an oversized Bunsen burner from a pile, still full of fuel, lit it. The flame ran at three inches and Isosceles turned it down to one and a half. After putting the burner in front of a stool and the bucket on the floor, he took his pants off and hung them across the inverted hook of a disconnected lab sink. He sat in tight white briefs, with his feet in a bucket of warm water and his hands held close to the flame of the burner, reading about Newton. His legs looked bleached white and his knees like elbows. The pain in his toes was unbearable, he thought he would have to call for help or get himself to a hospital and was not certain he could put his trousers back on and just then Jesus walked in the room.

Maybe Isosceles had fallen asleep or maybe he had lost his mind or maybe he was outside, still hobbling through a frozen stream. Maybe it was all three. There was no longer any way to be certain.

Jesus was wearing a thin loincloth and sandals, in his left hand he carried Isosceles' shoes, socks tucked neatly beneath the laces, and in his right was a knurled ash walking stick. His hair hung long and brown and had begun to form thick, nappy dreadlocks. He stopped, facing Isosceles, and spoke in a rough, archaic Latin. Isosceles had to listen hard to understand.

"Two thousand years ago, while hung from the cross, I had a vision. I was in a wintry wood. It was morning, a morning like today. A barefoot young man walked along a frozen stream toward me. I watched him come. I had never seen this man before, but looking at him I would know, know that this is the man I was supposed to teach all my secrets to. Since that day I have been coming to those woods every winter waiting to meet the man who walks barefoot along the stream. Today I was certain you were that man, but now, looking closely at your face, I can see you are not he, that I am mistaken. Anyway here are your shoes. Maybe I have the wrong woods, I'm not sure." With that Jesus walked out of the lab.

There was a moment of silence and afterwards a sound like a chandelier dropped from a great height onto a marble floor. There was a time of emptiness. Isosceles came to in a pile of glass and water. The pain in his feet had ebbed and they had regained their normal color. He put his pants back on and walked out of the lab and out of the building and to the train station and into a deep bitterness. Three days later he is in Key West and still confused and making his way to the Caribbean Islands.

He has three hundred dollars and a Bible. He drinks for three weeks straight and never opens the Bible. The clench in his jaw does not abate, his back molars grind down, occasionally Isosceles spits teeth particles onto the barroom floor. It is a month before anyone asks him his name, his business, his reason. When these questions finally come, they arrive with a six-foot-four Colombian, a professional scuba diver who works on massive oil rigs and drinks tequila. A life made of water, small beds, paychecks. His exact words are "Fuck's wrong with you?" Isosceles breaks his nose and his right knee and is trying to tear his eyes out when seven other divers pin him to a wall and take turns snapping first his fingers then his ribs then rowing him four hundred yards out to sea and throwing him overboard. They keep his money and toss him a cheap orange life preserver in exchange. A children's toy. He can neither hold onto it with his crippled fingers nor lie across with his shattered ribs. He is afloat for four days. Terrible visions. Later he will find a scar along his back in the shape of a scythe, over a foot long, and have no memory to attach to it. Never again will he like the taste of salt.

It is Pena who finds him and gets him to a hospital and pays the bill out of her own pocket. It takes doctors thirty-seven hours of steady massage before they can pry his legs from around the life preserver. They eventually use a car jack. He is in a mild coma. Before awakening he speaks in several languages, including ancient Sumerian, which hasn't been heard on this planet for almost three thousand years. No one knows what he said. Ten days later Pena hears his story, the only person he will ever tell, and checks him out of the hospital, putting him on a plane to Mexico. He walks alone across the Sonoran desert to enter into monastic servitude where he remains silent and brooding and devoted for ten years. Then he leaves for Baja. He did not attempt to found a ministry, he only wants a place from which to confront God. He begins studying physics again, ordering books by mail from America, when they arrive the postmaster brings them on mule back. Sometimes he practices self-flagellation.

Occasionally he takes in a repentant, puts him to work and to prayer. His church is built on strange sermons. Under the hard toil of his brethren the barren sand begins to birth thin, reedy vegetables. Hard corn, small tomatoes, and beans. After two years he can bake his own tortillas, starts a small business—some monks make liquor, his make tortillas. He inspires a deep devotion. It was said he baked his communion wafers from sand and punished slack with long dry walks in the desert. Around the monastery it is rumored that he once met Jesus. No one will ever ask.

Two months after Pena's death, when Isosceles crosses into America, he brings three of these men with him. They will chew glass for Isosceles, that is the depth of their faith. He has yet to ask them to, so far he has only asked them to find him an angel.

OFTEN THESE DAYS, ANGEL DREAMS OF
being out in the marshes, swatting mosquitoes, wearing a
ridiculous pair of knee-high yellow rubber boots at least
four sizes too big. Despite the odds and the boots, he somehow manages to wade and struggle to the same spot, night
after night, dream after dream; a place where the trees split
open above him and cool, clean air falls across his skin. He
comes to watch the lemmings in full tilt, their long march
to the sea, their annual tide. He doesn't, or hasn't, ever seen
them make it over the cliff, just a slow trudge out of a tired
bog. The parade passes at a sharp angle, three feet from his
muddy boots. Tiny feet make a wet smack, a sound like a
goose being plucked underwater. And the last lemming in
line, a gimp with eyes like Marilyn Monroe, struggling to
overcome bog and lily pads, pauses as he passes to say, "We
are not free, and the sky can still fall on our heads and the
theater was created to teach us that first of all." Which neither he nor the lemming know is an Artaud quote, but after
all, he's just a kid, the lemming a dream, and time and time
again he wakes from this laughing.

"What's funny?" asks a woman's voice.

He wakes to find his back against a tree and the wind
pouring over his face. It is still night. Someone is on the
ground near him, head resting on his leg and for some reason
he can't remember there is the sound of an accordion. He's
still drunk. It takes a little while for him to remember the
woman and how she held his hand in the darkness.

The Angle Quickest for Flight   *119*

"I didn't know you played."

But she doesn't answer and goes back to her lullabies as if from a distant country festival and Angel passes back to sleep with fresh daughters holding skirts high for one more dance.

Christiana plays the bandoneon in the old style. A cambric cover lies near her feet. The buttons are ivory in the pale, the bellows are oxblood colored leather, lush and sweet. As she plays she sways slightly, leafy and untethered. When the moonlight falls through the trees, brushing the instrument with a shadowy light, it's hard to see, but the tiny buttons are covered with carved images of Wuotan, the Teutonic arranger of wars and battles, an odd choice considering this is a Argentine instrument and long thick with the heat of that land. Her song is part canard, part tempest, a deep-throated ballad of the pampas.

The story is a familiar one, but only to a handful. The Great Cattle Jihad. It is the tale of a mysterious rancher from the Uruguayan highlands. He was lanky and heavily shadowed, with punched-out half moons for eyes and a black hat. His lands had been stripped, his great fields sold off parcel by parcel, the government wouldn't help, his wife dead, his sons gone. The earth had grown mean and cold and here was one of the last gauchos: baggy trousers and a guitar slung over his shoulder—he would not auction his pride. Instead, he drove his cattle, almost a thousand head strong, along backroads and quiet lanes for the better portion of ten days. He came over two hundred miles, traveling just out of sight of the highway to arrive on the shores of the Carrasco Beach. It was spring and the place was full of tourists.

Three hundred people were trampled. Tan men with clean nails, women who spent all winter preparing for their bathing suits, waiters in white tuxedos despite the heat. The gaucho took three shots in the belly and two through the heart. Some say God turned him to stone or mist or song. The cattle themselves were stout beasts, made in a tough land under the white heat of a flat sun. Though most died on the sand, rotten with salt water and shot down by the soon-to-be-arriving militia, a few are said to wander the streets of Montevideo, visible only on certain nights, on certain streets, when the moon is just right, still prowling with the courage and the fortitude that was once expected of them.

When Angel wakes again it is morning, he is stiff and sore and his head aches. It is as if some little portion of the heavens has opened above him to rain small rocks. He looks around for Christiana and doesn't see her and rises to look and pukes a thin stream into the dirt by his feet. There's bile in his stomach, something evil wanting to come out. His first real thought of the day comes to him between heaves. He still hasn't found the fisherman and he's no closer and no wiser and his thumb is resting on something sharp and cutting and he glances up from the ground to see he's actually bleeding.

Then he sees he's cut himself on a fish hook stuck through the tree's bark. A light yellow feather trails off its steel and a piece of folded paper is caught in the crook. He slides it off with his fingers, trying to keep the thumb upright, not bleed on anything important. The day could collapse on him at any time. His nose and throat burn. The note comes off and he staggers a few yards away on feet made of stone, legs of string. Has his head ever hurt this much? The note opens with a shake. It's only three lines and he stares at them for a long time before rolling over to vomit again.

Steven Kotler

YOU CAN SEE A MAN WALK DOWN THE
street, past the shops and the cafes and the bric-a-brac and
tomorrow he can jump off a cliff. It's as much a truth as
anything. Tonight the sky will stay clear and dark. That's
the way it was in his God's world and who is he to argue.

The snows have come early this year and though there
is still a month to go many of the Christmas decorations
were already up. Red and green tinsel wind around lamp-
posts, strings of popcorn lights hang over streets, one of
these days Aspen would have a winter carnival. Nobody
here would really know how to celebrate. They have too
much, thinks Johnii, they doesn't really need a festival.

He walks through town until a light snow begins, by
dawn there will be a foot of fresh powder at the top of the
mountain. Something to break their fall. How he can
already feel the adrenaline. It's getting cold, he wants a cup
of coffee and no matter, he isn't going to sleep much
tonight anyhow.

A white picket fence surrounds the patio. Inside, there's
a small crowd. He sits outside, under the hot angle of a heat
lamp, watching a woman across the way reading a book.
She licks her fingers before turning pages and her skin is so
white. His own hands are those of a Semite. Darker. One of
the better clues he has.

A waiter walks over and takes his order and brings him a
paper when he asks. Yesterday someone blew up an Israeli
school bus and in retaliation a group of soldiers went mad

with rage and drink and burned two Arab resettlement homes to the ground and beat one man to death as he tried to run from the fire. The paper says they used rifle butts and probably their feet and Johnii knew that if they were amputees they would have held matchsticks in their teeth in order to peck the man to death.

Across from him, she puts down the book and takes a sip of her wine. Copper hair in the lamp's light poking out from beneath a hat, a nose that drops off, shoulders that will never be straight, already she looks like a librarian. A woman you could pass on any street in the world and not notice. She licks a finger and turns a page. Not notice unless you were there to really look.

He finishes the paper and orders a refill and does the crossword puzzle. It's nearly nine when he leaves. A sliver of a moon hangs behind the mountain. The streets have gone soft with fresh snow.

There's a camera shop on the corner, a nook-and-cranny place with old Leicas in the front window. On the walls are photos of skiers taken fifty years ago. Men in heavy wool pants on wooden boards going down a mountain. Inside there is a couple debating zoom lenses and a young man going through a rack of postcards. The clerk looks up when he sees Johnii and says, "We're closing in two minutes." The whole shop isn't much bigger than a pair of park benches. Johnii leaves a small envelope beside the cash register, slipping it into a pile of other mail and papers, the day's business still unfinished, a little untidy over there. A little bell jingles over the door when he walks back into the night.

GABRIAL IS TALL AND THIN AND WHITE.
A white hassle of dreadlocks and white eyebrows and pale lips and the little coloring left in him lingers in his eyes. They are big, round, his pupils black rings that fold and fracture with white dots in the center and most people don't want him looking at them for too long.

Johnii's known Gabrial for five years, since they met outside the general store in Devil's Tower, Wyoming. A calm morning, the horizon long and sweeping. Johnii needed to learn to rock climb. Gabrial was a climbing guide, not picky, not much work for him anyhow.

"How many people want to be eight hundred feet in the air with a dreadlocked albino?" he replied when Johnii asked why.

"How many people trust a man without a past?" asked Johnii.

They slept in the desert. Gabrial ate well, got paid. Johnii learned to climb the ghost spires of Zion. The rock red and flat, the cracks so clean they looked man-made. In August, Johnii climbed twelve routes up Devil's Tower, set out like a clock dial. At the top Gabrial gave Johnii room for his magic. He understood that, Gabrial did, how one might need a little extra room every now and then.

Johnii knows the whole story, but isn't happy about it. Gabrial was born in Kingston, Jamaica—an albino child born to black parents in one of the worst slums in the Caribbean. A place thick with superstition. Gabrial a strange, quiet kid. One night, a couple of local women got strung out on rum and Red Stripe and too much smoke and took a razor and went looking for him. He got away, but they caught his mother. Cut her up pretty bad. She died for giving birth to a ghost and for being rude enough to try and protect him.

His father got soggy. Any excuse to be drunk and this one lasted a year. Gabrial hid in the jungle. One night, halfway up a mountain, sleeping in a abandoned coffee plantation shack, Gabrial woke to find his father standing in the doorway. The moon was at his back. For a long time neither spoke. Then his father told him an old African story of the white man, how the white man was just the black man stripped of his skin, how the white man would roam the earth unsettled, how he was unable to pass on quietly, how he must reclaim his black skin. They walked down the mountain. Gabrial got four hundred dollars and passage to America. He slept below the bed of an Italian waiter named Marco. Maybe three square feet in a world that smelled of rust. But he was fed and free and in the end Marco would take pity on him and send him to an uncle's house in Denver. He spent five months eating pasta and learning to read and growing almost a foot, but the uncle turned out to be afraid of him and rather than end up in an orphanage or back in Jamaica, Gabrial hitchhiked to Telluride and got a job putting people onto chairlifts. He shivered for four months, it was the first time he had ever been in snow.

The Hotel Jerome was built by silver miners nearly a hundred years ago and kept open and running when the ski trade arrived in Aspen in 1936. By the late sixties it had become a necessary luxury, by now it was more like a fraternity party than a bar.

At a back table, Johnii and Coyote play chess. Christiana sits beside them, hidden under a green fishing cap that she picked up in Montana last week. She is thinking about her little side trip and thinking about telling Coyote the truth. Her feet lie across an empty seat and her back is to the wall.

When Gabrial steps through the front door the room gets quieter. He is too tall, wearing a watch cap, with his white hair hanging loose beneath. Around his shoulders a heavy winter cloak, the kind favored by Franciscans. He looks the bad ending, like something come from the night to steal your soul.

A drunk at the bar scoops up a handful of Gabrial's dreadlocks, letting them slide through his fingers like rain.

"What the fuck happened to you?"

Gabrial doesn't bother turning around. He nods hello to Johnii. He's got a timetable all his own.

"Genetics," says Gabrial.

"You a Rasta?" he says, still holding Gabrial's hair.

Gabrial touches the guy's wrist. It happens so slowly that it's almost like watching a cinematic trick. Gabrial finds a pressure point and squeezes and uses the pain to flick the wrist over, spinning it too far so the pain shoots all the way to the tips of the fingers and the fingers spread and crimp as though struck by lightening. There is a look on his face like he just entered another world. A drink drops to the floor and the man drops to his knees. He tries to keep his wrist from snapping. Gabrial just looks down at him with a sad, quiet smile.

"All I asked was are you a Rasta?" the man whines.

"No, but I and I is," says a skinny dreadlocked black man stepping from behind Gabrial.

Two guys sitting at the bar start to stand and he just looks at them and shakes his head gently.

Gabrial releases the man's wrist. The other men sit back down.

"I and what?" says one of them.

Gabrial picks the man off the floor and returns him to his bar stool. He is still rubbing his wrist.

"I and I, meaning you and me, meaning we all in this together."

"Uh-huh."

"You like my fancy boy patois?" already turning and walking away.

Johnii stands and walks over to hug Gabrial.

"Thanks for coming."

"You call, I come."

There is a little more room in the bar now, everybody shrunk back into themselves. There are already empty chairs waiting for them.

"Everybody this is Sticky, Sticky this is everybody," says Gabrial.

"Very pleased to meet you," grins Sticky.

"Your name is Sticky?" asks Coyote.

"No. My name is Augustine Jacob Francis Montgomery. I am named Augustine after Saint Augustine and Jacob is my father's brother's name and Francis because my mother liked the way it sounds and Montgomery, my family name, coming from the great English family of tank drivers. Since I was small, they called me Sticky because, as my grandma used to say, 'the meat no stick to his bones.' "

Johnii offers him a seat and a drink. Sticky lives by a Nazarene code and won't touch alcohol but looks at the seat for a few seconds, looks hard like he's reading a book and finally slides into it.

He lives over in Telluride and plays in a band and teaches skiing at the ski school, but Telluride's so middle-of-nowhere, backwoods and hippied out that most of the time he just hangs out with children and tells them about the Lion of Judah and takes them into the steeps.

"Steppin," he calls it, meaning skiing and steeps and steps too, all together, sort of, but leading down not up and in not out. That's how Sticky skis, the harder the conditions, the better he does. For him skiing is a way to flow through the soul and sometimes he teaches this also. His kindness and patience with children is near legend. But Sticky is Jamaican and Rasta and his lines cross in ways that most people couldn't follow. He doesn't have many enemies, but when he isn't singing or skiing or teaching then people are right to be a little afraid of him.

HOW MUCH DID HE SLEEP, CAN'T HAVE
been more than four hours. A hazel light has already
started to fill the corners. It's a little room in a little house
at the end of a long road. A wall of pines for a front yard,
the whole of the mountains out back. Two bedrooms and a
kitchen and a big round table. Through a short hallway
you get a living room cut in half, subdivided into squares,
clean angles, little dust. A long couch that folds out into a
bed. Though Coyote didn't bother and slept long ways on
it. Still wearing his shirt and pants, tie loose and hanging,
hat over his eyes and legs crossed at the ankles. Hands
neatly folded and black silk socks.

The living room's other half has been made into a
small study. Bookcases, heavy wood. Johnii's stretched out
in a fat chair staring at the wooden logs running across the
ceiling. There was a fire in a fireplace but it's been out for
hours and there isn't even a spark to blow on.

A small table for his feet and stacks of books—seven
copies of the I Ching, commentaries in Chinese, English,
Arabic, Hebrew. A rare Sanskrit tome on the calendar as
map, an obscure idea even then. Sixty-four folders, each full
of notes and drawings. One in his lap, open, reading: Hexagram thirteen—community, Ch'ien over Li, the father and
second daughter, remember Li is the flame that blazes
upward. Wilhelm says it furthers one to cross great water—
unity helps in the crossing, his translation from the Chi-

nese. Fall ten feet for each of the lines. Five solid, one broken—five men, one woman. One man hidden—the photographer—though Johnii is not certain this is the right choice. In any taxonomy, where a time structure is based upon a nonfixed variable... and so on and so on. Almost fifty pages each, the records of a lifetime.

Christiana walks out of the bedroom, in an old robe too big for her so the sleeves are rolled at the wrist. Her hair hangs over three-quarters of her back and her eyes still wander through another world. She stands one legged in the hallway and rubs her fingers over her other foot until she finds the spot she wants. The heel rests on the edge of her knee and her foot arches slightly. Thirty seconds of direct pressure and her head clears and she heads for the shower.

In the living room, Johnii shuts his eyes and goes back to sleep. Christiana leaves the bathroom slowly, wringing a last few drops of water from her hair and feeling the rug beneath her. The towel gets dropped into a hamper and she puts on an old sweatshirt that somebody once wore in college. In the study, she takes the folder from Johnii's lap and closes it without looking, placing it with the others, a thick stack inside a short cabinet. Her fingers trace a line over his chest and onto his neck, it takes him almost thirty seconds to find his way back. There are worse things to open your eyes to in this world.

"Good morning?" Her voice comes from a place very few men ever go.

Johnii will never try. She is solid and tender together, a neat trick especially these days, but with something very momentary about her, like she could fade away, like she had built a lifetime out of fading away. He reaches up to touch her but she moves slightly. Besides a few more answers, she is the first thing Johnii has wanted in a very long time.

"Good morning," sitting forward and cracking his neck. "Are Gabrial and Sticky here yet?"

"They're meeting us at the lift."

"Forgot, can I make you some coffee?" his knees cracking as he stands.

"No, I will, wake Coyote," she says, walking towards the kitchen.

The sun has already begun to warm the air. She must have been a little girl once, small fingers and a mother somewhere, probably dead, but still a wonder of memories. Amazing, he can't begin to imagine it.

"WHAT'S UP WITH JOHNII?"

Sticky stands on a lawn of snow, looking at the sky. His arms are outstretched and a snowball sits in each hand. Gabrial is behind him, closer to the house, leaning against the corner of a pickup. The truck hovers in a thin bed of gravel and behind the truck is the house and behind the house is the dawn and behind the dawn—well, now there's a question.

"Not an easy question," says Gabrial.

He angles his skis into a tube tied to a post tied to the back corner of the truck. They will squeak some, on the snow-covered roads they will sound like crickets.

He turns to look at Sticky. "The I Ching is a book of possibilities. Sixty-four hexagrams, sixty-four possibilities. At first I thought Johnii was drawn to possibility."

"He who God blesses, no man can curse."

"What does that mean?"

"Johnii's got sixty-four things going on. Most people barely got two."

"Sixty-five."

Sticky wrinkles his brow.

"Johnii thinks there's a sixty-fifth hexagram. He's hunting it."

"That's what we're doing here?"

Gabrial nods. He's been running a file over the edge of Sticky's ski. Every three strokes he stops and touches the edge with his fingertip, testing for a sharpness he knows will emerge.

"How does he plan on doing this?"

"He's trying to enact each hexagram of the I Ching. It's a book of overlapping forces, Johnii creates situations," says Gabrial, smiling, as if this were the most natural thing in the world. "It's all that he does. He thinks that when he's created all sixty-four hexagrams perfectly then he will know where to look."

"The book will tell him?"

"Yeah."

Gabrial also knows how Johnii thinks of this sixty-fifth hexagram, a place where worlds fold together, a crease in the maps.

"That's what he's doing," Gabrial says finally. "What we're doing." Then he stops sharpening the ski for a second and looks up. "Welcome to your day."

A car slides down the street and its tires nip onto the edge of Sticky's driveway, catching the dry gravel. They turn to watch a rain of gray rock.

"So he's a little crazy," says Sticky with a smile.

Gabrial doesn't say anything. He doesn't know if Johnii's crazy, he doesn't think of him that way, he wouldn't even know how to start.

their palms and shake hands. It's something Pena showed Coyote some years ago. An old Slavic tradition. A people who would not break, who instead said, "Take it all, we'll remake our world from spit."

Gabrial and Sticky are already standing by the ticket booth, waiting.

Johnii watches the mountain's top as the three approach, even a little wind can topple a man, a strong gust could offset the trajectory, change the angle, snap the skiers in half. In Jerusalem they say as much, a place where they understood changing winds.

Johnii reaches into an inside pocket and comes out with a handful of lift tickets.

"You don't have to do this," says Sticky. "We can buy our own, it's a pleasure just to ski with you."

Within the I Ching are the categories of everything that exists. There is significant proof that the Chinese developed the sixty-four hexagrams as a calandar, a way of telling time through possibility. It was originally developed using complicated mathematics and having only one clue to go on, Johnii understands all of it. He knows that it was a system of binary structures, that sixty-four hexagrams actually meant thirty-two structures and an inversion principle. He understands that the probability of change is determined by a factor of six. He knows that if you look long enough at certain numbers they will tell you the color of Napoleon's underwear.

"Does it matter what order we ride up in?" asks Sticky.

This catches Johnii, makes him stop, skis dangling from a free hand. "No," smiling, "doesn't, thanks for asking."

The lift operator wears thick boots, watches everything like a hawk and doesn't speak. Johnii once saw a man try to tip him, hand him a hundred dollar bill to show off for his girlfriend. Twice as much as this man makes in a day. Five months a year he loads people onto a chairlift, makes sure they are safe as they leave his patch of the earth. One day a man tries to hand him a bill, to take something from him, and he stops the lift, stands there waiting and quiet until everyone in line, the whole noontime crowd can see, then he walks up to the man and straightens his coat around the shoulders, brushes a bit of snow off, takes the bill from him and tucks it back into the man's pocket. Then he starts the lift again and lets the day continue. You pay enough attention, the world will show you its secrets.

GABRIAL AND STICKY AND COYOTE SIT shoulder to shoulder on the chairlift. Gabrial is hunched over, trying to keep the wind from his face. He is staring at the iron grill, the painted blue pole, the world of white below. Someone with initials SB has been here before, left behind their thin metal scrape to prove it. Sticky rolls his neck, loosening muscles, his dreadlocks poking out from under his hat at a low angle. Beside him, Coyote stares straight ahead, his cheeks already flushed, his eyes beginning to water.

"How come," asks Coyote, "Johnii knows so much about the Kabbalah?"

Gabrial hears the question, but he's too cold and it takes him a while to remember to answer, to understand it as anything more than another part of the landscape. "Johnii comes from Jerusalem," looking up for the first time. "The promised land, it's in the water."

"Why doesn't he believe?" asks Sticky

"No, he believes," says Gabrial. "Johnii believes all of it. It just doesn't point in the direction he wants to look right now."

But for a moment nothing points in the direction either want to look, for a moment it's too cold and too windy and all around them tree branches hang heavy with snow.

THE APPROACH IS A STEEP SWATH MADE
broad and wide by avalanche years, emptiness, weight, by
the need of things to fall down. Enormous boulders border
the chute, jagged and ruddy, like the Gates of Mordor. Each
nearly thirty feet tall. Around them grow fir and pine,
whatever can take root and hold at such a lonely angle, their
roots curved and bent, improbable that they could stand so
tall. Needles crushed beneath snow.

It is a forty-foot chute followed by a sixty-foot cliff. It is
steep enough that their ski tips hang in open air and the initial twenty feet are hidden by the grade. From where they
stand, a ragged line across the top, the only thing visible is
the ten-foot patch of snow right before the cliff's edge. A
small, white island floating in a world of space. Far below
they can see their landing, a huge bowl empty and quiet. A
short trip really, just push off and hold steady and then fall
and then go on with the rest of their lives.

"Are we ready?" Johnii asks everyone at once. There's
no sense spending too much time up here, they're either
going to do it or not. The wind will blow either way.

"I'll count down from five, we go on one."

The seconds slip quickly. Sticky and Gabrial let out a
whoop. The sky looks like a woman Coyote once knew.

A FEW MILES AWAY, IN TOWN, A GAUNT, tall man approaches a table of tourists. A long nose, broken once, now a bad bump, the angles not lining up. He has a thick accent and speaks in measured steps. His jacket bunches a little at the waist and he is careful not to lean too far forward. He thinks that maybe he should have left the gun with his bags, but it is too late and anyway they don't see it and he will not show it to them. They are sorry but they don't know the street he is looking for, it is not their city, they too have traveled far. As they explain a waiter arrives and serves cocktails. He shakes his head no, he doesn't know either, he could ask around, but it's busy, it might take a minute.

"Don't be bothered," with a shrug and a smile to show them it's not all that important. "Please enjoy your drinks," he says before walking on.

THEY ARE AIRBORNE QUICKLY. UN-
checked acceleration really, the way they seem to hover
midair before they drop, and then so much speed. For a
moment the sky is very, very blue and then it is like a large
pane of glass breaking.

Gabrial has gone off cliffs before. A few times when
skiing, but never from this height. But as a small boy, in
Jamaica, his father taught him to wait for the tides and the
heavy waves and when to jump. The feeling still starts in
his stomach and grows until there is the fact that any more,
even one fat second, would be too much.

The air is cold. There is so much to be afraid of.

Christiana sees a bird rise before her, maybe a hawk,
but her eyes are teary from wind and she can't be sure. As
she passes it looks at her for a second, a quick question and
then folds itself into sharp flight, a mad up-and-away
dash—as if the only way out were the sun.

Coyote and Sticky land beside one another, a crush of
snow spray, a couple of tight smiles growing wider.

For Johnii it is always the same, the feeling of being a
part of a great vector. Six lines falling. Then it will be over
and the enormous quiet, a quiet that fills the sky, that
pushes at horizons will go away.

Slowly everything calms.

Then it is done and they ski away. Six quiet lines tracking through thick snow. Light flurries are beginning to drift

in, by morning everything they could have left behind will be gone. Soon they are out of sight and no one caught sight of the photographer sitting in a grove of trees on the south side of the cliff. His camera slides quickly into a backpack, his tracks angling away, and then, he too, is gone.

OUTSIDE HUNG A BLUE NEON SIGN
reading BAR in a straight legged script. If this place had
any other name then Coyote didn't know it. The snow had
started a few hours ago and it didn't take long to become a
blizzard. Coyote was giving Gabrial and Sticky a ride to
their car and the wind had turned the world white, so he
drove towards the first thing he could see and that turned
out to be a blue neon sign.

There were about ten people in the room when they
walked in and only one more had arrived after them. A big
man in a bad mood, now sitting alone with his beer. He's
pissed off and probably stuck, his car having gone off the
road, tires deep in a ditch. No matter, the bartender says,
there's a motel about a hundred feet down the road and
they have plenty of rooms and what the hell, they could all
sleep here, on the bar or the pool table. She's been the bartender for a few winters. Somewhere there are a few blankets stashed, this is Colorado, it wasn't the first blizzard
they'd ever lived through.

Sticky plays pool with a joint sticking out his mouth
and he'll pass it to anyone within range and what the hell
they're going to inhale the smoke one way or another, the
thing looks thick enough to outlast both the blizzard and
the millennium. He's been losing for over an hour, but
unless there's money involved he's doesn't pay much attention, mostly playing because he likes the sound of the balls
and the way they bounce, the angle of it all.

Gabrial and Coyote are at the bar drinking dark rum with lime. Coyote's playing a song on a harmonica, some mariachi number and Gabrial's got an empty bottle and an old pen to drum along.

"You guys would be pretty good if you'd bother finishing a song."

Gabrial and Coyote stop playing to laugh and wobble.

"The problem is you're too stoned," says Sticky.

"The problem," says Coyote, "is not that we're too stoned, it's that we're too drunk."

It's well after midnight when they cross the road and find the motel. It hasn't done much business this winter, too far from town to fill up. But the clerk has been expecting them. Coyote called earlier to make sure they had rooms and the man stayed up late waiting. He is thin, old, nearsighted with a bad cough. The lobby feels cold and small, a television in the corner, a brown rug with mountains in green and white, a broken couch.

"You want two rooms?"

"One's fine, double beds please," says Coyote.

The caretaker scratches a rail of stubble hanging from his chin.

"Got an extra person, I'm gonna have to charge for that," he says finally.

"And we'll be happy to pay, " says Coyote, lighting a cigarette.

"Sixty-seven big ones, cash or charge?" He passes the key over the counter and Gabrial picks it up.

"Cash," says Coyote, reaching into his pants. "Shit," finding empty pockets, "you guys go on up, I left my wallet across the road. I'll be right back."

"Anytime this century be fine by me," says the clerk snapping the television on with the remote.

Coyote's wallet sits on the bar, right where he left it.

"Nightcap?" asks the bartender.

"Wallet," picking it up with a smile. "Good night."

The bar door closes and the darkness is everywhere. Four cars are in the parking lot, their roofs bending beneath white piles. The snow is thick and crunchy, the sound of horses slogging through mud as he walks. He takes a few steps and then leaves his feet, something hard striking him from behind. His wallet flies away, dropping beside a tire. When he lands, some invisible hand reaches for him and he tries to roll away but his kidneys burn and somehow his forehead has been cut and the blood soaks into his eyebrows. He takes a hard blow to the chest and a harder one to his right thigh and falls into a short, dark tunnel vomiting blood as he goes.

He feels himself being dragged through the snow and then he's pushed into a sitting position against the rear tire of his car.

"Good evening, Coyote," says a voice of endless patience, a slight hint of an accent, something South American, hard to lock down. "Catch your breath, I can wait, we have all night."

For a while there is only pain and the thought that Gabrial and Sticky are fucked up and probably figure he's sweet talking the bartender and maybe he should have been. He spits out a clot of blood.

"Yeah, good evening," says Coyote. He still can't see more than tall gray shapes. It's very cold.

"We're not going to kill you." His words are slow.

"Some men traffic in fear, I prefer honesty."

"Because rules are rules," Coyote's voice crumbling as he speaks.

"Pardon?"

Coyote tries to wave off the question, but can't lift his hand.

"No matter, I'll get right to the point. I want the papers Angel took from me."

Coyote shakes his head.

"I want the papers Angel took from me."

"Who are you?"

"I am Padre Isosceles."

"What Angel?"

"I will ask one last time, where are the papers that Angel gave to you?"

"I don't know what you're talking about."

The man reaches down and lifts Coyote's left arm, he feels icy metal on his skin, his arms getting yanked to the right. He hears another click and then his arm hangs in midair.

"Those are police issue handcuffs, we're going to step inside for a little while, if anybody tries to rescue you I'll shoot them before they can, it'd be better if you just sat quietly and thought about your answer."

"I don't..." but he can hear footsteps moving away and hear the wind rushing down off the mountains. His gloves are fur lined leather, wet inside and out and starting to freeze. He can pick locks, but not here, too cold, not enough feeling, no precision. The handcuff's metal starts freezing to his wrist. So he sits, legs straight as logs, blood on his face, wind at his cheeks, snow piling everywhere. His throat burns and he feeds himself cold snow, waiting while it melts in his mouth before swallowing. He does it a few more times, but he must have landed on that arm and it hurts to lift. His vision starts to return and after a while it seems he can see the snow fall, one flake at a time. The wind sounds like an old man, after a while he realizes it's trying to tell him something. He listens for a very long time.

"I'm sorry you had to sit in the cold so long." Coyote didn't know when the man returned, he may have fallen asleep. "I want the papers, please tell me where they are."

It's hard to speak, his teeth are chattering too fast, chewing up his words. "I d-o-o-n't kn-ow wh-o or wha . . ."

"It's very cold out here, you're going to have frostbite very soon."

"I don't ha-v-e a-n-ybod-y's p-apers."

"Lying isn't necessary."

"Loo-k," suddenly angry, his voice flooding back to him. "I don't know what the hell you're talking about, so will you please leave me alone so I can get some sleep."

He hears it more than feels it, a soft tap, a hand on his throat, pushing him slightly back. He's getting dizzy, but he's not too afraid. It's very cold, but someone has found him, is dragging him to safety, he just wishes they'd grab his arms, leave his neck alone. Then it comes to him, he can't breathe. His free arm claws at something, but his fingers don't have any strength, any purchase. He realizes he's about to pass out and then one way or another he'll die. Something touches his chest.

It's almost funny, him dying like this, on a beach in the Caribbean, under a hot sun, watching a woman in a pale yellow bikini top and faded surf trunks catch a wave. A perfectly clear sky, can see for miles on a day like today. She's riding a long board, he can see its hot white and blue stripes from the beach and she has a small scar on the left side of her stomach, tiny railroad tracks like you see in cartoons.

The wind still blowing, still trying to tell him something.

THE CLERK HAD FALLEN ASLEEP WATCH-
ing television and woke to the whine of the desk bell ring.
Shapes come to him first, been that way for nearly thirty
years. Shapes first, then some color, then the image seems
to snap into place. Sixty-eight years on this planet and his
reward is to wake in time to see two gray shapes getting
into a blue truck. Maybe green.

"Fuck."

But he doesn't even try to stand. Piece-of-shit night it is
turning out to be and what happened to that guy who went
back for his wallet, now he's going to have to go pound on their
door, drunk sons-of-bitches. It's then that he notices the blood.

"Aw good goddamn," then he's around the counter and
sees the guy lying dead on his floor with a deep gash in his
forehead and the blood starting outside in the snow and
angling clear across the floor, a brown smear that nobody
will ever mistake for mud.

"Fuck kind of world is this? Come on fella, don't be
dead," reaching down, looking for a pulse.

He's been around dead people before, they don't scare
him like they scare some. The family business. What you
get with a mortician for a father, he used to say. But he also
got the endless stench of formaldehyde and teased at
school and some pretty strange dreams and eventually he
realized this wasn't a bargain he wanted to make. So he
traded it for a world of snow and it worked for a while, but
sooner or later death remembers and comes looking.

man stepped into the drifting night to climb twenty-odd stairs to the motel room where Gabrial and Sticky were sleeping, Gabrial sat, smoking cigarettes, listening to a story. The cottage had white curtains covering the window and the light fell softly, diffused, filling the room's center while letting the corners darken and gray.

As it turns out, Coyote isn't dead. He spends two days unconscious in the Aspen County Hospital. Tubes come out of him. A little dot on a screen keeps his pulse. "The watcher," Gabrial calls it and every time the nurses try to get him out of the room he wags a thin finger and says, "Yes, but who will watch the watcher." They really don't want to fuck with an albino Rastafarian anyhow.

Then Coyote is awake. He has frostbite, messed-up ribs, and a bad concussion. Twenty-seven stitches angling across his forehead and his legs still show black-and-blue marks, each bruise matching the toe of a size twelve work boot, but nobody seems to figure that part out. The police believe the hit-and-run story and don't notice the sheet of paper tucked into his breast pocket, don't notice much, not enough to put two and two together.

It's Gabrial who finds it, after the clerk had gotten him out of bed and the police had come. As they were loading Coyote into the ambulance, he saw something crisp and white sticking out of Coyote's jacket pocket. A clean, neatly halved piece of stationery, not the type of thing that stays in place when someone is hit by a car and sent spinning through the snow. It's a piece of stationery from the Hotel Jerome with six words written in blue ink. "Which are the prayers of saints."

"Do you know what it means?" asked Gabrial.

Coyote shakes his head no. He's lying in silk pajamas in bed at Johnii's place with Christiana sitting in a small, straight backed wooden chair on his left. Her fingers rest on Coyote's wrist, they have rested on Coyote's wrist for four days now.

"You're certain they put it there?" Coyote had told them the story two nights ago.

"Who?" meaning 'Who else,' meaning it still hurt to talk.

"Revelation, Chapter 5, end of verse 8. The whole thing reads: 'And when he had taken the book, the four beasts and four and twenty elders fell down before the Lamb, having every one of them harps and golden vials full of odors, which are the prayers of saints.'"

"And?" asks Coyote.

"Revelation, chapter 5, verses 1–10, when Haile Selassie was crowned emperor of Ethiopia in 1930 the Rastas in Jamaica recognized him as Ras Tafari, the King of Kings, Lord of Lords, the Conquering Lion of the Tribe of Judah, Jah—the one true God of the prophecy, the prophecy foretold in Revelation, Chapter 5, verses 1–10."

Outside, snow flees the heavens by the bucketful.

JOHNII HAD, AFTER ALL, TRIED IT
another way. He had a wife once, a lovely Persian woman,
but God had not wanted another life for him, had not
wanted much but for him to wander and search and well,
that was what he did now. In the end sometimes you drew
the lines, sometimes they drew you.

So, he's left in a nice cottage and a small study and a
desk huddled under a thousand scraps of paper. Nobody is
going to offer him too much pity. Sometimes, at times like
these, his dead wife would visit him. He is never to know
why, but he would ask anyway, talk in polite tones, she's
still very beautiful. It is a shame that all the rest of the
world can see of this is a tall man talking to an empty
room, but he has very faraway eyes and that counts for
something too.

They had been married in a small synagogue in
Jerusalem. She was Muslim, devoted to many of the Sufi
rights, and had no real business in a Jewish house of worship. They had fake papers and a well-paid Rabbi and anyway her belief was that in marriage, as in birth and death,
you must embrace one's enemy, must let love take you over
or past or through and who would want to disagree. Seven
months later she was dead.

Her father was one of the early supporters of the Aya-
tollah Khomeini, he had moved his house, his two sons,
and his lovely daughter to the city of Qom. He had told
them what many believed, that Khomeini was the Twelfth

Iman, the Awaited One who disappeared in the ninth century, a thousand years ago, and had just returned and that they were in Qom, in possibly the ugliest city in the world, living out of a concrete box, to serve him.

"If he wants anything from me, then let him wait another thousand years," read the note she left, then she left the house, the city, the country. She met Johnii in Jerusalem, they were in love, she had no regrets. A few months to make sure love was and a few more for safekeeping and then two weeks until they could find the temple and the rabbi and that was that. It took her father seven months to track her down.

It wasn't supposed to be murder, a simple kidnapping, tie her hands, and put her in a sack and in a car and bring her back to me. She was a Muslim, Khomeini was a prophet, and that was how things were done. It was late at night, moonlight and a stone staircase, she was upside-down in a burlap sack and her head bumped the stairs, for all she had done she probably deserved a few bruises. It was, after all, an accident.

Johnii didn't go to the funeral, he let the police bury her and sat at home, drinking wine, looking out a window, thinking life had already taken his past from him and now it had his future. The miracle is not that he had survived, people live through far worse with far less, but that he would want to. He would never again underestimate the miracle of curiosity, of wonder.

And now, almost seven years later, she is standing in front of Johnii in a cottage in Colorado, and he takes a while to notice her. He has a lap full of photographs: the ski jump from all angles, close-ups of faces in midair,

Christiana so calm she could be eating a salad. When he looks up, his wife is by the fireplace.

"Good evening, Soraya," says Johnii, but she has not spoken since her death and he doesn't expect her to start now. Her black hair hangs nearly to her waist. She at first appeared in her wedding dress and later in the burlap sack she had died in, both were too creepy for Johnii and he had told her if she was going to dress like that to not bother showing up and for whatever reason it worked and since then she's worn a long black evening gown with a scooped neck and side pleats and a looping pearl strand. Her skin much paler in death. Johnii can still taste the back of her neck.

"This is the thirteenth hexagram. The most common translation is community, stresses collective flow, persistence—such as that of an enlightened person. That last part, hedging bets if you ask me." He always speaks to her like he's taking notes, perhaps she's used to it by now. "New endeavors, serving needs of my fellow man—Coyote obviously needed to be in traction?"

Johnii spreads the ski photos across the floor, nearly a hundred in all, 8-by-10 shots, smaller cutouts from proof sheets, almost covers the whole of the rug.

"I had the photographer hide in the trees. The sixth line of the hexagram. I thought if everyone knew they were getting their pictures taken it would change things."

He can feel her behind him, peering down. She likes to stand among his life, see what it has become.

"Sticky and Gabrial talking. Me and Coyote skiing away, after the landing. Coyote in midair. The sky, before and after we pass through. Me in midair. Christiana—she is almost as beautiful as you." He continues enumerating the shots, but

Soraya stays with the photograph of Christiana. She stares for a long time and then looks at Johnii and reaches a hand for his cheek. He feels nothing, not even the shivers, and closes his eyes so he doesn't have to see her pass right through him. When he open his eyes again she is gone.

"SHE'S DEAD, ISN'T SHE?" STANDING behind him in the study. The chair is overstuffed, covered in an olive velvet, crushed now, since he's been sleeping in it for nearly two weeks. Christiana's fingers rest beside his left ear, pushing slightly into the fabric, writing invisible messages.

He hasn't spoken of his wife, not aloud anyway, for over five years. It was not a story he has practiced.

"She liked your photograph." Another thing he usually keeps secret, the photos, but for some reason he had shown Christiana a few, had let her know there's something he is looking for.

"What, exactly did she like?" she says, walking over to the desk with a smile that means, 'No, you don't have to tell me, but I am going to keep asking.'

He shrugs, looks back at the photos.

"So what are you doing?" asks Christiana.

"I'm a mapmaker."

"Meaning?"

"The sixty-fifth hexagram. I'm mapping the world of the I Ching."

"Hmmmm," she says, hers is a world so quiet, a world where even patience would be out of place. "Your wife still comes to see you?"

"You heard us speaking?"

"Now I know one of your secrets."

"If you've got to know one, that's not a bad one to know."

"How many of mine?" she asked without even arching an eyebrow.

"Only what Coyote told me."

"And what was that?"

"That he had been a businessman in the whole world sense of the word, a businessman in the way that he acquired things and made things happen and basically could do magic."

"If there was a special heaven for smugglers, Coyote would have his own throne," she says. "But he would not have told you that."

"No, other people did, all he told me was that he retired."

"But those aren't my secrets."

"And he told me that the two of you are pals and not lovers and he's not exactly sure why."

"That's true," she says, walking across the room and stopping before him. She crouches in front of the chair, looking slowly at him, waiting until she has his eyes.

Johnii can't help but stare. Like the man said there are blondes and there are blondes and there are blondes and she is none of these, she is not from that world.

"He is retired and we are not lovers," and she leans forward and kisses him. It is like falling. Her lips stay closed, mostly, just a hairline fracture between their purse, a slight suction to her kiss, a way of saying—stay, just one more second—and he stays and in less time than that Johnii feels his breath rushing out of him, rushing into her, and he feels the whole of him follow.

"MAN, I'M SORRY I'M LATE, I'VE BEEN working this Baptist deal thing and it's just taking way too much time."

Tall and thick and wearing a cowboy hat.

"Coffee, please," raising a heavy finger and then turning back towards Angel. "Where was I?"

Two booths, a Formica counter, and a cook who shows up twice a week to do the ordering and make lunch. Angel turns to look behind him and sees seven counter stools, red and plastic with short chrome legs in need of polish, and behind them a broken red neon sign hung at a bad angle in a front window that peers onto a gravel parking lot.

"I think you're . . ."

"You are Angel, aren't you?" frisking a mustache that looks like two trailer hitches making love.

Angel's in a diner in a place called Ten Sleep, Wyoming, four walls, and a roof in the middle of a long road in the middle of a big forest and nearly a thousand miles out of his way.

"Slow Drunk, pleased to meet you."

"Howdy," dragging the syllables, incredulous.

"Amo sent me. Told me I'd find you here," with a wave of his hand. "I'm just glad I caught you, been a change of plan, a delay of game, extra innings, the whole deal."

"What?" Angel's still reduced to monosyllables.

"Aspen, you're heading to Aspen, meeting with a Coyote, he's laid up, you got to hole up for a week or so, be there

The Angle Quickest for Flight   157

next Thursday after eight in the PM. Sorry if it screws you up. You need cash? A motel or something? I'd take you myself, but I got a load of medicine balls in my rig," jerking a thumb towards the parking lot. "Medicine balls, open the gate and a couple thousand of 'em will roll on out and over you, do some damage too, those things weigh in at a fighting size, anyway, they're going east and then there are Baptists going west and you're headed south."

The waitress brings his coffee and Slow Drunk drinks it in one shot, slamming the cup back into the saucer, when he open his mouth to speak steam pours out.

"Great coffee, is there a motel around here? I gotta get and the kid's gotta sleep."

"Does he ever speak in complete sentences?" her name tag says Sharon.

Angel just rolls his head sideways and smiles.

"I'm the only thing around here for fifty miles on a side, but I've got a couch upstairs that you can sleep on for the week," nodding towards Angel.

Slow Drunk tosses ten fifties on the counter. "Meals too," and Sharon nods.

"May the road rise up to meet you." Slow Drunk's out the door and Sharon and Angel sit looking at each other, listening to his truck pull away.

his way to Route 82, which runs crooked, its angles rhythm-less and indiscreet, from the main highway into Aspen proper. It is a forty-mile stretch of curves and ice. Heavy traffic. Just off the pavement are piles of tree branches, bro-ken and fallen from the winter's weight, that lie in rough bunches were the plows have driven them together. A nar-row world of fallen scarecrows. Angel gets a ride fast.

Angel doesn't know what kind of car it is, but inside the snow doesn't fall. Joe Temple from Pittsburgh, never been skiing before, sits in the back staring at the mountains as if they were cotton candy, alien landscapes, unapproachable. His arm hangs limp across the window, his chin denting the flesh, his fist clenched, at least he knows the danger of the road. Randy—"Just Randy"—drives by tapping fin-gers in dusty passes over the arc of the wheel and puffing his cheeks in and out like a blowfish or a chipmunk who can't stop talking, the kind of man who could chew a cud.

The radio plays static and Randy keeps leaning forward and fiddling and hunting. Randy is not the kind of man who can do two things at once. After about a minute of this, Angel picks Randy's hand off the dial and turns it to a station at the low end of the band. Plays old rock and roll, the kind everyone likes.

"Thanks man," says Randy.

The last time Angel was on skis was a brief stint as a lift operator at Telluride. It was his last time through Colorado, just before Santa Fe, when he needed a place to weather the winter, keep all his fingers and toes, a fireplace, the smell of pine and nutmeg. Then, like now, the mountains made him quiet.

COYOTE WAKES TO FIND CHRISTIANA

sitting hunched beside him. Her legs are tucked beneath her and her feet bare. His hand is pressed flat between her palms and when she feels him stir, she lifts an arm, pushing hair from her face. Her eyes are red from crying.

"Don't cry, baby," he says softly.

"I'm not," she says, smiling, tears falling down her cheeks.

It is morning, early, the sky the color of steel. There is a book on the nightstand, closed, unread, its pages unmarked. She must have sat here for hours, watching him sleep, wandering the angles.

"Did you sing to me?" asks Coyote. "In my dream there was song."

She nods, her hair falling back over her eyes, her hand pushing it away again. "Sticky came by, he said it would help you heal."

"Is he still here?"

"No. He didn't want to wake you. He had to get going."

He runs a hand over his ribs, tracing the bruise through the bandage, sharp tugs where he presses too hard. She watches him wince, lifts his hand away, setting it back in her lap.

"Why did this happen?"

"It's not the first time," says Coyote. "Don't worry, I'm a tough guy."

"You've got gray hair."

"Yeah, I noticed that too."

"You retired," a sigh coming with the words, a squeeze of the hand, exasperation.

"I did. I didn't. Someone found me, it happens, it was bound to happen. I don't know though, I don't think this has much to do with me."

"Not yet, at least."

"Well," says Coyote, grinning, "there's that."

Beside the chair is a small bowl of fruit. She picks up a pear and plays it through her hands and then puts it back.

"Are you hungry?"

"No."

She picks out a plum—where Johnii found plums at this time of year she will never know—and presses the skin against the edge of her teeth, pushing slowly, thinking her way through that first bite. Juice dribbles onto her chin. She sets the plum down, uses a corner of her shirt to wipe the moisture.

"What will you do now?"

"I will," says Coyote, "try to find myself an angel."

"You already have," says Christiana, lifting Coyote's hand to her lips and kissing his palm. Then setting it back down again, on the edge of the bed, tucking the fingers through hers. She has to lean forward to hold his hand this way, her back stretching.

"They want me to try and get Johnii out of Colorado," she says.

Coyote nods, lifts his hand from between hers. He touches her cheek and feels moisture on his fingers, the thin crisp of drying salt, her skin underneath.

"I could quit," she says after a while.

"No," says Coyote, "you can't."

"No, I guess not."

"So where will you go?"

"Johnii's been talking about Indonesia. He wants to go surfing. He has an idea that the jungle there is perfect for the next hexagram."

"Indonesia," says Coyote, "should be beautiful this time of year."

GABRIAL STANDS IN TWILIGHT, LEAN-ing against the door, white dreadlocks hanging past his shoulders, finally heading home. He has stayed with Coyote for the past days, made soup, told stories, sang, the most important things in the world.

"The miners used to say 'To hell you ride,'" says Gabrial, "But it got shortened to Telluride," he chuckles. "It is a good place for fools."

It is cold. The window is open and wind washes the room. Coyote stands without help for the first time in two weeks. He's wearing a stocking cap that Christiana bought for him and Johnii's robe, seven folded layers of varying materials—mostly silk, but warm somehow and covered with mountain streams and ancient, hobbling women. He has grown an enviable Fu Manchu and the hot light from the fireplace bleaches the gray a Teutonic white.

"Safe trip," clasps his arms around Gabrial.

"Nah sweat it. Johnii and Christiana are just driving me over the hill. We'll ski a bit, be back," he shrugs, meaning soon, meaning whenever, meaning who knows what's going to happen next.

"Bye baby," says Christiana, kissing him on the lips, her hand finding his wrist, holding it, the kiss, the whole world still, for a few seconds. Johnii winks out the door.

They have been gone five minutes when Coyote stands for a second time. His legs ache. The telephone is on a table in the hall, he shakes his head, nobody has a phone on a table in a hall anymore.

He dials eleven-, twelve-digit numbers, other worlds.

"Hello."

"The Great Bandoni," says Coyote, "how is the dry season treating you this year?"

Silence from the other end. Coyote pulls a deck of Luckies from his pocket and clicks his lighter open and waits.

"The man who called me that," says a thick Indian accent, "is no longer among the living."

"Parlor tricks, mad fakir magic," says Coyote.

"Pardon?" says the man.

"Because rules are rules."

"My God, Coyote," he can hear the sharp intake of breath, a moment of hiss and emptiness playing down the wire. "Well, welcome back from the dead."

He made eight phone calls, but it isn't much use, no one knows much of anything. Coyote likes the poetry anyway, he crawled out of a coffin to hunt down an angel. An odd world he lived in—sometimes his thoughts stopped right there.

Earlier, the stereo had played a couple of tangos and a rare Bartok quartet, but now there is only silence. He had wanted whiskey, settled for tea and cognac. Drinking out of an old tin cup, something that got hauled through this range on mule back, thick with dirt, long seasons. It's balanced on his knee as he sits reading in the overstuffed chair in the study: dark green, velvet, the one Johnii had been sleeping in. He reads a book on Haile Selassie written by a Polish journalist that Gabrial had given him after he had asked about the Lion of Judah. Outside the wind blows.

When the knock on the door comes, it is the only sound

in his universe. He lifts his eyes slowly, finishing the paragraph he's reading and marking the book. The .38 tucked into his waist untucks just the same.

"Bring it on," drinking straight from the bottle.

Coyote opens the door and finds himself with his gun pressed to the forehead of a kid, can't be much more than eighteen, shaggy hair the color of dust and sun, like a surfer, hanging loose a few inches above his shoulders. Freshly shaven. A sharp jaw running towards a small hoop in his ear, heavy black turtleneck sweater, holding a knit sailor's cap in his left hand and a thick notebook in his right. He stands tall, but slightly off-kilter, relaxed, not really a slouch, more like a body preparing, a body caught on the edge of some great motion.

"Jack Kerouac, nice to see you."

"Evening sir, I'm looking for Coyote Blú," not really noticing the gun at his forehead. Coyote has the feeling he is talking to a photograph, a feeling that will stay with him the whole time they know each other.

"You've found him."

"May I come in?"

"Absolutely," says Coyote, not moving the gun an inch.

"It might work better," without vexation, as if he had just hit upon the idea and is trying to be helpful, "if you find it within yourself to take a step or two backwards."

The robe's sleeve widens from Coyote's shoulder, a pasha's design, a light fluttering as his hand sweeps wide. The wind's hush as the door closes.

"And you are?" raising an eyebrow as he steps back.

"Angel." A slight nod, if he had been wearing a hat he would have thumbed the brim just then.

"Of course you are."

Coyote tucks the gun into his sash and wonders for a moment. He has his back to Angel for the twenty seconds it takes to walk down a hallway and into a room and when he stops moving and finds he isn't dead he knows a little more about Angel than he had before. There are certain things you have to find out the hard way.

"Drink?" asks Coyote. On his way to get the bottle of cognac, he spies a bottle of scotch in the study sitting beside a leatherbound copy of the great whaler—sometimes everything comes at once. The world always seems to flow towards Coyote.

"To you, Angel."

Angel takes a quiet sip and puts his drink down, his eyes have stopped twinkling, it's the type of thing you noticed in absence.

"Pena's dead," said Angel flatly. "She has left me her errand to complete."

Coyote freezes, feels wrong, feels struck by something hard and thick and long lasting, something much worse than the size twelve boot of some crazed priest. He sucks in a breath, tries to clear his head.

"She was one of the better ones," says Coyote finally.

Angel nods.

That's the thing about having the world flow towards you, sooner or later death turns up in the tide.

"When?" asks Coyote.

"A few months back, a monastery in Mexico, there's no grave, her corpse turned to birds and flew away."

Coyote takes it all with a nod and tries to walk to the window. A hard pain in his chest. Pena saved his life once, a long time ago, then she gave him a haircut, a fresh suit, a fancy tie, he already had a firm handshake, steady eyes, nerves that wouldn't fray—she gave him his job and told him it was always his job, that she had just been safekeeping it for a while. Even later, when he was just becoming a craftsman, she took him to meet a carpenter. Astounding how many places you could hide things: rocks, paper, scissors—things—inside a simple object, a steamer trunk, a car bumper, an extra flap of skin sewn onto the hip.

There isn't that much of a genealogy for smugglers, not like assassins, just a quiet apprenticeship, one friend teaching another friend a few things. No crown was to be passed. It didn't really matter, Coyote, even then, was the stuff of legend. If he came to you and asked, even if it was only for the weather or the time, well there's a story you can tell. No matter what, he would always owe Pena.

Turning back towards Angel, "She must have really pissed off the priest."

"No, I did that," tossing a notebook onto Johnii's desk.

He follows the flight and then turns back to Angel. Not quite cocky, thinks Coyote, just a flat confidence, a feeling that no matter what happens this kid wants to be there for it, wants to take point.

He glances at the desk and notices that what he had taken for a notebook is actually a folder stuffed with loose-leaf paper, like a collection of poems carried by some émigré poet.

Coyote takes a chair, waving Angel to another, it still hurt to stand too long.

It takes over two hours and all the while Angel sits very still, taking the whole of the time to finish his drink. It's an odd selection: background information on Pena and Angel.

A breakdown of Angel's movements—how he left his home and his parents, the color he dyed his hair, and the salary he drew from a short job as a lift operator. Where he lived and how he walked and how he met Pena in Santa Fe. A pretty thorough breakdown of Pena's life. Her past. Her present. Who she met and who she knew. Unreal really, Isosceles must have been watching her for years.

"You stole this?"

"Yeah, well, someone had to."

Yeah, I guess someone did, thinks Coyote. Damn impressive pile of information. Damn impressive theft for that matter. He sips his drink, turns back towards the pile.

Some simple studies of the Vatican's secret archives, nothing more than the information available at a good library, written as footnotes, touchstones, a memory system for someone who had long ago learned all this but occasionally wanted to look it over, see if there was something that had been missed. Copies of acquisition manifests, some dated from the fourteenth century, things that are hard to come by. The Vatican isn't liable to let just anyone see them, see that for over a thousand years they had stolen and thieved and managed to pick up one big pile of treasure.

There were some rough sketches of the old Roman aqueduct system, a blueprint of St. Peter's basilica, the Sistine Chapel, the Borgia apartments, the archives themselves. Then a whole ream of classical physics diagrams and equations. Coyote recognizes Bohr's work, some of Maxwell's, Planck's constant, Einstein, but to him it's like reading a language he does not speak well.

Coyote turns the page and finds the note that says "no one goes home." It stops him cold.

"Isosceles killed Pena?"

"You read it," tapping a finger towards the folder. "Isosceles didn't want anyone stealing his thunder. I think he was going to kill both of us. But no, he didn't kill Pena. She died before he got the chance and I didn't wait to give him one."

Coyote grins at him. "Looks like you stole his thunder to me."

A smile that could light a city, thinks Angel. Makes him feel good, no denying it, no one has smiled at him in a long time. Coyote shuffles through the pages again.

Towards the bottom of the pile, he finds an entire notebook devoted to the mathematics of Georg Cantor. An eighteenth-century mathematician, who, like so many before him, bent beneath the great shadow of the Roman Catholic Church. He didn't have it as bad as Galileo, but that's only a question of timing. His work concerned the actuality of infinity, not necessarily a new theme, but one close enough to the den of pantheism to raise a few eyebrows. Before him, the idea first surfaced in Aristotle's *Physics*—the infinite had only a potential existence. The idea that infinity was a mathematical quantity, that there were varying degrees, well suddenly it wasn't just about dividing up God's creation, rather the Creator himself—you see how quickly these thoughts lead down dark corridors.

Beneath the whole thing is another notebook, entitled the Sefer ha-Zaviot. Coyote recognizes the anglicized Hebrew, it isn't anything he had ever heard of before, but it doesn't take him long to figure out what's being asked of him.

The Kabbalah's a game, as Coyote understands it, one giant linguistical puzzle. The idea isn't even too hard to grasp if you come at it from the right angle. In the beginning was the word—words—what God used for Creation. God spoke the world into existence. You try creating something from nothing, imagine the things you'd say. The language of his creation is the Torah. Not the written Torah—the visible Torah as it is called—that being only one of an infinity of possibilities, but the one, true Torah. The words of God, the power to create. The game is in the permutations, to correctly pronounce the Torah, well there you have it, the power of God. That's been the course of Jews, a stack of lifetimes piled on top of one another, no wonder they managed to survive so long, how many billions of tries would they need to unscramble the Torah, to get it right just once.

Over the centuries they have picked up a few tricks, gotten a few things correct. This letter follows that letter and when you play the words through your mind it helps to see these colors, the words floating in a maroon sea, like soft, velvet smoke. It helps to hold fingers in this position, then in that. Maybe a certain direction should be faced. But the whole of the way was littered with distractions, pratfalls. There is the story of the four wise men, rabbis all, who took it upon themselves to study Kabbalah. Of the four, one went blind, one mad, one died and the last, yes, well he got some real knowledge but slowly he discovered he had no more use for this world. He had gotten a taste of another one, something sweeter, something to savor, so he sat around hoping that sooner or later something would come along, come along and pick him up and take him off to heaven.

Maybe what Pena noticed, so long ago, was that surety of spirit, the part of Coyote that said that this was magic and a treasure and it didn't belong in a locked dusty room, forever invisible, no matter who your God is.

Standing at the window, staring again. A night full of stars. Coyote stands and finds the scotch and refills Angel's glass, then his own. "Let's get drunk," the glass held high in his fingers.

Angel looks up, raises his glass, and smiles, he's going to go to Italy after all.

LATER, AFTER ANGEL IS ASLEEP ON
the couch, Coyote finds the section of the notebook that
talks about the Society. He knows all about groups like
these and he knows that whoever Isosceles is, he's not one
of them. If he were Coyote would be dead on the side of
that road, not sitting in somebody's living room with a bad
hip, bruised ribs, and a dull tingling in his toes. What that
means is that Isosceles and his henchmen came after Coyote alone and they found him alone. It means they had the
resources to find him. It also means that if Isosceles could
find him then he has to know who he is and if Isosceles
knows who Coyote is and still came—well then Isosceles is
one very crazy motherfucker and nobody's going to sleep
well for a while.

"WHAT IS THIS?"

The door hangs open, Angel's hand is on the handle pulling it through the low end of this February day. Less than twenty-four hours have passed since he met Coyote. In the background, sky the color of train's smoke. He went skiing, a boy at play in the snow, and there's something in him that doesn't want to give it up just yet.

"This," says Coyote, holding a newsletter from Pena's file, the same one that Angel and Pena spent an afternoon puzzling through.

"That, Coyote, is what we call a newsletter." He's still dressed for skiing. "Hold up a second."

Angel puts his skis and boots into a corner and hangs the parka in the closet, then joins Coyote in the living room.

"This is a problem," says Coyote, throwing the paper onto the chair.

With the door shut the room is dim. Angel can tell, just by looking around, by the weight of the blinds or the way the lamplight feels or something in the smell that Coyote's been in this room all day, sitting in one of these fat chairs, pawing through the angles. It snowed eight inches last night and Angel tried to convince him to come skiing, but Coyote shook his head. His ribs still hurt and his right arm is still swollen and purple where the cuffs had frozen to his skin.

"Tell me about it." His eyes move flat and cold from Angel to the newsletter and back again.

"Beer?" asks Angel, moving towards the kitchen.

"I asked a question," snaps Coyote.

Angel hears this and doesn't hear this, he's moving through the words and off towards the kitchen when they actually make contact. Angel can't really imagine Coyote angry, can't imagine what a man as big as a bear would do. He stops and pivots lightly on the ball of his left foot, it is a soft movement, a counterweight readjusting itself before crossing the room to where Coyote stands in his broad-shouldered hunch. Very slowly Angel reaches out a slow hand, touching Coyote's elbow, just the tips of his fingers making contact.

"You okay?" keeping his eyes level with Coyote's. Lately he's noticed something, that there's a certain power in reacting this way, in staying even and heading towards the center of the situation.

Coyote lets out a hard breath. "Cool," shaking his head. "Cool."

"And thirsty," says Coyote. He moves off towards the other room, saying 'I'll get it, sit down' with a rough pass of his hand.

Angel walks over and picks up the packet. Small words in a gray ink. Not more than twenty pages all together, but arranged as a newsletter, folded and folded and folded, a process, he thought, that would take time.

"Where'd Pena get it?" says Coyote, walking back into the room and passing Angel an open bottle.

"She never told me, sometimes things just came to her, just worked that way."

"Did she say anything at all about it?"

"As far as Pena could figure it comes out once a month, give or take a few days, but that's only hearsay. She said she'd heard about other issues but couldn't find any. This is it."

"Inside the Vatican," asks Coyote, a little mirth rolling through his voice.

"She figured it was being written by a Jesuit. The whole thing is a commentary on sacred books. Pena tracked all the books mentioned within this newsletter. None of them are supposed to exist anymore."

"So that's one very careful Jesuit."

"That's what she said," walking to the window and opening the blinds. He lit a cigarette and watched the daylight start to fade.

"Our only real clue and it's going to be a hard one to track."

"Work backwards," says Angel.

"I mean working backwards, unless of course you want to show up at the Vatican and wave this about just to see who gets killed first." Coyote pulls on his beer. "Who gets this thing? I mean, where does it go after it's published?"

"I have no idea, Pena could never figure it out either. She said it was like having a rope in your hand and not being able to find either end."

Angel lays his cigarette halfway in an ashtray and picks the paper up again. Small words in gray ink. Then it comes to him.

"Coyote, why is this ink gray?"

"What?" caught in his thoughts.

"The ink," pushing the paper towards Coyote, "it's gray. I saw it earlier but it didn't strike me, gray, not black, an odd color for ink."

"Odd," says Coyote slowly.

"Might just be odd enough."

"That, Angel, is one crazy idea." He smiles for the first time all day as he goes to pick up the phone.

GABRIAL SITS KING HIGH IN THE CABIN
of '49 Kenworth with 'Live Free or Die' plates and a chrome
grill like angry teeth. Inside the seats are plush enough.
He's got a leg curved against the dashboard's enamel grain
and his head cradled in the black sprawl of the leather, eyes
to the window, watching the signs. A little Buddha sits, impish and belly low, about six inches from his boot. It's glued to
the dash. He's been watching it since he hitched the ride, on
his way out of Telluride, thinks he's building up a relationship, like it might save his life someday.

Someone stole his truck and he can't find Sticky and
there's a burning in his eyes from lack of sleep. He spent a
week searching and waiting and asking and no one's seen
Sticky. He got a call from Coyote last night and left a note
on Sticky's door and really, he doesn't know what else to do.
He packed a bag and grabbed the old steel guitar and left.
The old guitar is now resting across his lap, his traveling
guitar, as he calls it, and he plucks out a rheumy reggae,
something by the HepTones called "Sufferer's Time." It's
only one out of a vast repertoire. His feet tap that soft shuffle,
that dread beat, and when there's pause enough in the
words he just throws out consonance, carrying the rhythm
onward, floating and unchained.

With his municipal railway pin stuck in the band of his
Stetson and a hard, thick jaw, Slow Drunk can drive with
the best of them. He's a smooth double-clutch. The whole

while playing stutter drums on the rig's wheel. Big, flat, heavy hands and he never tries to sing along.

"The world is carved by rightfully assigned tasks, my job right now is to drive, your job is to sing, that's how our world's gonna work for the next five hundred miles."

Slow Drunk, Gabrial finds out, received his name not because of a hard thirst, rather because of the idea that life is one long, slow drunk.

"I mean the mother of all drunks. Starts out clearheaded, a sweet taste, the fruit of the vine calling us onward. Sooner or later we're staggering, falling, laughing at a tree. Tomorrow there's greater inebriation. One day we pass out cold. Wake up someplace strange."

Gabrial sings dirges all the way into Utah. A world the color of rotting corn. They stop in Moab at a creaky roadside joint and kick dust across the parking lot with their boots. Slow Drunk "howdies" the entire room, then plows into the powder blue plastic of the booth.

"Get some grub and then we pick up the Baptists."

"The Baptists?"

"Yeah, they jumped ship in Nebraska, caught a plane in, and are meeting us here."

The whole room is staring at Gabrial and Gabrial's staring at the window, doesn't notice and doesn't notice Slow Drunk's jaw start to tighten.

"You guys got a problem?" Slow Drunk stands to his full height. "I got two-hundred-and-sixty pounds of a solution."

That wakes Gabrial up. He snaps his head hard towards the room, feeling two-weeks worth of anger looking for an outlet.

"Easy there, partner," Slow Drunk plunking a hand on Gabrial's shoulder, keeping him steady and in his seat. "We don't kill anyone until we have to."

And whatever that means, Gabrial's pretty sure Slow Drunk didn't just pull over and pick him up out of the blue. He doesn't know what the hell he's gotten mixed up in, but by now he figures Slow Drunk as one of the good guys and he's not going to get anywhere with him by asking. That much he figured out from being around Coyote. Ride this out for a while longer. He's put one thing together by now. The little reggae reference Isosceles left for Coyote. Suddenly Sticky, the only real Rasta for a thousand miles, is gone. Gabrial's going to find that Isosceles, going to find lots of things. A clench to his jaw and a grit in his teeth.

Eggs, sausage, bacon, a little butter on the toast, everyone in the room keeps their heads down and eyes forward. No one looks their way anymore.

"Baptists?" asks Gabrial finally.

"The New Orleans Baptismal Motion Conversion Consortium. Bunch of Christians got the idea that the Beatniks..." Slow Drunk stops speaking to shovel food in his mouth. "You know who they are?"

"Yeah," says Gabrial.

"Think these Beatniks are actually a secret Christian sect. Some kind of weirdo proselytizing thing. Someone gets the idea to put together a troop of sons and daughters, the oldest can't be more than fifteen, send 'em off to ride coast to coast in the back of eighteen wheelers, belting song. I got speakers strung alongside the truck."

The waitress brings more coffee. In the parking lot, the steel strings of the guitar glimmer through the windshield.

"When do they arrive?"

"Half-hour, eat, load up, seven hundred miles towards sunset."

Slow Drunk isn't lying, twenty of them and not one a day over fifteen. Children on an adventure, serious about something, Gabrial didn't have to think too hard to figure out what. He thought if he had the chance he'd teach them some reggae, maybe the redemption song. A little deliverance.

Slow Drunk drops it into gear and they pull out of the parking lot with the choir singing "Jesus Met the Woman at the Well," but softer than you'd expect, ghostly, like wind. "Mary Don't You Weep," " Precious Memories," outside the window the song hangs over empty desert. Miles of empty road. "The Old Ship Of Zion" and even Gabrial unclenched his jaw long enough to sing along.

Fifty miles pass, then fifty more.

"Can I ask you something?" says Slow Drunk, still thinking about the restaurant.

"Shoot."

"Things always hard for you?"

"Meaning my skin?"

Slow Drunk nods.

"The word albino comes from Alphos, a Greek word meaning dull-white leprosy, and from the word Alphito, the White Goddess. You read much Melville?"

"No, heard of him."

"*Moby Dick*?"

"That mad captain chasing a giant whale all over the ocean? The whale took a chunk of his leg and the captain wants revenge?"

"The very same."

"Uh-huh."

"Melville likes the contradiction of white: purity and grace on one side and on the other nameless horror: lepers, albinos, white hoods."

"So you bring out emotions in people?"

"The book comes from a time when people were just discovering that God was an idea that could be killed. Maybe. In *Moby Dick* the whale is the symbol of God. Ahab spends the book trying to kill God. But the thing to remember is Moby Dick's white. She's an albino whale, and when it's all said and done she wins."

THE WAILING WALL IS ALL OF WHAT
you would want to imagine. Old. Stone the color of desert
light, cut and caked into bricks the size of circus fat men.
Dropped down into the earth, so the square it rests on is dug
out, like an archeological site, letting the rest of Jerusalem
rise beside it. And rise they do. What a group of roustabouts:
hash dealers working the tourist crowd, pickpockets dressed
as Jews, Muslims, Christians, no matter. Eremites of all fla-
vors. The neighborhood crazy anywhere else in the
world—short and bushy and mumbling until white spittle
flies from dry lips, hair wound and tight into an antennae
of sorts, but with the Jew's sideburns, payos spiraling
below his chin, eyes meant for God alone. Regal women
with spines like rods of steel, eyes straight and hard, here
to bear their sorrow, but not an ounce more, others, women
so brought down by their God's word that they can do no
more than crawl in this hot sand. Mystics who levitate in
the privacy of their own home, who stick pins through soft
flesh, who walk the coals. Small children writing prayers
and promises and wishes—you could never count the
wishes. Everyone writes one or two on scraps of paper,
folded and tucked into pockets, crannies, every last space
on the wall and it's been going on for decades, centuries,
who knows where such tradition comes from, takes root,
takes the soul of all peoples—we may hate each other's
other ways, but sure we can hope, we can dream, we can
have that much in common.

And then, one morning, a small boy, a Semite perhaps, stands on his tiptoes. Maybe he's reaching a little higher than he should, how would you measure? Both his hands are stuck deep into the wall, thrust in past his elbows, into a hollow between stones, a tatterdemalion look in his eyes. It's the eyes that get you. The eyes stare on and on, how far do they see? How sure are you that the Kingdom of Heaven is within?

He does, eventually, pull his hands out of the wall. But it takes time for him to give up his purchase. Years pass. Pilgrimages come and go. Governments are in exile. Frontiers change. He holds on. The hottest part of the day doesn't sway him. It is as if he were dropped from a tremendous height and caught hold here. An arresting choice, but if he lets go who knows how far there is left to fall? How many things are you that sure of? What assurances can you offer?

When his hands do come out it's at night, when the dark has shrunk the distance, when it suddenly can't matter any more. He's been gripping a copy of the I Ching in his fragile fingers. A wipe of dirt on his sleeves. Has the book been inside the whole time? Has he found it by accident? Did he shove it inside himself and spend days baking its pages in hot brick? Even the hands, the palms, are strange, empty of lines.

He holds up his hands so she can see.

"A couple of hippie kids found me," says Johnii. Christiana across the room, eyes on fire, watching every word. Sticky had vanished, Gabrial panicked. She took a hotel room in Telluride and called Coyote. They spent the better half of the week looking. Wherever Sticky went, he wasn't to be found. Three days ago Coyote called, offered Gabrial a job, but he wasn't going anywhere. They spent two more days at it. Search parties on the mountain. Skiing all his favorite trails. Talking to the kids Sticky liked so much. No one knows anything. Coyote called again last night, this time Gabrial agreed. A few conditions. Johnii and Christian promised to stay around a few more days, keep looking, see what happens. They all know it's no use, not anymore, not in this game. Sure they can roll the dice, but some angles are just played out.

So now Johnii and Christiana have an extra day of quiet, the light soft on the curtains.

"It was the right time for it," says Johnii, "the middle sixties, I spoke English so they thought I had ducked out on my tyrannical parents who dragged their teenage son on a spiritual pilgrimage. They thought they were on my side, letting me camp with them for a while. It helped that I was toting this copy of the I Ching around, it was just getting big then, they thought I was ahead of my time. Scared them when they found out I could read Chinese, scared them even more when we all figured out I was fluent in five languages. Five languages and I didn't know how old I was, didn't know where I was from, what I was doing. I had over ten thousand dollars taped to my thigh and no one to count it with."

"How old do you think you were?" asks Christiana.

"Then, I don't know, twelve, thirteen, fourteen at the oldest."

God would he like to brush her hair, slowly, for years.

"Dreams?"

"I've looked at everything, for all I know the wall itself came up with me, the child of lost wishes, broken prayers, then spit me out." Johnii's smiling when he says it, a good game, his life, the past.

Christiana says, "You tell it very well."

"Not very often."

An inquisitive turn of her head.

"Gabrial knows some."

"And your wife?" Christiana can ask all the real questions, her mind goes right to them, and she can always get away with it.

"My wife knew."

"And now you've told me," coming closer to share a breath, holding his chin in her fingers.

"Run away with me," says Johnii, "just for a little while."

"Maybe longer," her answer.

ANGEL STANDS ALONE IN THE HALL-
way, lips dry from the thin air, too much coffee. Always up
early, feet bare against the floor, standing ready with the
fresh morning angling in all around him. He misses Pena in
the early hours, loosing her in the rest of the day, probably
just what she would have wanted.

Now, the house is quiet. No lights left burning. Coyote
still asleep. Angel fingers the small businesss card Amo
had given him. An area code, a number, a strange beeping
at the other end.

"Give me a shout when you're ready," Amo had said.
"I'll find you."

After the beep he dials the area code and the phone
number for Johnii's cabin, waits in the night for a call back
that never comes. In the morning there is nothing and not
the next day. Then a knock on the door.

"COYOTE BLÚ, YOHJI AMO."

"Heard of you," says Amo, "thought you were dead."

"Just retired. Heard of you too, you beat me out for those last few bottles of mead," admiration in Coyote's voice.

"They also wanted a particular vintage Homer, I had the only copy, it was a hedged bet, otherwise I wouldn't have had a chance."

"That's very kind."

"The truth."

"Homer, fine stuff that," Coyote smiles.

"Like leaves on a tree, so are the lives of men," adds Angel.

Amo winks at Coyote.

MUCH IS CONJECTURE. THE SEFER HA-
Zaviot is about as old and sacred as written things were going
to get. Not much thicker than a fat test tube, it would spread
out flat to give up fifteen feet of words and a small map. If
there is any truth to the rumors then the scroll was anointed
by magic and written in a special ink—a blessed combination of sacred waters and fertile blood and a paste made from
a sliver of parchment removed from the first Torah.

The words are part of the Kabbalistic tradition and
delineate a short cut through the thirty-two secret paths of
wisdom through which God created all words will ever tell.
They are, among other things, the unspoken names of God.
The map is of the earth if viewed as a quartered orange and
each quarter flattened and blurred around the edges and
then grown increasingly refined and detailed as its center
was sought. The lines are heavy and black and broken at
their edges like a plain of wild grass. It is drawn on yellowed parchment as thick as slab bacon. The effect is that of
fog or distance. Phantom words that have long since eroded.

Amo can't get enough of it: the old books, scrolls, hidden
knowledge. He's like a badger, a digger. Once, joking, he said
his was an exploration of the bowels of God, part
travail, part shit, but at least holy shit. He wrings his hands
late into the night after Angel asks for a history lesson.

They're drinking port in crystal flutes, cut with odd
snowflakes, an elegant braille to the touch. They left Colorado last night. Careful. Watching for a tail. A bus station,

a mall, underground parking garages, lots of sharp left turns. Finally the airport. They flew under fake names to Seattle, spent the night in a shoddy motel, then new identities and a bus to the Portland airport, more names, a fast flight to San Francisco. They've been nearly ten people since yesterday, no way Isosceles could have followed.

Now sitting in ragged chairs on a makeshift back porch, looking over a series of crushed gardens, not enough soil to raise a carrot but people have planted whole forests, tropical paradises in miniature, things that seem to grow atop one another. Discussing Kabbalah among inverted hanging gardens with the city all around them. They follow a palm tree up to silhouette. The lights of downtown casting a pale, bleached reflection, hiding most of the stars.

Amo talks the whole while. "Don't know anything about the actual scribe of the Sefer ha-Zaviot, except he was one of the Septuagint."

Angel shakes his head back and forth, slight and slow, just a mere whisper of a question.

"Septuagint was the title given to the delegation of seventy-two learned Jews, six from each of the twelve tribes of Israel, who went to Egypt about 250 BC to translate the books of Jewish law from Hebrew into Greek— the very first time the Pentateuch was translated. It was a trade: Ptolemy II freed a thousand Jewish slaves from his prisons in return for the translation."

The wind comes shifting through the gardens, Angel smells the night, watches small potted plants turn to arcacia trees on an empty veldt. He knows about small cells, old prisons, tries to imagine what a thousand men could do wrong.

"Ptolemy hated Jews," says Amo. "Loved books, hated Jews, this time books won."

Two brothers appear on a porch to the left, they speak Spanish but the night carries no words, only cadence. One, the younger, sits on the edge of a rye-colored banister, the wood creaking beneath his ten-year-old body. His brother stands before him wrapping white tape around his palms, thin tight strips covering olive flesh. He wraps slowly, doing a good job.

"In 640 AD, the library was burned by Amrou Ibn el-Ass under direct orders from Caliph Omar," Amo continues. "There were to be no words but the word of God and God spoke no more than what was written in the Koran."

Angel leans forward and pours them more port. The bottle is still full and heavy at this angle. The liquid is blacker than the night around and looks like molten tar coming out.

"The fires were said to burn for a month," says Amo, the words coming in hot stumps. It's been two thousand years and he's still angry. "The scroll was thought lost."

On the other porch the ritual of taping has been completed and now the boys stand before each other. Feet spread, arms raised, the older with flat palms held as targets, the younger hands turned to balls turned to weapons, but he's too young still and hasn't learned to weigh his punches, to shift his weight, to throw sequences and it is these things his brother has come out to teach him.

Angel can understand bits and pieces. Keep your guard up, stay moving, static targets are easy to hit, don't always lead with your right, save it, left jab, left jab, left jab, round house right, good, follow with a left upper cut if he's still standing and on and on into the night.

"In 1000 AD rumors surfaced in Jerusalem that three Jews had snuck into Alexander's great library prior to the burning. Of the three, one disappeared in the long sands of the Sinai, one was taken by the sea on a dangerous crossing to Damascus, and the last was caught by castle guards before leaving Alexandria. Whatever books he had been carrying he hid somewhere in the city. He was brought before the high council and asked a selection of questions. He chose not to answer the questions and in return they fed his body to the same fire that took the library to ash. It took most of an afternoon. They did it one limb at a time, starting with his toes. Of the Sefer ha-Zaviot it is said that once awakened, it walked out of Egypt on its own."

Angel stands slowly, he doesn't want to creak, doesn't want to disturb anything, he leaves his shoes off as he pads inside for his cigarettes. Past Coyote's room, he smells pipe smoke, heavy musks and cherry mixed with night odors. Coyote only smokes a pipe when he's thinking hard. Angel just smokes, doesn't have an excuse. When Angel returns Amo hasn't moved, preserve the silence thinks Angel, knowing how important it can be.

"It ends up in Jerusalem," Angel says.

Amo raises an eyebrow.

"Where else," says Angel, not even shrugging.

"Yeah, not for long," replies Amo. He pauses to touch a match to an offered smoke, Angel follows, two rusty lights bobbing on invisible hands.

"On November 25, 1095, at the Council of Clermont,

Pope Urban II brought holy war against Islam. The Seljuk Turks convert to Islam and seize the lands of Anatolia. Asia Minor. Took it from the Christian empire of Byzantium. Good plan, lousy timing. Urban unified Europe on their banner. Wanted the Turks kicked out, the lands cleansed with infidel blood, the long march to Jerusalem. He couldn't sleep at night thinking about the corpse of Christ buried on heathen soil. Early May 1099, a group of Jews and Moors boarded a smuggler's vessel and set off for Spain. It was a bad time for a crossing, summer storms just starting to heave, two hundred men left, a hundred arrived. The Sefer ha-Zaviot was hidden in a spice trunk. Said to still smell of sweet curried cinnamon. None of this happened a moment too soon.

"Two months later, June 7, 1099, the crusaders are a wanting and wanton lot. Most ride donkeys, steeds abandoned to the battlefields of Syria. Asses to asses, they stand outside the walls of holy Jerusalem. What a mess. They warbled. Seven times around these walls, they marched barefoot. There was much prayer. Some fasted. Siege towers were built. On July 15, 1099, they entered the city. One of the true miracles of Christianity. In two days the crusaders slaughtered every man, woman and child living in the holiest of cities. Jerusalem was a Vatican colony.

"The book gets three-hundred-fifty years of peace. Spanish Kabbalism flourishes. Southern France and Italy start producing great mystics. Everyone is writing books. Secret wisdoms. Nothing could touch the Sefer ha-Zaviot. The Zohar? The Bahir? They went the long way around. The running plays, ten in a row and what do you get? Field goal. The ha-Zaviot was the long bomb, the touchdown."

A cold forest wind winds over the bay, sweeping into the

city and on and on and into the mission where they sit until Angel smells knob pine and fir and Amo eucalyptus. They put out their cigarettes and inhale air in thick breathes.

"The map," says Amo. "The names of God are important, but the map is the key."

"Why?"

"It is the way to heaven, a biblical passage from earth to sky," he pauses and tries watching something too far away and can't see, but by then his eyes are scrunched with strain and the stars have begun to blur.

"A doorway," he adds finally.

"Why do you need a whole map for that, why not just coordinates?"

"From what I gather it's because the entrance shifts, the coordinates are not fixed, they rotate on an axis of their own."

Angel says nothing for a moment and Amo takes another cigarette from the pack and finds a lighter in his breast pocket, night pulling back from the flame and a slip of smoke furrows out of his nostrils before the lighter goes out and they both pause to blink the blackness from their eyes.

When it's gone Amo says, "They called it 'The Angel's Way.'"

"From Spain it wound up in the Vatican?"

"Like I told you when we met: the Spanish Inquisition. Long has the church been opposed to torture. But things change and in 1252 the use of torture was officially sanctioned by papal bull. God has become something definable through pain. In 1492 Christianity defeated Islam—the Muslim kingdom of Granada fell, the Moors were gone. It took three months of Christian rule before Ferdinand and Isabella created the Inquisition. In the beginning Jews were offered a simple choice: convert or leave the country. Many converted, it was easier, they stayed private Jews, secreted. They were called Marranos—crypto-Jews. The Christians were terrified of them. It was ridiculous. The Office of the Inquisition was created to uncover Marranos. It took twelve years, but the Inquisition poked and plundered. In the end it purged nearly 13,000 people, mostly Jews. During that time the Spanish Church paid its tithe to the Vatican with Jewish art and Jewish books, among the loot was the Sefer ha-Zaviot."

Did they know then? Angel wants to ask, but Amo has stood and stretched and left him alone on the back porch. Seven hundred years later and there are still men like Isosceles. Men capable of haunting. Angel thinks of Coyote's limp, he looks over the porch carefully, looks for a man willing to torture, to beat another man nearly to death on an empty highway in the cold of winter all for the sake of a little information.

Angel smokes another cigarette and watches the night and then swivels on his seat and watches Amo buttoning his coat in the living room. Angel sees only a dim refraction, a bit of brass button caught in a surface somewhere and bent back to him where he sat on the porch. Amo finishes buttoning his coat and runs an ivory lint brush over his trousers and walks out of the room and Angel hears the front door close and footsteps on the stairs and then silence. Angel stands and walks to the other room and stares at the lint brush which Amo left propped against a lamp on an end table. Amo was given the brush in Senegal some years back, along with a jade handled razor and a shaving brush made of tiger hair. He carries them in a smart black leather case and uses them daily. He's never told anyone how he got them and yesterday Coyote asked and Amo hefted the razor in his left hand as if it were an ancient puzzle and said that he could answer that question, but there was no way to do that in any language he knew.

COYOTE HUNCHES IN THE DARK HALL-
way, swathed in black wool, rolling back on his heels then
forward on the balls of his feet. Beneath him the cold floor
creaks. It is early in the morning, light just floating
through the slats and the moon somewhere, not having
dropped out of sight quite yet. Outside, the cough of an
engine disrupts his conversation.

"What was that?" back onto the toes while the information gets repeated. There is the small thug of the phone
being replaced in its cradle.

"The ink in question," says Coyote angling his eyebrows up and down in a mysterious fashion, "happens to be
of an extremely rare variety."

Angel and Amo sit in the dining room, mugs of coffee
and doughnuts, piles of doughnuts sitting in the middle of
the table. Amo's wearing a brown monk's robe made of lush
velvet. No matter how hard Angel tried, he can not look at
Amo and see a man who likes doughnuts. He still sees a man
who likes battle and fast cars and shipwreck yarns.

Two nights ago, Amo had taken them all to an old swab-
bies' dive behind Candlestick Park, a runt of a bar long low
on provisions. Angel and Coyote were the only white faces.
No one cared. Fishing tales and brave runs through the
Strait of Malacca and ghost ships haunting the Great Lakes
and Amo buying drinks and egging everyone on. They were
sailors, pirates mainly, and they'd traveled the whole world,
seen all kinds of things, even a few white people. Coyote

spent the evening leaning against a post, chewing a cigar. A man who understands the time for silence. Later, on the way home, Angel realized that most of those men had probably worked for Coyote, one way or another, even if none of them had ever met.

"Thirty-nine special ingredients needed to come up with this color and it has only one purpose—unless you want to count our newsletter as a purpose. This ink is used to repair palimpsests."

"Palimpsest?" Angel looking around for a dictionary.

Coyote reaches a hand into a pile of books at the table's edge to yank out a thick dictionary, letting the books stacked on top of it hang in midair for a minute before dropping down. He throws it to Angel, who catches it and flips through until he finds the entry: "Palimpsest, noun. A parchment or text from which writing has been partially or completely erased to make room for another text."

"Shitty dictionary," Coyote rolls his eyes. "In a palimpsest all the previous texts, everything that has ever been written on the parchment, is still visible. They're visible histories."

"So what's the point?" Angel asks.

"The point is that they are very difficult texts to repair. It's a pretty rare skill, a form of antique restoration or art repair, but more delicate, if you can believe that. The hardest part is in matching the color of the inks. You start filling in letters with the wrong color ink or with an ink that reacts badly to the parchment itself and you're finished. Whoever is our Jesuit, his attention to detail is tremendous. Among other things, this particular color of ink works best on manuscripts prepared in an arid climate over a span of roughly five hundred years."

"Which five hundred years?" Angel sitting suddenly taller and straighter.

"The five hundred years before the birth of Christ."

"The season of the throne," chuckles Amo.

"What does that mean?"

"The long dry season," says Amo with an arch in his brow. "It's one of the things that makes the Sefer ha-Zaviot unique. When it was written there wasn't anything like it. Back then the fundamental question in Jewish mysticism had to do with what God looked like on his throne. It's called Merkabah mysticism: throne worship. The throne existed pre-Creation, it contains all aspects of Creation."

"The Book of Enoch," adds Coyote, chuckling himself.

"You were in on that fiasco?" Amo looking slightly incredulous.

"Fiasco—a fine piece of work that was."

Angel leaning back in his chair, pulls at the few bristles he's been passing off as a beard. Amo's black eyes fix on Angel, a puzzle coming together.

"The Book of Enoch is part of a group of books known as the Hekhaloth Books, a blanket title that refers to all the books detailing throne worship, palace halls, what heaven looks like," waving a hand as if he saw that stuff every day. "The most famous book is the Book of Enoch. A really good version was edited in 1928 by a Swede named Hugo Oldbong."

"Odeberg," corrects Coyote.

"The whole system of heaven in Merkabah mysticism is divided into sevens. Seven spheres of heaven, seven palaces of the Lord, seven hallways, seven chambers, seven everything. The idea being there are seven beings who oppose the liberation of a soul, they have set up a series of gatekeepers to guard the entrance to the halls of heaven. A soul requires a pass to make the journey without danger. Each new stage of the ascension requires a new seal—the traveler seals himself within—in order not to be dragged into eternal flames by the demon gatekeepers. The seal also functions as a weapon, a way to fight one's way into heaven. The whole Christian notion of good behavior and absolution goes out the window. In the old days if you wanted to go to heaven you had to really work for it. These seals were an early version of the names of God, a preliminary mysticism that may have been off the mark but worked anyway. The Book of Enoch, though not the portion that Odeberg published, was supposed to contain the formula for obtaining the seven seals."

"So you had to get your hands on the original version if you wanted to figure out the seven seals?" Angel, a small half-smile, a tingle wringing his hands.

"I was in South Africa," sighs Coyote, "running guns. The place was a fucking mess. Everyone who could buy a gun was trying to start a revolution. The Afrikaners wanted everyone to believe they controlled all of the diamond mines, but that wasn't completely the case. The rebels would always start there, turn the workers against the owners, arm the insurgency, take over the mine for a few weeks. Mostly as long as they could hold it. They'd work overtime, round-the-clock shifts, trying to harvest as many diamonds as they could before someone came and took the mine away from them. Diamonds were good property, they bought a lot of guns.

"Word gets out that there's a guy who wants to see the

Book of Enoch. He doesn't want to own it, just wants to look at it, then he wants it put back. Willing to pay an unbelievable sum of money and he's able to pay this sum in diamonds. I wanted a break from guns. How hard could it be? The book was at the Hebrew University in Jerusalem, in a special vault in the archives. The vault had something like sixteen alarms and armed guards and was underground and hidden and nobody knew what else. We stole it, somebody noticed before we had time to put it back. My buyer didn't want it, was actually terrified of it. He offered to double the price if we would return the thing. I put a US postmark on it and mailed the damn thing back to Jerusalem."

Amo looks at Coyote. "Seven million."

"You made seven million stealing a book?" Angel shakes his head in disbelief.

"Three and a half for stealing a book, I made the other three and a half by mailing it back."

"Somebody leaked the story," adds Amo. "And every rare book fiend on the planet went nuts."

"I gave it back."

"That's why they went nuts, on the open market you could have tripled the money."

"Yeah, but then it would have vanished into somebody's private collection."

"Maybe, maybe not."

"I didn't like the odds. You know how I feel about it."

"It was a lot of money."

"Rules are rules," says Coyote.

Nobody says anything for a little while. Amo stands up and pours more coffee and sits back down. Angel reaches across the table for a doughnut but stops halfway and slides back Coyote's Zippo, his free hand fishing a cigarette out of a pack. The lighter clicks open, then closes with the hollow, flat clank of old metal.

"So the ink is rare, does that mean that we trace the shipment?" asks Angel.

"Not likely, the ink tends to be rare, but not obscure. This particular version is more common than some of the others. There are batches made from the spines of ground sea urchin, but ours isn't one of them. If we knew when it was purchased then maybe, but you can't date the ink that well. That's one of the reasons librarians like it so much."

"Librarians?" Now it's Angel's turn to raise an eyebrow.

"Who else repairs rare books?"

"Librarians," repeats Angel with a big smile.

"The kid's getting quick," says Coyote.

"Huh?" asks Amo.

"All we need to do," a sharp smirk edges into Coyote's mouth, "is get a list of the employees of the secret archives and figure out whose job it is to repair texts that were written during the Alexandrine age. Now how hard could that be?"

IN THE EVENING AMO TAKES ANGEL TO
an out-of-the-way bar on an out-of-the-way street and if
the patrons are the types to wonder who are these two new-
comers sitting in the back corner they're doing a good job
of hiding it. On one wall hang a few photos of boxers, old
black-and-whites with tin frames, and across the room
hang a couple of poets in similar frames. A waitress brings
Amo whiskey and Angel coffee and doesn't bother coming
back with their change. A pay phone stuck to the wall at an
off angle beside them rings once and stops. No one troubles
at this, phones are always ringing in their lives, nobody's
going to notice one more. Amo glances at his watch and
stands up. He looks once at Angel then walks across the
room and out of the bar.

Outside is another pay phone and beside it a young girl,
not much more than eleven or twelve, with a skateboard in
one hand. She looks at Amo as he walks up.

"You Amo?"

"Yup."

"Hang loose," then she slaps the board to the ground
with a fast twist.

"Nice deck," he says, as she vanishes around the corner.

He runs a hand through his hair and looks at the traffic.
An older woman in a housecoat steps around the same corner and walks up to him. She passes him a small envelope
and he passes her a cigarette and a match. They spend a

quiet moment cupped in the flame, then Amo looks at the traffic again and walks back inside.

"What's that?" asks Angel when he sees the envelope.

"Contribution."

"From?"

Amo offers a small shrug. "Book of the Month club." Then he slides the envelope towards Angel. "Open it."

Inside are sheets of paper a familiar list written in a neat block hand. "Did you follow me?"

"No," he says slowly, making sure Angel understands that he's not lying. "Look again. Red Lodge didn't make the list. This list belongs to Isosceles."

"You tracked him."

"Don't think Coyote's the only one who has a hand to play."

Which brings up a good point, thinks Angel, one he's been wondering about for a little while now.

"Amo, can I ask you a question?"

"Shoot."

Angel taps a cigarette out of the pack and lights it with a silver lighter. "Why are you in on this?"

"Long story, kid."

Angel puts his feet up on a chair and his hands behind his neck and looks at Amo. "No place I need to be."

"You like books, kid?"

Angel laughs at that, but says nothing.

"Me too. I was brought up by Jesuits. Ordained even. Somewhere I got a little white collar and a piece of paper with my name on it to prove it."

Angel smokes his cigarette.

"I thought it was what my mother wanted." Amo rocks his head from side to side, a slight apology for the error of his ways. "She went to a lot of trouble to get me to that monastery so I figured I owed her that much. But she split and I spent a pack of years on a frozen chunk of tundra for my effort."

"You ever see her again?"

"No, but I got a postcard once, from Argentina. So when I had read every book in the library and decided that Jesus didn't hold much more for me I split and made my way to Argentina to look for her. I asked a few questions and eventually met a guy who knew a guy and one day I had a conversation with a man named Earle Warren."

"Istanbul," says Angel. "Pena told me the story."

Amo doesn't say anything for a while, just sits there thinking. "I'm surprised she did." A wry smile and he goes back to his story. "Warren didn't have anything for me, he had never heard of my mother and didn't think anybody would, but he was looking for a guy to carry a bunch of books across a couple of oceans for him and the pay was all right and besides a postcard from my mother I didn't have much more than my socks. Earle got the postcard and I got the job and the books and me went on a long trip. Pena was at the other end."

The front door opens and Amo spins around a little too fast to look. Angel doesn't know what's going on, but he knows enough to unlace his fingers and put both feet on the floor.

"Sorry about that."

"Sorry about what?" asks Angel.

"I've been out of this game for a while." He picks up the envelope, placing the thin edge on the tip of his forefinger, testing it, seeing if it will cut him, "I'm not a hundred percent about our courier service. They got me the information about Isosceles, I just want to make sure Isosceles didn't get anything in return." Then he lets the envelope slip back to the table and moves his finger slightly, tapping the air. "You want another drink?"

"I haven't had a first."

"Then it's time you catch up."

When the waitress comes, he orders a pair of whiskeys and when they arrive Amo slides her a twenty and a look that says 'I want my change,' and he gets a look of his own in return. Angel feels the cool glass between his fingers, the weight of the liquor as he lifts it. There is a small chirp as they touch glasses.

Amo says, "You trust me?"

Angel watches him, the slight turn to his lips, leaning into the question, a ricochet laugh, a few heads turning.

"I trust all you sorry sons-of-bitches."

"Go ahead, take your time, think that one through."

"What would you like me to say? Pena trusted you. Coyote got hurt."

"That would be a start."

"Pena trusted you. Coyote got hurt."

Late at night Angel will climb onto the roof of the house. Amo has found him there, lying flat on his back at a precarious tilt of tile, lost to the stars. Each time Angel would continue staring at the skies, waiting for Amo to sit beside him, to take in the view.

"Nice night for a walk," is all he would say and then they'd lie there for a while, waiting until Amo got cold or restless, Angel never getting there himself, and then he would stand and help Amo up and say, "let me buy you a drink," and they would head inside.

"What about you?" asks Angel.

"When I met Pena she was still new to her game. I had delivered a packet of details. Kabbalah. What was in it?" Amo turns over a hand, stretches his fingers a bit. "Who could remember, but we stayed up pretty late talking for a few days in a row." Then he smiles and looks at Angel. "You fish in the right ponds, sooner or later something's gonna bite."

The wind creaks the door, but neither look. Across the room someone says something and a woman laughs in return. Things seem disjointed, as if they were all occurring one at a time. Amo, lifting his glass, watches the liquor slosh in slow circles. "Until that week I had never had a drink in my life, Pena gave me my first."

"Well," says Angel, "that explains everything."

"You know what Oscar Wilde said?"

"No."

"Was a woman who lead me to drink and I never had the courtesy to write and thank her."

The phone on the wall rings again and this time Amo answers it with a quick grab.

"Hello?"

"Remember me," he hears the excited voice of a little girl, "you liked my skateboard?"

"Yeah, I remember."

"Mom says come home now, dinner's burning."

Amo doesn't bother to hang up the phone. He grabs Angel and together they're up and moving towards the door and then across the street and past the traffic and into a taxi and another night passes away and Amo never does get his change.

TONIGHT THERE'S NO FOG AND EVEN IF there is it never creeps this far north. The streets are empty and cold. It's been years since Gabrial's been here, but he still knows his way around. Strange, quiet evening; the only sound he hears is a distant traffic and the low popping of his own boots against cement. It's even quieter as he walks down a road that used to be a river and past the monstrous church that is the Mission Dolores. The wind picks up and moves through trees. He wants a park bench to sit on and listen but doesn't see one and moves on. Instead he leans hip deep into a light pole wanting dinner or sleep or both and knowing that these things are far away. There's a funeral home on the corner, a clapboard white building rising two stories from the cement and midway through the second story is a black-lettered sign and midway through the sign, between the names of undertakers, a clock moves slowly through its pacings, counting down lives, one minute at a time.

At nine o'clock Coyote comes down the street, a perfect blue suit, 1940's juke joint elegance. Fantastic hat. No dust on his shoes. Under his left arm is a square box, black satin with a small brass hasp.

"Gab-ri-al," dragging the name out.

"Coyote Blú."

Coyote sets the box at his feet, they use all four hands to press palms.

"Nice to see you again."

"The same."

"This is for you," reaching down to gather the box. Inside is a brown fedora, brim exactly set. It is, of course, a perfect fit.

"Thank you."

"My pleasure."

"Seen Johnii?" asks Gabrial.

"Only when he left with you and Christiana. Christiana said Johnii was thinking Indonesia, where I don't know, how I don't know. After Sticky vanished," Coyote raises his hands in frustration, "a letter the next day saying goodbye, that they'd find me soon."

"Sticky," says Gabrial, still hot with anger.

Coyote nods, lights a cigarette, starts walking.

There have been rumors. The rumors have placed Johnii in Sumatra, surfing, sometime with, sometimes without, Christiana. The rumors have them leaving by bus in Mexico City. Some say her skin was darker, scented, edible, her hair longer, curly. There must have been a plane flight. Supposedly they are lingering together, driving mud trenched mountain paths through the tropical light. The scene is steep, pushed forward, descending at incredible angles, speeds.

Coyote misses them, but he keeps quiet about it. There's too much at stake and too many variables and he's glad she's a little out of the way. The whole deal goes too far, too deep, is too involved. Also, he can still feel his ribs as he walks, the sawbone edges. No matter what you want to believe this is still a game and there are still rules and now he's got a score of his own to settle. Isosceles scares him, but that is something else he keeps to himself.

Christiana left him a few of the details in her note, how

it would be nice to be someplace sunny. Coyote thinks California is pretty sunny, but he remembers the look on her face when he was in the hospital. He can see the place in the note where she stopped just short of asking him to come along. She has always known just when to stop short.

Johnii returns to the I Ching the same way explorers return to the jungle, needing the landscape of the unfamiliar, off center without it. It is an attractive quality, Coyote doesn't have to think too hard to see what Christiana sees in the man. Johnii and his book of changes. Coyote smiles at that, here he is, chasing his own ancient mystery because of what? A good kid? A bad priest? A debt to Pena? A little too much curiosity? What a strange life they have hammered together out of the odds and ends of the world's magic.

As they stroll the city begins to take on the affectations of a shipwreck: musky, thick scents, broken structure. Gabrial can't shake the feeling that if this were a dream the weighting would be different, as if, through the slightest miscalculation, the wrong angle of descent, even a missed foothold, and—down through the looking glass.

"Thank you for coming," says Coyote.

"I needed the work."

Coyote touches a hand to Gabrial's shoulder, then keeps walking. "So you're looking for your skin?"

"A fantasy—that's what you're thinking. That's how I think of it too, except I believe the fantasy is part of a certain history, important, but puzzling. Do I think I'm going to find a limp pile of black flesh that will fit snug? Something like Michelangelo's self-portrait in the Sistine Chapel? No, not really. But something like that, some skin of history, some way to affix myself, something to stop for."

Coyote nods, understanding, not understanding.

Gabrial stops and looks at him. "Johnii and Sticky are pretty much everybody I care about on this planet and now Johnii's somewhere in Indonesia and Sticky's door's been kicked in."

"What?" Coyote realizing he doesn't know all the details.

"As soon as we got back to Telluride I tried to find him so we could all go skiing. He didn't answer his phone and he missed a gig so I went over to his place."

"He lives alone."

"He did," says Gabrial. "I found a lock pick still in the lock on the back door."

"Police?"

"Yeah, I filed a missing person report and I showed them the lock pick. Look, he's a Rastafarian in the middle of Colorado, he shows up people notice. No one's seen him."

"What do you think?"

"I think a lock pick and a kicked-in door. I think Iscosceles wanted to send a message. I think Telluride is a big mountain and most of the snow doesn't melt until early summer and when it melts this year some poor hiker is going to find a good friend of mine tied to a tree and well-preserved and I'm very fucking unhappy about that."

Coyote doesn't say anything for a moment.

"We're going to find Isosceles?" Gabrial stopping to face Coyote.

"Or he's going to find us."

"One way or another."

"One way or another."

They've climbed to a zenith of sorts, turning behind, the cityscape is something Turner might have dreamed: the bay as mouth, buildings as teeth, and sky as lunch. Coyote doesn't say anything for a while and Gabrial calms down.

Gabrial says, "Looks like a child's map, someplace not yet visitable, something to wait for." Pointing towards the lights, "That's all a part of later."

"Comes with the business, mon ami." Coyote turns, profile, lighting a cigarette, match glow momentarily pushing shadows from his eyes. The smoke drags across his lips, new beard, over his fingers moving the cigarette away.

"The real problem lies within reconciling our lives to this. Understanding that $A+B+C$ equals D. That this is really ours, that these are really our lives, that every inkling we had of a future, every vision speaking through our childhoods never prepared us, never could have prepared us. Strange as it is, this is adulthood. These images aren't wrong, they're not the lies, somehow this is how things have turned out."

Gabrial says nothing, stands, hands plunkered into pockets, fedora askew.

"And then one day, you find yourself doing something, anything, and you say to yourself—didn't I do this, this morning—as if it were a faraway country."

SOMETHING HAS CHANGED. ANGEL paces through it in his mind, the ringing of a phone, the traffic, the cab driver's circuitous route. He's not certain. Amo doesn't tell Coyote what has happened, instead he comes home and sits on the floor reading in a shy mumble like something deep within him has started to tear and maybe these words are the way to glue it together again.

Later, after Amo has gone to bed, Angel picks the books up off the floor and puts them in a neat stack on the corner of the table. The books are written in other languages, but Angel knows they are all about the Kabbalah. He doesn't know how he knows this.

Coyote sits tired at the other end of the table with his hat in his hands. Angel tells Coyote about the evening. He starts with the envelope and ends with the present and Coyote sets his hat down and says, "This isn't good."

Angel has nothing else to say and starts to walk away.

"What do you think?" Coyote asks, speaking to his back.

The light rests flat on the floor.

"I think Isosceles knows we're in San Francisco." Angel doesn't turn around when he answers, "And I think sooner or later he'll find us."

"Or we'll find him," says Gabrial, walking into the room, standing at an off angle, shoulders set high.

When Coyote doesn't respond, Angel turns to face him. He sees Gabrial angry and clenched and the kitchen table, books stacked at one end and Coyote quiet at the other. He sees his world balanced like a teeter-totter.

AMO IS UPSTAIRS, PACING AND CHANT-
ing and making Angel nervous. Coyote walks in the front
door and hears the racket. Men are fixing something out in
the street and the cold whack of a jackhammer comes and
goes. Amo's voice plays over it, rising and lowering in the
spaces in between.

"It's a bad time to become a Kabbalist," shouts Coyote.

"Who's becoming?" Amo screams back.

Coyote tries to flip on a light, but the electricity is out
for the afternoon.

"Guy came round and said it'll be back on in an hour,"
Angel tells him.

Coyote shrugs and drops his coat on a chair. "Amo, can
you come down here a minute. I got a question for you
folks," shouting, but his voice suddenly serious.

The pacing stops, the jackhammer starts, Amo walks
down the stairs with an open book in his hands. Gabrial sits
quietly reading in the kitchen.

"Have any of you heard of Niko Tabak?" Coyote looking carefully at each of them.

Angel shakes his head no.

"Pena never mentioned him? Did you give me all her
files?"

"You've seen everything."

"Amo?" asks Coyote.

"No, I'd remember that name."

"In 1972, while the Vatican was going through crisis

214   Steven Kotler

after crisis, Niko Tabak disappeared in the secret archives. He was on loan from the University of Moscow and he vanished. The assumption was he was going to disappear on his own accord and the KGB got to him first."

"That is their business you know," says Amo.

"Yeah, but not this time. I was going over Isosceles' files, trying to figure out where he got his information. That same year Isosceles contacted a man I knew, a student of rare languages, this man didn't know anything but put him in contact with Tabak, who was working at the Vatican."

The jackhammer goes quiet and suddenly there are birds, a hint of a world not made by man, and the hallway light flicks on. Coyote sees Angel and Amo staring at him. Then there is a sharp pop as the bulb burns out. Once again they stand in darkness.

"I'll go find a bulb," Gabrial standing up, closing his book and walking towards the garage. Angel glances at the title, something about Georg Cantor.

"I've got a source inside the Kremlin, as far as he knows the KGB was going to make a play for Tabak, but they wanted him to finish his research first."

"What was he working on?" asks Angel.

"When Stalin started demolishing churches, a lot of little libraries were smuggled out of the country, much of that material made its way to Rome. Tabak was trying to catalogue the stuff. Someone in Moscow was trying to put the terror behind them, play the angles, assess the damages. The KGB wanted the catalogue, but apparently Tabak disappeared before he was finished."

"Where?"

"No one knows," continues Coyote, "There was a short

investigation. He was last seen heading into the archives, that is where the trail stops." Coyote pauses, opens the front door again to glance out at the street.

"There seems," says Angel, "to be a lot of that going around."

night stars. Gabrial pacing and puffing and nervous. Hair bouncing across his forehead, hands tangling through one another. Angel, bent limbed on the couch, tries to read, is unable to read, throws the book onto the floor. Gabrial stares at the spot it lands. Angel stares at the spot where wall meets ceiling, a place of unending whiteness, a place where the angles all blend.

"What's bothering you?" he says finally.

"What's bothering me," replies Gabrial, "is why has this book stayed hidden for so long. Why has nobody made a pass? Why are we the fools chosen for the job?"

Coyote strolls into the room, his tie black tonight, a dark silk that matches his shirt, his suit, his pants. Angel thinks about this, thinks he finally has made a friend who strolls.

Coyote sets a hand on Gabrial's shoulder and pries him away from the book. "That, my friend, is a good question."

"I mean how much money this thing worth?"

A short strum of laughter from deep inside Coyote. He moves with it, carried forward by its strength. At the window, he lifts a hand to touch the pane, tracing the patterns of light. The dippers, the myths, a finger connecting dots.

"See what I mean," Gabrial says and strikes fist against palm. "This thing is priceless. Even a church that big needs some extra cash now and again."

"The Vatican tries to sell it the rumors start." Angel still on the couch. "How many people know about this thing? A couple dozen maybe. But it hits the market and everyone's going to know. Sure folks won't know where it comes from exactly, but they can figure out where it doesn't. People start putting two and two together, they come up with the fact that there's probably a whole heap of treasure hidden in someone's basement."

"I don't think anyone knew it was around until Pena started digging. I'm not certain the Society even knew it was there. I think Pena's the reason." Coyote talks to the window, to the night.

Gabrial glances from Angel to Coyote. "Pena was a careful woman, but she made the mistake of going to Isosceles for information."

"Twenty years ago."

"The only thing that proves is that Isosceles has nothing to do with the Society," Coyote nods as he speaks, thinking it through. "If he's on the inside he'd have never rocked the boat this hard and there's no way Pena would ever have gone back there."

"No, he's not the Society," says Angel. "Pena believed in patterns. The I Ching, holy books, Earle Taylor, how she met Isosceles and Coyote and me, even her riddles. The Society was part of a pattern. She went back because she thought Isosceles was going to make a play, thought he was going to disturb some inner balance. Plus she needed his information and I think she needed me and I think she knew Isosceles was one way to make it stick."

Gabrial bends over and picks up the book and sets it on the couch and looks at Angel. "Why is that?"

"I've spent the better part of three months asking myself the same question."

"And?"

"And she was dying," answers Coyote.

Angel finds a cigarette, smoke coming out between words. "And I have no fucking idea."

"So you've got an insane priest chasing you across two continents for your trouble."

"Wouldn't have it any other way."

"Which leaves us with the fact that Isosceles is no longer patient."

"And he tracked me," Coyote absently rubs a finger across his ribs, "which means those monks he's got working for him are good."

Angel leans across the couch and grabs an ashtray off the end table. "You ask me, he's got an all-star team down there."

"They're still patient," says Gabrial.

"But not that patient, Pena didn't make mistakes," Coyote nods towards Angel. "If she thought Isosceles was going to make a break then he damn well was going to make a break. Isosceles is dogged and thorough and dangerous, but he's not the Society. I mean, this Society thing goes back over five hundred years, so they're obviously willing to wait."

Coyote tugs a string and drops the blind, the room falls dark. "The Catholic Church is a conservative organization. Careful and conservative." He has crossed the room and flipped on a table lamp. "Say you're trying to keep a secret in a world grown from secrets."

"Okay," says Gabrial, "so that's a boat you don't rock, but if the book marks a passage to heaven why not go yourself? You mean no one in the Vatican—no one with access tried to work the formula?"

"Who's to say somebody didn't?" Angel stands and walks across the room and pulls a copy of the New Testament from the bookshelf. "Got a whole history of people going to heaven right here. When they wrote the Bible who's to say they didn't leave out that little part—I mean they left out so much other shit."

"Or maybe someone tried and failed," says Coyote. "Maybe they failed in a big way."

Angel shoves the Bible back with a thump and turns to face Gabrial. "And maybe they left out that part too."

ANGEL DOESN'T KNOW WHOSE CADIL-
lac they borrowed, Coyote jingles the keys and winks. Fat
tires, white-walled convertible set into dark blue wheel wells.

"A deep, heady blue," says Coyote and he wears a fedora
to match. It's the first sunny day in over a week, Coyote's
jacket lies over the front seat. He wears suspenders, no belt,
a silk tie, also blue, with a ferris wheel at the bottom and
people, small people, not more than five dots and a sweeping line, people made from willow tree branches waiting
their turn in the silk sky.

They drive north along the coast, listening to clarinets
and drums and heavy applause, sounds taped through an
elephant's trunk. Past Stinson Beach they turn off and
drive roads that grow smaller and smaller with each turn.
Coyote parks before an iron gate and pushes a small brass
button and gets back into the car. The gate doesn't creak
when it opens.

The house would look perfect in a gale. Sunlight drops
across eaves at hard angles, making the whole picture an
impossibility. Heavy drapes hang alongside windows. The
door is mahogany, stained with a light cherry, as big as five
men. There is an iron knocker, an old man bent beneath a
terrible burden, in the middle of the door. Coyote brushes
his fingers over the old man's back, then over a silver
mezuzah shadowy in the door's frame, as he touches his
lips the door swings open.

They walk down a hallway and another and another and

into a large room. An unlikely man sits behind a desk the size of a small whaling ship. A man not much bigger than an umbrella stand sitting high and straight. Short hair oiled back over a high brow. Smoking jacket and a yarmulke. He's looking out a window. He turns and takes off a pair of round spectacles and looks at Coyote. Coyote stands very still. Angel stays in the doorway. A clean-shaven cement mixer in shirt sleeves stands in the corner, watching.

He looks at them as if they have made a terrible mistake. Then the man in the center wipes his eyes and smiles.

"I thought . . ." he says.

Coyote right hand hangs at his side, he raises it palm up, not much higher than his waist. The man nods and smiles again.

"Coyote Blú, he wouldn't skank, loved the mambo, did ghosts ships better and catered a beheading, how are you?"

"Samuel," says Coyote, removing his hat.

"How'd they ever convince you to cater a beheading?"

"It was my beheading," shrugs Coyote.

Samuel pushes back in his chair and folds his hands across his lap.

"Because rules are rules," says Samuel.

"Because rules are rules," says Coyote.

"I heard you went lockdown in Latin America."

Coyote shakes his head.

"Telling tales again?"

"My tales," says Coyote.

Samuel raises his left arm, waves Angel in from the doorframe, "Come 'ere kid, don't have to hide in the doorway. I'm too old to be much of a gangster."

Angel's shoes tap on the marble.

"What's your name?"

"Angel."

"Angle?"

"Angel," Samuel glances at Coyote, "Angel—Maimonides?"

"Maimonides," says Coyote.

"Angel, the luck of it, mazel tov," says Samuel.

"Maimonides?" Angel smiles that smile.

"Maimonides—old Jewish scholar, wrote a famous text known as the Guide to the Perplexed. He was a very truthful, rational man, Maimonides—it is true."

"Have you come for the name of God or would you like to have coffee with an old man?" asks Samuel.

"I am afraid the former."

"Then what is it you need?"

"Very current maps of the Vatican, good maps of the grounds above: streets, exits, guards, changing times, and security."

"Below ground?" asks Samuel.

"Below we need everything available—trap doors, secret panels, hallways, sewers, aqueducts, trenches, cracks, fault structures, stress lines, gnome tunnels, going at least half a mile outside the main wall, use the library and secret archives as the apex, work back."

"How long?"

"Two weeks, three at the longest."

"Give me six days and a Sabbath."

"Thank you, Samuel," says Coyote.

"Aach, would be sooner but most are in Europe, travel

time and the right escorts, who needs old maps anymore, the place I am going there are no maps. You won't tell me what it is you're hunting?"

Coyote shakes his head no.

"Because rules are rules," says Samuel.

"Because rules are rules," says Coyote.

"Shalom Samuel, 6 and a Sabbath and many thanks."

"Shalom Coyote, good to know you didn't lose your head."

Coyote takes a few steps towards the door and stops. "Samuel, have you ever heard of the Society?"

"What society?"

"Not a what, a the."

"The Society." Samuel runs a hands through his hair while he thinks. "No. Would that I were to look into it?"

"No, I think we need the quiet."

"Take care, Coyote."

"Good day, Samuel."

Angel and Coyote stopped at a small store on the way home and bought drinks and drove to the beach and walked on empty, hot sand drinking in cold, red sugary slurps.

"How can he get the maps that fast?" asks Angel.

"I've even got a grammar school Latin textbook with a map of the old Roman sewer system on the inside cover. Hide in plain sight. But more than that there's a whole network of people who like to know where things are and how to get at them."

"And Samuel?"

"Samuel's been a part of every network that ever was and he's been that way since the beginning of time."

Angel nods at that, walks a few steps and stops. Behind

him he can see the wind shuddering across the ocean. Coyote's shadow spreads wings across the sand.

"What did 'he wouldn't skank' mean?'" asks Angel.

"No drugs, I wouldn't run skank, one of my rules."

When they finish their drinks, Coyote takes Angel's from him and walks the cups over to a garbage can, the hatch is thin and sounds like a high hat when it closes.

THE ADVERTISEMENT RAN IN THE Sunday *Chronicle*. Angel didn't see all of it but he did read: "Roman villa: seven rooms, two-story library, windows looking towards heaven and so forth." Somehow this got rerun in a New York daily and then in a Roman newspaper and then the doorbell rings one afternoon and a messenger arrives. Angel opens the door and signs for the package and says good-bye to the courier and it's only after he glances down and sees that there's no address on the envelope does he bother to look up and notice that there's no truck, no postal vehicle, no sign of the deliverance.

"Too many networks," swirling the envelope into the middle of the dining room table with a flip of his right hand. "It's like living in two different worlds."

Inside, the curtains are drawn against this world, but a diffused light makes it past. Angel reaches through it, passing his hand up and down, feeling the stretch of heat.

"Cantor believed," each word working through Gabrial's throat, gathering speed, "that every number is actually two numbers, a finite and an infinite version of the same. A mathematical doppleganger. He called them realen and reallen, real or real."

"Funny way to make a point." Angel walks back to the table.

"Mildly unclear."

Angel picks his way around the chairs, working through some children's game, but halfheartedly and alone.

"The whole notion was so obscure that it made it neither into the French nor the English translations of his work. But the idea's the same. Two identical worlds: one temporal, the other infinite." Gabrial slides the envelope closer to himself and watches it for a moment before speaking. "Do you know what a monad is?"

Angel sits down, then picks his boots off the ground, and lays them across the table's edge. Gabrial, who, in the course of looking over the envelope has let his dreadlocks fall across his eyes, brushes them away and squints at Angel.

"Can't say that I do. Why are you squinting?"

"I'm an albino."

"I noticed," says Angel.

"Good of you. Rapid changes in light throw my vision off, I have to refocus occasionally."

Angel nods at that and glances down at the envelope, "Okay, what's a monad?"

"The concept was Greek originally, but it got picked up by later philosophers and managed to stay around a while. It's the idea that preceded the atom. A monad is something that constitutes a fundamental unit, a core or a source, but it was also stretched to mean an individual elementary being—physical or spiritual." Gabrial peeks at Angel to see if he's following along, but Angel gives nothing away. It's a new plan of his, to sit very still, to let all of it wash over him.

"What's interesting," continues Gabrial, "is that within each monad sits a tiny reflection of the whole universe."

"Electron orbits the proton, mirrors planetary orbits, that type of thing?"

"On a much larger scale." Gabrial picks up the envelope.

"It's like this, if you look at it, it mirrors an entire universe, subtle, but once you know a few things about this—how it was delivered or what's inside or that it can exist at all, you realize there's a completely different world out there, interacting with the one that you reside within, but not a part of it."

"But you can say the same thing about biology or particle physics."

"You could, are they separate worlds or are they just another way at looking at a traditional version. This world of Coyote's," holding the envelope high, "seems to come from an entirely different place."

Gabrial slides the envelope back across the table towards Angel. A mug of the morning's coffee sits in the middle of its trajectory and Angel lifts the mug to allow the envelope's passage and then extends his other hand, fingers uncurled, to catch it as it slides off the table. He pulls a small silver knife from his jacket pocket and slices it open. Twelve pages in all, including four photographs. The top of the first page lists four names: Ambrose Sepulchri, Giorgio Bruzza, Yves Renoir, Calvin Chumbawa. Two Italians, a Frenchman, and a Nigerian. All Jesuits. All employed by the Vatican secret archives for the repair and restoration of ancient scrolls, texts and tomes of the Alexandrine age. The pictures reveal two old Italians, hair thin and gray, faces that look deprived of daylight, squeezed by some secret vice. They are head shots taken against a plain background, like identification cards blown up. One wears thick square spectacles, silver frames and lenses over a quarter-inch thick. Both have sharp eyes. Neither smiles. The Frenchman smiles in his, but it's a thin, veiled angle of teeth. He's out of his robes, in a small Italian cafe, drinking wine with companions. The shot came from a telephoto lens and most of the background blurs. The photo of the Nigerian shows him striding down a hallway, dark robes billowing with his fast stride. His face dark, fierce, determined. He looks younger than the rest, late thirties maybe, but it's hard to tell in profile. He has a strong jaw and a goatee. His hands are outstretched at his sides, fingers wide as if he can grab the air and find handholds to pull himself forward at an increasing rate.

Angel yanks his boots off the table and stands up beside it. Moving the coffee mug, he lays the photos out into a roomy square. Men who had sold their lives to God. Who would have faith above the other choices. Who have agreed to a life, a tradition, to one right way. To, above all else, travel everywhere with a God who keeps secrets.

"Maybe we'll be lucky and Coyote will know one of them right away," says Gabrial.

Angel shakes his head. "No, he won't. Not these men."

Gabrial turns to look at Angel, maybe it's a trick of the light or the morning or the weight of the past few weeks, there's something in him that reminds him of the men in the pictures, but not quite.

Angel divides the dossiers into four piles, each overlapping the picture of the subject. "I'll take the Nigerian and the Frenchman, you take the Italians."

It is afternoon when Coyote comes back from another meeting with Samuel. He walks in the door with a large brown packaging tube, the kind used to ship posters or blueprints.

"More maps?" asks Gabrial.

"More of the same," replies Coyote. "We've seen six versions now, nothing's changed. The good news is the Swiss guards have fairly fixed schedules, they're thorough, but if our timing is on…" Coyote spreads his hands wide—a gesture of possibility.

"What do you think?" asks Angel.

"I think what I've always thought." Coyote walks to the table and picking up the picture of Yves Renoir. "Serious fellow." He walks over to Angel and plucks a cigarette from his shirt pocket, lighting it he says, "I think we try to find our Jesuit and follow him around, see what we can learn. Maybe—and I mean only maybe—we could turn him to our purpose. If that fails, we tunnel our way in and if that fails we'll probably all be dead and I hear there's plenty to read in the hereafter so why trouble ourselves over one little book."

Coyote lays the picture of Yves back down on the table and slowly picks each of the other photos up. He goes over them twice, just making sure. "What do the dossiers tell us?"

"Frenchman fought in WWII, found God in the Marginot line or the fall of it for that matter," says Angel. "As soon as Europe got quiet he signed on with the Jesuits. He doesn't seem to care too much about the old texts, his thing is craft."

"The text part doesn't fit, could be an act, but the gray ink is the kind of touch a craftsman would go for."

"If they've come this far, they're all craftsmen," says Gabrial.

Angel nods. "But Yves has taken it upon himself to create special tools." He lifts the Frenchman's papers, gives them a shake of authority. "Designed a curved pen like a scythe. Half blade and half pen, it allows him to dig into the parchment below the spoiled text. He thinks it allows the ink to dry more evenly."

"Is he ambitious?" asks Coyote.

"Can't tell from this, but I don't think so, I think he has come as far as he wants. He's the type who signed on to escape some terrible sin and if he rises too far he's only tempting the devil."

"Ambition comes in the form of Giorgio Bruzza," Gabrial holds up his photo. Giorgio and his thick spectacles and behind them darkness that roots out weakness. Coyote takes the picture and looks at the tight chin, the eyes, the flat, white background.

"Who does he want to be, the pope or something?"

"Too visible for Giorgio, this man is all Jesuit. But he definitely wants a higher position in the Jesuit order. Not father general, I'd wager regional assistant. The brains behind the puppet. He's more conservative than most of his brethren, but not a traditionalist. It's a good balance for an archivist. Views the new in the light of tradition, but immersed enough in the dust of things to understand that history is a passage."

"Is he the type of man to jeopardize his career? Is there an idealist inside? Secret guilt dating back to the Second World War? Anything that could cause a betrayal?"

"This guy was an orphan, he grew up on the streets for his first seventeen years: very hard edges. Got in trouble with the law and a judge saw that he had very little formal education and gave him a choice: strict Jesuit school or prison. He went to school and reacted really well to the discipline. Found out he was book-smart as well as street-smart; he's become a man who trusts books more than people. A perfect Jesuit. For a while nobody trusted him enough to let him do missionary work so they gave him library jobs and forgot about him. Worked his ass off and kept advancing and advancing. He's in his middle forties, though he looks older, and he's a senior archivist. That's not exceptional, but it's definitely fast track. For a man with his background and late start—he didn't finish his schooling until he was thirty-one: a quick rise. He's got the cunning to be our man and he probably has the resourcefulness to set the whole deal up. He wants power, he wants to prove he's better than everyone else, but it feels wrong. Disseminating information about secret documents, especially the way it's being done, has a quiet elegance to it. I don't think it's Bruzza's style."

"Whose style then?" There's something to how Coyote asks his questions, a certain cant of the head, a jaunty thrill of the tongue, a way of saying 'I have played this game several thousand times and I could play it several thousand more and please take all the time you need because we have all the time in the world and isn't it fun, aren't you glad you came out to play.'

And the whole time Angel knows that they don't have all the time in the world, they might not have more than an afternoon, a week, three at the most. They are making too much noise and somewhere Isosceles is listening.

Pointing at the photograph, Coyote says, "Tell me about our Nigerian."

"How did you know that?" gapes Angel.

"Trade secret."

"I don't care what trade, there's no way you could look at a photo of a black man wearing long robes with no ornamentation whatsoever and know he's Nigerian. He could be Senegalese or American or Brazilian."

"He certainly could," says Coyote, "but if he were Senegalese then why would he be striding down the central hall-way in the Nigerian branch of the American embassy?"

"Tricky," says Angel.

"What could you possibly have smuggled through the American Embassy in Nigeria?" asks Gabrial.

"Actually nothing," says Coyote. "I was involved with a woman who worked there, she had a nice accent and won-derful access."

"Access?" asks Angel.

"Access," says Coyote flatly.

"Our Nigerian," says Angel, very aware of the time to drop a subject, "Calvin Chumbawa plays a tremendous game of tennis. Born in Nigeria to a conservative aristo-cratic family. Sent to school in Connecticut, preppy boys school looking to attract foreign money. The school might have been happy to have Calvin, but he was a little too African for most of the students. He had very few friends, became chummy with another outcast, a Chinese student named Wayne Lee. Wayne was a devout Jesuit. It was a Jesuit school and Wayne was close to the priest. Over time two things happened, Calvin became a great tennis player, a fact which got him a lot more acceptance among his peers, and Calvin became close to his Jesuit priest. He was in the top one hundred players nationally when he gradu-ated, but on the suggestion of his priest, he headed for school in Pisa where he pledged himself to the Order of Ignacious and chose God over tennis."

"Tough call," says Coyote.

"He did some missionary work in Nigeria, about ten year's worth, but wanted to get back to Italy. Four years ago a clerk position opens in the archives, he lobbies for it and gets it. Two years as a clerk, he moves into the repair department. He's a natural. Within six months they're assigning him older and older documents, the rare stuff, the treasures. He's good. A few months later he joins the ranks of our three friends."

"But he hasn't been there long enough to publish our newsletter."

"It doesn't seem likely, unless an older archivist passed the torch to him before passing on."

"I'd bet against it," says Gabrial.

"So would I," adds Angel.

"I'll try to find out if anybody died or left the archives in the past three years who might be our candidate, but I'm inclined to agree with you," says Coyote.

"Which leaves us with Ambrose Sepulchri," says Gabrial. "Old and mean and bitter, but a really good possibility."

"Why?" asks Angel.

"German orphan, adopted by a Jewish family right before WWII. Spent the early war in hiding in a forest. Middle of 1944 the whole family got caught. He was around twelve or thirteen at the time. Sent to Treblinka. Both his adopted parents were killed. When the camp was liberated he walked from Germany to Belgium, turned up on the doorstep of a Jesuit monastery. They took him in and treated him pretty well. He may have managed to hide his anger, but be certain he never lost his hatred for the Nazis. The one sample we have fits both categories: old Kabbalistic document that would be helpful to Jews and a condemnation of the Nazis for art theft and the Vatican for coconspiracy."

Coyote's looking at the photograph. Tragedy shapes a person, adds hidden features: a tight line at the corner of an eyelid, a wrinkle just below the lip.

"He's our man." says Coyote, tossing the photo back onto the table.

"GENTLEMAN," SAYS COYOTE, STAND-
ing alone by the window, his back broad and lamp lit, "we
have a problem."

It is late, they have spent most of the day researching
the four archivists and are now tired, sitting in old chairs in
the living room. Outside, the moon a sliver, the sky black.

Nobody says anything, they have grown patient together,
able to bear the silences.

"We have no idea what the Sefer ha-Zaviot looks like,"
say Coyote finally. "I have tried every source I can trust, I
can find no physical description of it," he shakes his head,
crosses the room to pour a drink.

Amo, finally joining them after a day of study, says
nothing, smokes, looks tired.

Angel, sitting cross-legged on the floor, stands and
walks out of the room. The sound of him taking the stairs,
two-by-two, then back down again. When he returns he is
holding the folder he first stole from Isosceles, tapping it
against his thigh.

"I've been thinking about why Pena took me down to
Mexico in the first place. I was told it was for reconnaissance."

He tosses the folder onto the coffee table, glances at
Amo, waits.

"Do you remember how just after we met," says Amo,
"I took off for a while?"

Angel nods. "You came back and Pena and I left for
Mexico."

"I was in Brazil." Amo paces while he talks, glowering, his arm moving like a hinge. The webbed corners of his eyes catching the cigarette's light, going stiff in the sudden orange glow.

"Isosceles had a good contact there, when he started looking around for explosives, weapons, whatever, he went to Brazil. His contact was a woman—Alexandra Abriz—whom I had known for a long time. She knew nothing of my relationship with Isosceles. Nothing of Pena. When Isosceles was an undergraduate they were lab partners. He went to Princeton. She stayed in Brazil. For a while Isosceles' star was rising, he was eccentric, but still sane. She kept in touch, he vanished and she went to work for the government, built weapons, quit, but kept certain connections. When she took up a more interesting line of work Isosceles found her again."

"How did you know her?" asks Coyote.

"How men know women? I knew her a long time ago, before Isosceles, before she ever got to Brazil. I knew her in Argentina. She is one of the reasons I am a failed Jesuit." Amo lights another cigarette. "Pena asked me to go to Brazil, see what I could learn. I learned nothing, I couldn't find Alexandra, I couldn't come up with any leads, I came back to the States."

"Pena was uneasy, wanted to go down and see Isosceles, she was going to go alone. I told her to take you."

"And I went."

Amo nods. "Alexandra turned up while you were in Mexico. They found her dead, in some bushes behind an old church."

Gabrial swears under his breath, shuts his eyes.

"Sooner or later," Angel says, walking to Gabrial, giving his shoulder a soft squeeze. Lately Angel's been dreaming of Gabrial and Sticky, the club where they played together, the bars they drank in, things he's never seen, not with his eyes, things he can't really explain so why bother trying.

"Isosceles," Gabrial spits.

"I suspected, I didn't know. Now I'm starting to believe."

"Sooner or later," Angel repeats, a little mantra of his, something to carry them through.

"So this is personal," says Coyote as if he were taking notes.

"This," says Amo, "has always been personal."

Angel opens the folder, starts rifling pages.

"I always thought there was another reason I was down there, something Isosceles had that Pena wanted." He lifts a sheet of paper from the file. "Pena was a cautious woman, she wouldn't have risked my life down there, not unless there was something she had to have, something that was worth the bet. I could never figure out what."

Coyote takes the paper from Angel, looks at it, lays it back on the table.

"It looks like a handwritten copy of an old shipping manifest."

"When Pena first went down there, twenty years ago, she was looking for shipping manifests. Someone had hidden old manifests in that monastery. Isosceles had copied an old manifest and had put that copy in Pena's folder. It makes no sense unless he found what she was looking for."

He points to a line of writing, halfway down the page. "This word, quoin, and these dimensions," says Angel.

"Quoin is the external angle of a building," says Coyote.

"Those look like shorthand schematics, a couple of lines taken from an architectural blueprint."

"So someone was building something, so what?" says Gabrial.

"No shit," says Amo, his eyes opening like lampshades, his hands giddy. He walks over to the table where Angel has set the folder, squatting on reedy haunches, peering. "Sefer ha-Zaviot—Zaviot means angle."

"So those aren't building dimensions," says Coyote.

"No," says Angel. "No, they're not."

"Nice work," Coyote whistling low, smiling, the day finally brightening.

"But someone wrote them to appear as such," says Amo.

"Yeah, but why did they write them out in a manifest?" wonders Gabrial. "This should be a straight cargo inventory. Livestock and spices. Silks. Weapons. No one ships an angle, they ship stones or blocks or whatever, but not an angle. And no one ships an aleph."

"A what?"

"This letter, here," pointing to the middle of a row of numbers, "is an aleph, the thing that looks like an oversized N, it's the first letter of the Hebrew alphabet."

Amo takes a closer look. "Certain scholars believe that the name of God proceeds from the first Hebrew letter—aleph—pure breath."

"Except why would it be here, even if it's a description of a Kabbalistic book?" asks Coyote.

"Because Isosceles copied this," says Gabrial, "and in this case maybe it's not a reference to Kabbalah. Isosceles was pretty into Georg Cantor and Cantor used the aleph to represent infinity in numeric equations."

"Which means the book is infinite?"

"I don't know what it means," says Amo. "The whole thing is odd. If the Zaviot was written for the Library of Alexandra it should be a scroll and not a book. But nowhere are there references to it as a scroll. I just assumed. Everything we've learned says it's a book. Maybe it's not a book as we think of a book, but rather a collection of individual pages. Maybe Isosceles doesn't know how many pages there are, maybe the number could be infinite. It might explain why there are so many dimensions here. I mean look at this, even if this were an architectural schematic it goes on for way too long. I think these are all different pages. See this at the end, this string of single numbers followed by letters? When the Library of Alexandra was being assembled they used different colors of inks for different types of books. These numbers and the letters relate to colors. It was a rudimentary card catalogue. If we assume a one-to-one correspondence than each of these pages has a different color. It may take some time and we may not get it exactly, but if we go over these measurements, we'll at least have an idea of what we're looking for."

"Which is more than we've had," says Coyote, "and probably all we're going to get."

Outside the moon folds into a cloud, a last light fading, drinks are finished, repoured. Angel stays awake after the others have retired. Alone in a room with the folder. Copying the manifest into a notebook, working by hand, in the old way. By his count there are close to sixty pages in the Zaviot. Who knows. Not much of a book. A small collection of secrets. With each additional line something opens inside him, a deep falling sensation, but not falling, rising almost, but still the feeling of weightlessness, of precious excitement, of some thick and final motion. He copies the aleph at the begining of each line as a reminder.

ANGEL MOVES LIKE A BALLOON ON A
string, something waiting to rise. The air around him
crackles, as if the whelp of languages spoken here were
enough to produce a charge. Nothing is distinct. When he
looks he sees mostly Latins, their words coming in snaky,
dusk rhythms, but he hears other sounds, a goulash of
Korean, Chinese, Tagalog. English snaps at him like something fired from a rifle. He tries hard not to look, but usually does, and later that's how he notices.

Two days earlier, Coyote had bought them all new boots
and, not wanting to risk blisters later, had suggested long
hikes. The boots are heavy and black with inlaid brass eye-
lets now coated with grease paint, turning them to deep,
inky points, much darker than the boot's color. Angel spent
two days rubbing mink oil into the leather, moving his fingers in small, tight circles. The waterproofing spray in the
tall aerosol can lands in tight globules and takes ten hours to
dry. For some reason all of these gestures have meaning.

The Friday streets are crowded. He has walked all day,
making a diagram of the city. Maybe he hasn't guessed the
tree of life, but it's there all the same. Kether, the crown,
then left to Hokhmah—the wisdom of God—and three
hours later, deep into the high concrete, he turned at Tifereth and over to Binah.

"How much of the magic in our lives do we really
notice?" Amo had asked him on the day they met. "How

much is our own fantasy? How often does our desire call forth to empty rooms that will never fill with gods?"

But here, now, at the edge of the Outer Mission, on a newly annexed border street, Angel stands in a glut of life and sound. Hard eyes find him, but pass over—this is not the right time, right place, or he is not yet the right target. Perhaps he has walked a charm. The women here stand in groups. They gesture as they talk. Hands that worry and flap in tight knots. There is a feeling of people huddled around a campfire. Angel steps around, taking long, gangly strides. He's loose from his walk and starting to tire, he wants big motion and sound to keep him going. It has been awhile since he's heard English and when he does it's heavily accented, a thick, heavy Eastern European tongue coming at him from across a street.

There is a man staring at him from the flat, yellow light of a Korean bakery. A tall, heavyset man, his eyes like a swamp, and a thick beard the color of big-horn sheep, long as antlers. He wears a black brushed wool overcoat. Angel has a vision of a dark tower bellowing a mourner's kaddish. A Danish in his left hand. He looks familiar, but only at angles and in a strange way, like they had once shared a small secret. Angel steps back into a shadow between two fruit stalls. Across the street, the man takes a bite from his Danish. It has some kind of filling that dribbles onto his lower lip and the top of his beard and the man pulls a handkerchief from a side pocket to wipe his face. Could be conducting a symphony—Schostakovitz or Arvo Part. Angel puts one leg forward, about to move on. Beside him a woman drops apples into a small, plastic bag. She moves around, climbing over his extended leg. The step never comes, instead he has closed his eyes, his hands move like puppets. The man has been with him for too long, something out of the past, something that doesn't know it's time to move on, to forget. But he's not that or not quite and Angel opens his eyes again to look and the man is gone.

Back at the house, Angel sits on a stool eating curried potatoes in a heavy pie dough made by Gabrial from a recipe that runs in his family.

Standing in front of a blackboard full of equations and diagrams and meaningless scratches which double as mathematics, Gabrial tosses a piece of chalk between his palms as he talks. His hands are fast and from where he sits, Angels sees only a fleeting white parabola.

"Cantor's responsibility is to set theory, ordinal numbers, a whole host of things—but his goal was the infinite." Gabrial is drawn to this man, has been his entire life. Maybe that's why Coyote found him, maybe he knows or at least can figure the match. Coyote claimed it was for his skills as a rock climber, spelunker, but Gabrial figures it was Cantor. They are, all of them, so close to infinity. "Cantor took one principle leap: he was willing to consider infinity a closed set. Take natural numbers, the counting numbers: 1, 2, 3, 4 and so on—he was willing to say that despite their infinite extension that they were complete. He then said that infinite sets could have one-to-one correspondence, take the naturals, then take the even naturals: 2, 4, 6, 8, 10 ... they could always be matched against each other, for every natural there would always be a even natural, a one-to-one correspondence. They are both infinitely equal. This also means there are some sets that exhibit infinite inequality, their infinity is greater: the whole numbers, which comprise positives and negatives are also an infinite set, but they are larger than the naturals." He could go on talking through the night.

Gabrial, himself, came to this simple equation just over ten years ago in a very cold tent at the bottom of a big mountain. Kangchenjunga in the Himalayas. Gabrial found a waterproof plastic bag with a book on infinite mathematics sitting in the snow. Five members on the expedition and none claimed it. Gabrial never made it up the mountain, but he sat for five weeks in a small tent, smoking Nepalese cigarettes by the carton, listening to the blizzard wind, reading on as the snow fell and fell.

In the morning the slurp of the coffee pot drags Angel from bed. There is a ragged tide feel to the sound, something to drift in. The kitchen windows are still thick with frost. Gabrial and Coyote sit at the table, smoking quietly. Amo has already dressed and gone, as he is more and more these days. A small pile of weapons rests on the far end of the table, hand guns on cheesecloth. Coyote has been stripping and cleaning and rebuilding. He works very slowly, polishing until there is a luminous sheen of stored light and gunmetal. Coyote sits next to the pile, his left elbow resting on the butt of a Glock, doing the *Times* crossword puzzle. The porch creaks in the wind and somewhere a tree branch scratches. Coyote puts down the paper to listen, then picks it up again and fills in two answers, then puts it down and walks to the front door. As he moves, Angel notices the light falls away from him. When he opens the door he does it sharp and fast and Angel sees a man standing on the other side. Coyote doesn't seem to notice the man, he just throws his right arm out and leans forward—it is a slow graceful motion and Angel notices Coyote's feet slide, automated, like chess pieces, then he hears the flat crunch of the man's nose and sees him falling to his knees. Coyote reaches down to the man and takes something from his belt then stands up again and lifts his foot like a prancing horse until it smashes forward and into the man's chest. The man seems to hesitate for a moment, as if time has suddenly slowed and then starts up again at a different speed. The man flies backwards into the air and then the steps that lead down from the porch rise up to meet him and together they reach a point where noise and motion catch and cross and are indistinguishable. Coyote shuts the door and walks back to the kitchen before the man finds himself lying on his back in the street. Now there is a new gun in the pile of all the weapons that still need cleaning.

Then there is no more noise. Coyote has picked his pen back up but seems momentarily stuck so it teeters in his hand, caught at the edge. A snake of rope lies at Gabrial's feet and his hands work forward then back like a slow piston coiling and binding and loading the rope into a nylon bag. The rope is black with flecks of dark green and a lighter blue like a flag for a country that didn't last and instead got turned to other purposes. Gabrial finishes the coil and slides a clasp into place and the bag drops to the floor. He lights a cigarette and Angel follows and then Coyote, still stuck, trades the paper for a smoke and they all sit inhaling and exhaling and looking at one another until they start to laugh.

"I think we can safely say that our cover is blown," says Gabrial.

"And my fucking ribs still hurt, never kick anyone when you have bruised ribs."

"Good tip," Angel grins as he speaks.

There really is no way around it, Isosceles would have found them sooner or later and this time it just turned out to be sooner. In a far corner of the room Coyote pulls a pair of dice from a velvet bag, they look ivory in the light, no telling. Rolls, makes choices. Later he tells Angel some decisions are better left to chance and harder to follow that way. Then he spends an hour on the phone and they spend the morning moving to another house in an area just south of Golden Gate Park, Coyote calls it the mystery district, says nobody really knows what to call it, city fathers keep changing their minds. A null space, a place where things do not resonate as clearly.

"An empty set," says Gabrial, trying to carry six feet of chalkboard under one arm and hold a duffel full of climbing gear across his back.

Coyote is worried about Isosceles finding them again and about falling behind schedule. He has already called a man named Luigi and is starting to wonder when he's going to show up. A courier of sorts. It's time to get their gear out of the country and into Italy. He doesn't have good European connections anymore—too out-of-date as a theater of operations, not much fun left, hollow, unless it's just the money.

"Peru. Uruguay. Thailand. Burma," says Coyote, giving each word a full rest. "India," shaking just from the sound. "I once had tea with a man who had spent ten years learning to bury his head in the sand—literally and then he spent five more learning to put his feet flat on the ground, one on either side of where his neck entered the earth, and with hands clasped behind his back he would walk in circles. He said it was tremendous meditation technique, offered to teach me if I could help him. He wanted his daughter and his life savings brought to America. His wife had long left him and he did not want his only child growing up in what he called 'swami's poverty.' I asked him how he knew I was the right man for the job, he told me the Earth told him."

Angel smiles.

Coyote shrugs. "How do you argue with a planet?"

"Did you learn?" asks Angel.

"His daughter is now living in Evanston, Illinois. I took a detour on my way back to India and went to Jerusalem and met Johnii and ended up here and when it's over I promise you I'm going to India to find this guy and spend the next ten years with my head buried in the sand."

IT IS BARELY SIX. DAWN BARELY VISIBLE. Angel wakes suddenly and listens. A silence in the house, the feel of people asleep, of breath in other rooms.

He tells himself there's nothing to worry about or not yet at least.

There is no going back to sleep. He gets up and makes coffee and stands waiting with an empty mug in hand. He likes this house, the creaky wood, no porch, but they have a small square of grass that passes for a backyard. He has developed a little routine, drinking the first cup of morning coffee leaning against the door frame of the backdoor, watching for nothing. There is a feeling to the kitchen, a hue, that reminds him of the house he grew up in. He rarely thinks of his parents anymore, only thinks that he rarely thinks of them, but it stops there. Coffee is ready and he pours and walks slowly to the backdoor and opens it and sees Amo kneeling and naked in the middle of the backyard.

"What the hell?" nearly dropping his mug.

Amo looks up and shakes his head. "Be with you in a moment."

He is mumbling again, Angel thinks in Hebrew, garbled, he hears the word lasagna, can't be certain. He turns and walks back into the room and then turns and looks back out the door. Not lasagna, but something that rhymes with lasagna. Amo's still there and still naked and Angel still doesn't know what to do. Then Amo stands and walks to a small metal table, a rusted piece of lawn furniture left by a previous tenant. Folded on top of it is his brown robe. He lifts it slowly, wrapping it around him, tying the sash with a flourish.

"Meditating," he says, walking into the house.

"Naked?"

"Not anymore." And Amo walks towards the bathroom.

Angel finishes his coffee and laces on his boots and is out the door before Amo is out of the shower. Last night he dreamed of Coyote with his head buried in the sand, a sad, slow dream, the kind that means something or at least should mean something and whatever, he's got a little money and his life has been pared away, stripped, his choices now based on small feelings. His plan is to walk to a toy store downtown. So many ways to make a bad decision.

He has a long stride, a swing to his arms, his shadow curved and spilled across the sidewalk, his jacket open like small wings. The trees of Golden Gate Park arcing and high, the light green, cutting in shafts and angles. He makes it downtown before the store has opened. He tries the door and looks in the windows and sees an empty cafe in the reflection. He turns and walks towards it.

"Can I help you?"

She is thin and long, like his surfer girl, a ring on her finger and he thinks her too young to be married and then realizes he has the hands wrong. How long has it been since he fled Isosceles, since he has even talked to anyone his age? He is slightly jumpy as he walks in, wide awake, tapping fingers and ordering coffee and watching her fill the cup. Long curls of steam and dark liquid and the feeling of being alone in a room with a stranger.

"What time does the toy store open?" Pointing across the street.

"Ten." She has blue eyes.

Glancing around for a clock. "What time is it now?"

"Nine. You've got an hour to kill."

"So you want to go someplace?" Strangely grinning. "Maybe get a cup of coffee?"

Her name is Meliah and she walks around the counter and sits down at one of the tables and they talk about her time at art school and how she wants to be a painter and how hard it is to work at a coffee shop and see nothing but men in suits and women in suits and everybody so busy and moving and she says that is why she likes to paint, because it takes place standing still.

"Have you been to Italy?" asks Angel.

"No."

"The Sistine Chapel. He spent four years on his back painting that."

"That's a lot of stillness."

"A whole lot."

She looks out the window, into the street, nearly sighs. "I'd love to see that."

"Yeah, me too."

At ten he leaves and asks for her phone number and she writes it on the back of a napkin.

"I'm going to be out of town for a while, but can I call you when I get back?"

"Stillness, remember, I'll be around a while."

Angel smiles and says goodbye and as he is walking out the door she calls after him. "Where are you going?"

"Italy," he says, walking across the street.

Inside the store he finds what he wants on the second floor. A small shovel and a plastic bucket and a big red sandbox. He buys all of it and walks back outside with the bag strung over his shoulder. At a hardware store closer to the house he finds a bag of sand and slings that over his other shoulder. He thinks about taking a bus. The sand is already heavy, the bag whacking him with every step. But he's in training, sort of, and figures the hardship might be good for something.

Amo is gone when he walks in and no one else is downstairs. He walks into the backyard and opens the sandbox. Shiny red with a flat bottom and a rounded coping around the outer edge. He pours in the sand and sets the bucket and pail in the center.

"What are you doing, kid?" Angel looks up to see Coyote standing in the doorway.

"Bought you a present."

"You did at that." Coyote walks slowly over, bends to the sand, burying the fingers of his left hand.

Angel lifts the bucket out of the sandbox and flips it over on the grass. He sits on the edge and takes off his shoes, leaning back on his hands, letting his toes dig through the sand.

"Coyote?"

"Yup."

"We drink a lot of coffee."

"We drink other things."

"Like whiskey?" The bucket starting to bow slightly from his weight.

"That's another thing."

Angel gets off the bucket and pushes the sides back out, he kneels at the edge of the box, begins shaping sand into piles. "How come everyone thinks you're dead?"

Coyote pauses. Angel watches light travel, feels sand.

"You want some coffee?" Coyote says finally.

Angel grins at him.

"The world's greatest smugglers have always had an intuitive understanding of the need to look for things. The way that desire plays out. I remember a stretch of road we used to run near Tanzania. Six or seven different roadblocks were always set up. We used to get searched at each point."

Angel stays steady as he listens, folding in on himself.

"Tanzania's mostly open country, really wide spaces. So people get used to looking at things from a distance. When you came to a checkpoint, the guards knew this already, so they lingered on details. Cigarette lighters, wallets, small things hidden inside of bumpers and exhaust pipes."

"So you hid things in plain sight, as big as possible."

"Yes."

Angel stands and brushes sand from his knees, careful to aim it back into the box.

"Eventually," Coyote weighing the word in his mouth, trying to find a taste for those years, "people started figuring out where to look for me."

Coyote rocks back onto his heels, looks up at Angel.

"I became some kind of a king that needed dethroning, like if they wanted to run rhino hides through Zambia they needed to kill me first. I'm in Fiji, it's sunny, what the hell do I care what happens in Zambia?"

Angel realizes the spot where Coyote is kneeling is the same spot where Amo had sat naked just this morning.

"It didn't seem like I had the kind of business you could just retire from. Nobody wants to see a smuggler just retire. Smugglers need fancy endings, lifetime prison sentences, bad deaths, decapitations."

"So you faked your own death?"

"Give the people what they want. I staged my own beheading, in Bolivia actually, catered it myself. Then I just disappeared for a while. Pretty much stayed that way until Johnii showed up and invited me to join him in Colorado. Thought I'd fall in love, have a quiet ending in the country somewhere."

"Still might," says Angel.

"Damn straight."

Coyote stands and jams a cigar in his mouth, the match seesawing in the breeze.

Angel waits until the end catches fire, "Can I ask another question?"

Coyote glowers at him through the cigar haze.

"What rhymes with lasagna?"

range. Coyote wants Angel to learn basic rock climbing: how to build anchors, repel, move across different types of rock. The job falls to Gabrial. They spend a morning packing packs and filling the car with supplies and then they're gone. So little ceremony in the things that really change lives.

In a week Angel learns about a whole new California. Old mining towns abandoned to snow in the Sierras; hard drinking outdoorsmen in Truckee; near Soledad he finds immigrant towns and racks of pornographic magazines all in Spanish. But it is the climbing that catches him, draws him in. Pinnacles National Monument, at the base of a snaky talus climb called Portent, Gabrial dumps a bagful of gear on the ground. Friends, tri-cams, hexes, quick-draws, nuts, small spring-loaded devices called aliens, Angel runs his hands over them like each holds a magic all its own, feeling the odd angles of the metal, the secret power. They work through them slowly. Talking placement, possibilities. Gabrial passes Angel a harness: two legs loops and a waist strap.

"Keep the waist strap above your hip bones, if it's below and you fall and end up upside down you could slip out."

They practice knots in the desert sun: double fisherman for linking ropes together, water knot for tying slings, figure eight for attaching a rope to the harness, figure eight on a bite for attaching rope to an anchor at belay stations hundreds of feet off the ground. Gabrial makes him tie each one ten times with his eyes open, five with eyes closed and five behind his back. Gabrial's never tried to tie the knots behind his own back, but Angel gets it the first time.

Climbing is so much harder than Angel could have imagined. At three places on the route they wait nearly five minutes for his legs to stop shaking.

"Sewing machine leg," says Gabrial, "happens to everyone."

Angel finds little comfort. His hands sweat and pause, fingers working like mechanical claws trying for purchase. It takes him nearly ten minutes to move past the crux. When he reaches the top he spends long moments on his back. Then they repel back down and do it again. They climb for two days at Pinnacles and then up towards Tahoe. Another week they work at it. Angel's fingers aching with the strain of holding himself to razor cracks in the rock, feet splayed and strained, feeling a world made of fear. He goes quiet on the rock. Happens. People either speed up or slow down. Usually both, but at intervals.

At Lover's Leap, on top of a route called The Line, Gabrial tells him that awe is both beauty and fear, that it's a strange place, that most people aren't used to finding it inside. He taps his chest so Angel knows where he means.

One day, climbing a slick assortment of sport routes out on Mickey's Beach, something in Angel clicks. Gabrial offers congratulations after a series of nimble, balanced moves. Angel barely hears, watching light fall through fir trees, gone away with it. He almost tells Gabrial about his parents, about walking away and the long, cold nights in the mountains, but doesn't know where to begin and instead says only, "thanks for this."

Gabrial coils ropes, starting to pack the gear, looks up to see Angel bright, clear, somehow still a kid after all.

"Would you tell me something?" Angel taking the heavy pack, letting Gabrial carry the rope bag.

"Why do you always ask permission to ask a question?"

Angel stops and thinks about this but doesn't answer and instead asks, "How did they kill your mother?"

Gabrial's not surprised that Coyote hasn't told Angel the story, but still he thought Angel knew. It is a common error with him, the feeling that others know his intimacies—but that's part of his gift. He has it in him to know the secrets of others: Angel was a runaway, Amo's a bastard left to the church, Coyote used to wander the Texas range alone, looking for his father, telling himself stories about footprints that blew away with the evening. These are the things that come to him from others, but they are nothing he speaks about.

"I teach you to climb and you think you can ask me anything?"

"That's why I asked permission," says Angel.

"They slit her throat and hung her upside down to bleed. Her hands had been chopped off and the flesh boiled away to make talismans. I found her hanging from a branch."

"Uh-huh," says Angel.

"Uh-huh what?"

"You were a strange child, I mean besides your skin, you knew things you shouldn't. You scared people. Your grandfather left the village, saying you were evil, just walked off into the jungle and never came back."

"How did you know that?" stammers Gabrial. "I never told anyone that story."

"I dreamed all of it, last night: your mother's death, your grandfather, the last thing your dad said before putting you on the boat. 'You'll have a better chance in America.'"

"And this is where my better chance has taken me," says Gabrial, shaking his head slowly, watching the light in Angel's eyes.

"THERE ARE THOSE OF US WHO MIGHT actually be on your side."

A dull, low light is creeping over the city. Angel stands at the crest of Dolores Park looking north. Cascade of buildings then water, the glimmer of bridges, small things in motion. The sun is setting, he knows, somewhere over his left shoulder and the voice comes from the same spot. The voice is familiar in the same way as a place you've never been can be. He doesn't want to turn and look because he's tired and there's a dull ache in his hands that gets stronger if he tries to close them, he'd be lousy in a fight right now, and hadn't he just gone out for a walk to get away from Amo's mad chanting. All day long and for weeks now. Gets under his skin. He wants quiet, some fresh air, not used to his own petulance. Turning he sees the man from the bakery a few weeks before. Up close the face is a cracked brawl slapping outwards from behind a curtain of hair. He wears the same dark, long coat and has a newspaper rolled in his right hand and Angel can see the hard angles of a Cyrillic alphabet and feel the thickness of its words.

"Who are you?" The reflex of curiosity.

Raw iron fingers rise to his lips, part mustache hairs, twiddle away like the answer is some code kept in his gums. "I am a consequence, a probability. I am what comes when certain things get set in motion."

"Oh, of course."

Angel holds out a pack of Marlboros. "Smoke?" which, lately, seems to be the only response he's capable of.

"No, thank you."

A black Labrador comes trotting over, wiggling his weight between them. Angel plays his hands over the dog, rubs behind his ears, listens to his soft pant.

"What do you mean on my side?"

"Do you think you are the only one who has ever wanted to come up against the Vatican? You are another part of a grand tradition. I am part of what happens, kind of like an early warning system but for the good guys in this case."

"Good guys?" Which is a question to be asked with a certain amount of hesitation. He has images of Amo coming charging into the park, standing tall in the saddle, riding over the crest to the west, a silhouette to the rescue.

"Yes, mostly we deal in discouragement. Not every one is allowed a pass at the secret archives and most certainly not everyone is allowed to try for the Sefer ha-Zaviot."

Angel opens his mouth, but finds himself chewing on air.

"Don't look so surprised. It is the nature of Kabbalah, of all mysticism, there must always be a defense, an aporia. I am more a product of the word than I am of the light."

"I don't follow you."

"The word is the keeper of the mystery, the light, well, it just illuminates the obvious."

Angel shakes his head.

"I know I am not making this easy for you, let me simplify. There have to be controls, from outside the system, I'm a small part of that control. A traffic cop. There is a great history of us, we have networks that go back to the

Pythagorean, some say farther. Never been allotted the privileged of mysticism, simply the role of the guard. Some say it is a path like any other, I am too old for such hope. I'm only willing to play out certain scenarios, see what comes, but it has been many years since I've held my breath. In the Sefer Yetsirah it says, 'Sometimes, he will hear a voice—a wind, a speech, a thunder, and he will see and will smell and will taste and then will walk and levitate. This is the sleep of prophecy.' That would be a lovely sleep."

Fog has begun to cover the city like breath, a pulse, the love of some vast monster.

"You expect the Sefer ha-Zaviot to be different, to actually change something?"

"It is a hard question, is it not?" Tapping his teeth and gums again. "I traffic so close to the impossible, to believe in one thing above the rest? Madness, but perhaps not insanity."

"Why not make a go for it yourselves?"

"We could not, beside the blasphemy issue, the oaths we have taken, the long training, it is a matter of ritual and probability. For us to take an active role would change the nature of everything. Think of physics—the act of observing a phenomena alters the phenomena. No one is neutral. We could not risk it."

The sky has gone to milk. They have fallen in among shadows.

There doesn't seem to be an end point to the conversation, at least not one Angel can see. Eventually, he goes home. As he takes his leave the man offers a onion-stained hand, Angel shakes it. As he does he feels the faint edge of the man's great wool coat, just a light wrist rub, but he's expecting the touch of burlap, of shoddy cold-war craftsmanship, and instead gets something crossed between silk and mink. The softest thing he's ever felt.

"The Society is merely a shadow. There are not many left. They have a mean history, but now they struggle for control because it is easier to fight for what they have then to give it up and see what they get."

"Then why all this?"

"Because there are always a few. Remember that Isosceles is not one of them. He's worse."

"Worse?"

"He thinks he was chosen."

"That's worse," says Angel.

"Tell Coyote that the Russian says hello."

But he says it after Angel's started walking away and when Angel stops to look back, just a little surprised, he is already gone, great coat and all.

"Hey Coyote, I met a friend of yours, he says hello." Angel stands in the dim light of the front hallway, pulling off his boots. He can see through a cracked door Gabrial facing a blackboard full of equations, trouser leg full of chalk smears. Coyote sits in the living room, in an over-stuffed reading chair, thick light falling onto his silver curls, a brandy snifter at his feet.

"Who's that?" not looking up from his book.

"The Russian."

Coyote's face goes to a perfect idle, neutral, slowly looking at Angel. "You met the Russian?" More to himself than to Angel, "and you're still alive."

Angel finds he's not as surprised as he should be. "We have his blessing, their blessing. . . ."

"Then the rumor is true," says Coyote.

"Which?"

"The mystical protectorate, or whatever, they go by an acronym now, some say the Knights Templars were a splinter group, there is also a Jesuit connection."

"I got the impression he was a Jew."

"He is, that doesn't matter, this close to the source everything begins to blend."

Coyote walks over to a cache of bottles and glasses piled on a table, still not completely moved in, pours Angel three fingers of Orkney Island scotch, tastes like dirt and heat and a low groan.

"He is considered the greatest poisoner of the twentieth century, he studied under a man who was known only as Thousand Fingers—said to be the best ever. The thousand fingers of death. Great patience to be that good. They say that the only reason Hitler lived so long is that the Russian and Thousand Fingers were lost in the Amazon on the final leg of the Russian's training, lasted all during the war. He worked in Europe, Asia, Africa—I must have met him maybe ten times. Occasionally he used me as a supply conduit, I could get plants out of South America no one else could. We had tea once, Istambul. Pena knew him, which might be why he let you live, can't be sure. Fifteen years ago he retired—disappeared mostly. There was a story that he had been recruited by these sacred watchdog folks, the Society, it was the first I had heard of them."

Somewhere, between Coyote's words, Angel hears the sound of Amo upstairs. A slow Hebrew chant, ancient letters, obsession. Angel just doesn't want to sit by him on the plane to Italy.

"Tomorrow, when you meet Luigi, don't mention the Russian," says Coyote.

"How's that?" Angel trying to forget about Amo.

"He killed his brother, years ago."

"Why?"

"Most of the Russian's family died during WWII, his was one of the towns the Germans actually made it to."

"Luigi's brother was a Nazi?" asks Angel.

"No, Luigi's brother was a pilot like Luigi, good seaman too, very fair man some say. But he helped smuggle Nazis over to Argentina after the war. Two trips. As you already noticed, the Russian is a Jew. After the first trip the Russian warned him, but Luigi's brother took it as an insult, made a second run. Halfway through the run the crew began dying off, one at a time, leaving Luigi's brother alone, in the middle of the Atlantic, on a hundred-and-seventy-foot boat that needed a minimum of ten hands to sail. He got caught in a north swell, the boat was never found."

Angel says nothing, nods his head, always able to accept the impossible. Gabrial has stopped working his puzzles and has come into the room. He stands as a shadow in the doorway, hearing the end of Coyote's story. It's part of his fate, to always be close to the endings.

DOWN BY THE WATER IT IS WELL PAST the season of migration; today there are no great assemblages to be part of and only a few tight-capped fisherman work this far down the docks. Nothing but the slow cog of history at a distance marks this space. Give it no mind, this place is one of transition, an in-between that appears on only certain maps—much more of a waystation than a way.

Angel, up early, sits on a rough wooden stool in a tumbledown shack hidden behind a loading crane and a few small trucks drinking espresso out of a paper cup. Captain Luigi Peripatelli sits across from him, sipping coffee with eyes closed, humming the opening chords of the *Rites of Spring* between swallows. Wrinkles run over his brow, sunsoaked and sharp. He wears a white captain's uniform, complete with gold epaulets, and has a ring on each finger. The rings flash as his hands move and this morning his hands have been busy counting small bills, three thousand of them, that Angel's brought in an old gym bag. The bills came bundled in stacks of five hundred, all in twenties, and Luigi counts each stack twice. First in English, second in Italian. He spaces coffee sips between stacks.

"Everything, my friend, has its own internal harmony. The money, the espresso, even the morning form a perfect combination. It is our job, all humankind, to find that harmony, to match it." His accent is something to wade through or savor.

"Stravinsky?" asks Angel.

"Only today, this moment, this mood."

"You're counting in Italian and English."

"Yes, it's a good system, no? I think together, side by side, they match the music."

A small window behind the desk opens onto the bay. First light angles down and across, finding a corner of the desk and offering an empty spotlight. Only dust answers this curtain call. It reminds Angel of a dancer he once knew, a sixteen-year-old ballerina with small breasts and nipples that pushed at her leotard when she sweat. She taught Angel to kiss in a condemned theater, under a canopy of lime green paper stars cut out by children and hung with white string for a final performance of Peter Pan.

He said goodbye to her, that much he remembers.

Luigi finishes counting and humming and pulls a corncob pipe from a desk drawer. The sun has gone and a veil of clouds cross out the day. They stroll through the gray light, pipe smoke—musk and cherries, around the deck of the *Sergio Leone*.

"Damn good movies," says Angel.

"A true artist, a great vision, a wonderful sense of harmony."

"*Once upon a Time in America.*"

"They had no real link to the west. It was a place they came to only through imagination. Very mythical." His pipe has gone out and the ashes are a soft parade in the early breeze. "It is how I met Coyote, you know."

Angel turns towards him.

"*The Good, the Bad and the Ugly*, a friend of mine was the props master. Sergio only wanted original firearms, Coyote got them as far as customs, I got them in."

"That was a long time ago," says Angel.

"Yes, he looks good for his age. All that sunlight, maybe the senoritas down south took extra care of him, maybe they knew they had something special."

"You look good for your age, maybe the senoritas took extra care with you."

"Maybe they did." Luigi smiles into the wind. "Tell Coyote it was my pleasure to once again be of assistance."

"I will."

"You know him long?"

Angel leans onto the railing, feeling the wood against his fingers.

"No, I haven't known him long."

"Believe in the Coyote."

"It's a strange world."

Luigi raises up a hand in dismissal, but stops and thinks with one eyebrow raised like a cartoon.

"Strangers telling strangers to trust strangers," says Angel.

"We did business, drank coffee, you saw my boat, you get a sense of things—of the balance."

"Which sense is that?"

"The sea is the same," but he doesn't say any more and Angel doesn't say anything at all. Wind sweeps over the bay. A woman appears on deck, fixes something Angel can't see then disappears below. Angel and Luigi shake hands and Luigi walks away. He stops before he gets halfway to the boathouse and starts walking back to Angel.

"It was good of you not to ask for a receipt."

"Thank you," says Angel.

"You didn't disturb the harmony."

"I never thought of it that way."

Luigi walks back to the boat and hollers something that Angel cannot hear. The first mate appears, he is a tall, dark fellow, with a shaved head and a long stride. He leaps from the main deck onto the shore to untie the boat. Angel watches as it slips from the pier with Luigi at the helm sailing into the sunrise. The sails are down and whatever motor they have must be far underwater because Angel hears nothing but a softness and the play of the water. The wind, when it comes, rifles his coat open and smells of nothing. He feels the air carefully counting his ribs. This is how things have gone, this continual watchfulness. He has begun to see signs in everything.

The city is slowly moving. Angel lights a cigarette and starts towards his car. He gets twenty feet and draws up short. A pair of priests stroll towards the pier's entrance. They wear high collars and have long fingers that continuously creep into pockets. Long shadows play out from their robes. Twisted shapes that move almost on their own. What is it these grand men of God have come through the grist of dawn for; whose confession do they hear?

Angel drawls a shoe across cobbled stones and sea-damp wood. He does this unconsciously, this foot search for clues. Behind the priests and above, how far above? Fifty feet, sixty? Perched atop mud-slid cliffs are rows of houses, they look shabby to Angel, unsafe, not much in the way of refuge. Between the cliffs and the pier is fifty yards of broken glass and waist high weeds and beyond that a sharp rise to an elevated freeway. There's a gap between grass and pavement—could he make the jump, ten feet to the lowest railing, no shoulder on that road, just heavy exhaust and a low rumble and the beginning of the morning's traffic.

The priests have seen him and stopped. They've made a show of it, planting feet far apart and putting their hands inside coats. He can see the slick barrel of a long shotgun hanging down through one of the robes. It is shiny and black and looks wet in the half-light of the morning. If Angel had a backup plan now would be a good time to put it to work. He thinks of diving into the bay, of swimming for it, but to where and something about the feel of bullets finding him in the water, of the sluggish drift to sea bottom and sharks and drowning and a sea of pain as an ending is not appealing.

Six blocks away the door to Red's Java House opens into the shifting breeze. A lanky silhouette appears. He wears tight wire glasses that make his eyes appear gray. Eyes that are not just looking. No, not anymore, that time has long passed. Isosceles stands there, waiting, listening for a shotgun blast or a scream, but instead gets only silence.

Sumatra and watch that woman walk down the street. Whole cargo cults have come from less. A spring dress, something long-faded that has drunk glasses of twilight lemonade and been bleached in the passing of suns. When she turns or moves, the light finds the perfect angle, a touch of muscle, a hush, something to let you know.

Christiana walks through the market, stopping for a sliver of star fruit, wiping juice on the back of her hand. A man pointing to the dragon ring on a long silver chain hung round her neck showed her a whole case of jewelry. She bought earrings and shared a cup of tea. What a blessing to have her company for a minute, on an island so far away, something to mark this day a little bit.

She finishes her tea and walks on. The bar is at the other side of the market place, the last stop in town. Past its front door, no more than a hundred feet off, rises the wall of the jungle. Inside, it's cool and dark, a thatched roof, ten stools, a couple of tables, dust from the last century. Two old men playing a board game with curved pegs, drink tea, another has an afternoon beer at the bar. As she approaches, he stands up.

She kisses his cheek. "Hello, Emmanuel."

A radio above the bar plays a swoon. He should have worn a better shirt.

"Christiana," he moves to touch her, but she just isn't

there or his hand doesn't reach or whatever left him holding the air.

"A drink, miss?" asks the bartender.

"Bourbon, please."

She takes a small sip and undoes the clasp at the back of her necklace. The ring slides down and into her hand.

"It's big, you may have to wear it on your thumb." Then she shows him how to bend the dragon's tail, the small click as the head swings open. Inside, the ring's hollow and filled with a gray powder. "Twenty-five minutes," she says and drops the rest of the bourbon into her mouth.

"It's so obvious," says Emmanuel.

"Isn't it though." But there's something sad, not quite in her voice, for a moment. "Nice seeing you again." Out the door.

She spends the rest of the afternoon reading on the front porch of the bungalow Johnii has rented for them and when it is well past dark she pulls a black jacket around her shoulders and changes her shoes and goes off into the night.

The street's cooler now, rutted with the grooves of heavy carts, a lifetime of labors, entire histories as complicated as anything the world has ever known, all in a four-block radius. Christiana walks the opposite direction of where she had gone this morning, her green eyes fading in the night. Down an alley a drunk reels away from a garbage can, a cat creeps, thick prayers to Allah come from buildings far away. She walks six blocks and turns corners, deeper and deeper into shadowlands, around another bend and onto a thin street, everything closed for the night, the walls pushed high and whatever moonlight might have made it through is now blocked by strung laundry.

Something, at alley's end, opens, pouring light out onto the street, an open tea house, a little chatter, a hint of smoke, then the whisper of beads and the devil walks into the world. Skin like bitter milk, like wind. Bigger than the door he has stepped through. A black suit and eyes that find her immediately. Then whatever has opened now shut, just a plot of light from the door's jamb crack remains. Christiana sweeps her hair back with a hand.

"Christiana," and a voice that starts underground.

"In a world of beggars, I spy a prince."

"I cannot be a beggar, I am Russian, we are too tired to beg."

Up close he has a beard like a bonfire and a suit that looks almost ragged, but when she puts her arms around him her cheek rests on fine, thick silk.

"You have a poisoner's soul," running her fingers over his lapel.

"Do you know how they make perfume?"

Strolling down the street, away from light.

"They start with the most rancid smell available, something uniquely sinister and then hide it among beauty. The first order of the nose is warning, our alarm bell. The rancid smell is always there, something must catch our attention, tell us there is something here to be noticed."

"You inverted the equation," says Christiana.

"Sometime before the end of the century would you remind me to ask you to dance."

"Delighted."

Steven Kotler

They're working their way out of the town, the streets are wider now. They pass a burnt-out jeep, a forgotten war.

"Is he a gentleman?"

"Johnii?" turning her head to look at him. "He's a grace."

"Do you think he'll find it?"

"What? The sixty-fifth hexagram of the I Ching?" smiling at the thought of it. "He's a seeker all right, but who knows, who knows if it even exists."

"The hinge point of a revolving binary structure, a point of collapse—it's quite a good idea."

"Is he more of a problem than..." but she can't finish her sentence, something clawing in her voice.

The Russian stops walking, his body still, a small breeze to blow back his coat. "No, your assignment is still the same."

"When you contacted me in Israel all you said was you wanted me to meet Johnii, get to know him, stay with him, see what I could learn."

"And that is still your assignment."

"And I think I may have gone a little overboard," she says with a smile.

"These things happen," spreading his hands wide.

"What if someone decides Johnii's become too much of a problem?"

"They won't," his words hard and flat and final.

"What do you mean?"

"I pulled him out of the system, there's nothing left. I still want you with him and if he gets anywhere I need to know. You have my word, that's as far as it will ever go."

"What about the rest of the Society?"

"As for the rest of the Society, he was always a part of

my caseload, so I don't know who else really would remember him and now, strangely, his records seem to have disappeared...." He wipes his hands against each other, turning them up empty. Ahead is the sound of splashing water, already buildings have started to fall back, somewhere in front is the beach.

"Thank you."

"It is nothing," he glances over at her as they walk, sees hard lines formed around her mouth. "What else is bothering you?"

Christiana pauses, looking at him, "Will Coyote make it?"

He stops, a bit of moonlight caught in his beard. "It is hard to say, he is the first one we've let try in over a century, if he fails it is hard to tell what will happen. Also, we can't find Isosceles."

The Russian stops and holds up his hand, points out two reeling shapes on a slight rise in the far distance. Christiana can make out Johnii and Emmanuel, can see that they're talking but the ocean is louder here, sweeping away their words.

It's not a scene she wants to watch and she turns her back to it. The Russian puts a hand on her shoulder.

She shakes her head slowly, trying to get her mind around something, unsure, the smell of salt filling the air.

"Why are we doing this?"

"You know the story. He appeared before the Wailing Wall. He had a copy of the I Ching in his hands. It's just too much mystery."

Christiana says nothing.

The Russian shrugs again. "I was a poisoner, now I'm a

watchdog. I offered you a job, you took it. That is how the world works. Things change."

Christiana nods.

"If you want me to assign someone else to track Johnii I will."

"No," smiling again, "I kind of like that job. I just don't like tonight."

"Nither do I," says the Russian, "but what else could we do? Things got mixed up. Coyote has contacts we don't have. I had no idea Johnii was going to invite the two of you to Colorado, I had no idea he was going to Colorado. I didn't know Coyote would trust him as much as he did."

"So?"

"Coyote is very close to the Sefer ha-Zaviot. Pena was right in her choice of Angel. I met him, there is something to him, to the way things flow when he is around. I think Coyote has a chance and I'd like to let him have that chance. But when he decided to make a backup copy of his notes and send them to Johnii. . . ." He shakes his head in wonder.

Christiana watches him closely.

"I had no idea Coyote would ever send his notes to Johnii, but I have less of an idea of what Johnii might do with them."

"Even with me watching Johnii?"

"Even with you watching Johnii. I'm sorry, the risk is too high."

She stares harder at him, almost angry. "If you would have come to me before none of this would have been necessary."

"I was late, it was unavoidable. But you did good work. Someone had to get Johnii out of Colorado. With Isosceles around." Saddened by the thought. "What a mess. I'm supposed to watch over anybody who makes a serious play for knowledge. I've been assigned to Pena and Johnii for years. Nobody had any idea they would get tangled up together."

"But Pena's dead."

"We track ideas, not people. So now I'm assigned to Pena's lineage."

Christiana wants a drink, she looks up and down the road for an open bar, sees nothing. The Russain reaches into his pocket and comes out with a flask, his fingers delicate and slow unscrewing the cap.

"Thank you," she feels the cold sting of vodka on her tongue. "So you really think Johnii's onto something."

"I think he's obsessed. It could go either way."

"You're right, of course."

She passes the flask back, watches as he drinks.

"Isosceles," the word tight in his mouth. "Is Coyote okay?"

"His ribs hurt, the scar on his wrist will probably never go away, and he'll walk funny for a few more weeks, but yes, he's doing fine."

He nods, looking off towards the beach, then reaches into his jacket, and takes out a long envelope full of American currency.

"Here," he says, passing it to Christiana. "Thank you for going to find Angel in Montana. He was just getting lost up there."

With that he walks off in the direction of the beach and Christiana lies down on her back and stares at the stars.

Ten minutes later he comes back, holding a small cardboard tube, no bigger than a baby's arm.

"Go now, watch him sleep," nodding towards the beach.

"Good night," her fingers lost on his cheek. It's been thirty years since anyone has touched him that way.

JOHNII WAKES TO SOUND. HE HAD
fallen asleep beneath a flimsy boardwalk, just up from the
beachhead and the waves crash with the unmistakable sound
of exploding glass. The air smells of thick salt and rot. He
sees splintered light pushing through angled wooden slats
and smoke.

Sure, this is paradise, but only the outskirts, if it's buses
and taxis and crowds that you want, they're here too, but
they are in bed, asleep, many miles away.

Sumatra has yet to awaken. Johnii is alone with the
heat and the wet and the morning for a while longer. The
sun has blackened his already dark skin, making him no
more than an ash shadow against a naked horizon. One of
those people forever caught in invisibilities, penumbral.

He shakes his head with numb, jerky tugs. His beard
has grown crackly and long. One week of meditation,
buried deep in the jungle, in a world of insects. Sometimes
he chose wrong, the wrong hexagram, the wrong time, but
that was part of it too.

He came out last night, after a messenger had found
him, with a package from Coyote—and which courier system tracks eremites into the jungle? Then he wanted nothing but a bath and a quiet place to open it and Christiana,
mostly Christiana, and instead got drunk. He had stopped
at a bumba shack to buy a pack of smokes and a Sumatran
man had leaned over and spoken to him in perfect English.

"Last night I dreamed I was Fu Manchu."

And that was that and what did it matter now. The guy had a ring on his thumb, a wiggling dragon made from heavy, white gold. Later the man had told Johnii about some Gypsy fortune teller and how she hung out down at the beach and by then they were both drunk and had wandered down to find her and suddenly Johnii was very, very tired, like someone had tugged his bones out. The guy had gone off to some hotel to sleep it off and Johnii could barely stand, let alone walk anywhere so he slept right where he was and then it was morning.

"Shit." Where is that package Coyote sent him? He drops down to his knees and looks around under the boardwalk, but it didn't just slide out of his pocket, he had taped it to his leg and now it's gone.

"I am small but I am not that small."

Not more than four feet tall, with eyes the color of mercury.

"You are looking for me, yes? You want to play the angles?"

"Ummm?"

"It is a small island, sir," she says, folding her arms over the bundle of pregnant rags she wears for clothing.

"Johnii," sagging back to cross-legged in the sand.

Her tarot deck sits heavy on a lime green swatch of silk.

"You would like to consult the oracle, Johnii? You would like to gather knowledge? You would like to know the past and the future? You have come to the right place?" She arches an eyebrow over the last question, letting Johnii know it is a question.

"Yes."

"You mind answering background questionnaire?" Her

hands go rifling through a thousand layers of silk and satin and cotton and everything else on the island she could have woven into the veils upon veils she wears as clothing. It takes a while and eventually she comes out empty-handed, fixing Johnii with a very hard stare, as if it were his fault. "No pencil today, we proceed verbally, . . . yes?"

Johnii notices she has no teeth. "Sure," he couldn't help but come along.

"You are A mercenary, B have family on island, C wish to be someplace else, or D, are someone else?"

"Absolutely," still groggy, unsure, trying to figure out who is this ridiculous woman.

"Oh, pleased to repeat, A mercenary, B have family on island . . ."

"D."

"Next question, A your eyes have seen the glory of the coming of the lord, B you sleep on stomach, C you prefer doggie-style position, D you are surfer?"

"D," he says, still trying to get up to speed.

"A wish to visit Ulam Bator, B never eat fried foods, C have pets, D are a hoochie-coochie man?"

"D."

"A you are running down a long, dark hallway, B drink whiskey, C have foot fetish, D don't believe me?"

"B."

"Not D?" Wrinkling and furling and squinching up and down her old brow. "Are you certain not D?"

"Certain."

"Certain yes or no?"

"Pardon?"

"Yes or no?"

Lost now, shaking his head.

"Oh well, mucho ado, sorry cannot go on with reading, you argue with the cards," she says, shaking her head up and down meaning no saying yes.

"What?" His hangover neatly replaced by laughter.

Another thick veil comes down across her face, this one thick purple. "You ask for reading, no? I give reading. You no like style of reading, you take your questions elsewhere." And before Johnii can stop laughing she's down the beach, her scarves furling into the wind like the edge of a soft curtain that might eventually stretch onward to Singapore.

and sets out. He is tired and walks slowly, his steps high and long. It's been a long time since he's slept well and it's been even longer since Jesus had come to him. That's something he doesn't understand. He was chosen, after all. There is a throbbing in his temples when he thinks about it, an emptiness when he doesn't. One man should not have to bear so much.

He sees his men on the pier, they stand close to Angel, they stand and they wait. They are good Christian soldiers. What a journey they've had. Slick trick, Angel climbing out the window like that. A part of him was glad to see Pena die. She was too close, knew too much. He's glad he didn't have to kill her, glad she took it upon herself, but this kid—well, he'd know what that was about soon enough.

The blackjack is short and sweet. Made of hard leather, none of this new plastic for him. He likes his weapons old, with a history to be part of. His left hand finds the shaft and passes it to his right and then he stands at the edge of the pier. The sun passes into the sky from behind a cloud. It's a nice day after all.

Angel looks up and sees him or had he been looking up the whole time. There something in the way the kid looks at people, something that makes Isosceles' head throb, something too familiar.

As Isosceles approaches the men shift a few steps to each side to allow his passage. Angel sees the same cold eyes, the stork body, the blackjack. Whatever this brings, he knows this won't end well, but his thoughts stop there and he wonders why he isn't afraid.

Isosceles slaps him, but Angel sees a glimmer of brass in his hand and as he feels the angle of the earth tilt he realizes it wasn't just a slap. He is knocked halfway down and he comes up with a punch towards Isosceles' groin. The blow never connects because one of the other men has stepped forward and blocks his arm. Angel's never seen reflexes that quick. Then he hears a shotgun cock.

"No," says Isosceles, "not yet."

Angel rights himself and looks Isosceles square in the eye. "Asshole."

Isosceles grabs his throat, he feels the fingers lock tightly, he feels the air leaving his lungs.

"You stole from me."

"And how many were you going to steal from?"

"Now that," says Isosceles now smiling, "is a very good question."

Angel never sees the blackjack swing, he just sees the dark, crooked teeth and a mouth like a gravel pit, then he sees no more.

light left. All morning the wind's been carting dark, thick clouds down from the northern shelf—it's a cold, selfish visit and one that's come to rain on a parade.

Still, this rain falls and nothing is dry, least of all Amo. For Amo, it is a rain of frustration, of time lost and a dull weight that has lately come to play so heavily on his mind. Two days now, out looking for Angel, near panic, feeling responsible ever since Angel failed to return from his meeting with Luigi. Swearing and swerving. He's ten miles south of San Francisco, navigating through sheets of plummeting water, as Highway 1 whips through the hair-pin crevices blasted, long ago, through the foothills of mountains. The Pacific is visible at most places, though not today. Today Amo can see whatever he wants. There is no way to drive. This rain comes like an army. Amo parks, lights a Lucky. Above him, two hundred yards off the ocean side of the highway, perched on the welling brim of land's end rests Battalion Fire Control Station #6—the eyes of WWII's coastal guns. Built in the early forties, the foot-thick concrete walls were a dank home to five men and a horizontal azimuth indicator for nearly five years. From where Amo stands, now out of the car and staring, it looks like a giant two-headed duck.

He crosses the highway and walks up the first tentative steps of the path. It is very steep. The light comes in at odd angles. Rain blocks his vision, so he sees things in snatches.

The hill rises high and away from him. Cliffs, scrub brush, mud, ghosts from evenings past, times of sinewy moonlight, runaways and cherry brandy drunks gathering dust and age, young minstrels out of luck and song, the old and the forgotten and the mist that will always rise from the sea. But it is afternoon now, nothing to worry about.

He is wearing a nice suit, though he's not sure why. The path is too slick, twenty steps up the slick before his feet go out. Sliding most of the way down the slope, he stops just shy of the freeway. A car drives by, swerves, honks, a fan of water hits his head. He wags an erect finger at the passing brake lights, hollers a wet, "May the road rise up to meet you." A phrase which he has never totally understood.

How long does the climb take? He finds a small walking stick that sinks easily into the wet ground and offers protection against backsliding. Closer to the top, where the ground slows and levels out and Amo can stand upright with his shoulders back, proud stick in hand, gazing at the thin horizon, rain pelting his face, hair a black mat; there is a certain Lewis-and-Clark satisfaction that comes to him, that comes with such difficult passages, with conquest, with ruining good clothes in the pursuit of empty dreams.

Up top the walls are reinforced concrete. The two-headed goose turns out to be a pair of observation bunkers: one turned toward land, one toward sea, thin concrete slits for eyes and years spent watching for Japs.

Climbing inside is difficult. He eases out onto a thin ledge of dirt with the sea below going into the rocks and white salty spray rocketing towards his feet. The beach is called Devil's Slide, but he's trying not to look down. Instead, he raises a leg up and over, dropping inside through the lookout slit.

"About fucking time, Sweet Jesus, I was getting tired."

Amo slowly raises himself off the floor where he's landed.

"Get 'em up," feeling something jab into his ribs.

Sweat trickles from Amo's pits as he turns around.

"Hey, you're just a kid."

"I've been waiting for you since '43."

"Did you say 1943?"

"You fuckin' Japs, I heard what you did up in Brandon, Oregon. Little sneak attack there. So quiet it didn't even make most of the papers. Very, very tricky, that. I oughtta shoot you on sight, I have a brother up there, he could be dead you know."

"Shoot me. Yeah, good thinking," says Amo.

"Shut up."

"Hey you don't look so good. You look kind of gray."

"Shut up!" swinging the gun butt at Amo, which he ducks, but ends up on his ass for the third time in an hour, which is when he notices that 1943 or not the kid doesn't look a day over twenty and the entire left side of his head has been blown away. It wasn't noticeable it at first, but now that the light's better, everything clear from his left eye over seems to be missing. Just then it comes to him.

"You're Abraham ben Samuel Abulafia," screams Amo, now on his knees. "You have finally arrived. I am ready. I am ready." A vein is visible in his neck. There's mud on the floor, where he's pressed his forehead to the cold stone. In genuflection, he swipes for ankles. The boy tries beating him off with his gun, both end up passing through one another. Amo scrapes skin from his elbows.

"Just give me a clue," Amo says.

The boy is upright again, pistol in hand, a little shaky.

"Have you made your peace with Jesus Christ, our Lord and Savior?"

"Jesus?"

"Jesus does not make peace with Japs!" thunders the kid. "Where were you doing Pearl Harbor?" Weapon brandishing, glimmer in the old eye.

Where were you doing, odd word choice.

His name is Shame Finnegan. His father, Patrick Finnegan, raised eyebrows and rancid malt scotches in the muck and ire of Southern Oregon, until December 8, 1941, when, in the throws of a drunken Pearl Harbor-inspired rage, he set the cows to pasture, burned the barn, and mistakenly beat his wife to death with the caboose of an iron model train. Shame, carrying the family twelve-gauge out of the blaze, came upon Patrick not a second after that last blow was struck. He watched the slow arc of that train rising into the sunlight, falling with a muted whistle, the way his mother's forehead collapsed into a hot stream before he managed to get the gun to his shoulder, the long muzzle crack ringing into his ears, the way his father turned to dough, then the long trek to the recruiter's office, a Pacific tour, a war: Thank God, a war. Shame's plan was to kill as many Japanese as humanly possible, to become a whirlwind of death, the terror of the Asian world, to avenge his mother's death, his father's madness.

Amo hears a voice say, "There is no way to understand, not for you." It comes from deep behind his skull and it's said with so much compassion that Amo has tears in his eyes. He can see it all now. Lately this has been happening to him, the availability of other people's nostalgia—just another channel of information that will open to him, open like a long forgotten history lesson. Let him know that there is nothing here for him.

Amo starts to leave. He loops a leg through the observation slit, feet dangling, the cold concrete presses against his waist. Still, there is time for a moment of clarity or pity. Looking back inside, through the flickering light, his voice sounds funny, coming from so deep inside.

"War's over kid, go home already."

The storm's thinned out. Below him, a thin slice of beach is visible. A torn corner from some advertisement, private and pristine and kept away from the grubby fingers of the unwashed many. Amo, brushing dirt from his sleeves, watches the swell lines. The waves rise to fifteen feet and there are a couple surfers out there—must of snuck out past the guard at the gate and the sign. This is a no surfing beach. But what can that guy do? Just a rent-a-cop after all, not gonna go in after them. Not when it's cracking down this hard, not when he's got a wife and kids and this is just some moonlight cash, something to offset the paycuts at the factory and help with another baby on the way and the doctor bills for his hip, took some shrapnel in Korea, hasn't walked right since, can't even do it missionary style, has to let his wife be on top all the time and he hates that.

IT'S WAY PAST THE SEASON TO BE JOLLY, and if it's answers you want, well, it's almost too late in this game for cause and effect. The record of the next three days is blurry. Angel spends most of his time handcuffed to a bed with a cold chill in his arm.

There are hours of sad questions, voices without faces and faces without voices, a sharp pain when the needle goes in and a sticky chemical sweat. He has the distinct feeling of his beard growing—very little continuity. Often Angel wakes into light. A memory of Isosceles dangling above him at odd angles stays with him into consciousness. Certainly he gave answers, had no choice, but . . . he'll never really know.

One afternoon the guard falls asleep in a chair at the edge of the bed. Angel's right hand is hauled above his head, rests handcuffed to a bent iron rod serving as a headboard. There is a steady throb in his shoulder. His vision is bad, unsteady, the guard a soggy shape at the end of the room. He has little feeling left in his body, a cramp that starts somewhere near his feet and runs straight through his head. But he doesn't stop to think about that, knows he's not going to get another chance.

For how long? Ten minutes, twenty? Moments of silence and moments of movement. Isosceles could be back at any time. Angel's lungs hurt from breathing slowly, from trying not to pant. He works his cuffed arm as far down the post as he can, sliding it an inch at a time, trying to cover the squeak of metal with his body. The guard stirs, but does not wake. He manages to put both feet on the floor. A sharp fire comes into his left calf, he can feel the bones burning, the flesh coming apart and then it's gone and he has some feeling where before he had none.

The bed is not bolted to the floor, it's not much more than an army cot, thirty, forty pounds at most. He wraps his hands around the frame and tightens his grip. The cold, flat iron bites into his skin. His fingers curl through the place where bedsprings begin, he can feel the coiled metal ride and separate, tugging at the edge of a pinkie, a forefinger. Then he leaps, yanking the bed with him, his right leg kicking out, aiming for the guard's chin. There is a small pop as the jaw slides out of place and a second noise, a thump of sorts, as the guard's head turns sideways, the angle all wrong, moving into the concrete wall. He has fallen from his chair, a slumped pile, a little blood. Angel sees a broken tooth lying in a small pool of spittle and a cut runs across his toes where his foot must have slid into the man's mouth. The guard opens his eyes for a second, he rolls or tries to roll and Angel thinks about kicking the toppled chair at him but doesn't and the guard looks at him once more then closes his eyes and this time stays quiet.

The handcuff key is on the guard's belt. Angel's arm aches from bending and dragging and it nearly slides from its socket as he accidentally tilts the bed onto its side on his first try for the key. But then he stops and breathes and does everything slowly.

Angel has the gun out of its holster before the guard wakes again. It has a heavy, cool feel that reminds him of something, but he can't think too clearly and just tries to go on. Thankfully, no one is in the warehouse. He doesn't want to shoot anyone and doesn't remember much else. Outside it is raining. They had taken away his clothes and he's not going to get very far in his underwear. He is somewhere in San Francisco's gray area, wet and alone, stumbling the slums and darkness between Potrero Hill and Bay View. There are no bearings to be gotten. These are hard areas, not marked on the tourist's maps, kept out of sight by hills and intrepid inward passageways.

Angel finds a dirty pair of forest green army fatigues and an old T-shirt abandoned on a church stair. He had gone there with the sudden urge toward prayer, but now, standing in the lost glow of a broken porchlight, amid needles and glass, he can't take the cold press of watery cloth against his legs. He takes off his underwear and stands naked and cold before stepping into José Amable's last earthly possessions.

If he wanted to look, just sidestep over the porch, he'd find José dead, shirtless and pantless in the bushes that run across the baseline of the church's steeple. Dead of a hot shot, a broken heart and a fake green card paid for with the last remnants of his savings. Certainly it sounds like a nightmare or a fiction, but the needle's still stalled between his toes and if you were to crawl close enough there is the fabled smell of battery acid lingering around his once living flesh.

But Angel's not gonna look and it doesn't matter—José himself took the pants off Fernando "Cha-Cha" Inurera about a week earlier after a sloppy knife fight. Two weeks before that Fernando had won them in a football bet from Bigger Dan Washington, who, in turn, had gotten them from his brother Yo-Yo after the army sent Yo-Yo's remaining possessions home, put Yo-Yo in a box, and left him swollen in an El Salvadorian grave—where, if you'd think to ask them—he never was anyway.

Angel walks back into the rain, the pants triple cuffed and sagging, his boots squishing and his shirt stinking of Bay grime and fever sweats. People pass in cars, swerve at the last minute with headlights low or off; nobody around here wants any extra attention.

"Hey man, watcha need?"

Angel can't see a face, the voice floats low and off a broken porch.

"Coyote—is that you?"

"Man I ain't no fucking coyote, where the fuck you think you are?" There is some laughter in the dark.

"No, I mean have you seen Coyote?" Angel steps closer to the porch, wiping hair from his face, feeling very tired.

"You pretty far from home, hombre."

Angel just nods.

"Hey man, you okay? You look like shit."

"I just wanna go to bed, I'm gonna go…" but he never finishes that sentence and he never makes it to the porch. He slouches into a heap of rain. Somewhere, in the back of his mind, he feels his arms being lifted. A voice says, "Over here, outta this shit." But that's the last thing he remembers.

BACK IN THE CAR AMO TAKES A PISTOL out of the glove compartment, puts it in his lap. He doesn't know what's coming next, but he no longer has any intention of going around unarmed. He smokes a few cigarettes. The wind blows. He digs out a copy of the New Testament that he grabbed on the way out of the house, but it stays closed on the passenger seat beside him. A Bible and a gun. He looks over both and throws the Bible out the window, angles the gun into his belt. The book lands on the side of the road, rain soaking the cover. He starts the car and puts it in drive, heading back to the city. Hebrew words under his breath. An old language. Small prayers asking for a little guidance in a time of strife. After all, you never know.

shirt are gone. He's naked and warm, wrapped in an old Navajo blanket. He feels like rock bottom.

The room is smallish and stale, without windows or pride, simply a pair of mattresses angled into a corner and a feeble cross tacked above the bed. By now Angel has pulled his weight upward until he's rocking precariously in a sitting position. From somewhere, another room perhaps, he hears a soft moan and a throaty "Madré de Díos." He sees the small pile of clothes dry and folded at the foot of the bed.

The door creaks. "Morning sailor, want a date?"

Angel tries a feeble "Wait," but he's too weak and ends up falling out of bed and blanket and falls back to sleep on the rotting floor.

When he next wakes someone has left him a glass of water and some aspirin which goes down and stays down long enough for him to risk getting dressed.

It's a rotten morning. Miserable. He feels like crying. He realizes he's wearing all new clothes. Surprisingly, he can walk without too much pain. The hallway is dim and gray. He stops in the door frame to listen a moment, but hears nothing. A whorehouse of sorts, he's not really certain, a place of comings and goings. The hallway leads out and down, past a thin construction of ash walls and collected sweat. It is a place no one has lived, where the stairs creak underfoot and the lightbulbs illuminate nothing but darkness. The entire building is a parable for Angel. One he won't hear and won't remember later, but all the answers are available. So much so that a short-lived blackmarket has sprung up between the dust mice and the shadows, it's an insider's market to be sure, but information of a frighteningly pure strain is available at the right price.

Still, he doesn't stick around to bargain—just a rest point in a time of illness. As he stumbles into morning's light and the sticky breath of another day of his life, these markets collapse, leaving the house to fall into the slighted silence of pithy censure. There is nothing here he won't eventually learn the hard way.

FIVE DOLLARS ARE PINNED TO THE inside of Angel's right trouser pocket, enough for a cup of coffee, a pack of smokes, and the bus ride back into San Francisco. Somewhere, back there, is someone who deserves his thanks. A whore probably—one more connection that comes and goes.

He sits halfway to the back on the left side and for most of the ride the early sun lies across his seat. There are two women behind him speaking Spanish in a lilting falsetto and one more who is quieter and younger with black almond eyes and a smoky throat who rests her hand on his seat back. Angel watches the shadows angle and deepen between her fingers. She has thin fingernails, unpainted, and he wants her hands on his stomach. Moving slowly. It's been a long time since the things near him have moved slowly.

He switches buses on Market Street and rides standing and gets off a few blocks from the house Coyote had rented and walks the last quarter-mile with short steps. The house is the same small Victorian with two bedrooms and a back-yard with a small red sandbox. How long has he been gone? The stairs don't creak as he walks up and a breeze catches an antique wind chime as he passes, it quivers and a far-away dog barks twice, a signal, but to whom? The house smells like coffee and hurry. Piles of books spread across the dining room table. Amo's notes on Kabbalah run from page to page as if the act of writing itself was great and terrible but the idea of stopping worse. A chalkboard is full of Padre Isosceles' notes on Georg Cantor. Angel can't really tell, but he thinks Gabrial has made some progress with the equations. In the living room a hanging bag hangs bolted to the ceiling, a pair of Everlast gloves, red and old, lie on the floor beneath. There is a mirror across from it that Coyote uses for shadow boxing and beneath that a fantastic collection of tools: minijackhammers, explosive timers, wiring, headlamps, titanium shovels, maps, rope, backpacks, duct tape. There's more of this stuff in the hall, Angel steps over oxygen tanks and blasting caps as he goes.

He walks up the stairs and into one of the bedrooms. The window is open and the blinds chatter. He can see most of the city: paint-box houses, domed churches, the bridges, over and across onto green lands protected from people and held as forests and promise and the water of the bay, a windswept quivering flowing in, no out, out to sea and away, far, far away.

There is a purple welt rising above his rib cage and his fingers slip as he tries to untie his shoes. If he bothered to look he'd find matted blood where the blackjack connected and a cut on his jaw, but he doesn't make it that far.

The bed feels like water beneath him, the rocking slowly giving way to darker things but he slips into sleep before they reach him. When he wakes, it is to noise, but there's no placing it. The room is dark and cold. His dreams had been bad and there's a spot halfway down his spine where their memory waits. The door to his room opens, but the hallway light is off. Angel thinks to open his eyes and look but can't or not all the way and instead sees only a shift in the gray scale.

"Good to see you."

It's Gabrial's voice, but soft and unsure and not as far away as usual. Angel hears a match scrape and when he does finally look Gabrial is there, in the chalky door frame, holding an ancient hurricane lantern by his side.

He wants to ask after it, but only manages a few soft grunts and an eyebrow.

"Nice, huh," says Gabrial, turning his wrist slightly so the light sifts and plays across the wall. "It was in the garage, behind a broken radiator hose."

The glass is beveled and sectioned into octagonal panes held together at the top by rusted metal shaped into a mermaid. There's a dent in one of her arms and her tail, which curves upward as a looping handle, has been painted a deep red. Gabrial shuts the door with his foot and sets the lantern on the floor and slumps in a wooden chair beside the bed. Shadows cast upwards and catch his face.

"Had a rough time?" asks Gabrial.

"Yeah, I had a rough time."

"We found the warehouse where they took you. Empty. Morning paper had a story about two Mexican priests washing up down by Candlestick, said they got in a drinking contest with the ocean. None of the churches in the city claimed the bodies. I was betting on you."

Somewhere a phone is ringing.

"Did I have good odds?"

"So-so."

"Sorry to lose your money, all I did was get away."

The candle crackles and Gabrial turns his head to look but stops and sees the wash of the wall. He follows it down like a crack or a riddle until it blends into Angel and stops at his eyes.

"Do you want the credit?" says Gabrial, rubbing his chin.

"No," shaking his head.

They sit in silence for awhile. Angel falls back asleep. Gabrial, hands clenched and heavy, is telling him a story about Sticky, a small evening long ago, another thing Isosceles has done that he will not forget.

Angel stirs, wakes to Gabrial in midsentence. There's movement in the kitchen. Pots and pans, the sink.

"Amo?"

"Coyote," says Gabrial. "Amo headed down the coast to look two days ago, we haven't seen him since."

"Left his books on the table, he must have been really worried."

"Uh-huh."

"Something about those books..." But Angel's not thinking of Amo, he's thinking about Isosceles and suddenly there's not enough light in the room for him.

"Three nights ago Coyote said Amo recited the first half of Genesis in his sleep, first in English then Latin then Hebrew."

"In the beginning was the word."

There are footsteps on the stairs, Coyote's, and the beginning of a soft song.

"Did Isosceles leave for Italy?" asks Angel.

"Did Isosceles kill his henchmen?" asks Gabrial.

A chill runs up Angel's spin, the consequences of his action, his escape, but it's something he's known all along. He's never been responsible for anyone's death before.

"He killed them all right." Coyote stands in the doorway with a bottle of bourbon and three glasses clinking in his fingers. The noise is miniature, like a lost ballet in an abandoned theater. "Howdy ace, had a rough time of it did you?"

"Who told?" says Angel, managing a smile.

Coyote sits at the foot of the bed and tosses whiskey into the glasses.

"We have about a week, I just got a call from a Brazillian friend who said Isosceles landed in Rio and purchased a ticket down to Chile, there's a Vatican charter leaving late next Friday and Isosceles will be on it."

"What about the priests?" asks Gabrial.

"Tying up loose ends," replies Coyote, "a punishment for losing Angel. Maybe both. When they pulled them out of the drink they had Bible quotations placed in ziplock plastic bags and tucked into their shirt pockets. The police haven't released the actual quotes, but I know a guy who knows a guy who knows a guy."

"Shut up already," says Gabrial. "Just tell us what the notes said."

"The way of trangressors is hard," says Angel. "Proverbs 13:15."

Coyote startles, stares.

"He's right?" A slow smile creeps across Gabrial's face. "Isn't he?"

"How did you know?" asks Coyote.

But Angel can only shake his head, unsure himself.

A great bird flying high above in the thin cold passes over unnoticed. There's a creak from somewhere, the roof, followed by a hissing which gives way to silence followed by Father Yohji Amo crashing through the bedroom window.

He's wearing a WWII motorcycle helmet, complete with chin strap. There's a dent in its side, a fist-sized lunule, at the place where his head glanced off the sill. His suit is a ruin of mud splatters and secret tears. He is unconscious, in his left hand a small pistol. Glass has fallen to the floor beneath him and the wooden window trim, now splintered, sticks from the sill like miniature ramparts. No one says anything for a long time. Outside it starts to rain.

ANGEL LIES IN BED, THE ONLY LIGHT A small lamp on the table beside him. The broken glass has been swept up and a piece of cardboard is taped over the window. Above him hangs a dream catcher Amo had woven from some twine and feathers, but Angel has only slept in the darkness and silence from which nothing comes. There's an ache in his back from the drugs, but he's no longer feverish. Beside him, Coyote sits with his feet up on the bed's end, a cigarette in his hand, an ashtray by his feet. His face is long and drawn and hidden by the soft angles of smoke. They have been together most of the afternoon, turning the days around, trying to remember what Angel told Isosceles.

"Did we ever find out if anyone left the archives?" asks Angel. "Did any one die?"

"No one died, no one left, I checked it out."

"So we know it's one of the four."

"And Isosceles could know the same thing."

"He could," says Angel. "I tried to lie. That's all I remember, when they were drugging me, I remember telling myself to lie, then I don't remember anything."

"Lying is good."

Angel says nothing for a while, then "I'm sorry."

"No need, it could be a lot worse," stifling a laugh.

"Yeah, how?"

"You mean besides the fact that you're still alive, well, let's see, you could be dead."

"That might be worse."

"Yeah, might."

IT WAS LEIBNIZ WHO HAD THE FIRST
taste of the Book of Changes. Father Bouvet, a Jesuit
priest, passed the late seventeenth century in China and
while there corresponded with Leibniz from a place
called Peking. It's the idea of such a place that stays with
Johnii. Would Leibniz have known of Peking's existence
before the mail came? How does a man come to know a
place? Does he come to feel the world in the far corners of
his mouth?

They are in bed together, Johnii and Christiana, it is the
first time they have made love. The room is small and
white, the walls plastered with a kind of stucco that neither have seen before. Above the bed is a ceiling fan spinning slowly and a high window with a wooden shade that
opens inward. The shade and the window angle upward,
finally meeting in a small point like the nose of a fish.
Occasionally wind slips through rippling the pale mesh of
mosquito netting which hangs above the bed.

"Do you know what the Dutch said?"

"No," says Christiana, her head resting on his stomach,
tracing the line of his leg with her fingers.

"That the best place to learn a foreign language is
under the mosquito net."

"Is this a foreign language?"

"Hmm." He has been telling her stories, stories about
the I Ching, about Liebniz, about broken lines and solid
lines. They are the only way he knows to describe himself.

She rubs a piece of mesh between her hands, feeling the gaps, the points that almost allow entrance. "Where are you?" she asks.

"Sumatra."

"Sumatra." Christiana too loves the feel of place names. It has become a game they play.

Ask a Taoist what is the strongest thing he knows and he will draw a line in the dirt. It is t'ai chi—the unbroken line, the basis for all existence. It is the place from which all other places have come.

"Even Sumatra?" asks Christiana.

"Even Sumatra," stopping his telling long enough to kiss her, but that too becomes a point, a place, a map all its own.

ANGEL'S NEVER SEEN SO MANY COBBLE-
stones. Streets made for rickshaw nightmares, narrow and
curved and chockful of heavy stone, woven together like
thick yarn into a dark maze, mostly brown or black in color,
a shade past a bruise. As if long ago something terrible had
come to Rome, ridden a pale horse in terse moonlight
down these very roads and left behind something that
would forever linger in certain corners, some charming
terror, something to fulfill such nights.

They are staying in a small safe house, two blocks from
the Tiber, on a dusty Trastavere alleyway angling off the
river. Four blocks away, tucked into an alley, is an English
style pub, the Dog and Duck, a place where Americans
don't tend to stand out. Coyote bought everyone good shoes
and a new coats, they learn basic Italian from a twenty-five
page book for tourists: espresso, un brioche, dove es....

They do the walking tour of the Vatican. Angel wants
to feel the ground, the brush of innumerable shoes.

"Two thousand years and they've only come up with
pigeons and cowed heads."

"The rock that Jesus built," says Gabrial.

Coyote spreads his arms wide in benediction. "Welcome to the land of heavy columns."

Amo is worse. He spends the day on the verge of mumbling. Won't come inside, sits in the square reading, sharing his bench with men older than anything in sight.

In the Sistine Chapel, Coyote stands quiet and amused as

Gabrial and Angel argue the difference between a cupola and a basilica. Voice ringing across emptiness. No one else stands near. Angel's earring, Gabrial's white skin, hatred the oldest habit of all.

"Fuck 'em," says Coyote.

Time and again, they find themselves left alone in unbelievable places. But this much space empty has a different feel. Angel stops in the middle to press a cheek to the hallway's stone floor, to listen.

They climb a thousand stairs to the dome's peak.

"A million," says a small kid climbing behind them, listening in on their talk.

The view from the top of St. Peter's is one of the finest ever seen, as if they had hired the world's best gardener and manicured the earth, the air, the light itself. Coyote leans heavily into the railing, his hands on the banister, the paint beneath thin and white and chipped. He lifts a finger, his hand not moving more than two inches forward, not farther than a small poke. Angel follows the line, knows. The secret archives.

He feels it like dew on his back, a sparkle, they all do. In the distance stand rows and rows of umbrella pines. Giant trees, many over eighty feet tall and with their lower branches lopped off, the way the Italians like them, they look like cypress, like rainforest canopy with everything below swept away.

They go back down and wander through St. Peter's again. Somewhere, a choir sings Gregorian chants. Coyote says the whole thing made him feel like smoking and goes off to get a coffee.

That afternoon, under yawling clouds, Gabrial and Angel

prowl the outside of Vatican City. They move in slow steps, looking lost, looking around. Later that night pouring over maps of the same area, the four bend forward on elbows, just clearing the overhead light hung above the tabletop. The map is old, but there has been little change in the last thousand years. The Romans carved the whole city and Italy built itself anew atop the mess. Underground is a minotaur's field of passageways, tunnels, aqueducts. Hard to read. Squinting and pointing. Angel glances around for other references.

On the walls are more maps, bookshelves, a wall safe tucked behind an early American eighteenth-century landscape. A sunrise sweeping down from a mountain, dramatic river in the foreground. A fake, but a damn good one. Coyote has a small filing cabinet in the corner of the room. Hard wood, oak or maple. Inside, he keeps maps of every fraction of Italy. Lists of known contacts. Coastlines and escape routes. Schedules for barges and trawlers and obscure fishing vessels that haven't caught a perch in twenty years. A list of supply caches utilized by factions and splinter groups. Earlier, he tossed Gabrial a seven-hundred page booklet, a who's who of Europe, and watched as he paged through lists of names, wives' birthdays, favorite foods, scotches, cigars, suit makes, dress sizes, favorite flowers and which they were allergic to—all current and up-to-date. A smuggler's bible for currying favor. Even a list of the major missing texts: religious and mystical, and who would want them back and how badly.

"It's incomplete." Gabrial lifts his eyes from the book. "The Sefer ha-Zaviot isn't here."

Angel looks up from the map. "That just makes it a more closely guarded treasure."

Coyote nods.

They trace paths under the city, the apartment with the trapdoor into the floor and the basement that opens into the tunnel system, miles of mapped territory, but no one passageway that leads where they're going.

"May have to blast through about here." Coyote's finger wagging like a swollen tonsil. "What time does Luigi dock?"

"Two o'clock, tomorrow," answers Angel.

"Broad daylight," notes Gabrial.

Angel nods.

"Ambitious fuck." Amo's first words in an hour, but there's a sweet smile to accompany them and Angel relaxes a little.

Coyote pokes at a hexagram of lines. "He's bringing wet suits too, headlamps, air tanks, waterproof guns. If we do have to dive through an underground sea, we can. Amo and Angel go pick the stuff up. Amo, are you comfortable in Italian?"

"Enough."

"Good. Angel doesn't talk to anyone and I mean anyone," speaking as if Angel weren't in the room, "there shouldn't be any problems."

"Are we going to bother with Sepulchri?" asks Angel. "Or fuck the easy way and just blast through."

"These maps are only backup, Sepulchri is the way that keeps us all alive. I'm still operating on the assumption that's part of the plan."

"Alive is good," says Gabrial.

"Good," nods Coyote. "Then you should know that you are currently in the presence of Charles Merrick, esteemed archeologist and professor of ancient languages at Middlebury College, recently added to the faculty after a long and prosperous dig in Egypt."

"Congratulations." Angel dry and smiling.

Coyote reaches into his pocket and comes out with a letter. "Signed by the pope." He pulls the paper out of the envelope, but doesn't look at it when he reads "Please allow Professor Merrick every courtesy, access to the archives, a good point in the direction of Father Ambrose Sepulchri of the restoration department and ice cream and cookies when he's finished."

"You forged the pope's signature?" Angel stares at Coyote in disbelief.

"You think he really signs these documents himself?"

"You forged the signature of the pope's forger?"

"And not a bad job of it," showing the letter to Gabrial. Gabrial glances at it, then looks back down at the map. He follows a loose path with his fingers.

"How certain are we of the exact location of the Zaviot?" he asks.

"How certain are we of anything?" Coyote looks at the map for a minute. "Sixty, seventy percent certain, these are old maps but there hasn't been much reason for anybody to move it. Probably only the Society knows where it is."

"Or what it is," adds Gabrial.

"Either way no one's ever made a go at it and supposedly the Vatican added a new alarm system ten years ago, state-of-the-art so to speak and no one's given them reason to doubt it."

"Is it?" asks Gabrial.

Coyote looks but doesn't see.

"State-of-the-art?"

"No, not really," says Coyote.

Gabrial says nothing.

"We'll each be carrying twenty pounds in our back-packs," continues Coyote, "mostly fragile, so over the next three days everyone takes long walks. Wear your pack like a tourist, use books and water for weight. Do the hills, walk the busy streets trying not to touch anyone, practice turning sideways, getting a good intuitive feel for the pack's space."

He raises his hands. "We're in Rome, gentlemen, see the sights, you may never get another chance."

FATHER MALACHI KEALLY IS NOT AN old man, his father was, he saw what that looked like, he knows the difference. Still, he cannot explain the creak that holds his body at wrong angles, that curses through his bones. Rising to his full height, he walks toward the only window in his room. It closes quietly as everything here closes quietly. It's the Vatican, that's the way things work. The latch slides into place and he shudders a little as he walks back to his bed. He's amazed by his chill, he can't believe he'll ever get used to the Italian wind, the ballast of it, so different from his old country. His father would laugh at him for it, an Irishman bowing to the weather. But then again his father died of pneumonia, and in the end, supposes Malachi, it was probably the wind that got him.

So here he is, ten years later, his old trade long forgotten, most of the agility in his fingers probably gone. Malachi is a happy man now, happier than he can ever remember being. He's managed to grant his father his one dying wish. Who knew. Who would have thought his father hadn't wanted him to grow up to be an old thief like himself, who would have known he'd want a priest for a son.

The change weighs well on Malachi, he sleeps through most nights now and maybe someday he'll have to repay the people who helped him get from the county lockup all the way to the Vatican. He never would have guessed there were such people or that his father had known such people and, more than that, that such people had owed his dying father a little something. None of that matters right now, that day isn't today and this helps him at night too, the fact that someday he'll be able stand up under the weight of his debts. That, he thinks, is one of the things Jesus taught by example—you pay your debts, no matter who it is you might owe.

THE MAN KNOWN AS THOUSAND FIN-
gers stands alone in a long room talking on a phone. The
handle is made from ivory, the tusks of a great elephant,
the last of its kind. The elephant was killed in battle and
given a ceremonial burial and his tusks stripped and used
to make a few objects that were given to those who came
through long nights, as a way to carry on in the world. Out
of them came two phones and a small set of lint brushes.
Twenty brushes in all, given to others, also deserving of
such honor. The other phone is now far away, held in the
hand of the Russian, who speaks into it with his long voice
full of thick consonants. They speak slowly with each other,
Thousand Fingers and the Russian, two men who have
known each other for a lifetime, two men who have watched
the toppling of so much.

"I need you to prepare a gun," says the Russian. "I need
it done in the old way."

There is a deep pause on the line. The Russian can feel
the tick of his watch, a change in the angles between the
two thin hands of time. "It has been a long time, perhaps
something simpler?"

"No. Not this time."

There is another pause, but there will be no argument,
in nearly seven decades of such work they have never had
more than small discussion, the passage of information,
like minds working towards like aims. "What kind of
rifle?" he says finally.

314   Steven Kotler

"Hunting, sniper's scope, something elegant but untraceable. I will send a messanger to pick it up."

"Who?"

"A man of cloth, coming from Rome. A man you don't know, though you met his father once."

"Give me two days and have him arrive on a noon train, I will have Gretta meet him at the station."

"Gretta?" and then they laugh the laugh of two old men at play for a few last minutes.

IT'S ALREADY COLD AND DARK WHEN Angel and Amo reach the Dog and Duck. They order coffee correctos, coffee and brandy drunk early in the morning mostly, a quick way of putting another night behind.

No more than fifteen people stomp around. Men argue football scores, Italy's dismal hopes for a World Cup. A few students in a corner. The bartender and his friends at the end of the room. Old men and old women doing what they've been doing for so long that the time before seems to belong to someone else. And a young woman sitting alone in the middle. She wears jeans and a college sweatshirt and is pretty in the way only American girls can be pretty. So simple and uncomplicated it makes Angel want to stare.

They've walked to a far corner of the bar, apart from everyone else. Just two men having a soft conversation. They could be anyone. Anywhere.

"Are you ever going to tell me why you swung through the window?"

Amo slurps coffee, watches his breath mist. "Nobody believes in heat around here."

It had taken Angel over a week to recover from the beating Isosceles had delivered, Amo stayed at his side, reading to him in a soft voice. Even from where he lay in that bed, Angel would occasionally see a remnant. A sharp glimmer, light at angles, a lost edge of a broken pane. Amo never spoke of it. Besides a scratched hand and a thin cut on his leg he was, remarkably, unscathed.

Steven Kotler

"There was a lot of glass," which is not much of anything, let alone an answer.

Angel sips his coffee, thinks about the first time the two of them sat in a bar and drank coffee together. Who was that man then? Who is he now? He thinks about Pena sitting behind him in a movie theater on his fourth night in Santa Fe. He remembers crossing a highway in Colorado, the way the ice looked, the cold in his toes. There is no order to these thoughts. There is no way back and, actually, there isn't a map in the world that could mark their passage.

"It had been a long day, I wasn't thinking clearly."

"Do many clearheaded people dive through second-story windows? Does that happen where you come from?"

Amo sips his drink and looks at Angel. "You wouldn't believe what happens where I come from."

A woman comes into the bar selling roses. They're out of season and half-dead from cold but Amo buys one anyway. He closes his eyes and runs the rose over his chin. Angel watched him quietly, Amo becoming a man standing in two worlds at once.

"You should give it to her," says Amo, nodding to the girl at the bar.

"Why?"

"Have you ever given a stranger a rose?"

"No."

"It's something you should do," and he pauses, twirling the rose in his fingers. "It's one of the things to be done at least once in your life."

THE I CHING TEACHES THE TRIAD AS the basis for reality. A universe of three lines. It tells us that one produced two, two produced three, and three produced ten thousand things. Within the I Ching, there are eight possible triads and it is combinations of these eight that beget the final sixty-four. The end of all possibility. In no version of the I Ching is there a sixty-fifth hexagram. Sixty-five is a number for the faithful, the end of the line, of all the lines.

This is what Johnii knows, what has kept him going through his long nights. He had written these very lines on a sheet of paper, but how long ago? Long enough that he can no longer remember and Johnii remembers everything. He does not believe in trivia, for a man without a past nothing is trivial.

But where is that paper now?

He is going through his records and pages are missing: a diagram taken from the *Shuo Kua* which depicts the process of life as a closed series, and another found in the lectures of Richard Wilhelm, which shows six points arranged around an asterisk. If he closes his eyes he can still see them clearly. Following a clockwise motion they are labeled—the abyssal, keeping still, the arousing, the gentle, the clinging, the receptive, the joyous, the creative. A diagram of life unfolding in space and time.

There are many who believe the I Ching a calendar,

there are few, Johnii among them, who see it as a map and an incomplete one at that.

He is alone in the bungalow, Christiana gone out earlier, and he now sits with all of his notes, an entire suitcase of information, a lifetime of amalgamation—well, almost a lifetime. But things are gone and others have been reordered. After the fortune teller left him laughing on the beach he spent most of the day looking for the package Coyote sent to him. There were no traces. Nothing. He is beginning to wonder if ever there was a package or if the messenger was not who he claimed to be.

One thing is for certain, something is wrong with the network. He has never been so long without work. He still checks in, every other day, but there is nothing, no work, no need, nobody calling him back to Jerusalem. He even called Max just to see if anyone has been by, has asked after him, but Max hadn't seen anyone. He's not uncomfortable with any of this, his life moves in rhythms, that too he has learned from the I Ching, and there is no way to understand all of them.

Lately he has started to think about the small boy he once was, he can still recall the feeling in his fingers as he held them in the Wailing Wall, the thin angle of light bounding off high stone. He has built a life around the texture of this dust. Perhaps he has been wrong, perhaps one cannot move backwards towards the past, perhaps there is only one direction available to him. Then there is Christiana, a sign he can really attend to, something not entirely built of ash and mystery.

FATHER MALACHI KEALLY HAS NEVER visited the town of Valnerina before. He knows that somewhere close sits Umbrini, the oldest ruin in Italy, not much left now, a few walls of crumbled brick halfway up a small mountain. The remains of a few towers. Sharing the lower portion of the same mountain are farmers and fields, the bark of dogs—he does not know what grows here. The town itself is small, tucked into a long valley, visited mostly by students from the nearby college in Perugia. It is a place to come walk in the woods, a place whose time has long since passed. He had taken the train out of Rome and stopped at the Folgino station, another of the small hill towns north of Rome. It was here that the allies in WWII met their hardest resistance, it has always been so, a region well fortified, impossible to attack from the ground. At the station he is greeted by a young woman leaning against a small convertable. She has a glass of champagne in her hand, a sliver of fruit floating in the glass.

"Good afternoon, Father," opening his door with her free hand. "You had a pleasant journey?"

As he steps into the car he smells peaches. They drive on backroads, the wind picking at her hair, which she finally frees from the thin grasp of a small silver clip. It sails behind her, a twisting ebony cloak, things that make him feel young again. He is uncomfortable with the whole of the trip, wanting nothing more from life than the icy press of the Vatican's walls, wanting the peace and the quiet. A humble servant far enough down the chain of command that the sinister plotting, the throne of succession, the inner ticktock of the Christian empire leaves him mostly alone. He is here because he pays his debts, because a phone call came for him, the Russian's voice, the final task.

The woman does not tell him her name and he will not ask. When they turn into a long driveway and ride towards a large house perched on a high hill, he looks straight ahead. This is no longer part of his world, he does not want to begin to feel a tourist, does not want to open the door to such desires. They park beside an old barn beneath a large canopy of greenery. The barn is set far back from the house, a light breeze topping the trees, leaves like lapping waves, green tongues. The large door to the barn slid back, a slot of blackness inside, not much light.

She walks around the front of the car and opens his door. "Please go in," pointing towards the open barn door. "I will wait for you here. After your business is complete, would you like to come up to the house for lunch? Or would you prefer to head straight back to the station?"

"The station, please," already walking towards the barn.

He steps through the door and into a darkness not as deep or thick as he had assumed, more a trick of angles. He sees a light at the end of a row of stalls and is surprised to find horses inside some of them. He sees a tack room to his left and beside that the long tail of a chestnut mare twitching at the afternoon flies. He walks to the stall and looks inside, the mare ignoring him. A fine horse, he thinks to himself, a well cared-for horse, a horse meant for long days and hard rides. Someone here knows the value of animals.

"You like horses, Father?" the voice coming from

behind Keally. He turns and sees a tall man wearing a long smock. In his left hand he holds a long cane, though he seems to stand without its aid.

"I did, once. A long time ago."

"Are you staying for lunch? Perhaps afterwards you would like to go for a ride through the grounds?"

"I'm sorry, thank you, but I really do have to get back before I am missed."

The man raises a hand, a small gesture, an understanding between men. Keally sees a silver ring on his fourth finger, worn in place of a wedding band. He walks closer and sees what he took for silver is actually diamonds arranged as an intricate dragon, unusual and precise. He has seen the ring before, on someone else's finger, but he can't place it and already the man is leading him through a series of back rooms, down a flight of stairs, and places a key in a complicated lock. Keally looks closely at the lock, he has never seen anything quite like it and knows it is not one he could pick. Beside him, the man does something with the key, a final, difficult twist of his wrist and the lock opens with a hard clang.

Keally still hasn't gotten a good look at his host, as if the light never finds his features completely, as if he must put together a face from scraps and hints. They enter a workroom of sorts. Books and tables. A small sink in the corner and beside it a Bunsen burner and a set of test tubes and vials all capped with cork. He glances at the corks, sensing a pattern, and notices that in the center of each cork, burned into the phellem, rests the same image of the dragon and beneath that is an intricate band of hands or not hands, just fingers, a woven ring of fingers, too many to count. The man walks into another room and raises a finger, asking Keally to wait for just a moment and then returns with a large leather satchel. Black with a metal clasp. In his hand is a silver stamp and a thin envelope and a box of matches.

"These are your instructions on where the bag needs to be left and how to hide it and here are matches to burn the instructions when you are finished."

He reaches into a deep pocket and comes out with a small box, across the lid is an address and the postage already paid.

"You must stamp the earth with this," holding the stamp up for Keally to see, "and place the bag on top of it. After you are finished put the stamp in here and drop it into any mail slot. As I'm certain you have been told, this is a two-part task and as I don't know the second half I will not waste our time with guesses. The Russian will contact you and give you final details. Your help is much appreciated."

"Pick up a bag, drop off a bag, not much in the way of help."

The man smiles at him, maybe, maybe not, the future holds so many little things.

"Are you certain you won't be staying for lunch?"

"No, thank you."

The man nods once, placing the envelopes and the stamp in a large black cloth bag. He hands both the bag and the satchel to Keally and then guides him back through the rooms and the stairs and into the barn. "I imagined you would feel this way. You will find some sandwiches on the seat in the car."

"Thank you."

"You know," says the man, already walking back into the darkness of the barn, "I met your father once, in Ireland, he was a good man, he was a good thief. I am told you are better."

"Was better."

"Pity," and then he disappears around a corner and Father Malachi Keally is left alone, holding the bag.

THE CURATE LOOKS UP FROM HIS podium to find an exceptionally large man before him. He would guess early fifties, but the curate himself has lasted eighty-four years so he consistently assumes everyone to be younger than they are and knowing this about himself he instinctively adds five years to his calculations. As a system it's as good as anything else he can come up with. The man before him has short gray hair, curly and pulled off the forehead with some kind of gel. From what he's seen of the real world as of late this seems to be the fashion. Sideburns are short and well-trimmed, a tan forehead suggests authority and a particular intellectual prowess. Eyes hidden behind expensive glasses and a perfect charcoal gray suit, double-breasted and excellently sized—more noticeable in big men. The curate had found God and his mother's sewing machine at roughly the same age and for a short while they ran a close race. The only secret he keeps from his father confessor, the one tally he will have to settle alone with God, is a small closet full of handmade Italian suits. Once every two years he allows himself to spend a month's wages on a new suit that hangs in his closet, that he tries on at special times, that only twice in his eighty-four years has he dared to wear out. What a different life he might have had, but he stops his thoughts right there. On a list of things sacrificed for the Lord, he's certain his aren't quite near the top.

"Good afternoon, Professor Merrick."

"Good afternoon."

Which is how the curate learned that the good professor spoke a perfect Italian, with maybe a slight northern touch to his accent, but he tries not to be a snob like the rest of Rome. "Would you care to inspect the archives first or may I direct you to Father Sepulchri?"

"Father Sepulchri, if it is no trouble."

A very polite man for an American, but then the archives tend to make everyone meek. "Would you please follow me?"

The curate walks with a heavy step and a walking stick. Every part of him moves slowly, a creak of a knee, a crook of an elbow, a tiny step. Coyote finds himself standing still more than walking. It's too bad that Father Sepulchri's office is not accessible through the archives, Coyote would have liked a chance to glance around, but there's time for that later. One step at a time they pass up the center aisle of one of the reading rooms. A modern clock on the wall. An alcove with a small statue of the Virgin looking peaceful. Two rows of long tables and straight backed wooden chairs and stacks of archival books: cream colored leather binders wrapped around reams of parchment. The majority of the archives, contrary to what the name construes, is nothing more or less than a record of church transactions. Property bought and sold, trails and inquisitions, payrolls from the fourteenth century, lists of the mistresses of the Borgia, fines and levies, the occasional mysticism that led to the annointment of miracle status and later, perhaps, to the approval of a new saint. This is, thinks Coyote, the world's largest paper trail and I am being led through it by the world's slowest librarian.

This professor had never been to the archives before, the

curate can always tell. It takes a while to get used to and if that weren't enough, the rows of monks hunched over their work didn't make it any easier. Strangers, even very polite strangers, tend to gawk. "You have not been here before?"

"No, actually I haven't."

Two whole steps forward. "They are very impressive," says Coyote.

"The letter says you are both an archeologist and a linguist, it is strange that you have never needed to visit us before."

"Not strange for an archeologist, unless I had been working on early Christian artifacts, which I did not. I only became a linguist over the past ten years when I realized that the number of people left alive who would understand the relevance of my finds were few and far between. I needed fluency to explain the full merit of my work and thus to be able to continue to fund my digs."

"I see," says the curate. They slide slowly through two more reading rooms and down a long, dim corridor with doors that look to be shut and shut for a long time.

In another world, thought Coyote, the curate would be a man you would know a long time. Not any one particular man, just one of those who would turn up, time and again, who would never have more than one drink, who would wait a lifetime until you needed him and then he'd approach you in some East Indies cabana bar held together by pith helmets and roofer's nails and offer a short word or two of advice. Something like, "I've noticed the fishing boats run to Japan and Fiji from here." And you would take it and get off the island, because suddenly you knew that someone, somewhere was paying back a gratitude.

But that is not the case today, today the sum total of the curate's advice is "Some people never get comfortable."

"Pardon?"

"The archives, the weight of history I think. Maybe it is just us, the monks, the innards of a church that put some people off, it's hard for me to judge, I've gotten fairly used to it."

"I would hope so," says Coyote, but he's not smiling.

"The Vatican is its own country you know."

They pass through a medium-sized room with no windows and a collection of large tables. On the walls are various tools and reference books. Fluorescent lights line the ceiling but all of them are shut off, instead the room is lit by a bent arm desk lamp shining onto two men wearing long smocks and surgical gloves. They are stooping over a yellowed scroll spread open on a table against a far wall. Both are holding rulers and continually looking at an open book beside them. Neither are men Coyote's seen before.

"Measuring the distance of God's empire," says the curate, "one word at a time." He crosses the room and stops before an unmarked door at the back. The door, Coyote notices, has no handle, rather a brass push plate hangs where you would look for one. Beside the push plate is a small lock and beside that a deadbolt is visible in the crack of the doorjamb. The door itself is a frame of dark wood surrounding a large pane of beveled glass. Shapes and contours are barely visible through the glass, mostly as a mushy paste of flat angles and the only thing Coyote knows for certain is that a light has been left on inside the room.

"Ah, here we are." The curate pauses a moment and straightens up before raising a lean fist and rapping twice on the glass. The sound is louder than Coyote would have expected, especially from a librarian.

"Father Sepulchri has been with us a long time." But when Coyote gives the curate a blank stare he raises a long finger and touches his ear by way of explanation. "And sometimes his ears belong only to God."

Inside the room nothing moves, the curate knocks a second time. Still nothing.

"Has either of you seen Father Sepulchri this morning?" addressing the two monks at the worktable.

"No Father," says one, while the other shakes his head in agreement.

"Do you have a spare key to his room?"

"No, Father."

"Would you excuse me for a moment?" looking at Coyote. "Father Sepulchri occasionally works very late and has been known to fall asleep during his labors."

Coyote leans against a tall stool while the curate shuffles out of the room. Beside him stands an old apothecary's dresser, one broad sweeping shelf and below that almost fifty narrow drawers. Several of the drawers are half open and he sees piles of knives and scalpels, some still wrapped in factory plastic, a hot glint to their blades. Stacked on top of the long shelf is an assortment of adhesives, stacks of square glass plates, small silvery weights shaped like miniature pyramids. To his right a pegboard rack hangs on the far wall: brushes, paints, colored pencils, inks, and polished bone shards known as bone folders, close to a hundred of each arranged in suspended mason jars.

Though paper was invented in Asia over two thousand years ago, it didn't make its way to Europe until the tenth and eleventh centuries and it didn't gain widespread acceptance until the middle thirteenth. Instead, European scholars spread their thoughts across the more fragile papyrus and parchment. Coyote watches the two men carefully. An interesting choice, the life of a religious scholar. Most of a conservator's job, especially on manuscripts as old as those that pass through these rooms, is that of a puzzler. None of these items will ever see a display shelf and most would crumble beneath the hot lights anyway. Instead his job consists of filling in gaps in the text, of trying to refill the disintegrated, of attempting to find the words of another. The Jew's Torah is still copied by hand, one letter at a time, to make a mistake is to start over. A very subtle form of prayer.

They are trying to work silently, but Coyote can tell they are used to muttering among themselves, to a quick patter not suitable for men of God, and his presence throws off their rhythm. His earlier assumption had been right, they are, in fact, measuring lines of text or more specifically, they are measuring the gaps that exist between lines of text. Broken measurements. The idea, he assumes, is that a certain size space will only contain a certain number of words and a number of those words, will, by nature of all writing, contain an assortment of definite articles, the dead air of the written language. The trick then is to figure out how many real words can exist in the allotted space and knowing the prior text well enough one might assume that an author, with a predilection for such and such term would have written this here and in this manner. How many languages do these men read? He would have liked this job, the quiet halls, the light banter focusing upon one subject, no prying questions—he wonders why he never hid in a monastery. So many of his compatriots did and many of them at his suggestion. It's strange how much these men of God like to hide fugitives from another law.

In the corridor outside Coyote hears the gentle slap of the curate's step. The man wears very expensive shoes for a priest, a nice touch really. He appears in the doorway before entering the room. It's not that he stops or even pauses, just that his motion is so slow it seems to belong to another time, governed by an entirely different set of mechanics. In his left hand dangles a large ring of keys that he somehow manages not to clank together as he walks. As he reaches Sepulchri's door Coyote rises to meet him. He could have, in fact, risen to meet him several hundred times in the time it took that man to cross a floor.

"Sorry to keep you waiting."

"Please, it was no bother, fascinating to watch these men at work." Coyote's fingers brush over the air, pointing somewhere.

The curate sifts through the keys slowly, stopping to look at each one as if a hidden novelty waits in its notches. Some of them are of the skeleton variety, long, gray shafts and intricate metal boxes at their end. The one they want is nothing more than short, tarnished brass, not more than fifteen years old, but Coyote can tell, even from the cursory glance, that it is slightly longer than a normal key and intricately cut. Subtle ascents and slopes on both sides of the blade making it a difficult lock to pick.

The deadbolt slides back with a hollow click. The first thing Coyote sees is a stone floor, probably gray stone, but slightly brown in the lamplight. It appears someone has dripped ink across the floor in smooth, round dots. The ink makes a long trail across the room and over to the desk where Father Ambrose Sepulchri sits. Both his feet are on the floor and he is square shouldered with his neck exposed and head bent back to stare at some invisible spot on the ceiling. Father is not a large man, actually thin and frail, most of his hair gone and his eyes half-shut. It seems that his reading glasses have fallen and cracked and now lie submerged in a small puddle at his feet. The ink trails up from the floor and onto his robe. There's a large splotch spread across his chest and a wide smiling gash where his throat used to be.

"Jesus Christ," swears the curate.

The cut is almost four inches across and very clean. A scalpel lies on top of the desk and Coyote doesn't have to inspect it to know it's been used only once. Beneath the blade's tip is a small prick of blood like a leak in a fountain pen. Ambrose Sepulchri's eyes are half-closed and Coyote looks for an after image. It's just a myth, but myths have to start somewhere. But there's nothing there and there's going to continue to be nothing. Father Sepulchri is dead and cold and whatever he was looking at now rests somewhere higher than the ceiling of an old church.

A LITTLE RAIN TONIGHT. DOWN BY the wharf the watchmaster drinks from a fine bottle of scotch, the best he's had in months. He's got a small shack with wide windows and he can see the whole of the dock, watch the rain, the lap of waves, see if any new ships come in. It's a small port though, a few slips and some rust, not much going on. Inside the shack, he sits in a big chair in front of a messy desk and an old telephone. The telephone rings directly to the police station, to a fat desk sergeant with a bad lisp, a first line of defense if the watchman happens to feel something amiss. Certainly this should be the duty of the customs officials, but Italy is a busy country and a lot of things must come in and a lot of things must go out and sometimes customs doesn't want to know about all the minutia.

Beside the telephone sits a neat stack of magazines, just the type that you'd expect to find down by the docks. Sitting atop the magazines is where he found the bottle of scotch, tall and cool and tied with a slight red bow. It looks like a quiet night, he has to work straight through until eight in the morning and a little scotch will help the time go by. Beside the scotch, there was also a short note and a small stack of lire, but the lire seems to have been put away in someone's pocket by now. What's left of the note is right now turning to soot in a high metal ashtray, the kind that looks like a flying saucer attached to a two-foot pole. The top slides open by squeezing two levers together. Inside is an engraving of Marilyn Monroe, her breasts two sharp angles, her legs still long. It's a neat package, very elegant, almost like they have in fancy hotels. Isn't much of a message anyhow: a thank you note; enjoy the scotch; probably best to sleep off the hangover between five and six in the morning. There is a cot in the back, kind of sags in the middle, but perfect for such occasions.

THE CABS ALL LINE UP HERE, JUST
before the gate leading to St. Peter's Square, especially in
the thick dust around seven in the evening. A long line of
them presses against a high curb and just past their flank a
Roman traffic circle and near madness. The noise can be
terrific. Horns and shouts and a thousand tourists all lost or
tired or wanting supper. Everyone watching their pocket-
books and wallets, thieves love this square, and who would-
n't, such an easy place to make a fast living. Slightly to the
west of this rises a heavy Roman archway and beside that a
lone olive tree, some kind of symbol. The limbs are wet
with the beginnings of rain. Sitting under it, still dry on a
park bench, with a certain Coyote Blú, is a bare-legged girl
of eighteen. Long blond hair and a happy smile for Coyote.
She's wearing shorts and you know you can't enter the Vatican with this much Swedish flesh showing and her friends
are taking an awfully long time. Her name is Viveca. At
night, she dreams of America. In about two minutes a
phone beside the bench will start ringing and when he gets
up to answer it Coyote will lose Viveca to Francisco, tall and
swarthy and very Spanish, nice teeth, also wants to move to
the United States, but for now in Italy on vacation. Viveca
and Francisco will last more than half a year of long distance phone calls and train rides to some middle ground.
They'll decide they can't stand it and against the wishes of
their friends and families they'll elope to a small midwestern town where one day they'll get into a freak fender-ben-

der with Angel's parents. Nothing much will come of it, it's no more than a dent really, and they've all had to learn to live with life's little disappointments. Nobody will bother putting all this together and how could they anyhow, maybe for Coyote it would be possible, but he's busy right now saying goodbye to Viveca and standing up to answer a ringing pay phone.

Across the way tourists are piling into taxis, the lights coming on with a howl. Takes a certain bravery to continually drive through Roman traffic. Coyote holds the evening's newspaper on top of his head as he moves, the front-page headlines tell a terrible tragedy: a Nigerian priest, assigned to the Vatican's archival department, got run down by one of those very dangerous taxi cabs just this morning while walking to work. No one's identified the driver or got the license number and with so many taxis around probably never will. This is Rome though, Catholic Rome, where they truly do believe in hell—that's one driver who's going to spend all eternity in some very hot flames and they're sure of it.

Tomorrow's paper might hold another tragedy of the same type, a murdered priest found late this afternoon in the conservation department of the Vatican library. A real shocker, but it probably won't make the news. The Vatican prefers to handle such things quietly, they are, after all, a very proud institution.

The rain's thicker now, the drops audibly hitting the pavement, bouncing off at crazy angles.

"Are you enjoying Rome?" Coyote can hear Christiana just fine despite the long distance connection.

"How could I not, there are so many murky pleasures to go around."

"Do you remember the last time?"

"The sailor's scam, what a funny evening, he almost took all our money."

"He was really good." And then they both start laughing. It's the last bit of nostalgia they'll get to share for quite some time and well, why not tonight? Sometimes things come to an end, even when you're not noticing, even when there's no way to tell, even when you're on a wet phone in the beginning of a sweet Italian night.

"I have bad news for you," says Christiana after the laughter has passed.

Taking a breath. "Go ahead."

"I spoke to the Russian this afternoon."

"Isosceles made it to Rome?"

"It appears that way."

"How crazy is that man?" says Coyote. "He killed two Vatican priests in one day."

"That's the bad news," says Christiana, "he didn't kill two priests in one day."

"What do you mean?"

"The Russian killed one of them. He's been financing the newsletter from the beginning. It was his network to start with. You got too close."

"Why didn't you tell me?" says Coyote, his fingers tight on the phone.

"Even if I had known it wouldn't have been permitted."

"What do you mean even if you had known?"

"Johnii was working for that newsletter. The Russian hired him five years ago. A runner mainly. I didn't know until today."

"What gave?"

"The Russian called to tell Johnii that the network was blown and that their Vatican contact was no longer available for service, he was permanently predisposed."

"And Johnii told you?"

"We're in love, we don't have secrets."

"Congratulations."

"Thank you."

"And you put two and two together and realized that the Russian is playing both sides against the middle."

"That's my take."

"A tricky bastard," says Coyote.

"Tricky and proud," says Christiana. "He's very proud. You may have had permission to tunnel into the Vatican and steal a book, but when you decided to scrap that plan and find those priests... well, he doesn't want anyone infiltrating his network. He decided to set an example before you got too far, before anyone else noticed."

"Anyone else?"

"It's a big world, Coyote, you're not the only one who wants secret books."

"We've got two dead priests over here, which one did the Russian kill?"

"Sepulchri."

"Motherfucker," says Coyote.

"Are you going to go to the backup plan?"

"Hell yes."

"Are you scared?"

"Hell yes."

"Me too."

"Yeah, but I heard you jump off cliffs in your free time."

"I heard the same thing about you." Christiana pauses for a minute and Coyote stays quiet, listening to her breathing.

"Percent chance that it'll work?" she says finally.

"In and out and with the book and still alive?"

"It'd be better that way."

"The Russian going to leave us alone this time?"

"I'll ask him for you."

"Then I'd say fifty percent."

"Two to one odds."

"If I were a betting man."

"Sweetheart, you are a betting man."

Coyote sighs. "Before we left San Francisco, Isosceles got his hands on Angel."

"Damn."

"He drugged him, was going to kill him too, but Angel got away. We've no way to know what he told him. My guess is Angel gave him the names of the priests but somehow managed not to divulge which one was our target."

"So Isosceles decided to eliminate all possibilities."

"And he started with the Nigerian."

"There's always fate."

Neither of them say anything for a few moments.

"Coyote . . . "

But he cuts her off before she can finish. "You know my father was a minister. I probably didn't mention it."

"No, you never mentioned it."

"He was a kick-ass rancher mostly, ran horses mainly, but on Sunday he'd dress us all up and off to church we'd go. Workingman's preacher. You ever go to church in the Texas?"

"No."

"God is free."

"Pardon?"

"It's what he used to say, 'God is free,' meaning he don't cost nothing."

Christiana says nothing, she just holds the line and waits out the silence.

"He was a son-of-a-bitch. Ignored my mother and me. He liked horses and God better than people."

A busload of tourist hoots by and Coyote pauses to wait for the noise to die. In the distance the light has gone flat.

"Are you really in love?"

Christiana pauses for a second and Coyote can hear waves and ocean in the background. "Yeah, I think so. Are you impressed?"

"I'm so impressed I talk about you in my sleep."

Neither says anything for a moment. Coyote starts to speak and stops. Finally Christiana asks, "Are you really going to do this?"

"With Angel around, I can't explain it, but somehow I think we'll get that book."

"It's just one book. . . ."

"Please don't try to talk me out of this, Christiana, no matter what you would say I would still owe this one to Pena. She gave me my life."

"Because rules are rules."

"Because rules are rules."

"I'm crazy about you," says Christiana.

"But you're in love with another man."

"Details."

"I'll be seeing you."

"I'd like that." Then a soft pause, a moment of silence, before the light click of her hanging up.

His paper is ruined and he backhands it into a trash barrel and glances at the Vatican before hailing a taxi. It has grown dark and all that is left to see are the marble saints that line the rim of the archways surrounding St. Peter's Square. They and the small cross rising from the basilica, alight in the first pass of moon. Well, one thing's for certain, atop this rock, someone definitely built a church.

A TALL MAN STANDS IN THE HALF-
light of the Italian dusk. Beside him lingers an empty taxi.
The driver's door is ajar, open to a bare street. The car has
been left running and a little exhaust leaks from its tailpipe.

This road is far outside of Rome. A fence runs along one
side and behind the fence, set back far back from the street, a
factory of some kind—shoe leather or car parts. Across the
way sits an abandoned tavern beside an empty lot with only a
pay phone between them. The man is talking on the phone.
He wears a pair of grimy chinos, too big for him around the
waist and a little short in the legs. Beneath the cuff, a hint of
black sock is visible. His shirt is white and nondescript and
his blue union jacket is zipped nearly to the top. He is hissing
something, in a language that's not Italian, punctuating his
outburst with a sharp smack of the receiver against his palm.

The receiver itself is black, made of the same Bakelite
plastic that was so popular in this part of the world some
forty years ago. Another remnant of the war. They were a
poor country then, certainly Mussolini had gotten the
trains to run on time but when all was said and done and he
was hanging from a flagpole was there anything left in the
coffers? Certainly nothing to spend on telephones. So they
used what they had and they had some fancy phones in
their day. Every now and again, on empty backstreets
where no one bothers to go—certainly no one who would
recognize some rare art deco artifact from a war lost long
ago—but if you want to look, you can find them there.

On the other end of this phone is another man in another country standing very still and straight. He's not used to being yelled at and does not know how much longer he can maintain his composure. But yes, the monastery runs just as well as it ever did. Certainly the good Padre's presence is sorely missed. They are all praying for his mission and his safe return.

"Good night."

The man places the phone back in its cradle and walks to the taxi. On the front seat is a washcloth. At his feet are pools of dirty rainwater and he dips the cloth in a puddle. His hands are not what they once were and his knuckles still hurt from an unfortunate incident a few weeks back— more than a few weeks by now—and lately he has had trouble with the simple things. He runs the cloth over the interior of the taxi, slowly and methodically, cleaning off the upholstery. It's a newer cab and the trunk comes open with the push of a button hidden in the glove box. A long garment bag lies across the tire boot. There's no place to go so he changes right there in the street, taking off his dirty clothes and throwing them in the trunk. Inside the garment bag are the long robes of the Jesuit. He is now another priest in a city of priests. The trunk closes with a sharp click and the man flattens away any creases his robe may have accrued. When he's finished he makes certain all the doors are locked and closed and the car is shut off.

He stands to his full height, drops the rag into the puddle, and starts to walk away. He gets not forty feet when a thought occurs to him. Soon it will be night, in the distance he can see some of the lights of Rome start to turn on. He walks back to the puddle and picks the rag back up, careful not to let the dirty water drip on his clean clothes. There is no one around and he takes his time fitting his glasses on his nose and double-checking. When he is certain he walks to the front bumper of the car and runs the rag over that, paying careful attention to the left side, another unfortunate incident, one that really couldn't be helped. The smooth metal now bent at an awkward angle, a little dent from earlier this morning.

Glancing at the tires, he makes certain there isn't a lingering piece of cloth or a spot of blood. One can't be too careful. Then the rag goes back into the puddle and he walks back down the street.

Two blocks ahead is a trash dumpster shoved against the side of a building, he opens it and pulls out an old newspaper. He runs the paper over the taxi keys, wiping away any lasting fingerprints and then crumples them up inside the paper and tosses the whole lot to the bin's rear.

Certainly, Padre Isosceles had intended to kill the Nigerian, but not, at least, with a taxi. A debilitating injury perhaps, a broken leg, the drastic need for Iscoceles to get him into the cab, to rush him to the hospital. He would then be another man lost in transit. A short kidnapping, a round of questions. Sure, then he would have killed him, but by then he might have some of the answers he needed. Maybe the four names he got from Angel were wrong, maybe it was one of the other three Jesuits. What does it matter, there's no way to know now.

He rubs at a sore spot in his shoulders, tries to loosen his long neck. There are long days ahead. Such a simple plan. Four small deaths. Maybe a few more answers in the process. Leave Coyote with nowhere to turn, make certain he has to go it the hard way and save Isosceles the trouble. It could still work. Despite the heat of his earlier phone conversation, the men in his charge are good at their jobs. Now, he has a new plan. The gun he will need has already been arranged for and they have found him a new man with whom to visit, another priest, who will help him reach his goal, even if the man doesn't know it yet.

Isosceles runs a reedy finger down the hem of his robe, watches the sky for a moment. A small smile, who knows what the future holds. Perhaps there will be other priests to look forward to meeting. Just too bad he had never practiced running someone over before. He didn't really know the physics of that equation. Something to think about though, could be a useful skill in a holy war.

ANGEL STANDS AT THE DOCK AND watches boxes being unloaded. They're earmarked for a fashion show in Milan, but will never make it. What good would it do them, anyhow? Angel's never met anyone who wanted to wear plastic explosives. He listens to Amo and Luigi impersonate dock men. Voices made from gravel. Then soft again when no one's around to listen. A tall African walks between crates and Angel remembers him from San Francisco. There is a woman too, eyes that last and long hair and twin scars like tomcat scratches on her wrist, but Angel doesn't see her today. Luigi finishes talking to Amo and walks over towards where he stands. Today, he doesn't wear a captain's uniform, rather a roll neck sweater, black cashmere, and a pair of wool trousers. The effect is hearty sea dog and old aristocrat. In the distance, jazz plays on a small radio.

"Today is Chuck Mingus' "Wednesday Night Prayer Meeting," keeps a great time, no? A time all his own," says Luigi by way of greeting.

"*Mingus at Antibes?*" asks Angel.

"Yes, you own a copy?"

"No, my father did, I haven't heard it in a long time."

Luigi raises an eyebrow at that, it seems a very Italian reflex to Angel, but neither say anything.

"Would you'd like a copy?" before Angel answers Luigi shouts something in Italian to the boat and a shout comes back from the boat.

"Antibes," says Luigi, "is a great word, a battlefield of a word. A place to have a war of music. A place to tremble."

All Angel can do is smile.

"I own every live at Antibes recording ever made, play them back to back, a harmony of space."

"Grace?" asks Angel, hearing wrong.

"Ahh," with a smile the size of cherry pie, "you must be Coyote's friend, he too hears his own way, sometimes a better way. Grace is a most interesting place."

Angel glances over at the ship and sees Amo peering into one of the barrels, the African beside him.

"It is not too early for a cigar? We smoke, do the paper work, sit indoors for a moment so later we will remember why we enjoy the sunshine."

Which is fine with Angel because this morning's sunshine doesn't seem to do much more than provide light. He's freezing. His hands are so cold that Luigi has to clip the end of his cigar for him, ends up lending him a pair of Caligari gloves.

"Old gangster gloves, the zoot suiters wore them, big band era, our countries were at war then."

Somehow, there is really no proper way to respond.

They sit in the watchmaster's hut, a sloppy parcel of two-by-fours held together by nails driven at odd angles. Inside they have a pellet stove for heat and a desk that takes up most of the room. On the walls are nautical charts and posters of pinup girls. There is a filing cabinet with documentation and somewhere, Angel supposes, a safe with bribe money. The air a soup of blue smoke. The watchmaster is nowhere to be found—Angel is starting to wonder why he keeps ending up in these scenes, like some choreographed film treatment of his life, where everyone seems to know just when to disappear, just what to say, just what to do.

The crates get loaded into three different cars that leave through three different exits and take three different routes all leading to their flat where Gabrial is busy watching the street for signs of anything at all. Angel does get his copy of *Mingus at Antibes* and a rare couplet of Sarah Vaughan songs hidden at the tape's end. It's a nice gesture and one for which he'll never get to properly thank Luigi.

ISOSCELES WALKS DOWN THE ALLEY
and around one corner and then another. He passes an aimless array of Roman homes, the long wooden doors with their elegant knockers, simple touches for a city of such decadence. He finds the small fence and the small garden and opens the gate with a thin finger lifting the latch. There are plants he doesn't know, many he cannot recognize. A part of the garden is flooded. He sees a row of sundews, recognizing them from botany classes taken long ago. Carnivorous plants with long curling tenacles. The tenacles dotted with hundreds of tiny spines that are actually leaves and at the tip of each leaf a droplet of glue gleaming like nectar. Unsuspecting insects land on the tenacles, meaning to drink, and instead find themselves adhering to the plant. The tenacles then curl inward, trapping the bug in a mean fist. An acidic juice from the plant's glands liquifies the victim, then these glands slurp up the remains. A very famous creature. They were Darwin's favorite plants, which he often referred to as "disguised animals" because their sensitivity to touch exceeded that of any animal he had encountered. Once in a letter to another botanist, Darwin wrote that he cared more for sundews than for the origin of all the species of life on earth.

Isosceles had not know which plant the satchel would be hidden behind and had not known that the garden was meant for such life. He finds it fitting, though, to come to such a place to retrieve the gun he had requested. The stachel sits beneath a shaded iron bench, situated in the garden's northwest corner, with a black cloth draped over it. Invisible to anyone, even if they had been sitting on the bench. He folds the cloth and drops it into his pocket and sets the bag on the bench. Undoing the silver clasp, he sees the bright gleam of a rifle's scope and the separated parts of the gun below. In a side pouch are the bullets. As he turns to leave, satchel in tow, a cranefly lands on a staghorn sundew. Its thin legs are bowed at a painful angle, already struggling to pull free. There is nowhere to go, the tenacles already beginning their bleak curl. Survival of the fittest. Isosceles does not notice and does not stay to watch, another thing that passes him by. He also misses the small image pressed into the moist dirt beneath the bag. It has been slightly disturbed by the movement but is still visible. A complicated dragon held tight by a thousand fingers.

Steven Kotler

A LITTLE WHILE LATER THE PHONE
rings. Gabrial's alone at a small table in the kitchen of the
flat. Angel has gone down to the docks or is on his way
back, but they're being extracareful and there are new
orders and a circuitous route and it takes a good hour to get
home. Coyote is out, Gabrial doesn't know where. Gabrial
himself hasn't done many of the tourist sights this trip,
doesn't actually care for that much history to be that close
to him. The Vatican was bad enough. Instead he's at home
reading, he and Georg Cantor, two men who didn't much
care for Rome.

There's a little radio in the corner, a fat dial and a small
speaker, in an awful mustard color. Last night Coyote rewired
it, ran a thin antennae up a drainpipe, and all morning Gabrial's been listening to a Mediterranean calypso that's pretty
close to the ragamuffin bounce he remembers so well. Wailing songs meant for sailors and smugglers and the hot blue
waters, coming out of Malta or Algeria for all he knows. The
whole deal feels like pirate radio, fine with him, it's always
been outlaw music and he likes it that way.

Every ten minutes or so he gets up and shuffles round
the table with his head down and bobbing and eyes slitted,
the lazy two-step where arms move back and forth in that
fist-punching swing. A miracle he can stay standing, that's
what Sticky used to tell the girls back in Telluride when
Gabrial danced this way. Sticky knew all about it. He came
from West Kingston, more garbage dump than slum, the

meanest place ever. More than once Gabrial's heard Sticky say he just up and walked across the ocean. "From a place like that, how else you think I got here?"

Since arriving in Rome he has started to sense Sticky around, a dim presence, high above and watching, something that loosens the knot in his stomach, something that keeps him angry and focused and able. At these times he tries not to think of Sticky buried in the snow, rather he tries to think of him broken at some subatomic level, spreading out through the world in bits. When talking about Bob Marley, Sticky used to say, the measure of a man is how he's missed.

"He is sorely missed," says Gabrial, speaking above the radio's clatter. Something of a mantra for him these days, a way towards calm. He's never wanted to kill before, not even the women who killed his mother, like he wants to kill Isosceles.

So right now he's not dancing at all, he's looking at the radio, taking a few extra seconds to identify a new sound. Then it comes to him, that high cat's purr belongs to the ringing phone which Coyote has also rewired. It hooks into a small box with eight red lights in a constant flutter. If the lights all lock down and stay lit that means someone has bugged the line and then they have whole speeches prepared. Two nights back Gabrial got everyone real stoned and they sat around the table coming up with a world of lies. His favorite is the minicatapult and the expandable hang glider—land right on top of the secret archives and rappel down the outside walls.

"Good morning." All the lights are still flickering.

"Gabrial," and Christiana's voice rolls and floats, the gentlest thing Gabrial's heard in a month, "how are you, baby?"

"Hello, beautiful," says Gabrial. "Everything bone crazy round here. Never seen so many nuns. They got people over here whose only job is to approve miracles. Need two miracles and a good deed to become a saint. There's a committee."

"Does it pay well?"

"Don't know," says Gabrial. "But be willing to bet you that the bribes are pretty steep."

"Are you still going in?" asks Christiana.

"How you gonna stop a freight train?" Gabrial pauses to light a cigarette. "Tell me something, Christiana."

"Sure."

"How's my friend Johnii?"

"Why don't you ask him yourself." There is a moment or two of shuffle while the phone is being passed.

"Gabrial."

"Johnii Rush, missing you."

There's a catch in Gabrial's voice that Johnii hasn't heard before. "You making it?"

"Tell you what, I'd rather be skiing."

"Why aren't you?"

"Johnii," asks Gabrial, "you still running round the world trying to find the sixty-fifth hexagram of the I Ching?"

"Playing the angles," says Johnii. "Are you still running around the world looking for your skin?"

"You put it that way we both sound like fools."

"Passes the time."

"I was in the Sistine Chapel the other day," says Gabrial. "On the ceiling is the history of Judaica. I mean like twenty-centuries worth of history is painted on a fucking ceiling. Made me sad, but I realized something, with history you either stay on the outside or you get inside and crawl around. It's your choice. This is the first time I ever tried to crawl around."

"Worth dying for?"

"Nobody gave Sticky that choice."

"No, I guess, nobody did."

"You know when I said yes, I mean way back in Colorado, I agreed because I needed something to change. So I got to study a little more about Cantor and I got to teach this kid how to rock climb and I got chased around a bit by a priest and when we're done maybe I'll get to avenge a death."

"You know how I feel about possibility."

"I know how you feel about sixty-five possibilities."

"Sixty-six," says Johnii.

"I guess you like this girl."

"You guess right." Johnii pauses for a moment. "What I hear is this Isosceles isn't just any priest."

"In Jamaica they have a saying about any man who wants to change his life, who wants to break out. They say every man has his enemies and you can't beat them all."

"Beat them all?"

"That's what they say."

"Yeah, but what the hell does it mean?"

"I don't know. I like how it sounds."

"You sleep nights?" asks Johnii. It's one of their old standards and now Johnii's got a catch in his throat.

"You ever know me to sleep nights?"

But Johnii doesn't answer right away and after a pause Gabrial says, "I don't know, that day in the Sistine Chapel I felt something come loose. I can't explain it yet, but I felt like something is finally going to happen."

"Good or bad?"

"Good or bad," Gabrial says flatly.

"Promise me something, Gabrial."

"All right then."

"Promise me that when this is over you'll meet me in Wyoming and we'll climb Devil's Tower one more time and we'll camp up top and get really stoned and laugh all night."

"Just like last time."

"Just like it."

"It's a promise," says Gabrial.

"Christiana needs to speak to you again."

"I'll see you soon, Johnii."

"Yeah, you will."

Gabrial crushes out his cigarette and lights another one while Johnii passes the phone back.

"Hey Gabrial, would you please tell Coyote something for me?"

"Anything."

"Tell him the Russian says he has free passage."

"He know what you're talking about?"

"He'll know," she says. "Also tell him that for what it's worth the Russian apologizes for the bluntness of his action, he may have been a little rash, but he thinks he's got the weight of history on his back."

"He's not the only one."

She doesn't say anything for another moment and then, "I know sweetheart," and she doesn't say anything for another moment, "He also says good luck."

"Tell him thank you," says Gabrial.

"I can't," says Christiana.

"What does that mean?"

"It means I quit."

"You lost me."

"I know Gabrial, I meant to, but please tell Coyote that too and maybe he'll tell you the story sometime."

"All right then."

"Ask him to save me a dance," and then she clicks off.

PADRÉ ISOSCELES TAKES ONE FINAL
look at the heavily sleeping Father Malachi Keally and
shuts the door to his room. There is no one in the corridor
and even if there were his late hours are not exceptional.
The Vatican is a twenty-four-hour-a-day organization, these
men of God never rest.

The information his own network had provided was
exceptional. Keally's bag was in his closet as expected and
inside the bag was a small map of the Vatican's grounds and
marked on the map was a small door—represented by three
lines and three right angles—on the far side of the grounds
where Coyote and Angel and all the rest of them would
emerge if they were going to emerge at all. Isosceles had
taken a series of photographs of the map and the film now
sat in the inside pocket of his trousers, a little secret zip-
pered sector that he had sown for just such purposes.

Beside the film sits a plastic bag, tightly sealed and
wrapped around another bag and in the center of that bag
sits a small cloth smelling of a heady toxin. Something to
make sleep deepen, something he had placed over Keally's
mouth and nose—so fast acting that the man had not
awakened. The toxin moves through the body rapidly, lowering heart rate and respiration and numbing whatever
brain centers govern consciousness. It will pass through the
body in less than two hours and as a nice side effect leaves
behind a mild euphoria in the hours to come. It is a passing

gesture from Isosceles, not wanting to be thought of as a complete monster, and anyway he need Keally alive and available to help a few people through a small door marked on a small map with a tiny X.

JOHNII STOPS AT THE DOOR TO TAKE
off his shoes. He steps inside and sees their suitcases packed, waiting in a neat suture running across the bungalow's floor. In the room's middle Christiana sits in a straight backed chair, cheeks wet in streaks. Tears to remember. Years later, things will continue to remind him. Rain on the window of a restaurant, a frozen stream high in the mountains, a librarian's cough. An endless list.

She looks up at him, standing barefoot and still in the doorway. He wants to collapse at her feet, to weep forever.

"Can we go to Italy?" she says.

He walks to her, pulls her to him.

An angle of sunlight falls towards her hair.

He nods. He would go anywhere she wanted, but he knows, even now, what kind of treasure Italy holds for them. At his waist he feels the weight of the I Ching, but today is not a day for rolling coins or tossing sticks. Today, if it is an oracle he desires, there will be nothing to do but throw bones.

It is only later, after he has found a taxi and loaded their luggage inside, that he will wonder if he could have talked her out of it, could have changed her mind, what that would have meant for them. Still, he's not the type of man to do such things, people are not meant to be pried apart.

That afternoon the heat is like dough. They book a 3:30 flight from Sumatra to Jakarta and then on to Singapore, to Madras, to Damascus, to Italy. A lifetime's worth of adventure crushed within a day. He dislikes this squelch of possibility. He is a point-to-point man. The places in between hold too many things.

Her head rests on his shoulder, she has fallen asleep like this, waiting for their plane with the cheap plastic of the seats sticking to their legs. Outside it has started to rain in sheets. The afternoon monsoon. The time of year. The hanging weight of clouds.

Through the airport windows he can see the ground crew putting on their bright orange slickers, their rain shields and plastic caps. How much these Indonesians liked their uniforms, the sharp creases, the implications. Already puddles turning to moats.

When their flight is called, he considers lifting her sleeping body in his arms and carrying her aboard. How much he would like that. Instead, he kisses her, softly, stopping her breath with his own. She wakes smiling. On the plane he gives her the window seat, already knowing how beautiful these islands are from above.

She has not told Johnii that she'd been to Indonesia before, but before she had arrived at night, in the hot ink of darkness, on a plane without windows. She has not seen the islands from above before, the impossibility of their coastline. The plane is flying into the storm, the rain growing on the wings. A fierce wind pulls at it. An airpocket drops them far from the sky and Johnii looses his breath. The plane moans through the storm. The stewardess has strapped herself into a seat, today they will grow thirsty watching rain.

When the captain announces that they cannot land in Jakarta, that a river has overflowed, a levee broken, the

Steven Kotler

runway turned to sea, Christiana says nothing. They will land in Bali instead, reroute from there. She locks teeth to teeth and waits for the time to pass, no longer looking for the puzzle of coastline, not happy. Johnii watches in her stead. There are two surf breaks just before the Bali airport, they are so close to the runway that they are known as airport right and airport left for the proximity and the way that the waves curl. If you are lucky you can see surfers. But today there is too much rain and Johnii has to look away as they come in for the landing. It is after they have made it to the ground that they are told there are no flights available until the next morning.

"No one would ever choose to stay in Denpasar." Johnii holds her hand and talks lightly.

She smiles at his tone, at the effort he must be making. "It's okay," slipping her arm through his, "there's nothing we can do."

The cab driver cannot believe they want to go to Tanah Lot, it is raining too hard, there will be no sunset, why not try a nice hotel in Nusa Dua.

"Tanah Lot."

The driver says nothing more.

Christiana says nothing about his decision, doesn't ask after it. She sits still in the backseat, the storm having taken something from her. They drive through Kuta and Legian and Seminyak. Civilization begins to fall away. Rice paddies line the windows. The road gets bad. Then there's the long driveway that leads to Tanah Lot. The parking lot is too muddy and the driver stops in the street. They walk a gauntlet of stalls: masks and wood carvings, cloth and clothing, food and drink, bottles of magic sands and anything to scrape a living from thin air. People huddled in corners, out of the rain, drinking tea. Johnii and Christiana walk down a flight of steps and stop halfway.

"Where?" Christiana sees only foam, dark skies and fury.

Johnii points. It is always like this here, Tanah Lot eludes at first, an impossiblity that the eye does not see.

The temple is less than two-hundred yards offshore, built on an tiny atoll. It covers the entire island, extending over every inch of available land, rising some eighty feet from ocean to sky. Its bottom third carved rock, like the entrance to a fearsome labyrinth, a thousand different holes and ledges and twists of gray stone with water rolling back and forth between these fantastic caverns. The middle layer is covered in vegetation. Leaves sprung from stone hollows, leaves like clouds, hovering, with vines hanging long arms into open space, their tips reaching down to the waves. And above this foliage, rising through its center, are the layers of umbrella spires that mark Balinese temples. The stacked thatch crowns climbing into tonight's heavy sky.

"If you did not know it was here," says Christiana, "it would be a hard place to dream up."

They stand in the wind and the rain, watching the temple weather the storm.

"What do you think will happen to Coyote, to the rest of them?" asks Christiana.

"To them or to the church?"

"The church is built to survive, people will not abandon God because his servants were criminals."

"God has a history of pardoning criminals."

"If God makes a play for Coyote, I'm going after him."

Johnii had been watching the rain, but he turns at this,

turns to see how much of this she means. Something else he did not know about her.

"I think they have a chance, but not a very good one." He won't lie to her, even about this.

"And if they fail?"

"Remember, there are a thousand different ways to fail."

"And only one way to succeed."

FATHER MALACHI KEALLY KNEELS

alone in his windowless room, wearing the brown robe of the Franciscan order, an old Bible held in an outstretched arm. The book is thick, bound in frayed leather, an early English translation that his father had given him long ago. It angles across his left hand, his arm quivering under the weight. He has not moved for nearly an hour. His muscles are tearing and he worries that if the pain gets too severe he will not be able to do what he has to do.

Down the hall from him there is a knock at a door, the creak of age, a muffled thump. It does not startle him, still he has had enough. It is something else his father had taught him, that even in punishment there are endings.

The room isn't much more than an eight-by-eight cube, white walls, a hard cot hidden beneath a heavy wool blanket. Dark gray wool. White, empty walls with nothing to show for themselves beside a reedy, metal crucifix. Jesus' head curving down, hanging off his neck, nearly burying the crown of thorns in his own shoulder. It's unpleasant and Malachi likes it for just this reason.

He undoes the sash on his robe and steps out of it. His body is pale and young, he looks to be twenty or twenty-one despite his thirty-five years. He walks to his closet and pulls an old suitcase from the top shelf. Inside the suitcase is a false bottom. Underneath are a pair of black leggings, a long sleeved black shirt and a set of lockpicks in a black leather case held closed with a dark zipper. He had brought the lock-

364   Steven Kotler

picks along merely as souvenirs, never intending to use them. He thinks that after this he will probably not keep them any longer, he thinks after this he'll be all paid up.

Once he's dressed the lockpicks go into a flat pocket at his right hip, the pocket is held shut by two buttons that are separated by two inches of cloth. No matter how he contorts his body these buttons never rub against each other, never accidentally make a sound. He pulls the robe around his clothing, there is something old and familiar in this, a pleasure he has not expected. On the floor by his feet is a small leather satchel, not much bigger than a doctor's bag. He had come back to his room earlier today and it was sitting on the edge of his bed. A gift. He has only opened it once and he cannot believe what is inside, cannot believe what he has been asked to do.

Outside it is midafternoon, but he will not be going outside. Instead, he makes his way through quiet passages in the direction of the library. Malachi has not spent much time in the library, his duties lie elsewhere, but no one questions his presence. There are more books here than he can ever remember seeing.

In a lost room, in a far corner in the library, is a painting of the wife of Lot turned to salt. Behind her is a flattened plane—Sodom or Gomorrah, he does not remember which. Her grieving husband is no longer visible, there are no other figures in the painting, just a chalky form already crumbling in the hard wind and a charred horizon where the wrath of God has fallen. In this part of the library the lights are on timers, they switch on and off by sound. Malachi removes his shoes and checks the room again in his socks. Crouched in a corner, fingering the belt on his robe, he waits for the click and the darkness that follows.

The bag sits at his feet and he crouches beside it to open the latch. It is not the first time in his life he has handled a gun, but he doesn't like it any better this time. There is nothing he can do about that now. The gun goes into his waistband and he turns back to the shelves. They are open on both sides, the pages of the books face each other across the center. Where the volumes should meet an invisible gap exists, it is here that he places the doctor's bag. It is a perfect fit, for a moment he is stunned at the quality of information that someone, somewhere has made available.

He moves the painting from its place and leans it against a bookcase. The wall is smooth and white, he runs his fingers over it, directly behind the spot where Lot's wife once stood. There he finds a disk of plaster that is not plaster at all, some other material, a metal of some kind, painted the same white as the rest of the wall. It slides to the left on its silent hinge. Malachi takes a tiny pen light from his pocket and risks a fast inspection. He had been told that the lock would pose no major problems and he sees now that the Russian had been telling the truth. The buttons on his tights pop open smoothly, there is a satisfaction in knowing he still knows. He chooses his picks in the dark, not even needing to look. He had been a great thief, now he is a priest. Deep inside he knew they would never equal, but that is the way of some lives.

The pick finds its mark, he can feel the tumbler moving in its tiny orbit. He is sweating and his arms ache. There is a burning in his shoulders as he hurries. The tumbler slides again and somewhere a tension is released, don't ask him how he knows this, he couldn't answer anyway, there are some secrets that never translate.

There is a moment now when he goes deep inside himself, where he waits and this too is a trick of the trade. He hopes nobody has added a surprise to this door, a hidden alarm somewhere, perhaps a weapon of some kind meant to do its damage and then rehide itself, in Ireland he had heard stories. One thing is certain whoever build this portal was definitely as clever as any Irishman he had met.

"One, two, three," counting silently, in his head.

But there is nothing. The door opens inward, it does not go all the way to the floor as he suspected, rather, through some marvel of engineering the hatch matches the dimensions of the painting that has hidden it. He fits the painting back on its hook and starts to climb inside, stepping gingerly on the bookshelves.

This is, obviously, not the way to enter.

The shelving creaks under his weight and the noise turns the light back on.

"Shit."

He grabs the door and slides it nearly closed and then he sits very still, trying to hold his breath. There is a line where the light seeps around the edge of the painting and into the chamber. He stares at that until the edges blur, willing it away. He hears a thousand footsteps, conversations. There is no explanation he can offer and in the end one isn't necessary. The timer expires and the lights turn themselves off.

The passageway is some forgotten crawl space built sometime, certainly, but that is not for him to ever know. It goes on for nearly fifty feet before coming to a door. He knows that on the other side of the door is the real secret of the secret archives.

darkness, the twinkling canopy. Angel flat on his back on the roof again. Knees bent and rocking, feet splayed slightly, held at angles to hold himself still on the incline. Beneath him the rough poke of uneven tile, slight cracks from the added weight. A pigeon peeking around in a far corner, eyes twitching, wondering at this new creature come to share such a high perch.

"We should have never taught you to rock climb." Coyote pulls himself from the top of the fire escape over the roof's edge. A small rush of debris rolling down, bouncing over the edge, a long fall. He wears a nice suit, good shoes, a small rose tucked into a lapel. The pigeon disgusted, flying away.

Angel glances over, a small grin, a little more light in his eyes these days. "Nice night for a walk."

Coyote making his way down the slope, unhesitant, stopping only to push back his hat and clear the view. There's no point in asking what Angel's doing up here. He came up once to check the antennae and he's been coming back ever since. Coyote knows he would have found the spot anyway, in his need to fill his days with far things.

In the distance the sound of music, an accordion, the somber whine, the sound of a great extinction. It reminds Angel of another instrument, a song he would like to remember, a woman who found him drunk, who lead him out beneath the stars.

"Did you talk to Christiana?" asks Angel.

"Gabrial did, a few days ago."

"She played her bandoneon for me."

Coyote looks at him strangely, not understanding.

"A long time ago. We met in Montana, that was how I found you in Aspen."

"How?"

"That's what I was wondering, I forgot about it until just now, if I were a betting man I'd say the Russian sent her."

"I'd say you are a betting man."

Angel sits up. "And whatever gave you that impression?"

AT THE AIRPORT, IN DAMASCUS, THEY
have a two-hour layover. Christiana walks to the phone,
her stride quick, unhesitant. The floor dirty beneath her
footfalls, the light caught in bad pockets, trapped in the
angles. She dials a series of numbers and then another
series and wades her way through a circus of clicks and
beeps and pauses until a heavy Russian voice comes on at
the other end.

"Because rules are rules," she says.

"That's never been your code."

"No, I suppose it hasn't, but I miss him anyway."

"How is the future of mankind treating you, my dear?"

"I need you to do something for me," which, thinks Christiana, may be the first favor she has ever asked of anyone.

"You would like me to help Coyote." "Yes," knowing he
would already know.

"I was waiting for your call. I have already done what I
can."

"What does that mean?"

"I will help him get out, I cannot help him get in."

"Why."

"Because those are the rules."

"Because rules are rules."

"I will see what I can do," he says finally.

Christiana runs a hand through her hair. "I am going to
Rome, if you'd like to come claim your dance."

"I would be delighted, though, perhaps, you would consider Greece. It's lovely at this time of year."

"Perhaps afterwards."

"Perhaps. Have you ever seen the Vatican's museums?"

"No, I've never made it."

"Phenomenal collection, around the side, not so many tourists, private entrance, exit."

"God bless," Christiana says.

"Godspeed."

After she hangs up he stands alone, the silence of the dead line, a sound that is somehow close to his soul. The hollow, flat emptiness. He thinks it will be a very long evening indeed and he will have quite a few phone calls to make.

ISOSCELES KNEELS IN THE NIGHT. IT IS cold here on the roof and there is little to see. Around him is Rome—lights, angles—but he's not looking. His head is bowed in supplication, beside him a candle flickers and blows out, the smoke finding its own way skyward, another final plea gone sour. Isosceles is praying and a part of him feels he has been praying his whole life and it's always like this—cold, empty with something thin and hidden right behind him.

But tonight nothing waits behind him, nothing but Brother Anthony Jacari and he doesn't much care for Anthony Jacari—brother or not. Spanish by one lineage or another and Isosceles never had much use for the Spanish, he thinks them lazy and inconsolable and thinks the world might have worked better without them.

Jacari is a thick dog of a man with a hard chin and soft eyes. A man you would never notice until it was too late which is, after all, why Isosceles brought him all the way from Mexico. They have known each other for a long time, he was one of his first converts, if that word is even applicable, and Isosceles has kept him around for a reason and now they're here, together, on this Roman roof, two more pilgrims in a city of pilgrimage.

Isosceles would have rather come alone, that is how Jesus first came to him and this time he would like to get it right. Still, Jacari is fast with a knife and good with a gun and tonight he has both and as Isosceles kneels in silent vigil, Jacari runs the blade against a flat stone, turning the edges sharp and bright.

"You're certain they'll be coming out that door?" asks Brother Jacari.

Isosceles nods, says nothing.

"You're certain about the hallway?"

This time he doesn't even bother to look up.

After all a magician never reveals his secrets. Still, if Coyote makes it out of this church, he knows all about where. Isosceles wonders how Brother Keally is getting along, wonders how he felt after the drugs wore off. He smiles quietly, turning away from Jacari, hiding his teeth. Who would have ever suspected all those extra nights spent studying chemistry would have come in so handy. When this is over Isosceles knows where to look for Keally, knows how his body curls in sleep, knows what to do when the time comes.

Behind him Jacari coughs, Isosceles doesn't turn. He knows that this man has never become used to such long periods of waiting, or at least not yet. Maybe he just needs some more practice. Someplace to lie still for a while. Maybe, when this is over, he'll help Jacari on his way to heaven, right alongside all the others he plans on sending that way in the next day or so. Could be a busy time for those gatekeepers and as for Jesus, well once Isosceles has the Zaviot, then Jesus will just have to reckon with him one way or another.

IT'S AN AIMLESS ROMAN ROAD, A COL-
lection of cobblestones and scrapes that had outlasted ten
centuries of invaders and will probably outlast ten more. It
winds and creaks and doesn't have any of the charm of
other Italian roads, no place you'd ever really want to walk.
There's no one to notice this group of four strangers and
even if they did what would they see? A dark night.
Strangers wearing dark coats and gloves. None smoke. It is
cold enough that their breath fogs white.

Above them, a woman stands at a second-story window
with the drapes pulled back just so. An angle off center.
She has a crook in her finger and an ache when the rains
come from a lifetime of standing at windows and pulling
back drapes. She's an old Jew and Polish and at one time
had a husband who would have fought through three
countries to come back and be by her side. They said he
died on some French battlefield, but really he was a caught
spy and had died in Moscow—in some fucking Kremlin
basement—and she spat it out when she learned the truth.

He had been disguised as a priest and when the Russians
caught him they cabled the Vatican for confirmation and no
one backed him up. They were fighters, the Poles, and she
spent her war in cellars and behind panels. The crawlspaces
and secret rooms had saved her life, but for years, even in a
spring field, she would feel surrounded by walls. It's of little
importance. Just another reminder. The Germans took her

home and the Russians took her family and that is how war works and now she's seventy and will never forget.

Coyote likes her, she's the kind they all tell stories about. She's sad and long-nosed and has probably kept soldiers warm in her bed. The type of woman who holds the hands of the dead. He's glad this is her house and he's glad she was patient with her secret and has waited two decades for the right person to come along.

Coyote wants to ask her if she knows how dangerous this is, but doesn't. If he did she would only tell him that she's an old woman and what would they do to an old woman and he'd have to leave it alone.

When she sees them coming down the street she lights a lantern and walks down a flight of steps and opens the door a crack so they wouldn't have to knock. Then she sets the lantern on a table in the entrance hall and walks inside to sit in her big chair and drink one last port. For twenty years she has been doing the same, a dram of sweet, hot wine before bed—her last port. She has spent twenty years expecting each night to be the end. Some lives you just can't quit.

Italian entrance halls, their cavernous spaces, cold stone, white walls, dust, little else. Sometimes a piece of sculpture. He's used to America, a long tradition of fear of emptiness. He thinks you could make a study of such things, learn a bit about other lands, what it takes for people to feel safe, at home, in charge. That's what he should be doing right now, traipsing around the world taking photos of entrance halls, measuring widths and lengths, writing some coffee table book for obscure scholars—instead of feeling the icy angles, a cold prickle of what will come next.

The light from the lantern wickered and creaked. Coyote busy scouring the floor for the right stone, which is round and flat like all the others with a slight chip in the corner that faces the street. It presses inward and left, in a counterclockwise motion. There is a small click and a door opens into a stone pit not much bigger than a coffin. They take off their heavy overcoats and trade them for other gear. Angel pulls out a stick of greasepaint and wipes some under his eyes. Gabrial follows. This is a joke mainly, something to lighten their mood, a way to help them get there. Amo puts a stripe right down the middle of his face in the half-shadows of the entrance hall, he looks like both sides of a theater mask. Coyote shakes his head.

"Remember to wipe that shit off before you come out into the street." Then he reaches down and shuts the trap door leaving their four coats, two air tanks, and the breathing apparatus.

"I think we make a run for it," he says, eyeing them to see who disagrees. "I'd like to get through this all at once, but if we need to drill or head underwater or anything else I'd rather not push it. If we need the air tanks we'll come back tomorrow."

Angel and Gabrial look at each other. "How many times are you going to tell us this?"

Coyote just smiles at them.

"Do we have time for a cigarette?" asks Amo.

Coyote doesn't even look at his watch, just nods and fishes a pack of Chesterfields out of a waterproof bag in his inside pocket. He offers them around and everyone accepts. They sit watching the red shadows, the smoke pooling.

There's no noise from the street, not that there should be, but Coyote wonders after it. Maybe better to have come during the day, worked their way down the tunnels and waited for night to enter the Vatican. He doesn't mention it because he's already committed and Isosceles is already in Rome, somewhere, doing something, and that fact alone angers him. Leaves him cold in some unspecified way.

They walk into the apartment and through a couple of rooms until they come to a coat closet. There is another trapdoor in the floor of the closet and a space has been cleared around. For now it sits open, blackness moving back and forth like waves. Coyote puts on a headlamp and the others follow. The first passage is a set of steel rungs drilled into an old sewer line.

They try moving quietly, but it's hard. They're cramped

and hot and the headlamps provide too much and not enough light at the same time, like driving down a hilly road at night and over each crest stands a guy with a spotlight. The rungs have a deep, bouncing ring. Bootscrapes. They move down for what could be hours, no more than a hundred yards. The shaft ends in a tunnel, the rungs stopping four feet from the ground.

Angel lands in a splash. The water is three-inches deep, the color of slate. From the maps he knows this tunnel was built by Mussolini, that it goes a thousand feet, then dead-ends. One more thing left unfinished by a war.

They don't make it more than fifty feet. The tunnel is roughly eight-by-eight, square corners, struts running across the ceiling, I-beams dropping to the floor. At the second I-beam sits a stack of boulders. It appears as a wall, but around the bottom the placement is too uneven. Gabrial leans into it, a flat palm pressed against rough rock and feels motion.

They work in silence, forming a line, moving stones from place to place. Angel doesn't think about what's on the other side of the wall, it's nothing and something and at the same time. He understands this now, in a way he hasn't before.

It will be an hour before they clear it, they work the left side, just enough to provide a crawl space.

"And they all went to heaven in a little rowboat," says Gabrial, his hands striking cold air on the hole's other side, feeling a new excitement quiver through his palms.

Angel laughs, but says nothing. The laugh catches Gabrial cold, makes him turn and stare and wonder. He has heard it before, in fact has been hearing it on and off for years now, the same laugh that Sticky used in times of stress, the same laugh that has followed him these last weeks, that keeps him up at night, that makes him feel their task might just be possible.

"Not a bad last line of defense," says Coyote. "If we're running from something we'll know where to look for the hole." He doesn't bother to mention that if they make it through the hole first they'll be able to shoot anything that comes through after them.

The passage beyond is free of debris and intentional blockage. They never do find out what was being hidden behind those stones. The tunnel ends in a small mine shaft, no more than a four-by-four cube of darkness stuck into the back wall of a dank tunnel. Beside the opening hangs an empty birdcage, small metal bars, the door open. As if a long time ago whatever was inside was given one final shot at freedom.

Gabrial steps through the leg loops of a harness while Angel pulls a rope from his pack. It plays out onto the floor in a loose pile of loops. Angel loops a piece of webbing around an I-beam, a carabiner in its center. Gabrial threads a rope end through a figure eight, gets ready to drop into the hole.

"See ya boys," and a wink and the trickle of a light bobbing in a deep blackness. The headlamp has a range of roughly twenty feet and Gabrial sees nothing. Twenty seconds of silence then a cold thump and Gabrial's light is gone.

"You cool?" shouts Coyote.

Nothing.

"Fuck me," whispers Angel.

Amo in the corner, no light, his mouth moving without sound.

In the distance they hear singing, some kind of Slovenian drinking song. Coyote realizes this is an air shaft that, for some unknown reason, connects back into a separate network. A different city. He puts a finger to his lips and understands why Gabrial hasn't answered.

They wait in odd silence. Every twenty seconds or so the singing comes back.

Finally a triple tap comes rattling out of the shaft and the rest of them put on their harnesses. There is a flat click as Coyote locks in and descends.

Angel can't be certain, but it feels like the air shaft drops for half the rope length. A low breeze walks across his chest. At twenty feet there is another opening, smaller than the first and embedded into a far wall. He can catch a short flash as his light wipes across the metal portal. It runs horizontally into the earth, a matted abyss not even good for falling into—the song comes from there. It is in Croatian now, a language Angel can't remember ever hearing and he stops for a few seconds, a shadow hung in space, listening to words he will never know.

Forty feet below Gabrial's light hangs, a horizon unto itself. Angel thuds next to him and sees Coyote already checking the perimeter. Amo arrives in less than a minute. He takes the rope from him and pulls it through the topside carabiner. It falls with a hard slice through the air. They all cover their heads. Then Angel stands in the dark coiling rope.

"This is it," says Coyote, off in a distant corner. He has a faded map quartered in his left hand, his right is high in the air, sighting, counting—hard to tell. Angel finds that if he avoids looking directly at a light he can see a little better. Gray becomes shape, things that once hovered land. He can see that Coyote has found three Roman arches sitting side-by-side and forty feet to their left the earth drops away into a deep channel.

Coyote lies flat on the ground, his head lolling over the channel's edge. When he stands up he walks back towards Angel. Then he walks forty feet to the right. Then he does the whole circuit again. Occasionally he stops and tastes the dirt beneath his feet. Eyes the ceiling. A novelty act.

The archway curves a soft vowel. The stone the color of hard cider, gritty to touch. A dull breeze passes in and out, the breath of some dragon, long slumbering, anxious for return. It has a sharp smell, acrid, like it would eat through flank steak, shoe leather, bone. A tint of cayenne on the tongue.

"If we trust the map the first two arches lead to collapsed storehouses with five hundred years of civilization piled atop. This third one," Coyote points with his forehead, the lamp flashing up and down a patch of stone, "is unaccounted for, my guess is it follows the sewer gulch," a hand flickering towards the moat to the left.

Amo coughs and coughs again. He's had fits ever since the window, like something deep inside him got cut.

"You okay?" asks Angel.

Amo doesn't answer and instead his lighter blinks on and off and suddenly he stands smoking. "Smoke 'em if you got 'em."

"This is the old Roman sewer line, which, give or take a few earthquakes, should end directly beneath the Tower of Winds," says Coyote.

"Archive central," says Angel and they can all feel him smiling in the darkness.

HERE, THERE IS NO LIGHT. AMO stands straight legged, tall, feeling blackness like waves. Coyote, Angel, and Gabrial have already lowered themselves into the sewer trench, he watches as Gabrial slides from place to place, slowly, like there is something inside, some invisible power holding him in its soft hands. For Amo it is like electricity, a connection that flows through him as it flows amidst darkness, and all the while the emptiness inside him rises exponentially.

He is supposed to lower himself into the trench, can already feel the long wind on his face, the presence of old time, stale and hot like fumes. The soles of his feet ache and the stone floor seems to press back, at times trying to throw him. That too the Kabbalah has given him, an understanding of the depth of life, the subtle violence of it all.

Below him Coyote calls up, asks. Amo takes a step forward and tugs on the rope Gabrial has rigged. It's not more than twenty feet but it might be forever.

"Slower, more controlled," Coyote had said, using his hands to indicate he means descending.

Strangely the rope is heavy in Amo's hand, hard to lift. There has been a voice in his head for months now, a voice looking for words, but it will not speak. It is like a radio playing in another room. The noise weighs on him. The rope weighs on him. A deep spell and it carries a weight all its own.

He has always been good under pressure—a long time ago, when the loads got too heavy, he just seemed to shift all the weight around, rearrange it somehow, make it manageable. That was long time ago, he thinks, he's different person now. Then something snaps and he clips and drops and is suddenly standing beside the rest of them not able to remember what it was he felt so afraid of.

It is colder in the trench. They are standing in a small half-circle, lights trained on the distance. Coyote is busy pulling a map from his pocket and finding a flat, dry place to study it.

Gabrial steps closer to Coyote and calls back over his shoulder, "Can you coil the rope?"

Amo turns to find the rope's end and can't seem to, instead runs a hand over cold stone and his light follows. Something snags his foot. The rope rests in a impish pile on the ground, already tugged through. Things are cold and heavy again. He can't remember doing that and now stands very still, flexing his fingers, trying to recall the texture of the rope or the motion of pulling it down.

The aqueduct is made from heavy, square stones hewn at rough angles—bland weight—that forms tunnels much smaller than anything they've come through. Ten feet inside and all four of them are bent slightly, their necks starting to cramp. The air is dry and reedy and tastes like dust. Amo already hears dull thudding, a slow clock drumming in the back of his head.

They are into it now, already wandering through the tunnels. There are few markers and after twenty yards Amo realizes if Coyote's map is wrong they could end up parading beneath the Vatican for a very long time.

NOT LONG, MAYBE TWENTY MINUTES, from the beginning of the sewer line but each step has brought more water. They are moving down rather than up. They have turned their headlamps off to save the batteries and since now there's room, Coyote has lit a lantern. The small flame stains the narrow walls. They trudge down steep corridors, wrists and arms cramping from keeping guarded hands ahead of their faces, ever wary of running into something invisible in the dark. A cool wind rushes across their ankles.

"Hold up a minute," calls Coyote, he kneels down and puts his hand into the current. "Do you feel that?"

"Yeah," answers Angel.

"Stay here."

"I'll go," says Angel. "I'm smaller."

Coyote looks at him for a second, nods, steps away.

Angel turns his headlamp back on and moves forward slowly, watching the ground. It's not that wide of a pit, but it certainly is deep. Angel gets to be unlucky for a change and sets up another repel, careful to tie knots into the ends of his rope. He's only done this a few times, but knows that repelling into darkness should scare the shit out of him. It does everyone else. He feels little fear. Just the same deep curiosity that has always been there for him. Even so there isn't much choice in the matter and what the hell he thinks, how many chances do you really get to be so brave.

He descends one handed, the other hand held in front of him, constantly feeling for the wall. He can see it, certainly, but he's been night-blind before, knows how quickly everything can become deceptive. He drops for fifty feet. The wall's texture is rough and knobby, easy to climb back up if need be, which is the only good news as far as he can tell. At nearly seventy feet he hits the floor, a huge collection of scree piled against the wall's lip.

"Down," he shouts.

"We can barely see you," says Gabrial, seeing no more than a pale glow and the occasional shock of hair.

"Off repel, come down whenever you're ready."

The chamber, neither long nor wide, goes forward for not much more than thirty feet where it leads through a doorway and into a large room. Above, somewhere, hangs an invisible ceiling. The trough they've been slogging through ends in a pipe of sorts, but the pipe is sunk into the ground and completely full of water.

Coyote glances at the pipe then walks around it to lean against the far wall. He lights a cigarette and looks at the others as they walk forward to peer into the water. The pipe's mouth is almost six feet in diameter, some kind of strange stone which, under the new light of their lamps, looks almost white. The water inside is a deep blank sludge, black with the years.

"Show's over folks, nothing to see here," says Coyote dryly.

"Are we really going to dive through that?" asks Angel.

"Open to suggestion," says Coyote.

One by one they set out to explore the room. It's not much more than a twenty-by-thirty cube made of heavy stone. The far wall rises higher than the rest, but even with all four lights and the torch they can't tell. Thirty feet, maybe forty. At a glance the rock looks volcanic, bumpy and cold, but not damp to the touch. Angel is the only one who doesn't move, he stays still, his hand resting on the wall, staring into the pipe.

"That's concrete, isn't it?" asks Angel.

That stops Coyote, he walks very slowly back to where Angel stands. "Goddamn it is," kneeling down to feel the pipe's edge.

"The walls in here are dry," continues Angel.

"So what?" asks Amo.

"So why is this pipe so full of water if the walls around it are completely dry?"

Gabrial walks over and feels the rock, then he starts playing his flashlight along the room's ceiling. Everything is deceptive. His light finds a small crack running the length of the ceiling.

"Coyote, can I borrow your lantern?"

Coyote passes it to Gabrial who plays it along the roof. Upon closer inspection, the roof isn't flat, rather it slopes downward at a slight angle. The far wall, as they earlier thought, rises higher than the one above the pipe's mouth.

"Got good news and I got bad news," says Gabrial.

"Both," says Amo, meaning tell me both, meaning he's spent his whole life on both sides of the story.

"Bad news is if it rains outside and we are determined to stay in this room, we're going to drown."

"How exciting," says Amo.

"Not going to happen," says Coyote.

"How do you figure?" says Gabrial.

"Forty days and forty nights," says Angel. He walks across the room and takes the torch out of Gabrial's hand. "Look at this crack," raising the torch so Gabrial can see, "the rock is pretty rough."

"Volcanic," says Gabrial.

"Yeah, I know, but not if water's been pouring over it for a five hundred years."

"Smoothes out most things," adds Coyote.

Angel points at the far wall. "They were going to run a sewer pipe through here but didn't."

Coyote has stopped checking the blueprints, they're off the map. Wherever they are now is no longer. He thinks about this for a moment, all the preparation and to what avail? It's always been this way with mysticism, where you start and where you end, no matter the nature of the quest ...but he doesn't want to follow this through. Still it was good to see Samuel one last time.

"Probably because the rock was too unstable," continues Angel, "they sunk this into the floor, but stopped there. Probably not more than eight-feet worth of pipe and then it's a dead end. They ran a drainpipe off a main line above us, that's what's dripping into this pipe."

"It's right back here," says Gabrial, pointing to the place where the far wall disappears upward into continual darkness. "I'll bet it runs along the ceiling of this room and in towards the Vatican."

"What?" asks Angel and Amo at the same time.

"Sure," says Coyote. "That makes sense. Water flows down into this room. Not sewage, drainage. The Vatican put in this drainage system, not the city of Rome. They didn't finish it because they didn't have to, they hit this old aqueduct and that took care of the problem."

"And what is the problem?" asks Amo.

"The problem is they had a roomful of rare books sunk beneath the ground and no one's really supposed to know about and they wanted to make certain that if a pipe burst or Hurricane Jesus blew into town they didn't end up with a lot of soggy vellum."

"Which means," says Angel, "that somewhere above us is a pipe that leads into an aqueduct which leads almost directly into the place we want to go."

"And all we have to do is find a way into that pipe, crawl through it, into the aqueduct, through the aqueduct and we come to the entrance tunnels." Coyote has the torch in one hand and one of the maps in the other, trying to shake it open.

"I got the torch," says Angel, taking it from him.

Coyote opens up the map and traces a line across it. Angel and Amo are watching him choose a route while Gabrial scours the ceiling.

"Got it," says Gabrial.

"What?" asks Coyote.

"A way in," pointing upwards. "Here, take a look."

All they can see is a roof of black stone and a few lighter shadows where the light plays off the walls.

"See how the roof angles upward here, it and this far wall form a small chimney. That's why it's so dark up there." He targets his beam to a spot in the darkness. "Do you see how the light flattens out right there, how it spreads around a little more? It's concrete, because they dug a hole there, it's how they placed pipe along the length of this ceiling. Then they sealed the hole up and painted it when they were done. If we blast away at that cement we're going to find a larger drainage pipe."

"Any way one of us will fit in it?" asks Angel.

"Only one way to find out," replies Gabrial. "You shimmy up the wall, blow the hole open, and crawl on in."

"Why him?" asks Amo.

Angel has already started to put on his harness. "Because I'm still the smallest."

"I think you have to follow the crack along the roof," says Gabrial. "And then make your way around the bend and up into that chimney. Build some kind of anchor for yourself above the cement and angle the blast down."

Coyote opens up his bag and takes out four sets of thick headphones. "Before the blast goes off." He holds up one pair. "Unless you'd rather be deaf for the rest of your life." He reaches back into his bag and comes out with a blasting cap, a pencil eraser-sized ball of plastique, and a small plumb trigger linked to two strands of wire, each about ten feet long. "The wires go into the explosive, you get the fuck out the way, push this down, battery hits wires hit explosive goes boom."

"Thanks, I remember," says Angel, putting the things in a small bag that he clips into one of the equipment loops hanging from his harness.

Coyote puts a hand on his shoulder. "Can't blame an old guy for caring."

Angel bends down to step out of his boots and into a pair of sticky soled climbing slippers. He wears his headlamp and has a gear sling running like a bandoleer across his chest. The sling is full of protection. From his harness loops hang a small rock drill, fast-drying industrial strength epoxy, a collection of cloth slings, headphones, a small cloth bag with the plastique and the wiring, a few bolts and anchors, and an assortment of quick draws.

"You might need this," says Gabrial, passing him one end of a rope.

"Thanks."

At first Angel thinks it a simple task, but he's wrong.

"Shit."

"Toe in on your left."

He can't believe Gabrial can see to tell him, can't believe he's hanging upside down nearly twenty-five feet off the deck, can't believe—but why continue, the list is too long anyhow.

"Can you set a piece of protection?"

"The rock's wet," he grunts.

"Try anyway, you need to hang and rest."

His right hand is a balled fist, jammed into the crack above him. His left foot hooks over a rough flake and the toes of his right foot twist into a spot where the crack starts wide and grows narrow and because of this his knee can press into the sloped edge and lock off. It's painful, but it takes enough weight off that he can free his left hand to reach behind and come up with the Camalot. He squeezes the Camalot's trigger, causing its notched wheels to rotate in on themselves, shrinking the whole apparatus. He slides it upward, into the crack, and lets go. The springs pop the notched gears back into place. Angel's strength is starting to drain away. He's frantic as he grabs for the dangling rope. It slips from his fingers once, then he manages to click it through the carabiner attached to the Camalot's end.

"Take!" Meaning take up slack, meaning catch me I'm about to fall, meaning, among other things, I'd rather not die right now. And somehow, it works. Gabrial yanks in the excess rope and the Camalot doesn't slip out of the wet rock and Angel hangs thirty feet above them, shaking with excess adrenaline.

"Can you get another piece in before that one slips," says Gabrial.

"I don't have anything that'll fit."

"Take two of those chock nuts, the ridged ones, and stack them atop each other and wedge those. It'll work."

As Angel does this he notices a glint of metal on the far wall. It's ten feet from where he hangs and slightly higher.

"Got me?" he asks.

"Yeah, why?"

"I want to check something out, I'm gonna go another ten feet and do this again."

"Good to go," says Gabrial.

The crack opens here and Angel finds his rhythm. They can see his light running across the roof, but the roof angles upward, moving vertically, and suddenly his light is gone.

"Angel?"

Gabrial cannot feel his weight at the rope's end, but he's afraid to tug too hard, doesn't want to pull him off.

"Angel?"

"No shit," says Angel, somewhere above them. "They were really serious about this."

"What are you talking about?" asks Amo.

"Why is your light off?" asks Coyote.

"Not off," says Angel and suddenly it's visible again, but not as anything more than a yellow glow in a black space, "just around, the wall twists up here, there's no way to see it from below."

The glint that Angel saw turns out to be an iron rung, the same kind that runs up telephone poles, but it juts out from a depression in the wall so he could only see a corner and from the ground it's all but invisible.

"What are you standing on?" asks Gabrial. "Can you put some protection in, I'm a little nervous down here."

"I'm not standing, I'm sitting."

"What?"

"We were thinking that they were working up, but that's not the case."

"I'm not following you," says Gabrial.

"The sewer ran from the ceiling down, they built downwards. I'm sitting on a small wooden platform that they sat on when they drilled out the roof to shove in the pipe. I don't think we have to worry about blowing a hole in anything, Coyote."

"How's that?"

"Well, what we thought was concrete was actually the opening of the pipe and it seems like there's a ladder running up a length of pipe."

"Big?"

"About the same size as the one sticking out of the floor."

"They were really serious about that," says Coyote.

"You know," says Angel, "I don't know about that, this looks like a lava chute, like we're tunneling through an old cave system or a volcano or something. I think they found the hole already there, chipped it out a bit and dropped a pipe in. The stuff they chipped away was that big pile we landed on after the repel. They saw how high that pit was and realized it would take an incredible flood to fill. End of the line would be my guess."

"Now what?" asks Amo.

"Now I tie this rope off and smoke a cigarette while you guys climb up."

"What are you tying it to?" asks Gabrial.

"These metal rungs."

"Will you back it up with something, I don't know if I trust the rungs all that much."

"Already did it," says Angel.

They climb up one at a time, resting on the platform that Angel found, then moving out onto the iron ladder. The rungs are cold to the touch and covered in a flaky rust that tears at their hands as they climb. They move upwards for nearly a hundred feet and stop on another platform.

"I have no idea what comes next," says Coyote. "I have no idea if the Society knows we're coming and I don't know what they'll do if they do. But I can guarantee you that Isosceles knows we're coming and I'm pretty sure we all know what he's going to do."

They look at each other for a moment, then Coyote adds, "Shoot first, he would."

Amo looks back down into darkness. "Have we really come down this far?"

"No shit," says Coyote, but the laugh's back in his voice, the one that says—good, now that that's over let's go get in some real trouble.

THE TOWER OF WINDS WAS BUILT BY
Pope Gregory XIII in the middle of the fifteenth century
in response to the passage of time and the Council of
Trent. It sits above the Gallery of Geographical Charts, a
long corridor of vivid stylized paintings that show the
topography of Italy complete with dolphin-driving saints,
blue oceans and giddy sea monsters. The Tower seems
more of a temple than an observatory with its heavy stone
and dim, far corridors. All of its walls are covered in pictures, flaked and faded personifications of the seasons, all
taken from Biblical scenes in which wind is blowing, rain
falling: The Red Sea peeled apart; Saint Paul shipwrecked
on Malta; Elias nearly broken by prayer on Mount Carmel;
Christ with hard, flat, raised hands calming a tempestuous
sea; Ezekial seeing whatever it was he saw by the River
Chobar; Moses calling a burning wind; and the lost man
from Ecclesiastes who did nothing at all because the rain
did not come—the man with the unplanted corn and the
untethered oxen, standing gaped mouth and stock-still.

"He that observeth the wind shall not sow; and he that
considereth the clouds shall not reap."

On the ceiling of the Tower's meridian room is an
anemoscope, its angled metal fingers changing directions
along with the wind outside. It is a well-oiled piece of
machinery and never squeaks.

In a painting of the storm raging in the Sea of Galilee
there is a opening in the mouth of the figure representing

Steven Kotler

the south wind; through this opening light comes, pointing in different directions at different times of the year. It marks time on a series of meridians painted across the room's floor. Thin lines to guide our passage. Despite its antiquity, the calendar turns out to be remarkably accurate—erring a little over a second an hour. Twenty-six seconds a day, 9490 seconds a year, one day in 3,323 years. Vanished. Just like evaporation.

Less than fifty years later, when Paul Borghese ordered the centralization of all Vatican records into the collection known as the secret archives, the Tower of Winds became conscripted for that purpose. Hallways full of square wooden boxes, four sides to a box, ten drawers to a side, two small white, well-carved handles per drawer, eighty ways to pull open the history of a god. More words than any one could ever read, not in a lifetime, not even an army or a crusade.

It is also Paul Borghese, in the most secret decree of an already secret rule, who ordered a second edifice constructed beneath the Tower of Winds. A place not to mark time, rather to hold it. A place of abeyance. It was Paul Borghese who began the Society, who left the Society to guard the tower beneath the tower. And it is inside the hidden reaches of this place that Paul ordered all the truly mystical literature of the Vatican stored, including many of the remaining words of Kabbalah. Maybe there was a begrudged respect hidden somewhere in all of this, but more than likely this was just another thing taken from people and hidden for the duration and now none of it would ever do anything for anybody. Just another lost thing that even an omniscient god could not find.

To those few who know of its existence the place is

known only as the Other Tower. It is not a particularly pretty place and the only ornamentation is a single painting copied from the Tower of Winds—the ruined farmer from Ecclesiastes, the one standing very still. The one who learned the hard way.

HERE THERE ARE NO STRAIGHT LINES.
Passages dip and weave. Coyote's got the map and the faith and if either betray them then they'll just be four more bodies buried in a faraway land beneath a big church.

The air is damp and mossy. For nearly an hour they crawl through what must be a run-off pipe with a circumference not much bigger than Coyote's shoulders—but he doesn't seem to mind, he just slides along, as if he's been at this for years.

"Aqueduct?" is all Angel can say, but there's no doubt to his meaning.

"Fuck," says Amo in response. Because if it isn't and they have to go back or get stuck or any of the thousand little things he's been waiting for, well, what then?

They're going on only one headlamp now, trying to conserve batteries and to save each other the gasp of night-blindings, the absolute darkness that follows. More than anything Coyote fears rain, a small miracle is all he asks. They crawl on and on, joints ache, cold, hard to breath, harder to talk, alone in this. Ahead the passages widens and bends. Dropping over a rounded lip into an opening, not much bigger than a bathroom stall, but head high and suddenly all four are standing. In the dull light Gabrial notices Amo has gone to chalk. Pale sweat. Nobody has much to say. Gabrial drinks less, lets Amo hold his waterbottle, one less thing to worry, but it doesn't help. They all watch as he grows more claustrophobic.

By now, even the simple questions, Amo can't answer. He is far away, his eyes damp and blank.

The passage ahead turns out to be a narrow twist, like a slot canyon. The air grows thin and hot. If anything's blocking this passage they're just screwed, would take hours to blast the debris out and even so they'd never live, the only thing still holding these walls up is luck and most of the time luck and small explosions don't go hand in hand.

A hunched walk, back horizontal and head up, like a goose, cramps the neck but it's better than crawling. They've been moving over an upward slope, nobody can really remember for how long, ten feet, a hundred, all their lives.

Gabrial, still in the rear, feels Amo's hand on his chest, signaling a halt. They wait in narrow darkness. Coyote whispers to Angel who whispers to Amo and Amo turns around and leans close and tries to speak but in the end Angel has to duck beneath him and pass the message on himself. "We're moving in the gap between the aqueduct and the Tower, everything gets very steep ahead and the aqueduct branches into hundreds of tunnels that can lead anywhere, we're going in darkness, Coyote doesn't want to risk it, so stay together."

"YOU DO THE HONORS," SAYS COYOTE, stepping out of the way.

Angel walks into the Tower first, wearing the once sharp greasepaint like a bruise. Behind him the others are not much better. Soiled, clothes turning to rags, dirt packed under fingernails, in shoes, matted into hair—Coyote's silvered locks have gone muddy with soot and there's a deep rasp to Amo's voice where the pressure of the tunnels worked through his clothes and his throat and is holding out the air.

Inside is an impossible space, like being in a kettle drum. The hole is a small, stacked stone portal, dull gray and not much bigger than a rabbit hutch. Angel ducks, back bent and head low to wade through. The air smells of must and space, maybe a touch of cardamom. The opening's a trick that makes you stand straight and crane your neck, looking up into the Tower's impossible height. A hundred feet of stone and a reedy light to fill it all. Last light. Some pockets so dark they seem to have been black forever. They are the places to fall through, black holes and lost time and things deep in a different way. Places where the laws of the world don't work so well and others where the laws aren't strong enough to hold a feather still.

The place is hard on sound too, noise spinning off at all angles, odd echoes, points of diffusion, hard on everything by the looks of it. Too much height or stone or maybe there are weird acoustical tricks built into the design, Angel's not sure but it makes him not want to speak.

Maybe because there are no floors to break the space, just a thin metal staircase that leads a long black spiral up an endless wall. The walls are unbelievable. Everywhere are stacks of lore. Crates atop crates and tins and drums and mostly just stuff thrown against the walls like barricades. Two thousand years of lost gods and vanished religions and holy men covered in dust.

The center's just empty space.

"Like a hockey rink," says Coyote.

Angel raises an eyebrow and Coyote says, "We had ice in Texas."

"Jesus," says Gabrial, arriving beside them.

"You said it." Coyote talking and turning and helping Amo through the door. He stretches out a hand and finds Amo's grasp and feels a slight tremor in his flesh. Amo can't even look up at first, stands frozen, twitching, trying to break loose of his claustrophobia. Under his breath, softly, he is praying.

Angel crosses to him, places his hands on his shoulders, feeling soot on cloth, skinny bones beneath.

"You okay?"

Amo looks at him, his eyes unfocused, his hair slick with sweat, head moving slightly: yes or no or no way to be sure. Angel unscrews the top from his water bottle, a rusty squeak, makes Amo drink and breathe and keeps a hand solid on his arm until his breathing steadies.

The only light source a thin tallow candle, sitting in a high candlestick on top of an old wooden table. The table sits amid a raised dais, eighteen feet up and made from some kind of dark wood. A metal ladder is pressed against the platform's far side. Behind the table is a heavy chair, carved wood, delicate and too hard to make out from a distance. A relief carving: elves and fairies or Christ on the cross, it's too dark to see and anyway most of it is obscured by a man chained to the floor and sitting in the chair.

The chain runs from a heavy iron oval at the edge of the dais and is less than eight feet until it becomes a five-inch leg cuff drawn taunt around a rotten leg. The flesh beneath the cuff is all rubbed away and the bone shows through. Above the leg, the man is bent over a book, a long silver pointer in his right hand or what's left of his right hand. One empty eye socket, clean and white and glimmering in a pin of light. The left side of his body seems better preserved than the right, skin hangs in loose flaps, overlapping, like a spread deck of cards.

"What the hell is that?" another tremble in Amo's voice.

"Can't believe it all doesn't come crashing down," whispers Coyote, standing beside him, staring at walls of stolen history. "What the hell is what?" Turning slowly, taking out his gun.

"Son-of-a-bitch."

"Son-of-a-bitch what?" asks Gabrial.

Angel points.

"Son-of-a-bitch."

The floor is endless, a damp sheen that seems to prohibit movement. Coyote takes thirty slow steps then freezes to the spot. Just stands staring. Angel notices a pile of wax lapping the far table leg, the one beneath the candle. As he looks the pile seems to grow, until he realizes the wax has to be two feet in diameter and that the edge of the dais angles outward like a fin.

"That candle could burn for a year," says Angel.

"Probably does."

Coyote takes three more feet of steps and stops and shakes his head as if this is a simple trick of the light and not real or not really here.

"That's the ugliest thing I've ever seen," says Coyote, putting his gun away and walking back towards them. "Now we know what happened to Niko Tabak."

"Jesus," says Angel.

"Some Society," says Coyote.

"Gentleman," says Gabrial, "let's do this."

"Good by me,"says Angel.

"Amo?" asks Coyote, his eyes playing over the walls.

Amo looks around like a man waking after a long sleep. He walks over to the base of the staircase and follows it up with his eyes. He speaks very slowly. "If you can't find dates go to the first backup, look for books in Hebrew. Pay attention to paintings, dates on the back, in corners, beneath signatures." The stairs don't creak as he moves up them. Then he stops midstep and puts on a pair of gloves and speaks as if nothing has happened and he's been fine all along. "Oh yeah, be really careful what you touch, there's some serious shit in here."

Angel watches as Amo moves up to the shadows. He steps off the stairs onto a balcony, must be thin as a balance beam, a tightrope, a razor—Angel can't even see its shadow from down where he stands and the harder he looks the more it seems to bother him.

"Hey man, what's he standing on?" to Gabrial, who maybe doesn't have many of the answers but still takes his side in most things.

"Rain."

"What?"

"It's a Jamaican phrase. It means the only thing left for you to be standing on is the stuff that's already rained down on your head."

climb. In the distance comes the tight buzz of electricity. The stairs are a tight spiral of iron. A hollow ring comes with each step upward. All around them are brick archways like the catacombs of eighteen-century prisons and beneath their broken circles are frights of cobwebs. Insipid. Wrapped around crates of books. Imagine any ten libraries shaken loose of their order and piled haphazardly, something out of the witch trials, book burnings.

"Fucking awful," says Gabrial, feeling the same chill.

No one smokes and there is little more to say. Standing on miniature ledges of metal, two, maybe three feet across and below them the room open wide. They pry open crates black with soot. Words of all languages. Gabrial finds a crate of Arabic scrolls dated zero. The year zero. Imagine, in the juvenescence of that year came Christ the tiger.

"It makes you want to spit," says Gabrial.

Most of the books are holy books. The things we have told one another since the beginning of time, since before year zero, before the tiger, the things that have carried us through the dark nights. Carried all of us. Civilians, slaves, wives, and children, tired soldiers on the last watch, whole tribes left to die in cold mud—a thousand years of failed comfort. Boxes of it. If there's something that they haven't come prepared for, something they didn't think of, it is this kind of terror.

As his eyes adjust, Angel sees how deep the shelves go. Not

all the ledges are as thin as the ones below, higher up some rear backwards for thirty, forty feet. Every last inch filled with stolen words. He doesn't want to touch them yet and moves back to the stairs, rising slowly, watchful as he climbs.

Inside one book, Amo finds pornographic woodcuts from the second century. A nude man tied to a tree and a line of baby sheep before him. Ten robed woman stand and watch, wetting each other's fingers. The picture's border is made out of strange letters, a language, Amo is sure of it, but not one that has ever been spoken. He studies the drawing. Notices one woman standing off to the side who is not giggling, who is not aroused. Her eyes closed to slits and speech on her lips, there is no way to tell how he knows this, but he does. Which god has ordained this scene, he wonders, which has taken it away. The next drawing is blank, smudged from erasure. The third is a couple, he is in her from behind and she is sprawled in a wheelbarrow full of dirt. There is no writing around the border. He flips forward, every fifth picture or so is blank, the rest are more of the same. The woman with the drawn down eyes appears with some frequency, always trying to speak. Amo's shutting the book and turning to another when something catches his attention, makes him stop. A sound behind him, a low whisper.

Angel has climbed high enough, a dim shadow high above the others. It's then that he opens his first book and realizes what each one of them has already learned. There is no order to any of this. Every book he opens is written in Hebrew. He can only open a few thousand an hour, they all know what the Sefer ha-Zaviot might look like, Coyote made them memorize the shapes, draw them on the chalkboard in the living room, hours of it—the whole thing is

worthless. Angel tapes a line across the floor, starts in clockwise from it, moving with the room's giant spiral, just to
have something to do.

How long are they there? Fingers cramp from turning
pages, eyes strain against the bad light. Angel finishes one
bookshelf in an hour. Every sound pauses them. The dust
gets into lungs, the darkness weighs. Gabrial fights to stay
standing straight, his skin has been tingling for over an
hour, he feels a cool wind, but deep inside himself as if
someone has found holes in his skin and plays him like a
flute. He has already come across several hundred pictures
of people flayed alive, their hides hanging in every breeze
of the world: Arctic catabolics, the howl of the Khirgiz
Steppe, Mongolian horsemen in a hard trot, skins tied to
the tails of their horses—creating their own wind. And
any of them might fit him, might be just his size.

Angel notices it first, but it starts almost at his feet. A little
glow appears, a light passing fast through fog. Something
moves in periphery. Angel feels the room fill with silent
birds. They circle and land at his feet. But that's not what's
happening at all.

Amo, fifty feet below and on the other side of the circle
from Angel, feels the motion. A wet hand drawing down
his back. He can't see Gabrial or Coyote, there is a terror in
his stomach making it hard to move. He is sweating again,
feeling a terrible cold inside as his knees buckle. Close to
the floor the smell, the taste of wet leather. The heat of
bile rises in his throat. He tries to stand, but can't. His shirt
catches on something. He struggles anyway, ripping his
shirt half off before finally managing to crawl to the edge

where he pulls a long rope from his pack, ties it to a thin metal pipe welded into the wall, a railing of sorts but long out of use. The rope drops with a hiss.

Coyote stands shivering. He's looking through a thin leather volume. A collection of photographs of every man who has ever tried to kill him. The book is old too, dateless, the photos look like daguerreotypes. None of this is possible. Two men from Natal on the Atlantic coast of Brazil, the one with the green beard from chewing seaweed, the tempest from Paramaribo, the Red Devil himself with an armload of dahlias, just like Coyote met him in Bolivia that time. Men Coyote's never seen, who tried for him in the dark, who found themselves face down in barrels of rain.

He cannot ever remember feeling so afraid.

Amo hears something, a soft song, a cicadas drone—so far away. A thousand things to listen for. He pages through more books, a little hurried now, a little rushed. There are invisible things gathering inside.

Angel stands in absolute darkness. At his feet he feels a great assemblage. Things swoop all around him, but he stands stock-still and tries not to breath. Earlier he had seen a page tear itself from another book and slither across the floor.

The Kabbalists spoke of the hidden God, the other side of the God of religion. They said "in the depth of His nothingness." They would capitalize "His." This is the part of God that is beyond the unknown, it is beyond our ability to perceive, to imagine; this is not the very voice of Creation, but the voice that says, "So what's the big deal, you should see what I can really do."

Coyote throws the book aside, makes for the stairway.

The air presses in on him. He tries staying calm, calls out softly, "How's it going up there?" Climbing the iron rungs lightly, but two at a time, wanting to get to Angel.

"About what you'd expect," says Angel. Coyote sees him standing now, his head is cocked to a side, a slight smile. Coyote sees him and knows exactly what Pena knew that day long ago.

The scroll at Angel's feet grows whole. It arrives in tight sparks, visible from only one angle, but Angel knows its weight, soon he will bend to pick it up, take whatever comes, somehow the responsibility has fallen to him—but fallen from where?

The steps seem to drag out under Coyote's feet, it takes forever. The iron has a different timbre now, higher somehow. Below Amo shouts something, but sound seems to funnel away. Coyote climbs on. Fuck, when this is over he's going back to Greece, going to drink that funny Greek tequila on white beaches and play backgammon with olive-skinned women and fuck you if you're going to try and stop him. He wants warm, salty waters in his future. The Acropolis. Don't touch these dreams, don't even try to reach for them.

Finally, he's standing with Angel. Doesn't appear to be much above them, darkness, a ceiling of sorts. Still, they are far underground, some deep bowel. Above them is the whole of the Catholic Church.

establish. Things happen. Angel bends down to pick up a
book. He feels pages of soft vellum that indent slightly
under the pressure of his fingertips. There's a part of him,
somewhere, falling soft and away, that can't believe he's
finally holding the book, but it feels as if he's always been
holding the book, some distant part of him, something that's
always been there. He thinks he hears Pena's laughter, a
sound he hasn't heard since Baja, since Santa Fe, and this too
fades into some internal night. Above him something moves.
Perhaps a door opens, maybe a figure appears. A cleric, a
guard, an old hag with a wooden basket full of coins.

He sees a way out. Tries to nudge Coyote, point in that
direction. A door, not more than a hundred feet from
where they stand, topping a straight stone stairway, but
Coyote has already seen it and Angel's elbow finds only air.

Do they panic or do they just run? Have they gotten what
they came for? Amo hears thunder, wind and rain, leaps for
the rope. It's too dark. What can you really see? A miracle he
doesn't die. He still has gloves on, a white cotton made for
rare book collectors, made to keep oil and parchment away
from one another. They offer little protection and fifty feet
later they have worn through and his skin burns. Amo flings
them off, the pain makes everything worse. He hears shouting, thinks Gabrial is behind him, Coyote behind Gabrial—
doesn't know what happened to Angel. What can he do? Not
everything has to make sense. This is flight. Books slip

beneath his feet, go skittering across the cold stone, raise a racket. He runs past the table, the terrible empty eyes, the golden pointer caught in bony fingers and a fistful of candle-light. Someone is behind him, how many ways into this place, how many ways out? He spies the hole they crawled through, judging the angle, and dives for it.

He hears someone, maybe Coyote, scream something, instructions—go on or turn back, but there's no time to stop and check when all he's trying to do is get gone. Sweat pinches at his eyes. The tunnel opens two ways before him, he hadn't seen the other on the way in, and all he can do is guess. Behind him the hard slap of heavy feet. His flash-light shows only patches, musty, tea-stained doilies of light.

him, the cold slapping. He runs for miles. He starts to funk, turns round, runs back, but which way. The passages weave into one another, sometimes three or four come together in one junction. Things grow thin and dark, darker.

He stops for a minute, resting against cold stone. The light from his flashlight starting to dim, an impossibility considering he had just put in fresh batteries, had run them through a volt meter himself. They were, after all, supposed to double-check everything. But now, the light comes in gasps and what use is it anyhow, everywhere he looks the tunnels are the same dank and heavy underfoot, heavy in his lungs, full of voices.

Voices—that is what he has been hearing, voices, not footsteps. A sound unlike any other he has ever heard, voices like crashing airplanes, like lost maps. Louder now that he listens.

He walks on, fumbling in the murk, trying to head for the sound. Like walking through pitch, breathing it too. He holds his hands before him, they catch rock, splintered wood, start to bleed. Something wet beneath his feet and a smell like lust and old cabbage. He jams his right forefinger on a hard knob and the hand starts to swell. Stepping round a corner, with the light swung the wrong way, his foot crumples into a hole and he tears his left palm while stopping the fall. The gash runs down the middle, tissue and fat hang in flaps after he wipes away the blood, but the scar, even if he manages to get it stitched up, will obliterate the lines beneath. The pain comes in long washes and he has to stop and sit.

He doesn't know how long he stays still—does he pass out?—his light is gone—or has he gone blind?—there is no way to know. It is quiet for a while, but the lack of sound gets to him, makes it impossible to stay sitting. Every step he takes throws off his balance. He tries to move carefully. Occasionally he hears a voice in the dark. Far-off instructions, can't quite make them out. Madness rushes him from all angles. He takes a corner too quickly and a spike finds his thigh. He hears it break from the wall and grabs his leg and screams. The slow sound of rock cracking. It builds to an echo, it grows louder, even louder than the pain. He rips the spike from his thigh, more flesh tears, still the sound of rock cracking. Then the voices grow louder and panic returns. It is a blind stumbling and he starts to yell and cannot stop. The world fills with tar, turns into a terrible maze, offers nothing and nothing to guide him. He runs into walls, his skin flays, his head is wet with blood and one ear hangs loose after catching a spur. His shoulders rub raw and bone starts to show through. The spike in his thigh caught an artery and something soaks into his shoes. The voices are louder now, no longer around him, but inside him, in his head. They prattle on and on. They talk of the secret worlds of the Kabbalah, of deliverance, of a dead sealer's wife, and a thousand fingers and a dying priest.

And that is how the day ends for Father Yohji Amo, a million voices in his head and a mean blackness that tugs at his flesh, that will not end.

they are not that far underground. Above him he can see an open door and a figure dressed in black standing beside it. The figure whispers something, but Coyote can't quite hear and instead he follows Angel who has already begun moving up the stone steps in that direction.

Angel moves as if he is following a deep plan, something that has been inside, festering, waiting until it is time. Behind him he can hear footsteps and he knows without bothering to look that they are Coyote's. Somewhere there is a shout, something, a muffled, final prayer that will also go unanswered. A hand reaches out to grab him and he sees a young man's face, pale in silhouette, and he feels himself tugged from the last stair into an small rectangle. He thinks for a minute that he's in a tomb.

"Stay here."

His escort disappears back towards the stairway. Where Angel crouches it is pitch black, sticky with must. Sweat drips from his brow. Is it day or night? How long have they been inside? He has no way of knowing any of this and this freezes him for a moment, makes him cold in a way he has never been cold before. He cannot remember ever feeling this lost, a funny thought, considering he has the world's most treasured map clutched in his left hand.

There is the soft click of a door closing then his escort is back and Coyote with him. They stay like that for a moment, three crouched figures in darkness wondering how something like this is possible.

"I do not want to know who you are," the man says, speaking to both of them, "and you will not know who I am. My responsibility is to guide you from point A to point B and along the way we will try not to get killed."

Then he pushes past Angel, his hand almost brushing the Zaviot, but diverted at the last moment, moved by some unseen force from one trajectory to another.

"This way."

But neither of them move.

"We have to wait for the others," says Coyote.

"We have no time to wait and anyway they did not come this way."

"We wait."

No one says anything, then their escort speaks in a softer voice. "Look, I saw one light run into the tunnels below. I do not know how many of you there were, but the others have left by some other exit. I know nothing about what's behind that door. I am not a very wise man, but I know that there are some things I never want to know. The fact of that room is something I plan to forget as soon as this day is over. Your friends have gone another way and I can be of no help to them. Now you can either come with me or I will shoot the two of you right here and right now and maybe in a hundred years they will find your bodies and wonder at another of the desperate mysteries of this place. It is your choice."

THERE IS A LONG TIME WITHOUT TIME.
That is how it feels to them. They came out of an opening in
a wall, they stepped into darkness that became light. A long
room full of books. Angel does not look directly at their
escort, he does him this courtesy. They move quickly from
this room, only stopping to remove a dark bag from a space
between books. As they step from the room Angel glances
behind himself to see a woman turned to salt.

Then there is a procession of rooms, smaller and smaller
versions of themselves, like traveling through a series of
Chinese boxes. They walk on. In the half-light of a storeroom, they stop to catch their breath. Inside the bag are
three Franciscan robes which they slide over their clothing
and tie at their waists with long, tasseled belts. The man
hands them a cloth which he wets from a small bottle of
water. A small bar of soap smelling of tea rose. They wash in
silence, checking each other as mirrors. Through a window
in the storeroom, Angel can see out onto a courtyard.

"Sunset," though no one is really listening. Even in the
pale rutilance of the dusk it has been a long time since he
has seen that much light, that much open space, and it
pulls at him. Somewhere deep in his belly he feels something tugging at him, trying to lift him free. Free from
what, he doesn't know.

Coyote walks towards the window and glances out.
"The Pigna Courtyard," is all he says before they move on.

Angel knows where the Pigna Courtyard is, knows he is

near the northern edge of the world's smallest state and for the first time he realizes how he is going to leave the Vatican.

They walk in public now, not speaking, just moving down long corridors. There are people everywhere. Clerics and clerks and guards, all the inner mechanisms of the Vatican seem to prowl these halls. Coyote has adopted a different walk for this part of the journey. It seems to shrink him, to somehow, make his enormous bulk less visible. Through another window Angel sees a nun kneel to kiss the feet of a statue of St. Peter. There is the smell of incense and the coming night. They come to another doorway and their escort reaches for the knob, opens it, ushering them inside. It is another storeroom of sorts, more of a cleaning closet full of mops and brooms and against the far wall is a stack of old machinery. Angel notices a 1906 Smith-Corona typewriter with its long carriage specially built to accommodate a full sheet of newspaper.

Their escort sets down his bag and takes something black and shiny from his waistband. Coyote glances at the gun and then back at the man, it is the first time he has looked into his eyes.

"This is not for you," the man says as he tosses the gun into the bag and looks up to meet Coyote's gaze.

Coyote nods at him.

He points back at them and says, "Robes."

They undo their belts and slip the robes over their heads. The man takes them, sliding them quickly into his bag, the clasp latching beneath dexterous fingers.

"You go back out that door and down the rest of the hallway, at the end take a left. You will walk out into a courtyard, on the far side of the courtyard is the Vatican's museum entrance. If anyone stops you give them this. It is a letter of welcome for Professor Robert Hastings and for his star graduate student Jon Lacombe. Case Western Reserve University in Cleveland, Ohio. You are Egyptologists and have been visiting the newest wing of the Vatican's museums. Neither of you look the part, but the collection is vast so just look impressed and don't speak any Italian. Good luck. Now go."

"Thank you," says Angel.

Coyote lifts his hands and clasps the shoulders of Brother Malachi Keally. They stay like that for a moment before Coyote leans down to kiss each of his cheeks. It is a quiet act of humanity that will stay with Malachi for the rest of his life. Then Angel and Coyote are gone. Just another mystery this church will have to bear.

SO THIS IS THE VATICAN, THINKS
Christiana. In truth, she has been here before, but then too
she had similar thoughts. What a long time it takes to come
over to play at Peter's house. How many hours did they
spend in the air? She cannot remember landings, takeoffs,
perhaps they are still aloft. The long inch of the cab ride
from airport to Vatican. The pilgrimage of it all. Her life
ticking on. Now, it is getting late.

Again, they stand under black skies, yet another threat
of rain, at the far edge of St. Peter's Square. Already the
streetlamps have been lit, their flaxen glow falling onto
the departing. A priest strolls by, she can see the white of
his collar tickling his neckline. It makes her cold. She finds
herself looking into darkened corners, sifting angles, she
notices Johnii doing the same. Somewhere Isosceles is hidden, is waiting. Does he wait for them too? How much does
he know? Why did she wait so long to come here?

In another moment they too will turn to leave. To walk
to the building's side, to a hole in the wall, to sit and watch
a door in endless vigil. But not yet. For another moment
they'll stand shoulder to shoulder gazing up at the silhouette of Bernini's facade. It is holding them here, this
parade of holy watchmen strung along the lower tier of
the church's roof, not wanting them to leave so soon.

When Mother Elizabeth Bayley Seton, the only native-
born American saint, was canonized the cost was more than
250,000 dollars. Christiana cannot remember what she did,

this woman, to earn her wings. Somewhere, trailing beneath this world of stone, are four men—including Coyote with whom she has spent a good portion of her life. She would not like to live in a world without him. How much has she paid for her miracle? Has she paid enough?

"Upon this rock," she says. Her voice hoarse, charred.

Johnii would like to kiss her now, but doesn't. His lips have dried out, cracked, the dryness brought on by airplanes.

He is looking at her, she can feel the weight of his gaze, but she doesn't turn to him. She lets him see what he can see, this strange man who could forever amaze her.

He is watching her, rather than just looking. Somewhere a sign? The gold whip of her hair. The brush of her trousers and its hint of a curve, a hip, another secret she has kept. He wonders what hexagram this trip would represent, what point of connection and collapse has been passed. There are no photographs to document their passage, but he doesn't think he'll need them this time, doesn't think that whatever happens next is something he could manage to forget.

Christiana lifts her hand in his, looks at it for a moment, this one object made from two, their woven fingers, the light squeezed from their palms. She turns towards him slowly, smiling. It is a smile to topple empires and make no mistake, eventually, they will tumble.

"Well, we've made quite a day of it," she says.

COYOTE MOVES OUT INTO THE HALL-
way ahead of Angel. He sees the door at the end already
open and beyond it the light of the courtyard. For some
reason the hallway is crowded, but not with people who
work here or live here. They are people who lack a certain
intimacy and he doesn't feel a part of them, now that he's
tied to this place. It takes a lot of concentration to move forward, one foot at a time, to stay beside Angel, to try not to
call attention to themselves. He's waiting for everyone to
notice or point, despite the fact that there is nothing to see.
Two hundred feet he thinks, two hundred and a courtyard
and then all of the world to get lost in. For the first time he
thinks about the Zaviot and he thinks maybe he'll spend a
little time alone with it, just another scholar lost in a well
of words and he thinks maybe, if he's careful, there will be
a little more than one world to get lost in.

Because he's thinking this he almost doesn't notice, but a
lifetime of such moments, of long corridors and narrow
margins seems to direct his attention. A man on his left, stepping out of a group of people—tourists he thinks—looking
at a painting he can't quite see. But this man is not looking at
the painting and he's not with the tourists, he's looking right
at Coyote and he's holding a gun in his hand. Coyote sees the
man's eyes, slow, rounded eyes that under other circumstances would never give him away. Then he glances down
and sights the rounded hull of a silencer catching a trail of
light, a slow glimmer as the barrel starts to rise. Coyote starts

to move, to run, to what? For a second it seems as if they're both frozen, as if they're taken out of the play. It has never happened before, this moment of still time, the utter lack of available response. He has availed himself of all possiblities, he had forgotten only one. The barrel angles up a little higher and Coyote stands looking into the final dark eye, waiting for it to blink away his life.

But just then another man steps up to the first. Coyote doesn't see his face, the other man is wearing a Stetson, a size or so too big for him, and the brim shields his face. But then the man raises a hand to the other's neck and Coyote can see his profile and he realizes that this man in the Stetson is the Russian. On his third finger is a garish silver ring, a dragon of some kind, and out of the end of the dragon's tail hovers a small needle. The Russian's hand smacks into the man's neck finding a soft vein, a point of entry. Brother Jacari drops the gun and turns at the jolt, the last thing he feels in his life is the cold, stone floor of the Vatican rise up to meet him.

The Russian dissolves back inside the crowd and when a woman feels the heavy thud of the man dropping onto her leg, when she starts and gasps and the crowd looks away from the painting and onto the ground, the Russian is already on the other side of the group, taking the hat from his head, moping away a trickle of sweat that has formed there.

The Russian used a microtoxin of sorts, something taken from the jungles of Belize. On the exterior it does little more than bring a heavy froth to the mouth and a few pale shudders, but inside organs clog and misfire as if they are all simultaneously working backwards. The heart stops and the stomach jumps in on itself, tearing intestines apart and forcing bile into the lungs and the throat. Something happens to the lungs, but he cannot remember what. It is used to hunt large animals, usually bear, though the Russian has heard stories of African blowhunters felling elephants with its spark.

The Russian walks up to Coyote and says nothing, he simply passes the hat to him. Angel stays quiet, he's not certain what has happened and is waiting to follow Coyote's lead. Coyote doesn't react at first, as if something inside has suddenly turned off and he's looking for it, the switch, the way back to himself. When he doesn't move the Russian reaches out and places the Stetson on his head. All Angel can think is it's a good hat and a good fit and this makes him smile.

"You're the Society," Coyote says, "since the beginning," everything falling into place for him. "That's why..."

But the Russian cuts him off, putting a hand on his shoulder. "At your service."

"What about Isosceles?" asks Angel.

"I have called a friend. I believe that is one priest who will cause you no more problems."

Then he walks away and the last thing Angel and Coyote see of him is his heavy step walking the opposite direction of the way they are going. As he reaches a bend in the hallway, at a place where the light is not so good, where the weight of the Vatican seems to fill in and darken, a pair of Swiss guards move from the shadows. Angel can see them in silhouette. The sheen of their long halberds now gone. The yellow and black striping of their tights, their white frilled collars and great black coats dampened. They take their place on either side of the Russian and together they walk around a corner and out of sight.

SLOW DRUNK WANDERS THE ROMAN
backstreets at night. It's not the city of God he expected. But there's so little he expected. He never expected the crowbar in the Memphis alley, or the Baptists making off with his truck, or the drunken mess that followed.

In the truck stops along Route 70 they'll talk of an astounding Senegalese courtesan who lured Slow Drunk toward languid Maltese days. Later there will be new tales to add. How Slow Drunk smuggled her into Italy disguised as a farmer's wife. The possiblity he wore a straw hat and chewed long blades of grass through customs. How she left him in a large mansion on a large hill in the wide expanse of the Umbria countryside. How it is possibile that Slow Drunk spent a few nights drinking under the same roof as the fabled Thousand Fingers.

It is the stuff of legend. Thousand Fingers should be dead by now: bombed by his own people in Moscow; gunned down by an errant CIA operative in Salvador; then lost in a bad storm off the coast of Haiti, seen in Katmandu, Lombok, Uganda—but then these are only the heights of the rumors. Certainly they are both in Rome at the tail end of that long summer. Thousand Fingers is still dashing in a dark-eyed fedora way, steeled against fear, certain of his patter, never dogmatic, not worn or bitter. He carries a cane and dances in patent leather like Fred Astaire, but not as often anymore, no longer able to frequent the bistros and clubs he so enjoyed as a youth. These days, instead, he spends long evenings under old roofs drinking slowly, always preferring to be thought of as a craftsman.

"A vapor, a kiss—the end of a man can come in so many ways," he says. It is Thousand Fingers who teaches us that poison is only an adjective.

If he does meet Slow Drunk it is likely in one of his safe houses in the Italian countryside. Simple and elegant, styled to his taste. Women drinking champagne with slivers of fresh peach, long verandahs, soft tangos. If they speak—well, perhaps music, both are Delta men. And if Slow Drunk asks after his profession or his past he will be treated with kindness and Thousand Fingers will simply say, "Hers is the face I see when a certain night rolls in."

It is a difficult time for Thousand Fingers, though he hides it well. He has completed one final assignment as a favor to a friend. The very thing that once earned him his reputation. A severe poison, rare and hard to control, its origin deep inside Sufi mystery. A particular form of Islamic vengeance not seen on this planet for nearly a thousand years, more potion than poison, which causes the hands of the victim to sever at the fingers, for the joints to pull apart and the digits to take flight. Not a pleasant death and reserved for the most horrific of crimes.

The story goes that he learned the art from a book stolen from the Vatican collection, a rare occurance and another thing for people to wonder after. Certainly, he is the only man alive who knows such tricks.

As a point of pride he works by touch and sight and sense, decrying the use of beakers and measuring cups, preferring the odors of a task. But these days he feels a damp arthritis, his own hands grown inexact with age. A dimness to his vision and his memory of scents not what it once was. He fears that his measurements have been off, that he has failed for the first time in his life, failed in this one last task.

Or perhaps these are only rumors, perhaps it was nothing more than fate that leads Slow Drunk. He is alone now, drunk and reeling down old cobblestone alleys. There's a store up ahead, an old antique shop, and he pauses to look through the window at the shelves mossy with junk.

"Hello Buddha."

He's staring at an inch-and-a-half high statue of a laughing, fat man, the same statue that has ridden on his dashboard for years, the one Gabrial liked, the one that got stolen in Memphis.

He takes a few tentative steps forward, but since he's leaning on the window mostly he just shuffles his feet and coughs. There's still a bump on the back of his head where the crowbar caught him. It's been a while since he saw his little Buddah. He wants to sing but decides to save it for later.

"Want some whiskey?" talking to the statue.

He yanks a bottle out of his pocket, he's too drunk, moving too fast.

The window is old and fragile and the bottle goes right through it. Angles of glass fall at his feet. He's cut his hand but not badly and doesn't notice. He grabs the Buddah, putting the statue and the bourbon into the same pocket. They clank as he moves. It's hard to run on these streets, it's night and the cobblestones are uneven and how much has he had to drink anyway.

He finds what he's looking for six blocks away. The fire escape is old iron, black with years, it's retractable and squeaks as he drags the ladder upward after him and ties it off with rusty chain. On the roof, he spills a mouthful of bourbon over his shoulder for luck, puts the Buddha at his feet, and starts to sing. The songs just come to him, he's too tired to really think much about them. Factory songs and old blues and even a few of the choir's gospel numbers.

He's at it all night. Inspired. Dawn comes late. During the hot noonday sun he lies down on his back, watching the sky, still singing. Around 4:00 he stands up again. Neighbors, from nearby roofs, see him and wonder. Nobody really wants to get involved. Near sunset a policeman arrives. In the distance he can see the rooftop of the Vatican. From that direction, he hears gunshots, feels sadness. He sings softly now, his words floating on a wind hot with the weight of the dead. Not that this is unexpected, even Slow Drunk knows that if the beginning was the word the ending can be had for a song.

ALL AROUND HIM STRETCH THE QUIET,
long days of summer. The Romans are on holiday abroad
or frolicking through the noble countryside. A rough wind
has crept off the sea earlier in the day and stayed. Dust
sneaks around the cobblestone streets like some ghost
army. From the window, Isosceles can see the Porta Sant'
Anna and across the street, behind a patch of trees, an old
apartment building—he may not know which way they
went in, but he certainly knows how they'll come out.

The rifle is heavy against his shoulder. A small shelf
runs beneath the window and he puts the gun down, picks it
back up, puts it down. He munches on bread, small bites,
not much saliva left in his mouth. He went to three stores to
get this loaf. A city ordinance only allows bakeries to shut
down one day at a time during August. Most of the other
shops are closed. A traveling song runs through his head, an
old tune and one he hasn't heard since Brazil. There is very
little chorus or if there is then it has words he's forgotten.
Mostly it is a listing of places to go, places not tied to land,
places alone in their history, mostly better places.

Someone has been in the bell tower before him, left
behind a cheap Virgin Mary candle and scrawled "Not
Even Wrong" onto the wall. It's familiar to Isosceles, one of
the lines that gave Wolfgang Pauli his infamous reputation. It's what he said about errant scientists, that they're so
far off track that they're not even wrong.

A street sweeper strolls by. Isosceles raises his fingers to his hair and brushes it off his face with the slow grace of an old man long used to a gesture. The sweeper nods, thinking him a Vatican official. After he passes, Isosceles yanks the rifle from the shelf.

Below and not even a hundred yards away, there is a soft, velvet change in the light. This is how the future reaches us, a door opens, a light goes on, off, this is how men go to war and dynasties fall.

Isosceles wishes there were time for one final conversation, but that is only the dream of an old man. The day slows. A dusty boot punches out from the door. Two men walk into the street. Their faces are shadowed by the twilight and the angle of the sun and the very way they move through these final moments of the day. Isosceles raises the rifle. He can't tell who is who, it's a trick of the light, this distortion. It doesn't really matter.

Angel still has the Zaviot in his hand, but not as something he is holding, rather as something that is a part of him, that moves when he moves, that he can't even remember having to hold on to. He wonders why Coyote hasn't looked at it, as if it no longer interests him, but maybe there will be time for that later.

A cool breeze dips down the street, the first one of the day. Coyote takes the Stetson from his head, twirls it on his fingers, feeling wind for his last second in time. He's been thinking of the Alamo, where he once spent a West Texas rainstorm drinking Tequila Sunrises under the leaky thatch of a makeshift porch with a brush pilot's daughter. Also where Crockett and Bowie made their infamous last stand. Lately though, and he hasn't told anyone, Crockett's taken to whispering things to him, like right now, as he passes through the doorway—"Amigo"—that slow Tennessee drawl—"Remember the Alamo."

Isosceles sights and fires. The bullet hits Coyote in the mouth. He leaves the ground for a moment, his feet kicking out and forward and his hat lighting off his head and into the air where, somehow, he sees Angel's arm slip out to catch it. His front teeth shatter with the impact and a red mist flies from his mouth, then the back of his neck explodes, the brain stem severed from the spinal chord, and it was a great shot, not that Isosceles is that good of a marksman, but sometimes all the angles fall together into a single motion.

Coyote isn't really certain why he's suddenly falling. He's not sure, but it's a nice day and the air smells of olives, dust, the faint trance of good perfume. A girl sits atop a high brick wall. She's twirling a coonskin cap on an index finger. The wall runs around the Vatican and it's a strange place for a girl to be sitting, but he doesn't think of that now. For a moment he thinks he's heard a gunshot, Crockett whispering something—what—and then Coyote hears nothing at all.

JACK CRAWFORD NEVER DID FIND HIS end in a gunfight. It wasn't a question of bravery. He won a few hands of poker and left his hotel room and forgot to lock the door. Came home a little drunk and didn't notice. He died in his sleep, a queen of spades beneath his pillow. His sister failed to regain her sight. There are some angles that never get played out.

Steven Kotler

ISOSCELES NOW HUDDLES FROM THE new winds in the cramp of this stale church, his elbows, bent and raw despite his cossack's cloak, driven down into window frame brick, a deep ache in his shoulders and a strange taste round the corners of his mouth.

An elegant shot, his first one, and enough so that it caught him, held him for a second, watching the whole arc, the end of a man. He almost shakes his head in awe, but he has his purpose and there isn't much else to do but draw a bead on Angel. A soft tick forms at the edge of his left eye and he takes just a second to blink it away. The sky goes hard. Isosceles doesn't see this because he's still looking through the narrow tunnel of the sniper's scope, waiting for the right angle, waiting a moment for Angel to turn, to offer. Above him roars the driven darkness. A dragnet of havoc, but Isosceles sees only shadows fall and feels darkness.

The rifle grows suddenly hot in his hands and the joints of his knuckles stiffen, locking into place. The heat is sharp and intense. Smoke eases from his flesh and his fingerprints blister away. He doesn't notice that the sky has opened slightly and through the hole passes a pillar of light, not the golden sprawl you would expect, rather pale and silver, breaking through the broil of clouds, a thin finger reaching down to the earth.

At the moment the light reaches Angel, he is standing with Coyote's hat in his left hand and the scroll in his right, half-turned, looking at his friend. With his head cocked that way there's a bit of gunmetal grease visible on his collarbone and a slight, tender turn to his lips.

The exact instant Angel starts to rise, Isosceles feels a strange, hard pulling at the end of his arms and all ten of his fingers fly off simultaneously. In the moment before the pain comes, he falls backwards from the window, his head bouncing against the shock of a stone floor and the last thing Isosceles sees is Angel, the Sefer ha-Zaviot pressed between his palms, far away and high above, passing through a hole in the clouds, dragging a tail of silver light.

SHE IS AN OLD WOMAN ON AN OLD
street. Madame de Bruzini, but no one called her that beside
her husband and he has been dead for years. She is simply
the rose woman and these are simply her streets. For nearly
twenty years she has walked alone, carrying her bucket of
flowers, making a living off lovers and tourists and the pity
people always felt for an old woman with an old burden.

At the far end of the street she can see people gathering,
crossing themselves, she can see the body of a man lying dead
in the street. The angle of his fall. She has seen death before,
but doesn't like it any better for that and she looks away.

At the other end of the street she turns to see a young
woman, a rush of cornsilk hair, and a man beside her. It
takes her eyes a moment to see them clearly. It has been
quite a while since she has seen people running that fast.
Their feet lift and hover and their footfalls have hushed the
street. Then the young woman sees the body, the trail of
blood and gravity seems to shift for her. Her feet come out
from under her, but she is moving too fast. She begins to
crumble in midair. And somewhere, in the moments
between the beginning of her collapse and the rise of the
earth to meet her, Madam de Bruzini finds herself in the
eyes of that girl. She too knows that look and her heart
aches for the woman, but the only thing Madame can think
is how young she is, this fallen woman, but they always are,
the ones that another's death can still bring to their knees.

"There was a boy with him," says a voice behind her. It

makes her think of another boy in a bar a few nights ago, the one who gave away her rose to a stranger at the bar. But that was a long time ago and already she has another night ahead of her. This is one tragedy she can no longer stand to bear.

As she starts to take her leave she hears what they are saying about that boy, but she doesn't believe it. This is Rome, there is always such talk. Here, everyone wants to believe in miracles. She looks up the street again before turning to go. The dark-skinned man is gone, somewhere, but the woman is still there. She has fallen to her knees, the cloth of her trousers ripping and a little more blood drops onto these cobblestones. Behind her a line of cars has appeared. The early rush hour traffic caught too. But she does not notice them, her head is pressed between her hands and her face invisible. Just the slump of golden hair caught in the glow of headlights. Even the cars are all quiet. No shouts or horns, no radio plays through an open window. For a few moments the world has been stopped by a woman's tears. Now, there is only silence.

peace. It will come to her late in the day, alone and unarmed.
Earlier, she had tried the Russian, wondering, but he was
nowhere and his number is disconnected and the other
channels have shut down and that's never happened before.

The afternoon has grown long. The light here stretches
for uninterrupted miles. It is not quite a haze and not quite
golden. Some middle term, a compromise of sorts and one
that Christiana has no name for.

She has come back to the islands, has come far away. It is
one of the smaller ones in the Indonesian archipelago, the
map name and what the locals call the place are two different things. She will never again want to visit Italy. It is
another place now closed to her. Johnii is off surfing and she
sits sharing a park bench and a bottle of wine with a pair of
old women. Their faces are rubbery, dark, stretched by an
enemy that has long since rubbed their bones to sand. They
sip wine and giggle. Christiana wears an old Stetson on a
string. It is too big for her head and it rests halfway down
her back. She is careful as she sits, not wanting to damage it.
On the inside of the brim in an old script is the signature of
Davy Crockett, she wonders about this, but then leaves it
alone. Her taste for mystery has faded slightly now. Inside
her pocket is a felt tip marker and she takes out the marker,
holding its cap in her teeth. She pushes its point into the
hat's fabric, feels the ink start to catch and stain. With a slow

motion, just below Crockett's name she adds four others, a lifetime of connections on the inside of an old hat. She waits a moment for the ink to dry then puts the hat on her head. It hangs low, nearly covering her eyes and the women giggle at this too.

She fixes on Coyote's memory, on Angel and Gabrial and Amo who she never really did meet. Another thing she'll be left lacking. Strange how such things: the death of a friend, a boy risen through a veil of clouds, a lost book—how quickly the true mysteries of life pass on through.

The Society will go on, she knows this too, without her. Someday there might be a final reckoning, but it's no longer her concern, there are others better qualified to pass that judgment.

These days there's a song in her head, a few words that she hums aloud—"and they all went to heaven in a little row-boat"—words she likes more now than ever before, and if it's a summary you're looking for well that's there also, another thing caught in the final lines of this forgotten lullabye.

Inside her bag is Johnii's copy of the I Ching, it's gone on too long and though he can't do it himself he's asked Christiana to dispose of it for him. How much of a decision was it? Perhaps they have had enough of other people's magic for a while and they're willing to try for a little of their own. She wants to make a present of it to her new friends, but they won't take it and give it back quickly. The books weighs heavy in her hand and she slips it back into her bag knowing that later, around sunset, she'll find a high cliff and drop it into the ocean. She knows there is no one around who would want it, but it is why they came, here people have no use for such things.

The day moves on and the women drink more wine. They have never seen blond hair before and Christiana borrows a boot knife from a passing horseman to cut a few strands for them. This is one gift they will accept. There's been a birth in one of the villages just south of here. The child came with the dawning of a new star and astrology has a strong hold on these people. The strands are wrapped about a piece of driftwood, tied at the end with a luxurious knot, they will bring it to the new mother as a blessing.

GABRIAL DOESN'T REMEMBER START-
ing to run, but somewhere did. It has grown quiet. How
long has he been lost down here? Days—weeks, anything
is possible in this fog.

He pauses in a shadow, another in a series of points where
he's come to dwell. This is no place familiar. He misses Amo
and Coyote and Angel, strange that this thought finds him
here. Where are they? He keeps expecting to find them
emerging from behind whatever door he opens next, whatever lost corridor he tumbles through. What would a man
give for a little companionship, for something other than his
old, cold skin to wrap around himself.

Maybe this is what his father meant after all, but he
doesn't pause to follow this thought home. Instead, he
turns and goes on.

Here the tunnels narrow as he passes, turning slightly
upward in their slant. Corridors leading to more corridors,
an endless chambering that seems to spiral in on itself.
Sound falls away in pasty thuds. Walking on, Gabrial trav-
els through doors locked to men for a thousand years. Certainly he has had help, but none in a form most would like
to receive. Hands risen from a historic wait have come to
open locks, to brush cobwebs from secreted passages, to
allow entrance.

He passes through a door and up a short ladder atop
which waits an open hatch. His eyes have gone cloudy, his

Steven Kotler

sight failing. Somehow he has ended up inside the Sistine Chapel, pulling up short beneath Michelangelo's sprawl.

Inside, the light is dim. Today there are no tourists and no one to offer guidance. The priests are busy with other tasks and the chapel is empty. Gabrial brushes back a wet clump of hair. His knee is scraped and bloodied but he doesn't notice. A line of sweat stains his collar and his eyes take a while to focus. He hears a distant rain. The room is longer than he thought, shadowed in the corners and unnatural. What was once empty space is now full. Wooden benches are lined up, ten to a side, with small Bibles strung along them like popcorn lights. It's an odd sight since this room is seldom used for prayer.

His mother waits in the third pew. Directly above her is the Sacrifice of Noah, but she doesn't look. She appears haggard, longer than the years that have passed and no better for the journey. There is a chamomile shawl about her shoulders that draws tight at the throat. A pool of tears wait around her feet. She takes no breath.

A short flash occurs, near the point where Adam's fingers reach towards God's. Gabrial waits for a choir of angels, but gets none. Instead the light grows. A yawning spark that threatens to consume the entire fresco. Strangely, the fire seems to hover, not on the ceiling but not far below. It turns in slow circles like a burst, rusted carousal. Gabrial rushes towards the door, but the door too has vanished, leaving only a grayed wall, full of cracks and creaks, as if it has stood solid for more years than time itself. Somewhere above he hears a familiar laughter and he turns his eyes upward, look straight ahead and unafraid. He finds Sticky in the second row, his arms around Gabrial's grandparents, people he's never met, but still knows their location within his geneology. Then the room starts to rise, somehow unhinged and finally free of the earth. His eyes burn. Other voices occur in pockets, saying nothing or nothing in any language Gabrial has ever heard.

The last thing he sees, before his sight leaves him completely, is Sticky's eyes finding his. Then he stands alone, barren and blind, with little left to hope for while the room fills with generations of ancestors. He is the end of a long line, the final point in a small history. Above him floats a wall of bodies risen from fire, a tribunal of sorts, come to claim the last one among them. Slowly his sight returns, but doesn't return. His eyes have given way to another form, a view coming from somewhere deeper inside him. He tilts back his head, a portion of the fresco is still visible, darker now, and beneath that rows of floating bodies. Few are people he recognizes. He can feel his father's gaze upon him, but cannot pinpoint his shade. There is nothing he can do. He asks what they want but they say they want nothing more than his company and say it with such a laugh that he knows them as liars or gamesman at play in some primitive sport that he is not privileged to join. Soon it will be over.

Somewhere below is the Vatican, lives continuing, people he has never met, who he will never meet, the whole of existence as he had known it. Fire descends towards him, licking at his already torn clothing, picking off the soot of ancient books and tunnels and the whole of the labyrinth. The chatter above abates. Time funnels away. Occasionally a strong voice can be heard laughing, but the sound is quickly muffled.

Then Gabrial too laughs, a throaty chuckle and one that Johnii hears. So many miles away, on a small wave at the edge of a far country, just a lone man on a surfboard riding with the ocean. It finds Johnii at the day's end, a lost little chuckle carried on a wind all its own. Johnii knows it as a final goodbye, warming him against the waning light and a cool northern current, and raises a lone hand in return, held high above him, a small gesture in a big ocean.

Gabrial now sits in the row across the aisle from his mother. She makes sounds as if giving birth, but her loins have grown too frail and her limbs turn to mist with the effort. The pew has widened as if some invisible hand has inserted extra inches where before there were none. Prayer stools have vanished. The air smells of hazelnut and black-berry. An auburn glow now extends from Gabrial's feet and his legs, as if made of wax, have begun to melt. It happens without ceremony, just a quiet ending among his family and a great secret he will never understand. Strangely, there is little pain.

Gabrial picks up a prayer book and begins to read. The words are all Latin, not a language he knows. The passage comes from Ecclesiastes and speaks to the passing of gen-erations and the ends of people and the triumph of the earth—but the words are lost in a place where languages go after they have fallen from the common tongue and into the mouths of magicians.

ACKNOWLEDGMENTS

SANTA FE. ELIZABETH STOVER CAME TO VISIT and didn't quite leave on time and I was still young enough to not know of this book. We were still there when Howard Shack and Frank Miller put up posters reading "Our friends moved to Santa Fe, they're very lonely, please write to them." We spent a summer in a rain of odd words. They are all the best of people.

JERUSALEM. Another thing given to me by my parents. There are so many I could never make a list. I remember all of us laughing really hard, but I don't remember the moment the Wailing Wall began to put on weight.

BAJA. I didn't get there until after Howard Shack and Chris Marchetti taught me to surf, but before Chris died. At least that's how I remember it, though I'm still not certain. Time works a little differently on both sides of his passage.

ASPEN. Where I couldn't stop reading *Gravity's Rainbow* and didn't really make too many other friends. Chad Grochowski had lived in Colorado a while back and somehow that made it better. He was one of those guys who was there at the beginning of this book and there at the end and if our luck holds we might make it all the way through the next round.

SAN FRANCISCO. It was here that Tom Waits showed up and it is here I have to thank him for the "Gun Street Girl" and the "little row boat" and anything else I stole. I lived for a while in a room the size of a Volkswagen microbus and had to climb over my bed to get to my desk. It was John Eric Otter who kept me sane and laughing and pointed out the clock on the funeral home sign. It was Sheerly Avni who pointed out so much else. Sheerly never officially lived here, she just kept coming into town to help me sift through words. Like everyone else, but a lot more, the book would never have happened without her.

ROME. The best place in the world to lie on your back and stare at the sky, especially if you're indoors. I wish Rebecca Green had been with me, we would have laughed a lot, but then again, most places I go I wish for Rebecca.

INDONESIA. Which tried to kill me eleven different ways and was still nothing but grace. I would have never gone unless Miguel Postin had told me so many stories. It's one of his great gifts.

There are a few people who are off the map, but were still wonderful: John Barth was the first person who told me not to give up or give in and whose idea became an ending. Without the brilliance of my agent, Mary Evans, none of this would have been possible. She's a woman of implausible tenacity and fierce loyalty and there's no way to ever thank her enough. Kathy Acker, Chelsea Bacon, Steve Brodsky, Francis Chie, Jon Halpern, Rob Hill, Jim Jack, Daniel Kamionkowski, Joshua Lauber, Liz Olden, Jason Reiff, Lisa Rechsteiner, Gary Zieff—indispensable all. Bill Shapiro and Jim Nelson both took chances and gave me work and made my writing much stronger. I also have to thank my brothers Bradley and Matthew for all the years and all the love.

There are really no words to describe JillEllyn Riley. She is both my editor and my friend. She made this novel so much better than anything I could have dreamed up. Nobody ever believed as much.

Thank you all.

Steven Kotler